W9-ATW-136

*Center*

Steeple
Hill®

ISBN-13:978-0-373-65202-0
ISBN-10: 0-373-65202-X

9 780373 652020

50650

⊳ EAN

*Love Inspired*

## CLASSICS

# MARGARET DALEY

## Family for Keeps

&

## Sadie's Hero

Steeple
Hill

# MARGARET DALEY

## Family for Keeps

## Sadie's Hero

Steeple
Hill®

Published by Steeple Hill Books™

STEEPLE HILL BOOKS

Steeple
Hill®

ISBN-13: 978-0-373-65202-0
ISBN-10:      0-373-65202-X

FAMILY FOR KEEPS AND SADIE'S HERO

FAMILY FOR KEEPS
Copyright © 2002 by Margaret Daley

SADIE'S HERO
Copyright © 2002 by Margaret Daley

www.SteepleHill.com

**Printed in U.S.A.**

# CONTENTS

## Books by Margaret Daley

## *MARGARET DALEY*

feels she has been blessed. She has been married more than thirty years to her husband, Mike, whom she met in college. He is a terrific support and her best friend. They have one son, Shaun. Margaret has been writing for many years and loves to tell a story. When she was a little girl, she would play with her dolls and make up stories about their lives. Now she writes these stories down. She especially enjoys weaving stories about families and how faith in God can sustain a person when things get tough. When she isn't writing, she is fortunate to be a teacher for students with special needs. Margaret has taught for over twenty years and loves working with her students. She has also been a Special Olympics coach and has participated in many sports with her students.

# FAMILY FOR KEEPS

For I the Lord thy God will hold thy right hand,
saying unto thee, Fear not; I will help thee.
—*Isaiah* 41:13

I want to dedicate this book to all the nurses and doctors, especially my mother, Catherine, and my goddaughter, Ruth.

# Chapter One

"Lady, it worries me when I see a clown cry."

Tess Morgan looked at the giant who was leaning in the doorway to the waiting room, his left leg, up to his knee, in a walking cast. She blinked, releasing the last few teardrops on her lashes. Absently she felt the tears cascade down her face as she tried to compose herself in front of an incredible-looking—hulk!

*Oh, my, he's big.* He filled the doorway with his immense frame, thick-muscled neck, broad shoulders and chest. That was her first impression of the stranger, but it was quickly chased away by others—jet-black hair that curled at the nape of his neck, full mouth turned slightly down in worry, the handsome bronzed planes of his face; and his steel gray eyes, penetrating in their survey of her.

"Ma'am, are you all right?" He hobbled a few feet into the waiting room.

She knew she should respond, but in her weakened emotional state she was at a loss for words. He towered over her. She slowly craned her neck upward past the leg cast, the narrow waist, the wide expanse of chest, the solid neck, to look into his puzzled expression.

Words suddenly flooded her mind. She bolted to her feet, nearly knocking the man backward. "I'm fine. Really, I am. Nothing to worry about, but thanks for asking. Sometimes I just need a good cry. It cleanses the soul, don't you think?" She paused, fluttered her hand in the air and continued, "Well, anyway, it helps me to keep going when things are a little tough." As suddenly as she started talking, she came to an abrupt halt at the shocked expression on the stranger's face. Her cheeks, beneath the white makeup, flamed as red as her clown nose, which she'd placed on the table next to her.

The best possible solution to this embarrassing situation would be a quick retreat, which would be near impossible in her oversize shoes. She sidestepped the giant, muttering, "Thanks again for your concern."

As she clumsily walked toward the exit, she was all too aware of his perceptive gaze on her back. She could imagine it singeing a path down her spine, and she shivered.

She was about to hasten into the hallway and disappear with a small thread of dignity still in place when he said, "You forgot something."

Her pride, she decided, and spun to face the man. In his grasp lay her red ball nose.

"Oh."

She started to snatch it from his outstretched hand when his long fingers closed around it. He shifted closer, positioning himself in front of her. Disconcerted, Tess found herself gulping.

"Here. The least I can do is fix your nose. I can't do anything, though, about the makeup."

He replaced the ball on her nose. The brush of his fingers against her skin was amazingly gentle and extremely warm, too warm. The touch stirred a fluttering in the pit of her stomach, a sensation she hadn't experienced for several years. The scent of sandalwood swirled about her, setting off alarm signals in her brain.

Tess stared into his gray eyes, caught by the intense look he directed at her. The ball was on her nose, but his fingers hadn't dropped away. Five seconds. Ten. An eternity. She was sure he could hear her heartbeat clamoring against her rib cage. It seemed to drown out all other noise.

When his gaze slid away from hers, his hand returned mercifully to his side. "No decent clown should be without a proper nose," he said, amusement causing his eyes to glint like diamonds in sunlight.

Suddenly, always quick to find humor in life, Tess laughed. "The penalty at the very least would be a pie in the face, which come to think of it might not be so bad since I skipped breakfast this morning. I guess I could compromise with a fruit pie and cover at least one of the food groups."

His grin reached deep in his eyes. "Haven't you heard that breakfast is the most important meal of the day?"

"Yes, and I don't usually miss any meals."

His gaze trekked down her length. "That's hard to believe."

She blushed again, something she was doing a lot around this stranger. "My name is Tess Morgan."

"Peter MacPherson." He held out his hand.

She slipped hers into his grasp, silently preparing herself for his long fingers to close about hers. Nothing, though, had prepared her for the electric feel his touch produced, as though she had stuck her finger into a socket. She quickly removed her hand from his grasp and edged back to give herself some breathing room.

"Are you visiting a family member?" Tess took another large step back, sandalwood-scented aftershave lotion still teasing her senses.

"No, just a friend."

"I hope it's not too serious."

"No, Tommy should be leaving in a few days."

"Tommy Burns? You visit him often?" She would have remembered seeing this man. He wasn't a person anyone could easily forget.

"Several times, but I usually come in the evening. Today I'm getting my cast off so I decided to see Tommy before I went to the doctor's office across the street. Do you know Tommy?"

"When I'm not wearing all this white makeup, I'm a nurse on this floor. I dress up several times a week to entertain the children. It's a kind of therapy I've developed." The waiting room was warm, and she knew it had nothing to do with the thermostat setting and everything to do with the man standing in front of her. She was sure her white makeup would soon start running in rivulets of sweat down her face.

"How long have you been doing that?"

"Six months, Mr. MacPherson."

He grimaced. "Please don't call me that. My friends call me Mac."

"Okay—Mac," she murmured, wondering what it would be like to be his friend. In the next second she realized being his friend would be too dangerous for her peace of mind. He was a bit too overwhelming for her.

"What made you come up with the idea of clown therapy?"

"I read about a program back East and thought it was a good idea."

"Why were you crying? Something go wrong today?"

His questions, so full of concern, pierced the invisible armor she wore to protect herself. She wasn't sure how to answer him. The truth was she hadn't cried in several years—wasn't sure why she had today. Maybe she was tired of fighting to keep everything in. But how could she tell a stranger that?

"Are you all right?" Mac moved closer.

Every fiber of her being went on alert at his nearness, though he was still an arm's length away. She nodded, trying to put together an answer that would satisfy him.

"Not enough sleep lately. That's all," she finally said, realizing it was only a small part of the truth. She needed to focus on the good things about her job—the laughter, the smiles of joy and the reprieves she offered from pain. But she couldn't forget Johnny and the battle he might lose. The chemotherapy would work, and Johnny would go into remission.

"My, you are flirting with danger. No sleep and skipping breakfast," Mac said, a gleam dancing in his eyes.

"Tess." A man in a white coat stopped in the hallway and popped his head into the waiting room. "I just wanted to let you know Johnny is through with his therapy."

"How did it go?"

"Fine. He asked about you."

"I'll make sure to stop by and see him. Thanks for the update."

"A friend or patient?" Mac asked when the man left.

"Both." Tess thought about her struggle to get Johnny to smile this past week. She wasn't sure Johnny felt she was his friend, but whether he wanted her to or not she was going to stand by him.

"Johnny must be someone special."

"Why do you say that?"

"From the expression on your face when that man was talking about him."

"I've only known him a week, but he's become important to me in that short time. I know I shouldn't become emotionally involved with a patient, but sometimes it's so hard not to. Johnny doesn't have any family. No one comes to visit him." And that was the reason she was drawn to him, Tess realized.

"How old is he?"

"Ten going on forty. He's a ward of the state." Tess glanced at her oversize watch that didn't keep time. "And if I don't get moving, I might be looking for another job. It was nice to meet you." She backed out of the room, glad she was hidden beneath tons of makeup and a red wig. If she stayed much longer, the man would have her whole life's history. It was too easy talking to him, and the last thing she wanted to do was become interested in any man, especially one who made her heart pound.

Tess started down the hospital corridor, her oversize shoes slapping against the linoleum floor. She was conscious of Peter MacPherson following her undignified exit with his sharp gaze. The hairs on her neck tingled, and the fluttering in her stomach intensified.

She had to get a grip on herself. Peter MacPherson was a man she would probably never see again. But she vividly remembered the warm, gentle touch of his fingers as he adjusted her round red nose. A gentle bear, she thought as she hurried to the nurse's locker room to remove her makeup.

After scrubbing the makeup off and dressing as a nurse, Tess left the locker room, determined to put the gentle giant out of her mind. She had no time in her life for a relationship. She was trying to piece her life together after the disaster in South America.

Pandemonium greeted Tess with a cold blast of panic when she approached the nurses' station.

"Tess, am I glad you're back. I was just going to page you," Delise said as she rushed up to Tess. "Johnny wasn't in his room when I went to check on him."

"Have you notified security? Looked all over this floor?"

"Yes. Yes. What should we do? We have medications that have to be given out."

"There's nothing we can do until we've given out the medications. I'm sure security will find him before we're through," Tess said in a calm, controlled voice, though her stomach muscles were tight as a fist.

What if Johnny had collapsed somewhere unconscious? What if he had a reaction to the therapy? What if— She had to block from her mind what could happen to Johnny. He would be all right, she told herself as she put a bottle of medicine on the counter, closed her eyes and breathed deeply. But the antiseptic-laced air underscored in Tess's thoughts her fear that the child might not come out of this all right.

Mac stared at himself in the mirror in the men's room, an image of a clown stealing into his thoughts. A picture of her tear-streaked face with rivulets of black paint ruining her white makeup materialized in his mind. He remembered how she'd drawn in a deep breath, her hands clasped tightly in her lap to keep them from shaking. Slowly, while they had talked, she had pieced herself together, but the effort had left a vulnerability in her eyes that struck a chord deep in him.

What did she look like under all that white makeup and the red curly wig? He knew she was tiny, but that was about all. His curiosity was aroused. He wondered if he could fit his hands around her small waist. Shaking his head, he looked away. He would probably never know. Besides, he wasn't looking for a relationship of any kind.

He couldn't image finding anyone to take the place of Sheila. As he remembered his deceased wife, his throat constricted, making it difficult to swallow. In the past few years his life had changed drastically, and if he hadn't known the Lord's love, he wouldn't have been able to hold himself together for his daughter.

A noise behind him brought Mac up short. He'd thought he was alone. He glanced at the stalls, cocking his head to listen.

Crying?

The muffled sound filled the air. Someone whimpered. As quickly as his leg cast would allow, Mac hobbled to the stall at the far end of the bathroom.

"Are you all right in there?"

Silence. Even the whimpering stopped.

"Is everything okay?" Mac asked, alarm beginning to form in his gut.

A sound as if someone was falling launched Mac into action. He threw his body against the stall door, and it would have crashed open except that Mac stopped it. Carefully he swung the door wide. On the floor lay a boy, his pale face streaked with tears, his eyes fluttering closed.

After checking for a pulse, Mac stooped, picked up the child and cradled him. His small chest rose and fell with each shallow breath. Mac quickly carried the child from the bathroom down the multicolored corridor toward the nurses' station.

As Mac approached, he caught sight of a tiny nurse whom he somehow immediately knew was Tess. She was like a pixie with short brown hair feathered about her oval face, a cute turned up nose, a mouth meant for laughter and dark brown eyes he could imagine sparkling with mischief. It was those eyes that had given her away and drew him to her.

When she looked at him, her gaze widened, and her hand halted in midair. For a few seconds he saw fear in her eyes. Then a professional calm descended.

"Delise, notify Dr. Addison. Please come with me, Mr. MacPherson."

Mac started to correct her use of his name but stopped when he looked at her. He sensed she needed her professional facade, that it was the only thing that held her together. He followed her to a room across from the nurses' station, placed the boy on the bed, then backed away while Tess checked the child, her movements precise, efficient. But he saw the slight quiver in her fingers, as though the effort to be businesslike was taking its toll on her.

"I think he'll be all right," she said, the rigid set of her shoulders easing.

Mac started to ask about the child when the doctor came into the room. Mac quietly left to stand outside as if on guard at the door. He wanted to appease his curiosity about the child and the tiny woman who had touched him deep inside.

With his body propped up against the wall, he tried to ignore the ache in his leg. In his old profession he had certainly dealt with his share of pain. Massaging his tight muscled thigh, he focused his thoughts away from the dull throbbing and onto one nurse clown who captivated him more than he wished.

He remembered the helplessness he'd felt when he'd seen her in the waiting room crying, her face streaked with the evidence of her tears. A strong urge to comfort had drawn him into the room before he could stop himself. Her vulnerability had moved him, causing him to forget his losses for a short time. Seeing her again renewed his interest. He wanted to know what had put that look in her eyes that declared she'd seen more than her share of pain and suffering. He wanted to get to know her, ease the burden he sensed she carried.

Whoa, there, Mac. What do you think you're doing? Getting to know her? As a friend? Or, something more than that? He had more than he could handle right now in his life. Relationships were out. He'd been blessed by the Lord with one great marriage and wasn't looking for another.

The door swung open, and the doctor left the room.

Mac waited another minute, then decided to go inside. He was never good at waiting, he thought with a smile.

Tess pivoted at the sound of the door swishing open. Her startled gaze took him in, running down his length, before she returned her attention to the boy on the bed. "Thank you."

Limping to the bed, he smiled at the child whose eyes were full of caution. "I'm Mac. I'm the one who found you. I just wanted to make sure you're okay."

For a full minute the boy stared at Mac as though he had sprouted wings and was going to fly about the room any second. "I'm okay." The child frowned and looked at his feet.

"Good. What's your name?"

Silence.

Mac glanced at Tess, a question in his eyes.

She started to say something when the child finally mumbled, "Johnny."

So this is the child Tess was concerned about, Mac thought, a tightness in his chest. He was reminded of himself when he was Johnny's age, trying to carry off a tough, couldn't-care-less attitude. God had been his salvation. "Well, Johnny, I hope you'll let me come see you."

Plucking at the white bedsheet, the child shrugged. "Suit yourself."

"Johnny, I still have some medication to give out. I'll be back to see you in a bit. No more stunts, young man." Tess motioned for Mac to follow her from the room.

"'Bye, Johnny." For some reason Mac was reluctant

to leave. The child seemed so young, yet so old at the same time. Tess was right, in a way—Johnny *was* ten going on forty. But Mac suspected Johnny wanted to be ten years old and do whatever ten-year-olds did.

In the hallway Tess turned toward him. "Where did you find him? What happened? How did—"

Mac held up his hand. "Wait. Give me a chance to answer the first question."

Tess sighed. "Where was he?"

Mac couldn't take his gaze off the tiny frown that dulled her eyes and wrinkled her brow. He found himself wanting to smooth it away and make her laugh. Before he realized what he was doing, he raised his hand to her face and grazed his fingertips across her forehead as though that action would erase her concern.

Her eyes widened, and two patches of red fired her cheeks. "Mr. MacPherson, where?" she asked in a breathless rush.

"You look lovely when you blush."

Her brown eyes grew rounder, and she tried to step away, but the wall blocked her escape. Mac knew she was unnerved by the trapped look that appeared in her gaze. She doesn't hide her feelings, he thought and liked that. Sheila hadn't been able to, either. That comparison came out of nowhere and unnerved him.

"The men's restroom by the elevators," he finally answered.

"What happened?"

He supported himself against the wall with one hand

braced by her head to take some of the weight off the leg with the cast. He could smell her scent, theater makeup and lilacs. "It's too long a story, and didn't you say you had medications to give out? I'll explain over dinner tonight." One part of him was as surprised at his invitation as she looked. It was as though there was another man inside him. Hadn't he decided he wasn't ready to get involved with another woman? Sheila had only been gone three years. And yet, he sensed a fragile composure in Tess that drew him to her. He found he was having a hard time resisting her.

"I don't date."

"That's okay. I don't, either. How about seven tonight?"

"I'm washing my hair. Sorry."

"Well, then, I suppose the story can wait until tomorrow night." The clean aroma of her hair perfumed the air.

"Nope. I have to scrub my bathrooms." A spark of mischief lit her brown eyes.

He laughed, leaning closer. "Then you tell me when."

Her head tilted to the side, she appeared deep in thought. A moment later she flashed him a sassy grin before ever so politely quipping, "How about we go out when pigs fly."

Chuckling, Mac watched her leave. He always liked a good challenge, and suddenly Miss Tess Morgan was daring him to discover the woman beneath the clown makeup and colorful uniform of a pediatric nurse. He limped toward the elevators. It was just as well she'd said no. He didn't have time for a relationship. He had a daughter who needed him and a large family that depended on him. No, sir, he had no time for a woman even if she was an intriguing, beautiful, caring one.

"Do you know who that is? Of course, you don't, or you'd have never let him leave." Delise pointed at the retreating figure of Peter MacPherson as he stepped onto the elevator. "He's *the* Mack Truck. He used to play for the Denver Broncos as a running back until he retired several years ago. He's a legend around here." Delise felt her friend's forehead. "Have you gone mad? Women would die to go out with him, but since his wife's death he's retreated from public life. From what I heard her death hit him quite hard. Left football. Started his own business, does something with a foundation and volunteers at a halfway house. Quite a family man, from everything I can gather about him. That's so appealing."

Tess shook her head, trying not to feel empathy for Peter MacPherson because that emotion would lead to others she definitely wasn't prepared to feel. "My, you could write his biography. Where in the world do you come up with all this?"

Delise fluttered her hand in the air. "Oh, you know, magazines, newspaper stories. The usual places. The bottom line is that he's one of the hottest items in Denver even if he doesn't want to be."

"You make him sound like a piece of merchandise."

"Oh, you know what I mean. Or has your eyesight gone with your brains?"

"They're both intact, thank you very much. Now, don't we have a job to do?" Tess walked to the counter and picked up her tray of medications.

"Did he ask you out?"

Tess realized she wouldn't get any peace or work done until she satisfied her friend's rabid curiosity. "Yes. And before you ask, I refused. Three times."

"I'm sure Dr. Smith can see you in emergency."

Tess sighed heavily. "Not every woman in this world is man crazy like you."

"Okay. I grant you maybe a visit to the shrink isn't necessary. Are you just playing hard to get? That might work, Tess. In fact, that's a brilliant idea. Be mysterious. Act uninterested. Keep him guessing." Delise snapped her fingers as she rattled off her advice.

"Whether I like it or not, I'm an open book. And I am not interested in that man." As Tess spoke, she tried to force conviction into her voice, but it lacked the ring of truth.

Tess didn't wait to hear her friend's response. She took her tray and entered the first room. If she was lucky, which she was beginning to doubt, Delise would tire of the subject of Peter MacPherson, and Tess could finish her shift without thinking again about that man.

But it wasn't Delise's questions that caused Tess to dwell on Peter MacPherson. She saw a boy with a cast on his leg, and she instantly thought about Mac and his gentle touch as he had replaced her clown nose. She saw an orderly who was over six feet tall, and she thought about Mac towering over her. And when she visited Johnny, he forced her again to think about the man.

"I would never have been found if it hadn't been for that man," Johnny declared as he twisted the white top sheet into a mangled ball of cotton.

"You're lucky he did."

"Why? I hate this place. I hate it!"

Tess swallowed the lump in her throat. "Hopefully you won't be here much longer."

"Then I'll just have to go live with some dumb old stranger."

"Mrs. Hocks is trying to locate your relatives." Tess hoped Johnny's case manager would find someone to take him in.

Johnny turned away from her onto his side and stared out the window, his shoulders hunched. "I don't have nobody."

Those words knifed through her, mirroring her feelings. She didn't have anybody, either, but that was the way she wanted it. Johnny needed a family. He needed love. Suddenly she was afraid he would pull another stunt like today. "You aren't going to try to run away again, are you?"

He didn't say anything.

"Johnny?" Tess moved to the other side of the bed and looked at the small child. His eyes were closed. She wasn't sure if he was asleep or faking it. It didn't make any difference, because if Johnny didn't want to talk, he didn't. Quietly she left his room, drained from the child's brief emotional outburst, from the day's events and especially from not trying to think about Peter Mac-Pherson. He occupied her mind, threatening the fragile defenses she'd finally erected around her heart.

## Chapter Two

A film of sweat covered Mac's body as he struggled to finish his leg exercises. Ten was all he could do with his mended leg. The soreness bore deep into him as he got up and limped to another machine. Absently he did arm curls as he mentally tried to psych himself up. It was only a matter of time before his left leg would be as good as new.

Three sharp raps at the door drew his attention. "Yes?"

His housekeeper stuck her head into the room. "Your sister is here."

"Which one?" Mac finished his last arm curl and put the weight on the rack.

"Casey."

"Does she have that troubled look on her face?"

"'Fraid so."

"Tell her I'll be there after my shower. Fix her breakfast. She's way too thin."

"My thoughts exactly," Nina said as she closed the door to the exercise room.

Fifteen minutes later Mac hadn't stepped one foot into the kitchen when Casey started in. "You wouldn't believe the fight Mom and I had. All because I don't want to start college in the fall. You've got to talk to her, Mac. Tell her I'm an adult now and capable of making my own decisions."

"Do you think I might have some breakfast first? Say hello to my daughter."

Mac scooped up Amy and whirled her around. The three-year-old giggled. When he started to put her in her booster chair, she said, "Do it again. Please, Daddy."

Not able to resist such a plea, he swung her around and around until he became dizzy. "Enough. I'm gonna be seasick, and we are landlocked, young lady." He settled his daughter in her chair and sat next to her, preparing himself for his sister's onslaught.

Casey gulped down half of her orange juice. "I don't want to go to college. Mom will listen to you."

While he watched Amy finish stuffing a piece of toast in her mouth, Mac took a bite of his omelette. "Why don't you want to go?"

"I want to go, but not this fall. I need some time to decide what I want to do with the rest of my life. I'm not like you, Mac. Everything in a neat little box."

He took his napkin and wiped his daughter's jelly-smeared face, then bent and kissed her nose. "Pumpkin, you're as good as new."

Amy jumped down from the chair and threw her arms around Mac's neck, kissing him on the cheek, then doing the same to Casey. "'Bye, Aunt Casey."

Amy raced out of the kitchen. A minute later he heard the television. He glanced at his watch and realized her favorite show was on. He liked to watch it with her, but he needed to appease his sister or he would never be free.

"Casey, you think my life is in a neat little box?"

"Sure. You always know what you want and go after it. If it hadn't been for your determination, none of us MacPhersons would have had a chance at college. I just want my chance a year later than the others." Casey reached across the table and took Mac's hand. "Please talk to her. I don't want her mad at me, especially since Dad's death."

Mac felt the familiar emptiness at the mention of their father's death. He had not only been Mac's father, but his best friend, as well. Facing two deaths in the past three years had been very difficult, and without God's love and guidance Mac wasn't sure he would have made it. He thanked the Lord every day for being in his life, his salvation when life overwhelmed him.

Casey squeezed his hand. "Please, Mac."

He focused on his sister, pushing the pain of his father's and wife's deaths to the background. "Casey, it's your decision. I'll have a talk with Mom."

She hugged him, a wide grin on her face. "Great! I knew I could count on you. The best time to talk to Mom is tonight at dinner. You're coming, aren't you?"

"Of course. I wouldn't miss Steve's birthday."

"You're the greatest! I'll let myself out. You just sit and finish your breakfast. 'Bye, Nina."

When Casey breezed out of the kitchen, Mac shook his head. He never had a moment's rest with his family. One child, three brothers and two sisters kept him hopping.

As his housekeeper poured his coffee, she said, "I know it's none of my business—"

"But you're going to make it your business anyway."

Nina ignored his interruption and continued. "Ever since you fell off that roof at the halfway house, you've been shut up here, working in that office of yours. You only go out to volunteer at the halfway house. You haven't gone out socially much in the past couple of months, not even to do things with your family. Now that the cast is off, get out. Enjoy life. Stop trying to do everything for everyone else. Do something for yourself. That's the way your father and Sheila would have wanted it."

"Whoa! Since when did you become Dear Abby?"

"Since I've been watching you draw in on yourself after Sheila's death. I think you used the accident to avoid seeing people socially, except family. I know how hard your father's death was on you, especially on top of the accident."

Mac scooted back his chair and stood. "I appreciate your concern, Nina, and I'll think about your advice. Now if you'll excuse me, I'm going to enjoy some time with my daughter, then I have a date at the hospital."

"A date at the hospital?"

"With a ten-year-old boy. So get that gleam out of your eye."

"Think about what I said," Nina called as he left the kitchen.

In other words, get a life, Mac thought as he sat next to Amy in the den. Until yesterday, when he had been drawn to Tess crying in the waiting room, nothing much had touched him. It was as if the numbness was slowly fading, leaving in its wake a prickly awareness of one tiny woman.

There was absolutely no way Tess could sneak up on the children in the rec room with her oversize shoes announcing her approach from a mile away. But when she stepped into the room, ready to go into her clown routine, every child's head was bent over one piece of paper, and Peter MacPherson was in the middle of the group, drawing something on the sheet.

Is he a closet artist? Tess wondered, and moved into the room. Every child was looking at the paper and listening intently to what Mac was saying. Maybe Mac was a budding Rembrandt.

"Really!" one girl said in awe.

"Yeah. Here, let me show you what I mean. Brandon, you stand over there…." Mac's words died in his throat as he straightened and looked into Tess's eyes.

Instantly a finely honed tension streaked through her as the heat of his gaze sealed the breath in her lungs. No matter how much she fought it, she couldn't deny the fact that this man heightened her awareness of how alone she was in this world, but that wasn't how she had planned it all those years ago when she had dreamed of her future. She had wanted a husband and a large family.

The girl who had been in awe came over to Tess. "Do you know who he is?"

"Yes, someone told me he used to play football for Denver," Tess said without thinking, her gaze still connected to his smoldering one. Oh, why in the world did she have to admit that she had been talking about him with someone?

"I strongly suspect, guys, this clown here doesn't appreciate the finer points of football." His statement was accompanied by a wickedly charming grin as he threw her to the wolves.

"You don't?" the oldest boy asked, his doubts about her sanity evident in his tone of voice.

Tess narrowed her gaze on Mac, wishing him bodily harm. "Tell you the truth, I've never been to a game."

"That's un-American!"

"You're joking!"

"Yeah, she has to be. Everyone has seen a football game."

Would a group of kids attack a clown for not having been to a game? Tess looked from one face to another and seriously thought about her chances of escaping in shoes four sizes too big. They'd tackle me at the door, she decided.

"I'm not into sports," Tess offered in the way of an explanation. It went over like water on a grease fire. "I've been out of the country for the past few years, and in high school I preferred to study on Friday nights," she added, aware that her explanations were bombing faster than bad jokes in a comedy act.

Her gaze fastened onto Mac's, and she wanted to lynch him. Crossing his arms over his massive chest, he was watching her and enjoying every minute of her discomfort with a huge grin on his face.

"I think she just needs someone to explain the finer points of the game to her," Mac finally said as all the children tried to tell her what she was missing at the same time. "I'll be glad to offer my services, say, over dinner tonight."

"Yeah, that's a great idea," several of the children said at once.

"Everyone should know about football," the oldest boy added.

Tess was speechless. Her refusal stuck in her throat.

"Come on. Say yes to him," the girl said.

Mac smiled an infuriating smile as he strode to her, leaned toward her and whispered, "Unless you're one of those people who judge something without knowing anything about it."

She stepped quickly away as if his breath had scorched her neck while struggling to control the shivering sensations spreading down her body. "I'm not!"

His smile broadened. "Then prove it. Have dinner

with me. We'll be eating with a whole crowd of people, so you won't even be alone with me."

Tess swung her gaze from Mac to the children, all eagerly awaiting her answer. There really wouldn't be any harm in one dinner with him. He was the complete opposite of what she would be attracted to in a man, so she was perfectly safe. Wasn't she?

She looked him straight in the eye. "Fine."

He chuckled and whispered for her ears only, "It looks like a pig has just taken flight."

She smiled sweetly at him. "I'm sure anything is possible where you're involved."

"Is that sarcasm I hear in your voice?"

"Me? Never!"

His eyes twinkled. "It's interesting how you like to hide behind either a nurse's uniform or white makeup. Why is that?"

Tess felt the gazes of the children on them and sidestepped toward the door. "Would you all excuse us for a moment?"

"You want to speak to me—alone?"

Tess took a deep, calming breath and said through clenched teeth, "Yes, please."

"Kids, we'll be back in a moment."

Out in the hall Tess leaned toward him and lowered her voice, conscious of the children in the room not three feet away. "Why are you here?" Don't you know I'm trying to avoid you? You aren't making that easy for me.

"I thought it was obvious. I'm visiting the children."

"Why?"

"I thought that was obvious, too. To spread a little joy and happiness, the same as you."

When he said "the same as you," Tess felt an instant bond with the man that she wanted to deny. She would have to endure their date that evening, but she didn't want to be around him anymore than was necessary. "Well, since you're spreading all that joy and happiness, I'll get back to my nursing duties." She started away.

"And miss all the fun?"

She glanced over her shoulder at him and saw six pairs of eyes glued to her. The children were framed in the doorway, intent on Tess and Mac's conversation. She figured she had done enough entertaining today. "I'm sure there are some bedpans that need to be emptied."

The sound of her shoes slapping against the floor echoed down the hallway as she made her escape, embarrassingly aware of the gazes trained on her. She was seriously thinking of deep-sixing her clown shoes for some sneakers—a fast pair that could take her away from a very dangerously appealing man.

By the time Tess's shift was over, several hours later, she couldn't wait to get away from the hospital. She felt the walls closing in on her. She wished for the thousandth time she didn't throw herself so totally into whatever she was doing. It took a toll on her that once nearly did her in. She couldn't let that happen again.

Inside her apartment, Tess stripped quickly out of her

sky blue pants and multicolored shirt, as though shedding her uniform would help her cope with the emotional treadmill she had been running on. But she felt wound up. She filled the bathtub with water so hot she had to force herself inch by inch into it. She eased back against the cold marble and laid her head on a plastic cushion, staring at the white ceiling, the evening with Mac looming ahead of her.

She wished again she'd somehow managed to refuse her date with Peter MacPherson. She wasn't looking for any kind of relationship. Once was enough for her. She'd left her broken heart in the Andes Mountains. Pain, buried and best forgotten, sliced into her, piercing her protective shell.

Determined to forget, she closed her eyes and blanked her mind. She concentrated on the heat seeping into her, stroking away her stress, the scent of lavender wafting to her, easing her tension. Slowly she drifted off….

*She faced a line of eleven huge men, bent on taking the football away from her. She crouched down, staring at the opposition with the meanest look she could muster. The ball was snapped. With her hands about the oblong pigskin, she dropped back, looked for a receiver and froze.*

*Mac hurled himself toward her. She ran forward, desperately trying to avoid him. Through the sea of men she rushed toward the end zone. She heard Mac behind her. With a quick glance back, she nearly tripped. He was only a yard behind her and gaining on her. She pushed herself to go faster, to cross the line before he plowed into her. Ten more yards. Five. She dove for the end zone at the same time she felt Mac's arms encase her. She fell forward, the air swooshing from her lungs as she hit the ground. Suddenly water was all around her, and she was gasping for breath.*

Tess shot up in the tub, spurting, coughing. The man had entered her life, and she'd nearly drowned dreaming about him. She had to do something about this. She couldn't allow herself to care about another man, not after Kevin. They would have been married by this time with possibly a child on the way. Now all she had were memories. Always the memories.

Running her hands up and down her arms, Tess pushed away the images that threatened to invade her mind. Never again would she love like that. She would never allow herself to become involved with someone who could touch her heart. She couldn't live through the pain of losing again. It nearly killed her the first time. Being an all-or-nothing kind of gal was awfully hard on the emotions.

The water was chilly as she focused on the present. She shuddered from the cold, empty feeling that encased her like Mac's imagined embrace in her dream. She stood and toweled dry. She rubbed hard, as though she could erase the last vestige of her old self.

She was determined to build a life here in Denver completely different from her old one in South America.

She quickly dressed for her date, hoping that her casual attire of black slacks and a simple peach knit top would send the man the right message. Nothing serious.

By the time he picked her up, she'd paced a path in her living room that left a trail in the carpet. His warm greeting did nothing to ease her tension. While leaving her apartment, she found herself responding to his smile with one of her own and instantly wishing she could find fault. But he was the perfect gentleman, down to opening the car door for her.

As he started the engine, he peered at her and said, "You look beautiful. Quite different from the last time I saw you."

She remembered the incident in the playroom with the children and how he had maneuvered her into going out with him. She tried to muster some resentment toward the man but couldn't, especially when he looked at her as though she were the only woman in the world.

"How's Johnny doing?" Mac asked as he negotiated through traffic.

"Sulking most of the time. He has little to say when I visit him."

"I know. I stopped by his room before visiting the other children. I think he spoke three words to me the whole time I was there. I felt like I was carrying on a conversation with myself."

"Yeah, that's the way he is with everyone. I wish I could reach him. But things haven't been easy for him."

"Well, I haven't given up. I'll make a point to stop by again. I'm a pretty determined guy when something is important to me."

Tess could imagine his determination. He wouldn't

have become such a good football player without it. But she was a determined lady, and he wasn't going to get her to do something she didn't want to do again. Even as she thought that, there was a part of her that realized she'd wanted to go out with him or she wouldn't have allowed the children to talk her into this date. That realization startled her.

When Mac pulled his car into the driveway of a house, Tess sent him a wary glance. "Do you want to show me your etchings?"

His laughter filled the small confines of the car, warming the already heated air. Tess was caught by his silver molten gaze and held in its spell. This is a mistake, she thought frantically. It's way too dangerous for me to go out with him. He's too overwhelming.

"What if I said yes?"

"Then I'm not moving from this car." She felt herself being drawn into his web of male charm, held together by an incredible smile and the most beautiful eyes.

He grinned, his arm sliding along the back of the seat. "That'll be all right by me."

The air became unbearably hot. Tess felt prickles of heat slip down the length of her. She stared at that incredible smile of his that no human being had a right to and wanted to melt. She didn't know if she would be able to move from the car if her life depended on it.

Even though his arm didn't touch her, she was acutely conscious of it only inches from her. Her skin tingled as though electrical currents flowed between them. She found herself leaning closer to his arm along the back of the seat as if she needed to establish tactile contact with him. *Oh, my, what's happening to me?*

Suddenly she bolted upright, staring straight ahead, determined not to look at him. "I think you'd better take me home."

His laugh was low and full of warmth. "I never figured you for a gal who went back on a promise."

She threw him a surprised look. "I'm not. I went out with you. It was just an incredibly short date."

His chuckle danced along her nerve endings. "I suppose technically you've fulfilled your obligation to the children, but you're missing the intent of the date."

She quirked a brow. "Oh, and what is that?" she asked, confused by the way his laughter seeped into her bruised heart and demanded she forget everything but him.

His hand touched her shoulder, urging her back against the seat. "Stay and relax. All I want is for us to get to know each other."

The way he said "for us" made her breath catch and belied the meaning of his words. She wasn't good at this dating stuff, having done little of it in her life. She should never have let the kids at the hospital bully her into going out with Mac, even if there was a small part of her that had wanted to go.

"Friendship is about all I can handle in my life," he murmured, his voice low and throaty.

"Now I'm really comforted." Vividly aware of his hand near her shoulder, Tess sat stiffly against the seat cushion. Her senses registered everything about him, his clean male scent, the silver gleam in his eyes, the dimples at the sides of his mouth when he smiled.

"If it would make you feel any better—" Mac stopped talking as a car pulled up behind them in the driveway and a man, woman and child got out of it.

The man approached Mac's car and bent down at the open window on the driver's side. "This has got to be a first. I don't believe it, Mac. You've never been early for anything. Turning over a new leaf?"

"Funny."

"Are you coming in or do you plan on celebrating out in the car?" The man's gaze slid to Tess then back to Mac. "I'll admit I wouldn't blame you."

"Tess, this obnoxious guy is my brother Justin. His wife, Mary, and their son, Justin Junior, are standing behind him."

"Brother?" Tess's voice was full of puzzlement. Her cheeks still flamed from Justin's comment.

"Yeah, I was about to tell you that this is my mother's house. We're celebrating my brother's birthday tonight, and the crowd I told you about at the hospital is my huge family."

"See you inside, brother dear. Don't take too long. Mom probably has her binoculars trained on you as we speak," Justin said.

Tess watched the couple and their son walk to the front door and go inside. She should be angry at the way Mac had deliberately misled her, but she couldn't muster the feeling. Relief washed over her. She knew in the brief ride to his mother's that she couldn't handle being alone with Peter MacPherson. She would have to remember that, and avoid the situation at all costs, she told herself as she clutched the door handle, needing to escape. She realized she didn't trust herself around Mac.

"Why the rush, Tess? The rest of the family isn't even here yet. Let's talk. Get to know each other. Believe me, once we hit that door, we'll get very little time to talk alone together."

"I know all I need to know." Is that my voice that sounds panic-filled? Tess, take deep breaths and calm down. So he makes your heart beat a bit faster and all your senses vibrate with awareness. It will pass, she assured herself, thinking back to the handful of guys she'd dated in her life and realizing she was definitely out of her league.

"There you go again, judging me before you even know me."

She angled to face him in the small car. "I'm not judging you."

"Aren't you?"

"I'm just not interested in any kind of relationship."

"Even friendship?"

"Is that what this is all about?" Strangely, that was what frightened her. His offer of friendship was the most appealing aspect about him, she was discovering as she spent time with him.

"Yes and no. I'm not going to deny you interest me."

His hand settled on her shoulder, kneading the taut muscles. "There's something between us even you can't deny. But, Tess, what I really want is to get to know you as a friend. No one can have too many friends."

Her eyes closed for a brief moment as she relished the feel of his hand on her, massaging the tension away, creating delicious sensations in her that went down to the tips of her toes. My gosh, she thought. He's good. Too good!

"I don't think casual is in your vocabulary." She pulled away, plastering her back against the car door, grasping anything—however fragile—to break the hold this man was weaving over her. "You say you want to be my friend, but something else is going on. Like you, friendship is all I can handle in my life right now."

"What happened, Tess? What are you running away from?"

## Chapter Three

"I could ask you the same questions," Tess said, wanting to avoid the direction the conversation was headed in.

Sighing heavily, Mac opened the car door. "I think it's time we go in. Justin's probably right about my mother and the binoculars. I think I see sunlight glinting off glass from the living room window."

For some reason Tess couldn't let the question drop. "Are you avoiding my question? Why won't you answer it?" she asked as she faced him over the top of his car.

"Probably for the same reason you won't answer mine. It's not easy for the two of us to share our pain, is it?"

She blinked, nonplussed by the way he could hone in on what she was all about—and in such an incredibly short time. "I think you're right. We'd better go inside." She headed for the house.

A petite woman with gray hair opened the door before Mac could reach around Tess and put his hand on the knob. "I was beginning to think I'd have to send Steve out to get you."

"Mom, not everyone is here yet."

"But still, I wanted some time to get to know your friend before the rest of the horde descend."

With that declaration Tess found herself being studied by Mac's mother's sharp gaze, much like her son's.

"As you've probably surmised, this woman is my mother, Alice MacPherson. Mom, this is Tess Morgan."

Tess shook Alice's hand. "Pleased to meet you."

"The pleasure is all mine. When Peter called to tell me he was bringing a date, I was frankly very interested. Ever since Sheila—"

"Mom, where's Amy? I want Tess to meet my daughter."

"She's in the den with her cousins."

"I'll be back in a sec. I can trust you, Mom, not to say anything too outrageous while I'm gone."

"Why, son, never." Alice signaled for Tess to precede her into the living room. "I'll just get acquainted with your lady friend while you're gone. Take all the time in the world getting Amy. We'll be just fine, Peter," Alice called as she winked at Tess. "I wager he'll be gone no more than a minute, if that long." Alice gestured toward the couch. "Are you from Denver?"

"No, I grew up in Maine but after my parents died, I decided on a change of scenery." Tess sat on the couch across from Mac's mother, feeling as though she were being interviewed by a pro and determined not to mention the year she'd spent in the Peace Corps in South America. That might lead to questions she didn't want to answer.

"I must warn you, in a moment this place will be chaotic. Do you have any brothers and sisters?"

Tess's chest felt tight. She drew in a fortifying breath and answered, "No." She had always wanted a lot of brothers and sisters. She was completely alone in the world. There had been a time when she had wanted a large family with Kevin. Now that wasn't possible, but the empty ache still hurt.

"Well, Tess, I'm not sure you missed out on anything," Mac said as he joined them in the living room, carrying an adorable-looking little girl in his arms. She had huge brown eyes and dark hair. "As the big brother, I have to put up with a lot of nonsense."

"Oh, sure, you think you're the only one who has suffered." Justin entered the room with another young man. "Steve, you tell our big brother how we have to constantly live up to his legend. It's very hard to at times."

"Justin, be kind to your older brother," Alice said with a laugh.

"Yeah, bro." Mac put Amy down and watched as his little girl walked to Tess.

Amy cocked her head, her brow knitted, and asked, "Who are you?"

"I'm Tess Morgan, a friend of your father's." The second she said the word *friend* she felt Mac's smug glance touch her face and wished she could stop her cheeks from flaming scarlet just with the thought of the man looking at her. She must learn to control her reaction to him.

"Daddy has a lot of friends," Amy announced, then wandered to her grandmother and sat next to her.

Tess was trying to decide what the little girl meant by friends when another man came into the room, quickly followed by a young woman. Suddenly the room was filled with people of various ages, from a baby to Mac's mother. Tess felt inundated. The people were all interested in her, kidding each other and enjoying the moment. By the time everyone had introduced themselves, Tess counted fifteen people. She was never good at names, so she found herself reviewing their names as she listened to the conversation flowing around her.

Mac walked behind the couch and leaned over. "I have something I'd like to show you before dinner."

She smiled. "Those etchings finally?"

His chuckle was low, meant only for her. "Not here. Never any privacy. It's something outside. You just have to put your trust in me and come with me to find out."

The thought of putting her trust in Mac's hands didn't alarm her nearly as much as she thought it should. That knowledge sent a bolt of pure panic through her. Since South America she'd lost her ability to trust.

"Coming?" Mac asked, his hand extended toward her.

Fitting her hand within his grasp, Tess followed him from the living room, aware of a lull in the conversation. She suspected his family had stopped talking to watch them leave. Another blush tinted her cheeks as she realized they would be the topic of conversation after they left.

Mac confirmed her suspicion when he whispered into her ear, "I thought I would spice up their dull lives and let them talk about us for a while."

"Are you always so accommodating to your family?"

"Alas, you've found me out. I'm a doormat when it comes to them." He opened the back door and motioned for her to go first. "My daughter has already figured out how to wrap me around her little finger."

On the patio, the warm spring air felt good. Tess took a moment to relish the clean fresh air laced with the hint of honeysuckle. "What did you want me to see?" she asked when Mac came up behind her and stood close.

"This." He spread his arm wide to indicate the beautiful sky at dusk.

Mauves mingled with pinks and reds to feather outward to all reaches of the heavens. The light, cool breeze, carrying the scent of pine, ruffled the strands of her hair. The quiet just before night descended filled Tess with a momentary sense of tranquillity she wished she could bottle.

The sunset was a vivid backdrop to the tall peaks. Tess loved the mountains. Standing on top of one was like standing on top of the world. That was one of the reasons she had chosen to live in Denver, even though the memories of the Andes Mountains sometimes got to be too much for her.

"When I'm over at Mom's, I love to come out here in the evening and just enjoy the sight. This is what life's all about. God's creation," he whispered close to her.

Tess turned slightly so she could look at him, surprise in her expression.

He laughed. "Don't look so stunned. I can appreciate beauty as well as the next guy."

"Why did you play football?"

"I love the game. It gave me a lot."

"How did you break your leg—playing football?" She made the mistake of letting her gaze trail downward. As she took in his great physique, her face flushed. If she had to use one word to describe his body, it would be *powerful*.

"I've broken a couple of bones over the years, but I didn't break my leg this time playing football. I haven't played the game since I retired."

"What happened to your leg?" She turned and put some distance between them. Suddenly the cool air was warm, too warm. The space between them was filled with yearnings. She balled her hands at her sides, resisting the strong urge to run them over his massive shoulders. His body was a rock-hard force that spoke of his former profession.

"Nothing much. I was helping to roof a halfway house at which I volunteer and fell off the ladder. Now it's your turn. Why haven't you seen a game? You admitted to the children today that you know nothing about football."

"Kids take risks they shouldn't playing that game. I've seen firsthand some of the results as a nurse."

"Life's a risk."

"And life is much too violent without a game like football." She stared at the sunset quickly fading behind the mountains. She had seen enough violence in her life as an emergency room nurse, then as a Peace Corps volunteer in South America. An act of violence had claimed the man she'd been engaged to marry.

"Are you really being fair to the game?"

His presence behind her pulled her from memories that were always just below the surface. Potent power emanated from him, threatening to overcome any resistance she had. She steeled herself against that lure and said, "In high school I had a good friend who played football."

"And you never saw him play?"

"My studies were too important to me. He asked me to, but sports wasn't my thing. His second year on the team, he caught the ball in the end zone for the winning touchdown. Three players tackled him. My friend never got up. He had to be carried off the field and to this day is paralyzed from the waist down."

"Football offered me a way to go to a good college. It opened up the whole world for me and consequently my family. It has given me a chance to use my status to spread the word of the Lord. Through my foundation I have been able to help a lot of people I wouldn't have been able to. Football gave me that chance." Mac came around to stand in front of her.

"What is your foundation?"

"I've used my connections in the sports world to raise money for the Christian Athletes Foundation, which I started a few years ago. Through this foundation I can fund certain projects. The Lord has provided for me. I want to provide for others."

"What kind of projects?"

"One of my more recent ones was establishing scholarships for students who don't have the money to go to college. I want to make sure others have the opportunity that I had through a good education."

"Education and football?"

"Yes, and football, but I don't want to talk about football. Let's talk about where we're heading, Tess."

The way he said her name, like a caress, was a silent plea for her understanding. She couldn't resist him. She wanted to understand him in that moment more than anything else.

"There's a connection between us I can't deny. I think you need a friend more than you care to admit." He reached up and cupped her face in his large hands, his touch electric. "Go out with me Saturday night. Just you and me. No family between us."

She laid her hands over his and stared into his silvery gaze, which radiated intensity. She felt lost as sensations she had never experienced washed over her.

"Will you go out with me?"

The question was a whisper between their mouths as he leaned closer to her, his breath anointing her lips. One of his hands fingered her hair then slid to clasp the nape of her neck. She was surrounded by him, his power shoving everything aside as her senses centered on him.

"Answer me, Tess," he whispered against her mouth.

An emotion deep inside her stirred, an emotion she'd buried forever, she thought. "Yes, I'll go out with you."

She waited to see what would happen next, half anticipating him kissing her. His gaze locked with hers, and she felt a part of herself disappear.

"Mac, dinner's ready."

He lifted his head and muttered, "I'm gonna have to talk with my sister about her timing."

Slowly Tess's senses calmed enough for her to think rationally, to step away from him before she became lost again in his gaze. She welcomed the cooling breeze of evening as her heartbeat returned to a normal pace. He was a force she had never reckoned with or needed in her life. And in a moment of pure insanity she had promised to go out with him again Saturday night.

"I guess we'd better go inside or no doubt my whole family will come out to investigate…the sunset. They feel just because they're my family they have a right to know every little detail of my life, and then if that doesn't satisfy them, they make up a few tidbits."

"And you probably love every minute of it."

He lightly touched the small of her back as she went through the door. It was a casual gesture, but nonetheless it unnerved her.

In the dining room the adults were seated at the long table. The children were at a smaller table in the living room. All eyes were on Mac and Tess as they entered the room and quietly sat, Mac at the head of the table and Tess to his right.

"Mac, will you do the honor of saying grace?"

Bowing his head, Mac clasped her hand as well as Casey's, who sat on the other side of him. "Heavenly Father, please bless this food we are about to partake and give us the wisdom to see our path in this life."

She felt comforted, and strangely a sense of peace descended, his fingers about hers and his simple prayer filling the room with his conviction.

"It's about time you two came in. I'm starved, and we've been waiting ages for you guys," Casey said as she started passing the platter of ham around.

Mac shot his younger sister a narrowed look. "Watch it, kid, or I'll forget our conversation this morning."

"Casey, you didn't go over to Mac's to get his help concerning college?" Alice asked, clearly upset by the frown on Casey's face.

"Yes, I did. He's the only one you'll listen to. Besides, it's his money that's sending me to college. I thought he should know I don't want it right now."

Tess ate her dinner while the rest of the family debated the merits of going to college right out of high school or waiting a year. She loved listening to the bantering among family members. She hated discovering Mac's generous nature when it came to his family. He had done so much for them, which, against her will, only endeared him even more in her eyes. It was going to be hard to stay away from the man, because she felt the same pull he did. And he was right. She did need a friend. She had avoided getting close to anyone for far too long.

After everyone had shared an opinion on the subject, Alice stood to cut the birthday cake. "Mac, what do you think?"

"It's Casey's life. It's her decision. It's something, Mom, she has to want to do." He took a sip of iced tea. "But I want Casey to know right up front that I believe a college education is the way for her to go when she's ready. It opens so many doors."

His mother gave the first slices to Steve and Tess. "Then it's settled. Casey, you'll have to find yourself a job if you aren't going to college right away."

Tess was amazed at how rapidly everything had been decided after such a diverse and lively debate. In the end it had been Mac's opinion that counted. She got the impression he had become the father figure for all his brothers and sisters. What a wonderful burden to feel so needed by so many. Again she thought of her plans, which had died that day on the mountaintop in South America, and her throat constricted.

When the dinner was over, Kayla and Casey, Mac's sisters, started clearing the dishes while everyone else moved toward the living room.

"Can I help you?" Tess asked, needing to feel busy before her thoughts of the past took over.

"Sure. The more the merrier," Casey said and headed for the kitchen.

Tess picked up her plate and Mac's. He whispered as he left, "Don't believe a word they say about me. They've been dying to get you alone all evening. You just fell into their trap."

"Since I don't listen to gossip, you don't have a worry," Tess quipped as she strode away. The truth of the matter was she didn't want to know anything else about him. The more she discovered the more she liked, and she couldn't afford emotionally to become involved with anyone, especially him.

It didn't take one minute for the sisters to start the interrogation. "How did you two meet?" Kayla asked casually as she scraped food off the plates.

"Mac hasn't been too many places since the accident," Casey added.

"Sis, give her a chance to talk."

Tess smiled. Casey obviously didn't know all the finer points of an interrogation. "We met at the hospital."

"Hospital?" Kayla's forehead creased with a frown. "What was he—oh, I know. It must have been when he went to see Tommy." She looked expectantly at Tess for confirmation.

"Yes, he mentioned a little boy named Tommy."

"Mac hates hospitals, but he still visits the children whenever he can. Hospitals remind him too much of Dad and Sheila." Casey cut in with another tidbit of information.

It was clear to Tess that if she ever needed to know anything about Mac it was Casey she should pump for information.

"It was hardest on Mac having to watch Dad die slowly. They were so close," Casey continued as she opened the dishwasher. "Then of course, when Sheila delivered—"

"Casey, aren't there any more dishes on the table?" Kayla asked, exasperated at her younger sister.

"No, I don't think so."

"Go check anyway. Then see if Mom needs anything. I think we can manage."

"But…"

Casey's protest died on her lips at the look her older sister gave her. She went meekly out of the kitchen.

"Casey is the kind of source the *National Observer* would love to get hold of." Kayla cast a glance at Tess. "But it is true Mac was pretty torn up about Dad."

In other words, Tess dear, you'd better have honorable intentions toward the man or get lost. "You have nothing to worry about from me," Tess answered the unspoken question as she began to load the dishwasher. My intentions are to get lost—just as soon as the next date is over.

Mac peered into the kitchen. "Tess, I'm sorry to interrupt you two getting to know each other, but I have an early day tomorrow. Ready to leave?"

"Yes," she answered, hoping she didn't appear too eager.

"Thanks for your help," Kayla said as Tess joined Mac.

"I figured when Casey came into the living room you were in big trouble," Mac whispered when they were alone in the hallway. "Kayla fancies herself my protector from the female population."

"So, you don't have an early day tomorrow?"

"I always have an early day. I think dawn is the best part of the day."

"Where's Amy?" Tess asked, hoping the little girl could act as a barrier between Tess and Mac on the ride to Tess's apartment. Tess was beginning to feel she needed all the help she could get to stay away from Mac. Her acceptance of a second date was proof she had a hard time resisting him.

"She's staying with her grandma tonight. So it's just you and me." He winked at her as he turned to say his goodbyes to his family in the living room and kiss Amy good-night.

Mac hardly gave Tess time to say her own goodbyes before he whisked her away from his large family. In the small car she was reminded of his powerful presence, which saturated every inch of the interior.

"I'd forgotten how overwhelming my family can be to a newcomer."

His family overwhelming? There's no way they compare to him. "Protective is a better word."

"We almost scared off Mary when Justin first brought her around to meet the family."

"I'm not easily scared," she said, then wondered why she had.

He looked at her, his gray eyes penetratingly enticing. "I can see that."

The words, spoken in a husky timbre, tore at her already battered defenses. His study of her was so blatantly male that an ache deep inside threatened to rip the last of her defenses to shreds.

"You more than interest me, Tess. You're intriguing. One part of you is so innocent. The other I suspect has seen things that would make my stomach wrench. We'd better go. This certainly isn't the time or the place for this discussion."

Discussion? More like a temptation to forget everything she had promised herself, Tess thought and clasped her hands so tightly her knuckles turned white. But still she felt his lure—a lure that spoke of happier times, if only she could forget and forgive herself.

The drive to her apartment was done in silence. All of a sudden Tess felt physically and emotionally exhausted. She was beginning to wonder if she would have enough energy to walk to the front door.

At her apartment, Mac stood between her and the door. "I'll pick you up at seven. Dress casual."

"I can meet you at the restaurant."

"Is there a reason you don't want me to pick you up here?"

"Makes it seem like a date when aren't we just two friends going out to dinner?"

He stepped closer, slowly raising his hand toward her face. "Friends do go in the same car to places. And while we're on the subject of Saturday night, I'm paying for dinner. No Dutch treat, if that was what was going to pop into your head next."

"Fine," she murmured, deciding her brain had stopped functioning. She couldn't move an inch, so entranced was she by his presence. There was nothing friendly about what she was feeling.

When his fingers finally touched her cheek, she wanted to lean into him and seek his support because her legs felt so weak. For a few blissful seconds she wanted to forget her past, but reality was always just under the surface, ready to invade her thoughts. She felt again the pain of losing Kevin, of holding him in her arms as he lay dead. She felt again the anguish she had experienced when she had survived and no one else had.

Finally sanity returned, prodding Tess away from Mac. She fumbled for her key. "Thanks for a nice evening. It's late, and I do have an early morning." The words tumbled out in a coherent pattern that amazed her because inside she felt as though she were trapped in an English garden maze, lost and alone.

She finally found her key in the bottom of her oversize purse and quickly inserted it into the lock. "Good night. Thanks again."

Mac laid his hand over hers, the touch warm, intimate. "We're still on for Saturday?"

She needed to say no. She said yes, turned the knob and escaped inside. Leaning against the closed door, she listened as he left. With each step he took, she felt more alone, the way she wanted it ever since Kevin's untimely death. Then why did it bother her that such a nice man was walking away?

# Chapter Four

Mac listened to the recording for a second time as though that would erase the words on the machine. "Mac, this is Tess. I'm sorry I've got to cancel our date this evening. Something has come up."

He frowned, rubbing the back of his neck while he played the message a third time. Yep, he was sure of it. Something was wrong. He could hear it in her voice. That settled it. He was going over there, and if she answered the door, he would act as though he hadn't received her message. The quaver underlining her words drew him to her. He had to go and make sure she was all right.

The pounding in Tess's head matched the pounding of her heart. She reread the letter from Kevin's mother, the fine, neatly written words leaping off the page as if the woman was in the room with her, shouting at her. Tess squeezed her eyes closed, remembering the last time she had seen Kevin's mother, at his funeral. She had created a hysterical scene in front of everyone in her congregation, wanting to know why Tess had survived when her son hadn't.

Tess's hand shook as she carefully placed the letter on the coffee table then switched off the lamp next to the couch. Relieved that the shadows of dusk crept into the room, she stretched out on the sofa, hugging one of the throw pillows to her chest. The letter had restated the woman's ramblings at her son's funeral. Again.

Tess stared at the ceiling until the blackness totally swallowed the light and she couldn't see anything. She kept her mind blank, needing to think of nothing at the moment. But slowly thoughts slipped inside to torment her. The rebels had left her to die, but she hadn't. She had survived when no one else had.

For the past two years she had run from what had happened at the mission, but it was becoming more difficult to hide from the memories, to forget—to forgive. Weariness weaved its way through her, making her eyelids droop. Her grip on the pillow eased as the lure of sleep engulfed her.

*Tess threw her head back and took a deep breath of the crisp mountain air, clean, fresh. Not a cloud in the sky, and the temperature a perfect sixty-five. What a glorious day! She looked at the ring on her left hand, its diamond glittering in the sunlight. In a few short months she would be married.*

*Someone called her name. She glanced up.*

*Kevin stood in the middle of the Indian village nestled at the bottom of a mountain. He waved to her, a wide grin gracing his mouth. She started toward him, eager to share her news about the little girl brought in that morning who was finally responding to treatment.*

*Crack!*

*Kevin's smile crumpled as he collapsed to the ground, a bright red spreading on his white shirt.*

*She froze, her eyes widening at the pool of blood around Kevin. Then her world completely shattered as a horde of rebels from a mountain stronghold descended on the village like a swarm of locusts.*

*Screams pierced the clear mountain air. The scent of gunfire accosted her and propelled her forward— toward Kevin. Ten feet away. Five.*

The insistent ringing wormed its way into her nightmare, pushing Tess toward wakefulness. She blinked, trying to focus on the present.

The sound persisted, filling her mind with urgency. She rolled to her feet and fumbled for the switch on the lamp next to the couch. Brightness flooded the room, causing her to blink again.

Shaking the haze of sleep from her mind, she started for the door. When she peered out the peephole, she saw Mac standing on her front porch and immediately opened the door, forgetting to mask her dismay at seeing him.

"Are you ready—" His smile of greeting died when he looked into Tess's pale features, her eyes lackluster and pain-filled.

"What's wrong, Tess?"

She combed her fingers through her hair, staring at a place over his shoulder before swinging her gaze to his. "I left you a message. I can't—" Her voice broke, and tears welled into her eyes.

Mac stepped into the apartment and shut the door behind him. He drew her into his arms and pressed her head to his shoulder. "I know. I ignored the message." He'd had every intention of letting her believe he hadn't received the message, but suddenly it was very important for him to tell the truth. "I could tell something was wrong. That's when a person needs a friend the most."

The way he said *friend* made the tears flow. She had been running for the past two years and had avoided getting close to anyone. Now suddenly this man wasn't allowing her to remain aloof, and she was found she didn't want to. She needed to know someone cared, if only for a short time.

She felt the dampness of his shirt against her cheek and the strong stroke of his hand down the length of her back. She smelled his scent, sandalwood and soap. She heard the steady beat of his heart beneath her ear and felt as though its soothing rhythm could erase the remembered sounds of gunfire that echoed through her mind. And for a while it did. It had only been one of her nightmares. This was reality. Denver. The children she helped. Peter MacPherson.

"Do you want to talk about it?"

Tess shook her head, her throat still too tight to say anything, her fragile emotions raw and near the surface.

He continued holding her for a few minutes while she drew in calming breaths and tried to right the chaos she had felt deep inside since that day her life had changed. When she pulled back, still loosely fitted in his embrace, she peered at him through red-rimmed eyes.

"I must look a sight." She swiped her hand across her cheeks to rub away any evidence of her losing control. This was the second time he had found her crying in their short acquaintance.

His mouth quirked in a smile. "Maybe a sight for sore eyes." His arms fell to his sides.

Again she fingered her hair, trying to bring some order to its unruliness, and returned his smile. "If this is your way of cheering a gal up, it's working."

"Good, that's what I came over here to do. Give me some coffee and I'll regale you with stories of my family. That ought to make anyone thankful they don't have to walk in my shoes."

"I hear your teasing tone, and don't forget I've met that family. They are dears."

He tossed back his head and laughed. "Dears? My, I've never heard them referred to as dears."

His infectious laughter spread through her, warming her inside. She imagined his younger brothers, all over six feet and broad-shouldered like him, and knew they wouldn't want anyone to think of them as dears. "Well, at least your mother, daughter and sisters are."

"Oh, but the trials and tribulations of being the head of a large family. Casey was over at the house first thing this morning wanting me to help her find the perfect job. I said something about working at the foundation for me, and she immediately said no. She wants a job, but she's being awfully picky about it. Says she can't work for me."

"What does she like to do?"

"She likes working with people and she's good with computers."

"We have an opening on our floor for a unit secretary if she wants to apply at the hospital."

"I'll mention it to her. She loves children so she might go for it."

"Come on into the kitchen. I'll put some coffee on and even fix us something to eat." She stopped after only taking a few steps and turned to him. "That is if you haven't had anything for dinner yet."

"Nope." Mac followed her. "Do you have a roommate?"

"Yes, but Delise is gone for the weekend. She went to see her parents in Aspen. She wanted me to go but I—"

"—had a date."

She paused at the counter and glanced over her shoulder at him. "Well, yes, that, too. But I promised Jan I would work for her tomorrow. She needed some time off while her son was home from college."

"How long have you been a nurse?"

"Seven years."

"Have you only been a pediatric nurse?"

"No." Tess turned her attention to making the coffee, concentrating on keeping her hands from trembling.

"What else have you done?"

She hadn't heard him approach, but he stood right behind her. She sucked in a deep breath and held it for a long moment. "A little bit of everything," she finally answered, aware that her voice quavered.

He laid his hand on her shoulder and squeezed. "I'm sorry. Have I hit a taboo subject?"

She swallowed hard. "My first job as a nurse was in the emergency room in a large city hospital. I saw more that year than a lot of people do in ten years. I moved around after that, but I've decided working with children is what I want to do from now on."

He positioned himself next to her, lounging against the counter with his arms crossed over his chest. "I see your fascination with clowns extends to your home."

After putting the coffee on, Tess leaned next to him and looked about her. Her clown collection overflowed from the living room into the kitchen as well as her bedroom. "I started collecting them when I was a little girl. I can't go by one in a store and not buy it."

"I can tell. How many do you have?"

"I stopped counting after a hundred."

"Well, I know what to get you for your birthday."

"Yeah, I'm easy to buy for." She tried to ignore the implication of his teasing statement, but she couldn't. It suggested they would have a future. She saw how at home he appeared in her kitchen, and her wariness pushed to the foreground.

"Of course, a friend has to keep straight which clowns you have, and I'm sure there will come a time when you'll have everything there is to have."

She shoved away from the counter. "I always say if you're going to do something you might as well do it right."

"An all-or-nothing kind of person."

"Yeah, I'm afraid so. I tend to jump in with both feet."

"What happens when you discover there's no water?"

Tess went to the refrigerator, some of life's painful lessons washing over her. "It hurts when I land."

One side of his mouth lifted in a self-mocking grin. He bent and rubbed the leg that had been in a cast the week before. "Boy, I can attest to that."

She chuckled, glad he was putting the conversation on a light note. Searching her refrigerator, she came up with the makings for ham and cheese sandwiches.

"Can I help?"

"You can set the table while I make the sandwiches. The plates and glasses are over there, and the silverware is in that drawer." Tess pointed with the tip of a butter knife.

While she prepared their light dinner, she listened to Mac move about her kitchen as though he had visited her often and knew where everything was. Again the impression he was comfortable, at home in her apartment besieged her. That thought brought a halt to her movements as she slid a glance at the man who dominated any room he entered. He filled the space with his muscled body, but mostly his presence radiated confidence and determination. He had a direction to his life that Tess envied. Once she'd had a path to follow, but she'd lost her way.

"The coffee's done. Do you want any?"

His question broke into her thoughts. "Yes, please." She hurried to finish the sandwiches, realizing she was thinking too much.

When she sat at the table, the scent of brewed coffee wafted to her. She inhaled the fragrance, much too aware of the man next to her. After adding sugar to the coffee in her mug, she lifted it to her lips and took a sip.

He picked up the salt and pepper shakers and examined them. "Clowns. My daughter would like these."

"Most kids respond to clowns."

"Is that why you started your clown therapy?"

"Yes. I wanted a way to take their minds off why they were in the hospital. Most of the time I succeed." Tess began to eat her sandwich, enjoying the sharp taste of aged Cheddar cheese and the tang of the mustard.

"But not all the time?"

"Every once and a while I run across a tough cookie."

"Like Johnny?"

"Yeah, he's been a challenge."

"He's had a lot of hard knocks for a ten-year-old." Mac popped a potato chip into his mouth, then took a bite of the ham and cheese.

"I just hope Mrs. Hocks finds a relative for him to live with."

"Who's Mrs. Hocks?" Mac washed his meal down with a swallow of coffee.

"His case manager."

"What's gonna happen to him in the meantime?"

"He'll live with a foster family. He leaves the hospital on Monday afternoon."

"What does Johnny think about that?"

"He tells me he would rather be on the street taking care of himself."

"Do you believe him?"

Tess tilted her head to the side and thought about the last time she saw Johnny, his mouth set in a defiant frown. "Yes, I'm afraid he believes he's better off by himself. He's been shuffled between foster parents before."

"Then, do you think he'll run away?"

"He has a habit of doing that when faced with something he doesn't like."

Mac speared her with a sharp gaze. "Most people do."

She was close to squirming under his unrelenting stare. She felt as if he had delved into her mind and glimpsed her innermost thoughts. She dropped her glance to her plate and fingered what was left of her sandwich. "Sometimes running away is the best thing for a person. The only thing."

"Do you really believe that? Do you think that's what's best for Johnny?"

She lifted her gaze to his probing one. "No, it isn't. He needs a home, someone to love him. But he doesn't need to be shuffled between different foster parents just because he may be a little difficult."

"I agree." Picking up his half-eaten sandwich, Mac took another big bite and chewed slowly, the whole time his attention fixed on her face, a thoughtful expression in his eyes.

She blushed, wishing she could read what was in his mind. Or maybe she didn't want to. The flare of interest was more than she could handle. She wanted no complications in her life, and Peter MacPherson was definitely a complication. She looked away before he saw more than she wanted him to see.

Mac covered her hand next to her plate, forcing her attention to him. "I hope his case manager will find a relative to take him in."

"They've been looking for over a year, since he became a ward of the state. There may not be anyone. Johnny doesn't say much about his family. He won't talk about his mother, who died last year, and I don't think his father was ever around much. From what Mrs. Hocks has said, he abandoned them long ago." She slipped her hand from Mac's grasp, feeling the imprint of his fingers as though it was a brand.

"No one should have children unless they are willing to take care of them. They're too precious to ever take lightly."

She didn't want to get into the subject of having

children. That possibility had vanished for her when Kevin had been taken from her. Their dream of a large family was just that, a dream. Twisting her napkin in her lap, she searched for a topic of conversation that wasn't so painful. "Tell me about your work at the halfway house. You said you were fixing the roof and fell off the ladder when you broke your leg. Do you work there often?"

"I don't usually do those kinds of things at the halfway house, and after that accident, I'll make sure I hire someone to do it from now on. Being a handyman isn't my area of expertise."

"What is?"

"I usually hold counseling sessions several times a week. I spend most Monday, Wednesday and Friday afternoons there."

"Counseling? You're a counselor?"

"I majored in psychology in college, and after I quit football, I went back for my masters."

"I thought you were a businessman."

"That, too. I have investments and the foundation to look after. But my love is counseling. I wish I could do more, but I do have those other obligations that are important to me, too."

"Why the halfway house?"

"I've seen what drugs can do to people."

"So have I. Some of those emergencies I told you about my first year were drug related. Not a pretty sight."

"Then you understand why I have to do something. I had a friend in college who got involved with drugs. I couldn't help him. He died of an overdose. I promised myself then I would make a difference."

"I think that's why I became a nurse. Like Casey, I like people and found I wanted to help." Tess relaxed in her chair and sipped her coffee. She liked Mac a lot. He cared about others and wasn't afraid to show it. "In school I was good at science and for a while thought about being a chemist. Then I decided in college that I didn't want to be stuck in a lab, working with test tubes all day. I wanted to work with people, particularly children."

"I think my most rewarding work is with the youth group at church. Some of the most confusing, trying times for children are when they are in middle school. I find myself looking forward to teaching them each week about the power of the Lord's love. It has sustained me through a lot of rough times."

The devotion and intensity emanating from Mac reminded Tess of Kevin. She frowned and looked away, not wanting to remember anymore that evening. "I'm glad God is a comfort to you." She finished the potato chips on her plate as though it was important that she eat everyone of them.

"What happened, Tess?"

"Let's just say I was abandoned in my time of need and leave it at that." She stared at her empty plate.

"If you want to talk, I'm a good listener."

"The counselor in you?"

"The friend in me."

"There's nothing to say. I would rather leave my past in the past."

"Well, did I ever tell you about the time the kids in the youth group had me skateboarding in the parking lot?"

She shook her head.

"I crashed and burned several times. I'm surprised I didn't break my leg that day. I will say those kids make me feel young."

Tess laughed. "You are young."

"Sometimes when my body protests and creaks, I don't feel young."

"How old are you? Thirty-two? Thirty-three?"

"Thirty-four."

"Oh, what an old man you are," she teased, enjoying the heightened color that crept into his cheeks.

"Okay. Turnabout is fair play. How old are you?"

"Didn't your mother tell you never to ask a lady her age?"

"Yes. How old are you, Tess?"

The mischievous gleam in his eyes made her heart beat faster. "Twenty-eight. *Much* younger than you."

"I'm robbing the cradle."

She tensed, realizing how easy it would be to fall in love with Mac. She wouldn't do that to herself again. "But we aren't dating."

"This was supposed to be a date. Remember?"

"Yes, but I canceled."

"I'm here. I didn't let you cancel."

"Well—" She couldn't think of anything to say to

that declaration. She snapped her mouth closed and stared at him.

"But you're right—this really isn't a proper date. So you owe me one. Let's say next Saturday night, and don't leave any messages on my answering machine begging off."

Tess rose, busying herself by taking her plate and cup to the sink. "I'm sorry. I am busy next Saturday night."

"Washing your hair?"

"No."

"Cleaning your bathroom?"

"No, I'm working. I'm pulling double shifts for the next few weeks. We're shorthanded at the hospital."

She listened to the scrape of his chair across the linoleum, then his footsteps covering the distance between them. He placed his dishes in the sink next to hers, his arm brushing against hers. Tension whipped down her body as she turned on the water, her hands trembling.

"Thanks for the sandwich. I'd better go. I'll be seeing you."

Surprised—and somewhat disappointed—that he gave up so fast, Tess dried her hands and followed him from the kitchen. "I appreciate your understanding about this evening." She opened the front door and leaned on it while he stepped over the threshold.

Turning, he smiled. "Any time. Good night, Tess."

She watched him walk toward his car, perplexed at her reaction to him leaving so abruptly. Wasn't that what she wanted? To be left alone? Then why did it bother her that he didn't fight longer for a date with her?

Mac sat in his car staring at the closed door to Tess's apartment. Like her heart. Closed to the Lord. Closed to people who cared about her.

*Heavenly Father, give me the guidance and strength to help Tess through her hurt and pain. She needs You. Help me make her see that.*

As he started his sedan, he suddenly knew what he would do to help Tess. In the dark, he smiled.

# Chapter Five

Tess stared out the picture window that overlooked the hospital parking lot, the mountains in the background. "Where is Johnny?"

"They'll find him, Tess." Delise laid a reassuring hand on her shoulder. "Where would a ten-year-old boy go?"

"I knew he was going to run away."

"And you told Mrs. Hocks your fears. That was all you could do."

"He's been gone for two days. It still gets cold at night here."

Delise's tightening clasp on Tess's shoulder conveyed her support. "I know. About all we can do right now is pray."

Tess rejected that option. She had tried it once, and it hadn't helped. She whirled. "I can do more than pray. I know that when my shift is over I'm hitting the streets again."

"You were out searching for Johnny the past two evenings. You don't even know where to look. Let the police handle this."

"I can't sit home and wait. I have to do something. Even if it's driving around looking, it's better than sitting home and waiting for the phone to ring." Or worse, the phone not ringing. Tess ignored her friend's worried look as she headed to the nurses' station.

Delise followed her. "I can't go with you tonight. I'm working a double shift. I don't like you going out looking by yourself. Some of the places we went last night weren't too safe."

"Delise, I'm—" Tess pivoted to face her friend and halted in midsentence. Mac stood behind her roommate. "I'm a big girl. I can take care of myself." Some of her words lost their punch as she stared at Mac.

Delise glanced over her shoulder at him. "I'm glad you're here. Talk some sense into her. She won't listen to me. She shouldn't go out by herself looking for Johnny."

"What happened to Johnny? Did he run away?"

Tess nodded.

"How long ago?"

"Two days." Seeing Mac made Tess's heart lift. Somehow she knew things would be okay.

"I'll go with you. When are you off?"

"In an hour. Why are you here?"

"I brought Casey in for an interview about that unit secretary's job. You should have called me and told me about Johnny disappearing two days ago."

"I—" Tess didn't have anything to say to that gentle scolding. She'd dialed his number once and hung up. She'd known he would help and that he would want to know about the child's disappearance, but she didn't think she could handle being around Mac. He overwhelmed her, and this situation with Johnny made her emotionally vulnerable.

"Tell you what. I'll call Mrs. Hocks, talk to her and see what I can find out. Then I'll be back to pick you up in an hour. We'll go from there."

"I'll be ready," Tess murmured as she watched him stroll away.

Delise whistled softly. "My, what a take-charge kind of guy. He's a keeper."

And that was what Tess was afraid of. How do you resist an irresistible guy?

"I'll take some more of that coffee." Tess held her empty mug out for Mac to refill. "I know it's April, but it's cold out there." A shiver flashed up her spine as she cradled the warm cup between her hands and stared out the windshield. She savored the aroma of the hot brew and relished the steam wafting over her face in waves.

Then she thought of Johnny, out in the cold by himself, and frowned. "Why did he do it? Leave a safe haven for this?" She gestured toward the vacant parking lot.

"He thinks he's alone. We'll have to show him he's not."

"They're talking about a chance for snow tonight." Another shiver assailed her.

Wind blew the limbs of the trees, shaking the tender new leaves in its angry grasp. Pieces of trash swirled across the deserted parking lot, the glare of the street lamp nearby casting a harsh light about Mac's car as though it were a spotlight.

"Where else do you think we should look?" Tess took a tentative sip of the hot coffee.

"I'm fresh out of ideas. We've been to every place Mrs. Hocks could think of. Of course, the police have already checked those places, too, but it didn't hurt to look again."

"And again, if need be."

"Tess, you need to prepare yourself in case they don't find Johnny." Mac caught her gaze and looked long and hard into her eyes. "He's street smart. There are a lot of places a kid can hide in this town."

"He's sick and weak. We've got to find him."

Finishing his coffee, he started the engine. "Then we'd better get moving. We'll drive around the area where the police found him the last time he ran away. Maybe we'll get lucky, Lord willing."

Tess listened to the strong faith in Mac's voice and wished she had it. But it hadn't been the Lord who had rescued her in South America. It had been her hard determination to stay alive in the face of tough odds. That same determination came to the surface as Mac steered his car onto the streets.

"Johnny's lucky to have someone like you on his side," Mac said, making a turn onto the road where the police had found Johnny a few weeks before.

"I wish I could take him into my home, but as you know, the apartment I share with Delise is small. And besides, we both work quite a bit. Johnny needs someone there for him, especially at the beginning."

"Maybe Mrs. Hocks will find a relative."

"I'm not sure that's the answer. Johnny has told me he doesn't want to live with relatives he doesn't know. To him they'd be no different than foster parents."

The blare of Tess's cell phone cut into the silence. Startled, she jumped. "I forgot I left it on." She fumbled in her purse and pulled it out, flipping it open. "Tess here."

"Johnny's been brought into the hospital. He's down in the emergency room right now. I thought you'd want to know."

"We'll be right there, Delise. Thanks for calling." Tess clicked off and told Mac about Johnny.

He made a U-turn in the middle of the road and headed for the hospital. "At least he'll be warm tonight."

"And from now on, if I have anything to do with it," Tess said, not sure how she was going to follow through with her vow.

"He's lucky he didn't freeze to death." Tess stared at Johnny asleep in the hospital bed, his face pale and thin, dark circles under his eyes. "How do I make him realize he's not alone, Mac, that there are people who care about him?"

"With the Lord's help." Mac came up behind her.

She felt his presence down the length of her even though he didn't touch her. She stiffened, resisting him, resisting his words. "I'm going to depend on my powers of persuasion. You can depend on God."

"I've asked you before what happened to make you turn away from the Lord."

"He let me down when I needed Him the most."

"Are you so sure of that?"

Tess spun and took a step back to put some space between them. "Most definitely." She kept her voice low, aware of the child in the bed behind her.

"Do you say that because He didn't do what you wanted? Sometimes, Tess, we have to put our faith in the knowledge that our Lord knows what is best, not us."

Her fingernails dug into her palms. "All I wanted was for a good man who served God to live to continue his ministry."

Suddenly the room seemed to stifle her. She fled into the hallway and leaned against the wall, drawing in shallow breaths. The click of the door closing brought her head up. She stabbed Mac with a narrowed look and hoped he got the hint. She didn't want to talk about it anymore. The pain speared her heart, and she bled all over again as though the wound was fresh.

"Tess—"

She held up her hand. "Please, Mac. I didn't say that so we could start a discussion."

"I stand by what I said. We don't always know what the Lord wants of us or our loved ones." He lifted his hand toward her. "Now, let me walk you to your car. You need to get some sleep."

Combing her fingers through her hair, she avoided his touch, knowing its enticing lure. Instead, she attempted a smile that she knew failed and asked, "Gee, do I look that bad?"

"No, but you do look exhausted. Those double shifts are beginning to add up."

"I'm staying. I need to reassure myself that Johnny will be here tomorrow morning. That he won't somehow get up in the middle of the night and escape before I can talk to him."

"You can't be with him all the time. There comes a time when you have to put faith—"

She pressed her fingers against his mouth and instantly regretted touching him. She dropped her hand and moved away, her back coming in contact with the door into Johnny's room. "Don't say it. I'm staying. Good night, Mac."

"Then I'll stay with you and keep you company."

"You have a family at home."

"I have a live-in housekeeper who takes excellent care of Amy. She'll be fine. You, on the other hand, I'm not so sure about."

"You aren't my keeper."

"I know that. You've made it perfectly clear to me and everyone else that you want to stand on your own two feet."

Her chin came up a notch. "And what's so bad about that?"

"I hate to say a cliché, but I'm going to anyway. No man, or in this case woman, is an island. You aren't alone, just like Johnny isn't alone. How can you make Johnny see that if you don't believe it?"

His words struck her with the truth. She didn't have an answer for him. Most of her life she had depended on people around her to complete who she was, first her parents, who died one after the other, then Kevin, who was murdered. She gave Mac a look that told him to back off. "I depend on no one for my happiness. Johnny will need to learn to depend on himself, too, when the time is right. The time isn't right for him."

Determined not to let her emotions get the best of her, Tess decided the only thing she could do was ignore Mac as much as possible. Behind her she fumbled for the handle and quickly opened the door to slip inside Johnny's room—she hoped alone. The sound of Mac entering behind her made her stiffen her resolve to put as much distance between them as possible. But then she realized the only comfortable place to sit down was the love seat on which Mac was already seated. Her legs trembled from exhaustion. Reluctantly she eased down next to him after pacing the small room for fifteen minutes.

In the dim light the hard lines of Mac's face were softened, and she could see the weariness etched into his features. She fought the urge to brush her fingers over those features as though that action could erase the deep lines of fatigue. Clenching her hands in her lap, she sat up straight, her shoulders thrust back.

He touched her arm. "If you don't relax, I'm afraid you're going to shatter. If you sit back, I promise not to think you're depending on me."

She whipped her head around, meaning to say something scathing, but the words lumped together in her throat. His look melted her resolve, and she realized he was only trying to help her and Johnny.

He smiled, his eyes sad. "It's gonna be a long night, Tess."

The tender concern in his look moved her more than she cared to acknowledge. It had been a long time since she'd felt such companionship. His offer of friendship was a temptation she found unable to resist. She leaned against the cushion, her body nestled in the crook of his arm. "I'm afraid you're right."

"Then you and I should be as comfortable as possible on this hard, incredibly small couch."

She grinned at him. "I think you have a point, but this love seat is much better than that chair over there."

Mac inspected the chair with a wooden back and a cushion that had little padding. "True." His attention returned to Tess. "What would you like to talk about?"

His whispered question flowed over her in enticing waves, beckoning her to get to know him better. Danger lay in that direction. "The weather? It's beastly out there for this time of year."

"Oh, yes, beastly. But you're from Maine. You should be used to the cold."

"I'm finished with winter and definitely ready for summer."

"Well, now that we've explored the weather, what else do you think is a safe subject?"

"Not politics."

"Nor religion."

Tess started to sit up when Mac's hand on her shoulder stopped her.

"I shouldn't have said that, Tess. But one day I hope you will open up to me and tell me what has put that look of sadness in your eyes. Did I tell you Casey got the job?"

She latched onto the change in subject matter, easing again into the crook of his arm. "I'm glad she will be joining us. We have a great group of people working on this floor."

"She's excited and relieved. Mom hasn't let up since the birthday party about her getting a job. She doesn't believe in idleness."

"What's Casey been doing since high school graduation?"

"A little bit of everything. She doesn't know what she wants. Ever since she graduated from high school in December, she has been going from one job to another."

"She's still young. A lot of young people her age don't know what they want to do."

"Were you like that?"

"No, I always wanted to be a nurse. How about you? Did you always want to play football?"

"I love the game. I got paid well for doing something I enjoyed. Can't beat that."

"Then why did you quit?"

A shadow fell across his face. Tess felt the tension in his arm. He had taboo subjects just as she did.

"My heart went out of the game. When I first started, I told myself I would quit while I was on top, so I did."

"What happened?"

For a long, breath-held moment Mac didn't say anything. The stark expression on his face conveyed the struggle he was having concerning what to tell her. She knew what it was like to have a past that haunted you. She reached out to place her hand on his arm to impart her support. He spoke in a low, barely audible voice.

"We were in the playoffs, and the score was tight. My wife went into labor early. No one told me until the game was over. By the time I got there, she was in surgery. I never got to say goodbye. I was too late."

"I'm sorry," she mumbled, knowing how inadequate those words really were. Beneath her hand his arm muscles bunched.

"I just couldn't play football after that."

"No one told you?"

"The game wasn't here in Denver, but that hour would have made a difference. The coach didn't realize that."

"I know how important it is to say goodbye. When you can't, you feel there's unfinished business between you."

His gaze swung to hers. "Have you lost someone close? Not been able to say goodbye?"

"Yes, my father had a heart attack. He was fine one day. The next he was gone. My mother pined away and died within a year. They were so much in love she just didn't want to go on without him."

"How old were you?"

"Eighteen. My parents were older when they finally had me. They had tried to have children for years. I was a surprise, because they had given up. I think by the time I came along I was an intrusion." The second Tess said the last sentence she wanted to snatch it back. She had never voiced that thought to another human being. She hadn't allowed herself to think it because the implication hurt.

He brought her close to him, his hand massaging her arm. Silence reigned in the hospital room, only the occasional sounds from the hallway intruding. Tess laid her head on his shoulder and thought about what she had told him. In a short time he had learned more about her than most people she'd known for years knew. That in itself should warn her to stay as far away from the man as possible. Before long she would be telling him about Kevin and reliving those painful memories when all she wanted to do was forget and maybe in the process forgive herself.

In the dim light Mac shifted on the couch, stretching his long legs in front of him. The feel of him next to her comforted her. Tess nestled closer to him, her eyelids drooping as the exhaustion she'd held at bay took over and sleep descended.

* * *

The scent of sandalwood washed over Tess, teasing her senses. Then she noticed that her body ached. Her face was pressed into something hard, angular. Her eyes snapped open to bright sunlight streaming through the slits in the blinds and forming stripes across the linoleum floor and the hospital bed that held Johnny.

Blinking, she straightened, her actions awakening the man next to her on the beige love seat. Her heartbeat began to race as his sleepy look took her in. She resisted the urge to brush a wayward lock of hair that had fallen onto his forehead. Much too intimate a gesture when she was trying desperately to keep this man at arm's length. One side of his mouth hitched up in a lopsided grin.

"Good morning, Tess."

The way he caressed her name caused her heart to beat even faster. She drew in a shallow breath, then a deeper one while she struggled to stand and put some space between them. She plowed her fingers through her hair and said, "I hadn't intended to fall asleep."

"You were tired." Mac leaned forward, resting his forearms on his thighs. "Besides, Johnny is here and still sound asleep."

She stared at the small boy in the bed, his features ashen, almost gaunt, and something twisted in her heart. She knew she couldn't save all the children, but what was it about this one that touched her so deeply? Kindred spirits? "I guess we weren't very good guards. Sleeping on the job."

"I'd better not add surveillance to my résumé, then."

His teasing comment eased the tension she'd experienced from waking up beside him on the couch. "I know it wasn't likely Johnny was going anywhere last night. He was very weak and dehydrated, but I just had to make sure."

"How about some coffee?"

"I don't want to leave yet."

"Then I'll go get us some and bring it back here."

"That would be great. I take cream and lots of sugar."

"How much is lots?"

"Four or five packets."

His eyes widened. "You drink hot sugar water with a little coffee flavor. You ruin a perfectly good drink."

"That's the only way I could drink coffee when I was younger. The habit has stuck with me. The coffee in the room behind the nurses' station is good. Get it there."

She watched him walk to the door and open it, a casual grace about his movements for such a large man. From what she had discovered about him on the playing field he had been surprisingly quick for his size. Not that she would ever tell him that she'd asked about him.

When he left, she stretched her arms above her head, then twisted from side to side to try to work the kinks from her body. She rarely slept sitting up and was surprised she had even though she was exhausted. But she could vividly recall the warmth and comfort she'd experienced when Mac's arm went about her shoulder and he held her close to him.

Out of the corner of her eye she saw Johnny move, trying to take the IV out. She rushed to his side and placed her hand over the connection. "If you think you're going somewhere, I have news for you, young man. You're staying put. Got that?" She schooled her voice into a no-nonsense tone, making sure he didn't hear the fear behind her words. Johnny was smart enough to use that.

The corners of his mouth turned down in a pout, and he glared at her.

She hovered over him like a mother hen protecting her young chick. "Understand?"

"Guess so," he mumbled and looked away.

Tess pulled the one hard-backed chair in the room to his bed and sat. "Good. I lost three nights of sleep because of you, and I don't know if I can keep that up. People count on me to be sharp when I work."

He turned his head to stare at her. "You did? Why?"

She gentled her stern expression. Johnny really didn't understand that she cared about him. She could see it in his confused look. "Because you're important to me. I care what happens to you. Why did you run away?"

"I ain't gonna stay with strangers. I can take care of myself."

She wanted to hug him to her and knew he would be upset if she tried. "With luck Mrs. Hocks will find a relative soon, and you won't have to stay with any strangers."

He huffed, his glare back. "I don't have no relatives

I know. My grandma died a while back, and she was all there was."

Tess leaned forward. "Please promise me you won't run away again."

He clamped his lips together, his eyes narrow, his mouth set in a frown.

"Johnny?"

"I ain't gonna promise something I can't keep. My word is important to me."

"A man of his word. That's a good trait to have in life, Johnny."

Both Tess and Johnny glanced at Mac who stood at the end of the bed. She'd been so intent on the child she hadn't heard Mac enter the room. He smiled at her and held up a cup.

Taking a sip of the coffee, she welcomed the warm, sweet brew as it slid down her throat. She needed the time to compose a response to Johnny's declaration. "What if we can find someone you know to stay with?" she asked, desperate to keep him from running away, but not really sure how she could.

"Maybe." Johnny dropped his gaze from Mac who came around the bed to stand next to Tess.

"I'll have a word with Mrs. Hocks. I might be able to work something out." Tess toyed with the idea of taking care of Johnny but still didn't think that would be the best solution. He needed a family. He needed someone who would be there for him.

Johnny pulled the white sheet to his neck and turned

slightly on his side away from Tess. Mac nodded toward the door, and she rose. In the hallway Mac stopped her with his words. "I'll have a word with Mrs. Hocks about taking care of Johnny until she finds a permanent home for him."

Tess whirled. "You're a stranger. That won't work any better than the foster parents he ran away from."

"Since the nurse at the desk told me Johnny would be staying a few days in the hospital, I'll make it a point to get to know him."

"Just like that?" She snapped her fingers, not sure why she was upset by his solution. No, correction. She knew why. In order to get to know Johnny, Mac would have to visit him a lot at the hospital, and she was working the next few days, which meant she would see Mac a lot more than she wanted to.

He stepped closer. "Yes, just like that."

"He's a tough one to crack."

"I know that."

"Then how do you plan on doing it?"

"By being here for him. I'm not easily discouraged."

Another appealing quality about him, Tess thought, and wished she could find reasons not to like the man. "I need to go home and change. I'm on duty in less than an hour."

Mac headed for Johnny's room.

"What are you doing?"

"Getting started on getting acquainted with Johnny. See you in a while." He opened the door.

"Mac!"

His gaze found hers.

"Thanks for helping last night."

His smile lit his eyes. "Any time."

When Mac disappeared inside Johnny's room, Tess inhaled a deep, cleansing breath. Her legs felt like jelly, and her hands trembled. Exhaustion, she told herself, but that really wasn't the truth. Peter MacPherson affected her on many levels. Somehow over the next few days she was going to have to get real good at avoiding the man, because every time she was around him she felt herself weakening and dreaming of much more than friendship.

## Chapter Six

You would think this pediatric floor would be big enough for the both of them, Tess thought, not for the first time that day. She fixed a polite smile on her face and said, "Johnny shouldn't be gone too much longer, Mac." *Go find something to do that is useful. Quit driving me crazy.* She wanted to add the words but remained silent, proud of herself.

"Do you think he'll like this?" Mac placed the handheld video game on the counter in front of her.

"Are you using bribery to win him over?"

"I'll use any means I need to in order to keep him off the streets." Mac slipped the game into the pocket of his navy blue windbreaker.

"You could regale him with some stories of your days playing football. The other kids seem to enjoy them."

"I've done that. It didn't work, and he leaves

tomorrow. I asked Mrs. Hocks not to let him know just yet that I'd be his new foster parent."

"Chicken," she teased, not daring to let the man know how elated she was about him being Johnny's foster parent. Mac's family and home would be perfect for the child if Johnny would allow anyone through his tough shell.

Mac propped himself against the counter as though he was staying for awhile. "Okay, any bright ideas?"

Shaking her head, she laughed. "No, the video game is great. I haven't found a boy who doesn't like them." She glanced toward an orderly who was wheeling a patient down the hall. "And you'll get your chance right now to see what Johnny thinks. I have to get back to work before they fire me."

"They wouldn't do that. You're too valuable. I've seen you work with the kids. You're a natural," Mac said as he headed toward Johnny's room.

Tess really tried not to feel pleased by his compliment. That would only endear the man more to her, but his words warmed her. *You're a natural.* She repeated his words in her mind, her heart constricting. Memories of the times she and Kevin had discussed the family they were going to have inundated her, and for a moment she was flung back in time. She gripped the counter and closed her eyes, trying to right her world.

She forced herself to concentrate on her job. She had several temperatures that needed to be taken, then some notes to jot down. Work had been what had gotten her through the rough times before. And it would again, she told herself as she made her way toward a patient's room.

Half an hour later she stopped by the counter to grab a chart and saw Mac leaving Johnny's room, a frown etched into his features. Avoid him. She could have slipped into the examination room next to the nurses' station and gone unseen by Mac.

Instead, she walked up to him and said, "The video game didn't work."

"So much for your theory. He acted like he'd never seen one."

"Maybe he hasn't. He's never had much. What are you going to do now?"

"Try something else. I'm not giving up."

"What?"

He raked his hand through his hair, a frustrated expression on his face. "That's the problem. I'm fresh out of ideas."

"You were a boy once. What would you have liked?"

He thought a moment then his face brightened with a smile. "That's it! Thank you, Tess." He clasped her by the upper arms, drew her close and quickly planted a kiss on her cheek before hurrying away.

Tess stood in the middle of the busy hallway, stunned, her fingers caressing the place where his mouth had touched her skin briefly. She could swear it tingled. Beneath her hand she could feel the warmth of her blush as she thought of his kiss. Oh, my, what would she had done if he had kissed her on the mouth? Fainted?

* * *

Perplexed, Tess frowned. Why would Mac bring Amy to visit Johnny? Not ten minutes before, the two of them had disappeared into the boy's room. This was Mac's big idea to win Johnny over? Okay, maybe he knew something she didn't. He'd been a boy once. But a three-year-old girl?

Finally, after ten more minutes had passed and no one had left Johnny's room, Tess decided she couldn't wait any longer. She headed toward the door. Okay, so she needed lessons in how to avoid a man, but she was dying to see why he had brought Amy to visit Johnny. Usually a patient woman, she had to acknowledge she had no patience where Mac was concerned.

She pushed open the door and heard children's laughter spicing the air with warmth. The sound wiped the frown from her face and lifted her spirits. Maybe the man knew what he was doing, after all. She stopped inside the room and took in the scene before her. Amy sat on the bed with Johnny, listening intently to him as he read a Dr. Seuss story about green eggs and ham.

Johnny finished the book and flipped it closed, setting it on his lap. He peered at Amy, a smile on his pale face. "I forgot how funny that story was."

"Daddy, I want green eggs 'morrow." Amy turned the book over and opened it. "Again—please."

She looked at Johnny, her big brown eyes framed by long, dark eyelashes, and Tess figured the little girl had made a conquest. Johnny wouldn't be able to resist that sweet, innocent face or those dimples in her plump cheeks as she smiled at him.

Johnny sighed heavily. "Okay. But only one more time."

Amy clapped. "Oh, goody. You do such a good job."

While Johnny started the story again, Mac slipped out of the chair and took Tess's arm to guide her from the room. "Is there something wrong?"

She shook her head. "No, it looks like you have everything under control. But I don't understand why you brought Amy here."

"Once when I was about eleven I was in the hospital because my appendix had to be removed. The one thing that made me feel better was seeing my family—even my sisters. Little children have a way of making a person forget about his troubles. I was hurting but I didn't care. I put on a front for them, and before long, I forgot about my own pain and enjoyed their company. I thought Amy could help Johnny."

"I don't believe it. It's working."

"It's a start. She brought her favorite book to share with him, and when she asked him to read it, he couldn't say no even though I know he wanted to."

"How many times has he read it?"

"Three. Actually Amy could recite it for Johnny, but the last time he started using different voices for the characters, and she loved that. I don't quite get into the story like he did."

She cocked her head. "And why not?"

"Because I've read that book probably three hundred times. After the first twenty times it kinda loses its appeal."

She chuckled. "I can see what you mean."

"I'd better get back inside. Amy can overstay her welcome. I want to win him over, not chase him away. Oh, by the way, Casey starts work here tomorrow."

"Good," Tess said and wanted to groan. Another MacPherson in her life. At this rate she would never be rid of the man.

After Mac and Amy left, Tess paid another visit to Johnny. He plucked at the sheet, his gaze fixed on his lap, his forehead wrinkled in deep thought. He didn't even look up when she entered the room.

"Amy's quite a character," Tess said.

"She's okay for a girl," Johnny mumbled, his head still down, his hands twisting the sheet.

"I know she enjoyed you reading that story to her."

"Yeah, I guess so." Finally Johnny looked up. "Why did Mr. MacPherson bring his daughter to see me?"

"He's taken an interest in you."

"Well, I don't need no one to care."

Tess straightened the bedding, needing something to do with her hands. The urge to pull the child into her arms was so strong she was afraid she would act on it and really upset Johnny. He wasn't ready for that. She didn't know if he ever would be. The shell about his heart was tougher than hers.

"Do you know what Amy said to me? She said she

had lots of cousins but no brothers and sisters. She wants a brother and sister, but she knows her dad doesn't like to talk about it."

"Is that right?" Tess's hands trembled as she fluffed his pillows.

"She says her mommy is in heaven watching over her. She told me mine was doing the same thing."

"She's right."

"Then why isn't my mother doing a good job?"

The question caught Tess off guard. She didn't have an answer for the child. Why did children like Johnny suffer? There was a time when she would have readily been able to answer him. Now her doubts about the Lord plagued her and made her wonder why, too.

She pasted a bright smile on her face and said, "I know, Johnny, you'll get better. I know that in here." She pressed her hand over her heart, fighting the tears clogging her throat. "Everything will work out." She had to believe that. She didn't want to give the child false hope, but neither could she tell him that bad things happened to good people.

"Sure. You have to say that." He turned and presented his back to her.

She reached out toward Johnny, wanting to connect with him, but she knew he would reject any attempt on her part to touch him. "No, Johnny, I don't have to say anything," she murmured and left the room. She hoped that somehow Mac could reach this child, because she couldn't seem to.

\* \* \*

"May I join you?"

Tess glanced up to find Casey standing beside her table with a lunch tray in her hands. The young woman wore a hopeful expression on her face, and Tess could remember her first day on the job. So much to learn, so many new people.

"Of course." After Mac's sister sat, Tess asked, "How's the job so far?"

"Great. A bit overwhelming, but then I expected that since it's a new job." Casey popped a French fry, smothered in ketchup, into her mouth. "I was supposed to meet Mac here for lunch, but I guess he's running late. He wanted to get everything ready for Johnny."

"When's he going to tell Johnny?"

"This afternoon when Mrs. Hocks visits." Casey took a bite of her hamburger, chewed it quickly, then leaned forward and said, "I'm so glad he's decided to do this. Being a foster parent will be good for Mac. He's great with children. He wanted a whole bunch of them with Sheila."

The aroma of onions and hamburger made Tess wish she had gotten what Mac's sister was eating. Tomato soup and tossed green salad were good for her diet but didn't do much for her appetite. "Well, he's still young."

With a frown Casey munched on another fry. "I don't know. When his wife died, something happened to Mac. He doesn't talk about it, but he took her death especially hard. I think—"

"Casey, I see you couldn't wait for me to eat lunch." Mac swung into the chair between his sister and Tess.

Tess tamped down the disappointment she was experiencing at Mac's untimely interruption. Everyone was so guarded about Mac and his relationship with his deceased wife. On the outside it appeared as though he had moved on, but Tess got the feeling that really wasn't the case. He was still dealing with her death as Tess was with Kevin's.

"You're late. I have a schedule to maintain now."

"Sorry. Traffic. I had to sign some more papers at Mrs. Hocks's office." Mac shifted his attention to Tess. "How's Johnny today?"

"Not saying much, which really isn't that unusual."

"Well, now that I have everything signed, sealed and delivered, I'm gonna tell him about the arrangement I have with Mrs. Hocks."

"Good luck." Tess looked around. "Where's Amy? I thought you might bring reinforcements today to help bolster your case."

Mac chuckled. "If this is gonna work with Johnny, he'll have to accept me. We might as well see how receptive he is to the idea of me being his foster parent."

"Besides, this is Mom's day with Amy, and nothing interferes with that. You can't get Mom near a hospital," Casey added, stuffing another French fry into her mouth.

"Do you want moral support when you tell him?" Tess asked, trying to ignore her mouth watering at the quickly disappearing fries on Casey's plate.

His eyes crinkled at the corners, a smile deep in their depths. "I'd love it."

"Then let me know, and I'll try to be there."

"How about now?"

"Fine. I have fifteen more minutes of my lunch break." After downing the last few swallows of her iced tea, Tess rose.

"You guys gonna leave me to eat alone?"

"Casey, if I know you, you'll have a whole flock of people around you in no time." Mac picked up Tess's tray to place on the conveyor belt near the exit. "I'll stop by and see you after I talk with Johnny."

Tess saw the nervous smile Mac sent his sister and knew he was concerned about this meeting. She took his hand in hers and said, "Kids can tell when someone cares. That's gonna mean something to Johnny."

"Will you come to dinner tonight?"

Tess blinked, surprised by the invitation. Words of refusal lodged in her throat.

"I could use your support during his first night with the family. A familiar face will help."

She choked back her refusal and nodded. Releasing his grasp before she became too comfortable holding his hand, she went through the swinging cafeteria doors and headed for the bank of elevators.

On the ride to the pediatric floor Mac lounged against the stainless-steel wall with his arms crossed over his chest. "What time do you get off work?"

"Three."

"You could follow us home."

"I rode with Delise."

"Then you can ride with us, and I'll take you home later tonight. We'll have an early dinner since I'm sure Johnny will be tired his first day out of the hospital."

"How are you going to prevent him from running away?"

Pushing away from the wall, Mac prepared to exit the elevator as it came to a stop. "If he wants to, short of locking him in his room, I can't. All I can do is show him I care about him and make him a part of my family."

"I hope that's enough." Remembering how pale and drawn the child had been after his last bout on the street, Tess chewed her bottom lip, worried that no one would be able to stop Johnny from running away again.

When they reached the child's room, Tess hung back, realizing Mac would have to be the one to convince Johnny he wanted to be his foster parent. The boy saw both of them, slipped the video game under the top sheet and frowned at them.

"Did you want something?"

Mac pulled the hard chair close to the bed. "To talk."

"What about?" Johnny narrowed his eyes on Mac.

Mac inhaled a deep breath and said, "About you coming to stay with me and Amy."

Johnny's gaze widened for a few seconds, then slid from Mac's face. "Stay with you?"

"I have plenty of room. In fact, my house is too big for just Amy and me. We were hoping you'd share it with us." When Johnny remained quiet, Mac added, "Mrs. Hocks has given her okay. You have to stay with someone. I'd like it to be us."

Tess watched Johnny ball the white sheet in his hands, the video game slipping off his lap. It would have fallen to the floor if Mac hadn't been quick and caught it in midair. Mac didn't say a word to Johnny about the game, just set it on the child's lap, his gaze fixed on Johnny.

The child latched on to the video game, his grip tight. "Okay, for the time being."

"Great! I'm gonna make the arrangements, then I'll be back to pick you up. Tess is going home with us after her shift is over at three. I need to call Amy and tell her you're coming. She's so excited."

"She is?"

"She told me not to come home without you."

Johnny stared wide-eyed at Mac as he left the room, his hands clenched around the video game so tight that his knuckles were white. "Did you ask him to do this?"

"No, he came up with the idea all on his own. I think it's a good idea."

"It's only temporary."

Tess's heart ached. She came to sit where Mac had been and took Johnny's hand. She felt his tremor as he curled his fingers into a ball. "We don't know what the future holds for us. Things will work out," she said with more conviction than she really felt.

Johnny gripped her for a few seconds before he

realized it and released his grasp. "Yeah, they always do," he mumbled.

Tess hated to hear sarcasm in such a young child. He was world-weary and only ten years old.

"We're home," Mac called as he stepped into his house with Johnny and Tess beside him.

Amy came running from the den and flung herself into Mac's arms. He picked her up and planted a big kiss on her cheek.

"Look who I brought home, pumpkin." Mac put Amy down.

The little girl swung her attention to Johnny and smiled. "Good. I want to show you my toys." She took his hand and started for her bedroom. "Daddy said we can get a puppy."

"Daddy said we will talk about it," Mac replied to the two retreating backs. He turned to Tess with a helpless expression on his face.

She shrugged. "Don't look at me. Personally I think a dog would be great. I wish I could have one in my apartment."

"You don't have to convince me. I've left it up to Nina. She'll be the one cleaning up its messes."

"And I haven't decided." Nina walked into the foyer, wiping her hands on her apron. "Where's Johnny? Did I miss him?"

"Amy's already captured him and dragged him to her room to show off her doll collection."

"Something I'm sure the boy is dying to see. I'd better go rescue the child." Nina headed for the hallway that led to the bedrooms.

"Come on. Let's go into the den. It won't be long before Nina brings them in there."

"How long has she worked for you?"

"Before I was married, and since Amy's birth she lives here. I don't know what I would have done without her help. She's priceless and she knows it."

Just as Mac predicted, Nina brought the two children into the den a few minutes later. From the expression on Johnny's face Tess realized the boy was probably shell-shocked. Amy was still chattering as they walked into the room.

When Amy saw her father, she went up to him and asked, "When can we go pick out a puppy? I told Johnny he could name her."

"A her, is it?"

"Yes, so she can have puppies."

"You have this all figured out?"

Amy nodded.

Mac looked at Nina. "What do you think?"

"I think this weekend would be a good time," the housekeeper answered.

"You heard Nina. We'll get a puppy this weekend."

Smiling from ear to ear, Amy turned to Tess. "Will you come, too?"

"Well—" Tess searched her mind for a reason to say no, but she couldn't come up with one, especially when several pairs of eyes were glued to her waiting for her answer. "Fine. What time on Saturday?"

"I thought we would go out to Colt's farm after church on Sunday. Why don't you go with us to church? We can make it an all-day outing."

Tess glanced at Amy then Johnny and couldn't refuse, even though the outing was turning into something she wasn't ready to deal with. "Okay," she answered slowly, feeling as though she'd been cornered.

"Good. Church begins at nine-thirty. I'd better warn you. The whole MacPherson clan will be at church."

"Whoa. I'm not sure I remember everyone's name."

"That's okay. I'll help you," Amy said, climbing into her father's lap.

"How many are there?" Johnny asked, his eyes round.

"Too many to count. We'll just have to stick together on Sunday, Johnny."

"Tess. Tess," Mac said, shaking his head, "don't scare the child away. I know my family can be a bit overwhelming, but there are only thirty or thirty-five of them."

"Thirty? Thirty-five? You don't know how many people are in your family?"

"Well, it depends on what you want to classify as family. I have a few first cousins you haven't met yet. And then there are my second and third cousins."

Tess raised a hand to stop him. "That's enough. I'll never keep everyone straight. I have a terrible time with people's names. Faces I can remember. Names go in one ear and out the other."

Mac grinned. "I'll help, too. And, Johnny, my large family just means you have a lot of children to play with. My family's looking forward to meeting you."

"They are?" Johnny squeaked, a bit overwhelmed, a stunned expression on his face.

"Come on, pumpkin. Let's show Johnny his bedroom. You look like you could rest before we have dinner." Mac rose and set his daughter on the floor.

When Johnny stood in the doorway of his room, he scanned the area that had obviously been decorated with a boy in mind. There was a blue bedspread on the double bed and a few toys on top of it. A computer sat on the desk with a fish tank on a stand next to it. The light illuminated several angelfish and some other types of fish for which Tess didn't know the names.

"This is for me?" the boy said in awe, taking a few steps into the room and slowly turning in a full circle.

"I didn't want to do too much. You can hang whatever posters you want." Mac settled his hand on the boy's shoulder. "Go on and make yourself at home."

Johnny walked to the navy blue beanbag in the corner and sat in it, bouncing a few times. Next to it was a bookcase with books on two shelves. He perused the titles. "The Hardy Boys?"

"I know those books are old. They were mine when I was growing up. We can get you some books that you like to read. Amy and I go to the library once a week. I hope you'll join us."

Johnny didn't say anything. He just stared at the

Hardy Boys mysteries on the shelf next to him, running his finger along the spines of several to them.

"I think it would be a good idea if you rested for a while," Tess said, noting the dark circles under Johnny's eyes and the ashen cast to his skin.

Tess knew he was feeling tired when he didn't protest but lay down on the bed and closed his eyes. Everyone backed out of the room, and Mac quietly closed the door.

"Do you want to see my room?" Amy asked, taking Tess's hand and guiding her toward the door next to Johnny's.

"I'd be honored."

"While Amy shows you her room, I'm gonna help Nina get dinner ready. Come into the kitchen when you're through with the tour."

As Tess crossed the threshold into the little girl's bedroom, she glanced at Mac disappearing down the hall. He stopped at the end and peered back. The smile that lit his face melted her insides, and she knew she was in big trouble. He was even more appealing on his home turf.

# *Chapter Seven*

Tess held Amy and Johnny's hands as they left the sanctuary. She sensed Mac behind her with members of his family flanking him. Alice grasped Amy's other hand. The mass of people leaving the church slowed as they approached the pastor and stopped to say a few words to him.

Pastor Winthrop's message still rang through Tess's mind. "Wherefore I say unto you, All manner of sin and blasphemy shall be forgiven unto men; but the blasphemy against the Holy Ghost shall not be forgiven unto men." The Bible verse from Matthew described the power of the Lord's forgiveness. Then why couldn't she forgive herself for surviving and continuing to live after so many of the people she'd cared about had died?

When she laughed, she thought of Jorge, who would never be able to tell her one of his silly jokes again. When she helped a patient, she thought of Kevin, who had devoted his life to the Lord and medicine, feeling the power of both could do anything…except save his life.

The family ahead of them moved on, and Tess came face to face with Pastor Winthrop. Her hand trembled as she reached out to shake his and say, "Your sermon was thought-provoking."

"Good. That's what I want to do. Get my congregation thinking about the Lord."

"I'm Tess Morgan, a friend of Mac's. I'm just visiting for the day."

"I hope you'll come back. We always love to have new faces around here. Alice is a great one for recruiting people to help with various tasks that need to be done at the church. Don't be surprised if she calls you up. Before long, you might become a regular."

Mac's mother laughed. "Now, Pastor Winthrop, I'm not that bad. But I do run a tight ship where the Lord is concerned. His house must be kept tidy."

"And I for one appreciate all your efforts."

Mac leaned forward. "You ought to see what she has planned for the spring festival."

"Speaking of which, I need to talk to you about some of the plans." Alice stood to the side to allow her large family to file by while she remained to speak with the pastor.

"Tess, let's get everyone into the car. We have about an hour's drive to Colt's farm." Mac touched the small of her back.

"Who is this Colt?"

"He was a teammate of mine, a few years behind me. When he retired a year after I did, he bought himself a farm and takes in stray animals."

"I thought you were going to get a puppy."

"He has several puppies, but he also has other dogs that need a home."

"Be careful. You might come home with more than one." Casey came up behind them, clasping her brother on the shoulder. "You were always a sucker for a stray animal."

"I'm not the one who adopted a baby squirrel, a robin and a fox, and that wasn't that long ago."

"You know, come to think of it I would like to ride out there with you."

"And do what, young lady?" Alice said, joining the small group.

"We don't have a dog. I think it's about time we got another one."

"That's what I was afraid you thought." Alice turned to Mac. "Don't let her bring home anything bigger than Amy."

"Then I can get a dog, too?" Casey asked, surprise evident in her expression.

"With our growing family, it would be nice to have a dog for the children to play with when they come over. Did you hear the news? Kayla is pregnant. With Mary due in a few months that'll make two babies born this year to the MacPhersons. Not a bad year, if I say so myself."

Mac saw Kayla with her husband, Paul. He swept his

sister up and swung her around. "Way to go, Kayla. Your patience has finally paid off."

"I gather Mother told you the news."

Tess hung back as the members of Kayla's family congratulated her. Tess held Johnny's hand, but Amy was in the midst of the adults in her father's arms, joining in the festive activities. Mac glanced at Tess and Johnny and stepped away from the group. He took Tess's arm and pulled her and Johnny into the family.

"I know that we arrived late so I didn't get to make the introductions. This is Johnny. He'll be staying with me and Amy. Some of you have already met Tess at Steve's birthday party."

Mac went around the group surrounding them, giving each person's name and the relationship to him. By the time he had finished, the spacious foyer of the church was filled with thirty members of Mac's family. Johnny yanked on Tess's arm, and she leaned down for him to whisper into her ear.

"Am I supposed to remember all these people?"

"No one expects you to. Now, me, they probably do. I'll let you in on a secret. My mind stopped at the sixth name. We'll work on it together."

"It probably won't make any difference. I won't be here that long."

She saw the corners of the child's mouth twist down in a frown. "Why do you say that?"

"Because it's the truth. I have no home. Since my mother died, I never stay long in any one place." Johnny sidestepped, the look on his face discouraging further discussion.

Tess still feared that Johnny would run away. She hoped that wasn't what he meant and realized she would have to let Mac know what Johnny had told her. She wanted this situation to work for everyone, because Mrs. Hocks wasn't optimistic that she would locate any of Johnny's relatives willing to take a ten-year-old boy.

As the members of Mac's family moved slowly toward the double brass doors that led outside, Tess peered at the entrance to the sanctuary. There was a time when she would have gone into the church and prayed to God to keep Johnny safe and to find a home for him. Now she was afraid to ask—wasn't sure how to. Her prayers before hadn't worked.

"We'd better leave for the farm if we want to get home by dark," Mac said at her side.

She glanced at him. Mac glowed with self-confidence. In that moment she felt everything would work out just as she had told Johnny it would. "Lead the way."

Mac waved his goodbyes to the rest of his family. "Casey, you hop in back with Amy and Johnny and behave yourself."

"Me? I'm always good on road trips."

"Don't get me started on that one." Mac opened the door to the passenger's side for Tess. "Remind me to tell you later about our family trip to the Grand Canyon."

"That's not fair. I was only four at the time."

"She started out by getting sick all over me."

"If you get car sick, you can sit up front." Tess twisted to add, "I don't mind riding in the back."

Mac laughed. "She didn't get sick because she was riding in the car. She got sick because she ate a whole box of chocolate candy an hour before we left."

"A whole box!" Johnny buckled his seat belt.

"To this day I can't eat chocolate. It makes my stomach churn."

"That's awful. I can't imagine not liking chocolate."

"So, Johnny, you're a big fan of chocolate, are you?" Mac pulled out of the parking lot.

"Any way I can get it."

"Then you're gonna fit right in. Amy and I love chocolate. How about you, Tess?"

"Yep, I have to say I have a hard time passing it up."

"Okay, you guys, if you're trying to make me feel left out, you're doing a great job."

"Never, Aunt Casey. I love you." Amy threw her arms around Casey and gave her a hug.

"I love you, too, squirt," Casey said, tickling the little girl in her side.

Tess settled back, listening to the giggles and laughter. Before long Johnny was drawn into the fun with Amy and Casey ganging up on him. The three only calmed down when Mac threatened to stop the car in the middle of the highway.

"Casey Leigh MacPherson, I knew it was a mistake to bring you. Contain yourself for the children's sake." Mac's amused tone belied his words.

"Aye, aye, sir. Just as soon as I thoroughly orient Johnny to the Tickle Monster."

Another burst of laughter sounded in the car, prompting Tess to smile and say, "I think your sister is a lost cause."

"One of my many burdens," Mac said with an exaggerated sigh.

"Thank goodness we aren't too far from the farm."

"Uncle, uncle," Johnny called between giggles.

"I think he's thoroughly oriented, Mac." Casey sat between the children as though she hadn't caused a major upheaval in the car, her back straight, her hands clasped together in her lap, an innocent expression on her face.

"Now I'll get a good night's sleep." Mac's gaze twinkled as it found Tess's for a brief moment before he returned his attention to the highway.

His look continued to undermine her determination to keep an emotional distance from Peter MacPherson. Tess focused on the beautiful mountainous terrain and tried not to think of the man next to her or the atmosphere of camaraderie that abounded in the car. Its lure tore at the barriers she'd erected around her heart, making her think of all kinds of possibilities.

Thirty minutes later Mac turned off the highway onto a dirt road that led to a log cabin set at the base of a mountain and nestled in a grove of pine trees. Tess counted five dogs and three cats in the yard as he brought the car to a stop in front of the house. A huge man, taller and bigger than Mac, came onto the porch and waved.

"What was Colt's position on the team?" Tess asked, staring at the man who made Mac look small.

"Tackle. He's six-seven and weighs three hundred fifty pounds. He prides himself on saying it's all muscles."

"Oh, my," Casey whispered from the back while Colt left his porch and approached the car.

"Good to see you, Mac. Glad to see your leg has finally mended," Colt said as everyone climbed out of the vehicle.

Mac shook Colt's hand, then gestured toward the group behind him. "You know Amy."

"She's looking more and more like Sheila every time I see her."

"That's what Daddy says. I'm the spittin'—" Amy screwed her face into a thoughtful expression. "Spittin'?"

"Image, pumpkin."

"Yeah." Amy craned her neck and grinned at Colt. "You're tall."

"And this is Tess, Casey, my sister, and Johnny." Mac pointed to each person.

"Well, you all are in luck. I have a nice selection of puppies for you to look at." Colt began walking toward a barn about a hundred yards from his log cabin. "I hope you'll stay for lunch."

Tess scanned the barn, the scent of hay and animals filling the air. Along one side were stalls, all empty except one with a horse in it. Various pens were along the opposite wall with rabbits, a coyote and a hawk in them. A calico cat came up to Tess and rubbed its body along her leg before ambling over to Colt, who picked it up and stroked it, its purring added to the other noises the animals were making.

The children were drawn to a pen with six mixed-breed puppies waddling around. They were brown and black, and two of them were fighting over an old slipper. One nudged its nose under the bedding until it had managed to trap itself. It couldn't figure out how to get out. Colt stepped over the wire fencing and rescued the puppy.

"Can I hold her?" Casey asked, climbing into the pen.

"Me, too, Aunt Casey."

Tess noticed Johnny leaning over the fence and petting the runt of the litter. "Go on and pick her up."

Johnny threw her a look of uncertainty, straightening immediately as though caught doing something wrong. "I might drop her."

Tess reached into the pen and lifted the runt out, thrusting the puppy into his arms. "No, you won't."

The boy hesitantly took the squirming puppy from Tess and held it close to his chest. She began to chew on his finger, content in Johnny's arms.

"I may have a problem here," Mac said, coming up behind Tess.

"What?"

"Look at Amy and Johnny. Both are falling in love with different puppies."

"You could always get both of them."

"And have Nina walk out on me? How would I ever survive without her?"

"I suspect Nina can be won over. I think she'll take one look at Johnny and Amy with their puppies and won't say a word."

"I like your optimism. If she says anything, I'll tell her you assured me she would be okay with it."

"Daddy. Daddy, I want this one." Amy picked her way through the rambunctious puppies and held hers up for him to look at.

Johnny's grin of delight vanished, and he put his runt in the pen, then shifted away from the fence. Tess's heart twisted at the closed expression descending on his boyish face, the hunched shoulders and folded arms.

"How about if we pick two? Which one would you like, Johnny?"

Mac turned toward the child, whose chin rested on his chest.

Johnny's head came up, and his eyes brightened. "You want me to choose one, too?"

"Sure. The puppy will be your responsibility if you want it."

"I—" Johnny gulped. "Yes."

Mac retrieved the runt from the pen and handed it to Johnny. "Is this the one you want?"

"Yes." The boy buried his face in the puppy's fur, rubbing his cheek against her. His grin was ear to ear.

"We get two puppies! Neat, Daddy. Then Johnny can

name his and I can name mine." Amy cradled hers in her arms. "I think I'll call her Buttons."

Mac lifted his daughter out of the pen while she still held her puppy. "But both of you have to feed them and make sure they have enough exercise."

"I will," Johnny and Amy said, almost at the same time.

"Well, now that is out of the way, let's go up to the house. I have some stew on the stove. I hope you guys brought your appetites. I don't get to cook often for guests and I think I went overboard."

Everyone filed out of the barn, the two puppies left in their pen until later. Tess paused outside the large double doors and took a deep breath of the mountain air, perfumed with the scent of spring. The sun warmed her face while a light breeze blew strands of her hair as though dancing on it.

"I always enjoy visiting Colt. Sometimes I wished I'd moved up here, away from the hustle and bustle of Denver."

"Why didn't you?" Tess asked, slanting a look at Mac who stopped next to her while the rest headed for the log cabin.

"One word, family. They depend on me, and this is just too far away."

Tess would have given anything to be able to say that. She'd wanted a large family, and now that didn't seem a possibility. Her dream had died on that mountaintop in South America as surely as Kevin had, but that didn't stop her from wishing.

"And then, of course, there's the halfway house I volunteer at and the foundation I run. I suppose I could manage to run the foundation if I lived here, but I wouldn't particularly like commuting to Denver and I can't see giving up my work at the halfway house."

"That's important to you?"

"Very. A lot of the people I work with have lost hope. I try to give them their hope back."

"How?" She wanted hers back, but didn't know how to go about finding it.

"Through the Lord, Tess."

"What if the Lord took your hope away?"

"Only you can do that for yourself." He stood in front of her, blocking her view of the log cabin. Taking both her hands in his, he continued, "Let me help you, Tess. I know you're hurting. I'm a good listener."

His words tempted her to tell all, to open up the wounds and bleed again. Maybe then she would heal. Where would she begin? Fear held the words inside.

"The Lord's a good listener. If not me, then talk to Him."

Tess yanked her hands from his. "I tried, and it didn't work." Her throat closed. Her tears, which lately had been so close to the surface, threatened to flow again. She couldn't cry in front of Mac. She swallowed several times and said in as cheerful voice as possible, "I don't know about you, but I'm hungry." She stepped around him and hurried toward the cabin and people who wouldn't demand something of her she couldn't give.

"Tess," Mac called.

She didn't stop. At the door into the cabin, she glanced back and saw Mac standing where she'd left him. She thrust open the door and rushed inside, desiring to hear sounds of other people. The scent of baking bread, meat and onions saturated the air, making her feel welcome.

She paused a few feet inside the cabin and surveyed her surroundings. She felt as though she had stepped back in time. There was one large room with a massive fireplace along the back wall. The kitchen and dining areas were off to the side of the main room, and two doors that probably led to bedrooms were on the opposite side. The oak furniture was simple, sturdy and fit well into the rustic environment.

Casey and the children were setting the long table with enough benches for eight people to sit on. Johnny laughed at something Casey said while Amy tugged on Colt's pant leg. When he looked down at her, she indicated she wanted to be picked up so she could peek into the large black kettle on the stove.

The door behind Tess opened and closed. She felt Mac's presence, the air charged with his vitality the second he entered the cabin. Her heart reacted by increasing its beat, and her mouth went dry. The hairs on her neck tingled, and she knew he was staring at her, probably trying to figure out what made her tick.

"Daddy, Colt let me stir the stew and taste it to make sure it was ready for us to eat." Amy raced across the large room and tugged on Mac's arm to lead him to the group. "I'm gonna ask Nina if I can help her, too."

Tess heard Mac mutter as he passed her, "Nina is gonna be thrilled to hear that. I remember that last time you had more flour on you than in the bowl."

"Ah, Daddy, I was two then. I'm bigger now."

"That was only six months ago."

"Yeah, but I'm all grown up now." Amy straightened her small body, adding an inch to her height.

Tess hid her smile behind her hand while Mac answered his daughter with a grunt that could mean just about anything.

Johnny spied her and said, "Tess, Colt has two new puppies that he has to feed himself. Someone left them on the highway. Come look." He waved her over to a cardboard box sitting in front of the fireplace. "They can't be more than a week old."

Tess looked inside at the two white balls curled together, sleeping on an old terry-cloth towel. "They're lucky he found them. They wouldn't have made it on their own."

"Why do people discard animals like that?" Johnny said in a whisper as if he was afraid of waking up the puppies.

"I wish I had a good answer for you. Some people don't value life very much." She thought of the men who had invaded the mountain village, shooting at anything that moved.

"Come and get it. Lunch is being served," Colt announced.

"No one's gonna hurt Frisky. I'll make sure of that." Johnny straightened, a fierce expression on his face.

"Is Frisky the name of your puppy?"

He nodded, his hands clenched at his sides, while his gaze was riveted on the sleeping puppies. "She won't be the runt for long. I'll take real good care of her."

"Then that's all she can ask," Tess said to Johnny while they found a bench to sit on.

After everyone was served, Colt bowed his head and said, "Heavenly Lord, bless this food and watch out for the animals who need help. Send them to my door and I will provide. Amen."

"How many animals are you caring for right now?" Casey passed the basket of homemade bread to Colt, who sat next to her.

"Gosh, I'm not sure." He silently counted on his fingers, then announced, "Thirty-one if you excluded the two puppies you're taking back to Denver."

"Make that three. Except that Mom requested a dog, not a puppy." Casey lavished butter on her piece of bread. "Do you have any dogs that need homes?"

"I have seven you can choose from."

"The ride back home should be interesting. Five people and three animals." Mac shook his head as though he couldn't believe he had agreed to do this.

"What made you take in stray animals?" Tess asked, sipping her tall glass of iced water.

"It sorta just happened. One day someone dumped some puppies out on the highway. Then I found a stray cat that was pretty beaten up. The rest is history. People around here know that if they don't want an animal I'll take it in and try to find it a home. I think my reputation is spreading. Every week I get more and more. I'm gonna have to take on help if this pace keeps up."

"I want to help," Amy said after stuffing a spoonful of stew into her mouth.

"Me, too," Johnny chimed in.

"Hold it, kids. I think that would be great, but Colt lives too far away for that to be practical. Sorry." Mac handed his daughter a napkin to wipe her mouth.

"We gots to do somethin', Daddy."

"You are. You're taking in two puppies who need homes."

"But I want to do more."

"Sorry, pumpkin. It's not possible."

"Tell you what, guys. I'll bring you out here one Saturday, and if Colt doesn't mind, we can help him." Casey threw a smile toward the man in question.

"Mind? The more the merrier."

"When, Aunt Casey?"

"Soon. I need to check my schedule at the hospital."

"We could do it some other day."

"No, Amy. Johnny will be starting school next week." Mac took the last bite of his stew.

"School! I ain't going."

"That's not an option."

Johnny pouted. "I won't know nobody. Besides, I don't feel too well."

"The doctor told me you could start next week half days." Mac's features firmed into an expression that told the child this was a battle he wouldn't win.

Tess remembered the comment Johnny had made about not being long in any one place. She would definitely have to say something to Mac this evening so he would be aware of what Johnny was feeling. She hoped the child wouldn't do something drastic to avoid going to school.

"Well, I don't know about everyone else, but I'm ready for dessert." Colt rose and took his plate toward the sink.

"What is it?" Amy asked, her eyes growing round as Colt brought a plate with a top over it.

"Chocolate cake."

Casey groaned while the rest cheered.

"I think they both are finally asleep." Mac entered the den and sat across from Tess. "Johnny insisted his puppy stay in his room with him. Frisky is in the box, but I won't be surprised to find the puppy in bed with Johnny later on."

"Where's Amy's?"

"In the utility room."

"How did you get her to agree to part with Buttons? I thought they were attached from the time she got in the car with her."

"Not easily. Of course, when she finds out Johnny slept with Frisky, I'll have a problem on my hands."

"You couldn't say no to Johnny?"

Mac shook his head. "I tried honestly, but the boy has had so little in his life. All I could think of was how I felt about my first puppy, and the word yes just came out." He gave her a sheepish look. "I really do know how to draw the line. Honest."

"I believe you," Tess said with a laugh.

The grandfather clock in the corner chimed nine times. Tess glanced at it, surprised at how late it was. She had to get up early tomorrow and work, and yet she hadn't talked to Mac about what Johnny said. "Speaking of Johnny, he said something to me today that I think you should be aware of, Mac. It's probably nothing, but he said he wasn't going to be at your house long. Do you think he's planning anything?"

Frowning, Mac plowed his hand through his hair. "I hope Frisky will change that. If he feels responsible for her, he might think twice about running away."

"So that was your motive. Good plan."

"Actually my plan is to make him feel part of this family."

"What happens when he has to leave because Mrs. Hocks has found a relative to take him in?"

Mac's brow creased with a deep frown. "We don't know how long that'll be, if ever."

"That's true. Have you thought about all the possibilities?"

"Like what?"

"What if Mrs. Hocks never finds a relative, what then?"

"That's easy. I'll take care of Johnny."

"What if she does find someone? Are you prepared to let him go?"

Mac drew in a deep breath and released it slowly. "I'll have to. I've placed this in God's hands. This will work out for the best for Johnny."

"I sure hope so. The child has been through so much in his short ten years. He's so afraid to care."

"I know, Tess."

The look Mac gave her spoke of his concerns, which went deeper than Johnny's fear of getting close to another. Her own fears connected her to the child, and both she and Mac were aware of that. If only she could turn her life over to the Lord, then maybe…

"I'd better get home. It's a long day tomorrow." Tess stood abruptly, needing to leave before she broke down and told Mac her life story. It was a boring subject she wanted to avoid. Spilling her guts wouldn't change what had happened.

"When will I get to see you again? How about coming to dinner one night this week?"

Tess bent and picked up her black purse, hoisting it on her shoulder. She was so tempted to accept his invitation, not just because she would be able to see Johnny. But she needed to toughen her resolve to put some emotional distance between her and—who was she kidding—Mac. "Not this week. Sorry. Extra busy."

"Well, then, I'll see you at the hospital."

"You will?" Her grip tightened on her purse strap. Why was he making it so hard to avoid him?

"I've worked out a visiting schedule with the child life specialist, Cindy. I should have done something like this sooner. I'm organizing some of my football buddies to help."

"Oh, that's good. The children will love that," Tess replied, aware the enthusiasm she should be feeling wasn't present in her voice even though she pasted a bright smile on her face.

"Cindy was excited about it." He escorted her toward the front door. "So I guess you'll just have to get used to me being in your life."

The twinkle in his eyes emphasized he knew exactly what she was trying to do and that he wasn't going to let her. Her smile faltered. "I'll wave to you while I'm working. Some days I'm so busy I don't even get a break."

Mac held the front door for her. "I'll be sure to wave back. Good night, Tess, and thank you for sharing your day with us. It meant a lot to—" he paused for a few seconds "—Johnny."

Tess felt Mac's gaze on her as she walked to her car, parked in his circular drive. Reaching to open her door, she noticed the quiver in her hand as it clasped the handle and pulled. He was deliberately undermining her resolve, and she wasn't going to let him get away with it. But as she slid behind the steering wheel, she wasn't sure how she was going to stop him.

# Chapter Eight

Mac heard muffled voices then a giggle coming from Johnny's room. Pausing in the hallway, he listened. Thirty minutes before Amy had dashed through the den with a box, saying hi and bye all in the same breath. Then not ten minutes after that Johnny had hurried into the kitchen, retrieved a bowl and disappeared to his bedroom with not one word of greeting as he passed through the den. All this after they had put their puppies in the utility room. What were those two doing?

Mac knocked on Johnny's bedroom door, waited a few seconds, then pushed it open just in time to see the boy throw a blanket over the box, then sit with Amy in front of it. One look at the children's expressions told Mac everything he needed to know.

He fisted his hands on his hips. "Okay, what are you two hiding in that box?"

"Nothin', Daddy." Amy stuck her thumb into her mouth, a clear sign to Mac that she wasn't telling the truth.

He riveted his attention to the ten-year-old. "Johnny, do you care to explain?"

Johnny dropped his head and mumbled something Mac couldn't understand.

"I'm sorry. What was that?"

The boy lifted his gaze to Mac's, his lower lip protruding. "Amy and I found some baby rabbits out back."

"You shouldn't have taken them from their nest. They need their mother." Mac walked to the children and knelt next to them to peek into the box at two tiny balls of grayish brown fluff.

"We've been watching them for the past few days. I think their mother abandoned them." Johnny hovered over the box as though he was going to protect them.

"You don't know that for sure."

"Yes, Daddy. We saved them just like Colt. They're hungry."

"That's why I got them a bowl of milk, but I can't get them to drink."

Mac sighed heavily, tunneling his hand through his hair then rubbing the back of his neck, his muscles taut beneath his fingers. He wasn't sure what to say or do. He noticed that one rabbit's eyes weren't open yet as they squirmed together, nudging each other for comfort.

"Can we keep them, Daddy?"

"Oh, pumpkin, I don't know if that's what's best for them. We can't have animals like Colt does."

"Why not, Daddy?"

Mac stared into her big, brown eyes and couldn't come up with a reason she would accept. *Because I said so* wasn't going to work with her or Johnny. "We'll discuss this when I get home. I'm due at the hospital. I'll call Colt and talk to him about this on the way."

"What should we do about them being hungry?"

Johnny looked at Mac as though he would have the answer. What to do? He scratched his head and tried to think of a way to feed the babies something until he could find out what to do with them. When his daughter stared at him, too, her thumb still in her mouth, he retrieved his cell phone from his pocket and punched in Colt's number. He had to leave a message for the man to call him back. When he slipped his phone into his pocket, he faced the two children who were waiting for a solution to the babies' problem.

"I'll get an eyedropper and you can try to use it to feed the rabbits some milk. But don't do anything else until I return. Maybe Colt will call me back by then. After you feed them, put the babies in the box and leave them alone. Is that understood?" Mac looked from Amy, who nodded, to Johnny, whose pout deepened into a scowl. "Johnny?"

"Yes," the ten-year-old muttered, clearly not happy with the order.

"Are you gonna see Aunt Casey?"

"I think she's working today. But I'm going up to see the children on the floor."

"How about Tess? Is she working?"

Mac was surprised by Johnny's questions. "I don't know. I'm not sure about her work schedule," he said, hating to admit the woman was avoiding him. "Have you talked to her lately?"

"She called yesterday to see how I was doing. She said something about taking me out for some ice cream."

"She did?"

"Yes, and me, too, Daddy. I like ice cream."

"Does she call you often?"

"Usually every day."

How is she? The question was on the tip of Mac's tongue, but he bit it back. He hadn't seen her in several weeks and was determined to change that fact. "You know I like ice cream, too." Now why in the world had he said that?

"Then you can go with us." Amy peered at Johnny. "Right? Just like a family."

The hard edge in the boy's gaze softened as he looked at Amy and nodded. "We'll need to ask Tess first."

"Oh, she won't care. She's a nice lady."

Mac hoped Tess didn't care, because he was going to use the opportunity the children offered to be with her. He'd never seen anyone run as fast as she was from relationships and people. She was hurting inside, and he was determined to help her. The Lord had given him many blessings, and it was his duty to be there for others in need. And if he kept telling himself that was the only reason he wanted to see Tess, he might just come to believe it.

\* \* \*

The children were all gathered around the table in the playroom, their faces eager. The nursing techs had managed to squeeze in two hospital beds with a boy and a girl who were bedridden. Quiet reigned where only a moment before laughter had filled the air when Tess had botched a magic trick. The deck of cards lay scattered all over the floor.

Tess allowed her gaze to peruse the colorfully decorated room before it settled on a little girl near her. "Kelly, you can be my assistant for this next feat of magic." From inside her oversize coat she pulled out a flattened top hat and popped it open, the sound punctuating the silence. "I want you to hold on to this hat as tight as you can." Nodding, the child took it. "Now, I'm going to pour this glass of water into the hat where it will disappear into thin air," Tess said with dramatic flair.

After emptying the glass, Tess took her wand, tapping the sides of the hat while the little girl held it above her. "Abracadabra and all that mumble jumble." Tess swept her arm wide, her gaze pinning each child for a second. "Now, who would like to wear this beautiful hat?"

When no one volunteered, Tess scanned the faces of the children again, making the corners of her mouth turn down in a frown. "Okay. I admit my last trick didn't work, but this one will."

One child in a wheelchair giggled.

"You don't believe me. Well, I'll prove it." Tess

grasped the hat high in the air and then plopped it down onto her head. Water cascaded down her face, dripping into her eyes and splashing onto her clothes and the floor.

The children burst out laughing.

Through the strands of wet red hair obstructing her view, Tess saw Mac lounging against the door into the playroom. She flipped the hair back and gave an exaggerated sigh. "Oh, my, what could have possibly gone wrong?" She held out her hand toward a nursing tech. "A towel, please."

The woman handed her a tiny swatch of cloth to dry her face and clothes. Tess mopped at the water then twisted and twisted the cloth to wring it out, managing to squeeze out a few drops of liquid. While she sidestepped toward the door, her shoes made a funny squeaky noise that draw more laughter from the children. As she escaped down the hall, trying to run in her oversize shoes, she felt Mac's gaze on her as well as several of the children's. She came to a screeching halt at the door into the employee locker room, turned toward the playroom and tipped her top hat before disappearing inside.

She leaned against the door and let out a rush of air, the pounding of her heart having nothing to do with her swift getaway. Quickly she began removing her wet clown clothes, then her white streaked makeup, trying her best not to think about the man in the playroom. But all she could picture was his smiling face. All she could hear was his deep, rich laughter complementing the children's. And she could swear she had smelled sandalwood as she'd raced by him. Avoiding him certainly hadn't managed to diminish his effect on her.

So what was she going to do about it?

She didn't have an answer for that question. She wanted to be involved with Johnny, and the child was living with Mac. She was going to have to bite the bullet and put up with the man if she wanted to see Johnny. It wouldn't be easy, but surely she could be around Mac and his family and not have visions of having a family herself.

With her determination firmly in place, Tess marched down the hall toward the playroom and the sounds of children's voices excitedly talking. When she peeked into the room, intending to check out what was going on before heading to the cafeteria to grab something to eat, she saw Mac signing his name on anything and everything that was thrust at him. One little girl insisted he write "Mack Truck" on her bare arm, and her peals of laughter drowned out all the other children's voices.

"That tickled. Do this one, too. Please." The little girl smiled at Mac.

Mac took her other arm and made a big production out of it. All the other children quieted and watched. When Mac finished with a flourish, he scanned the faces of the boys and girls, his gaze finally coming to rest on Tess in the doorway. One corner of his mouth lifted in a lopsided grin while the room erupted in giggles and talking. Tess responded to the mischief twinkling in his eyes, returning his grin.

A boy in a wheelchair tapped Mac's arm, pulling his attention away. The child pointed to the cast on his leg, and Mac immediately signed it. Tess took the opportunity to move away from the playroom. If she walked fast, she could be at the elevator and on her way to the cafeteria before Mac realized she was gone. She punched the button and waited, glancing back several times as though any second he would appear and she would be dazzled with his presence, unable to escape. She made it safely onto the elevator, rode to the ground floor and hurried to the cafeteria, finally breathing a sigh of relief.

While she inspected the array of salads before her, she sensed someone come up behind her. The faint scent of sandalwood drifted to her seconds before Mac whispered close to her ear, "Did you think I'd let you get away that easily?"

Tess peered over her shoulder, smiled and said, "Whatever do you mean?"

"I saw you hurrying to the elevator. I thought I would let you think you'd escaped my clutches. But alas, Casey told me where you were going."

"I knew I was going to regret your sister working on my floor."

Tess grabbed the salad nearest her and slid her tray down the counter toward the hot entrees. When she glanced at what she had put on her tray, she frowned. Macaroni salad wasn't one of her favorites. As she told her order to the server, she noticed Mac pick up a tray, select a salad and move down the counter toward her.

Tess took piping hot roast beef, mashed potatoes and broccoli from the lady. She wondered if she could attribute the perspiration on her upper lip to the steam floating from the serving line. The server eyed Mac and heaped an extra large portion of roast beef and mashed potatoes on his plate, then drenched them in brown gravy.

"I guess she thinks you're a growing boy," Tess said as she pushed her tray toward the checkout person.

"Do I detect a note of envy in your voice?"

Tess stared at the food piled on his plate, watching him add a large slice of pecan pie to his tray. "I think I'm gaining weight just looking at your meal."

"Just so the nurse in you doesn't get too worked up over this high-calorie meal, I exercise every day. I usually don't eat this much."

"I'm worried about you." Tess handed the lady at the cash register the money for her lunch.

"Why?"

"You came to a hospital to overindulge in food? Hospital cafeterias aren't known for their culinary treats."

Mac followed her to a table in the corner near a large ficus tree. "True. But Casey told me this one has good food." He slipped into the chair next to her. "My sister is a fountain of information when it comes to this hospital. And now Amy has decided she wants to be a nurse. She's been practicing on her dolls. Her bedroom has been turned into a hospital."

"You have a beautiful daughter." Tess heard the wistful

tone in her voice and hoped Mac didn't. She didn't want to get into a discussion of children and families.

"That she is. She's my life." Mac stared at his plate of food, the hand that held the fork poised in midair as though he were caught in a moment of reflection.

Tess clenched her teeth together to keep from asking questions about his deceased wife. It wasn't her place to delve into his past, and yet she wanted to know everything about him. She cleared her throat and asked, "How's Johnny doing?"

"I think he's settling in."

"Has Mrs. Hocks had any luck finding a relative?"

"No."

Tess took a bite of roast beef. "What if she doesn't?"

"I want to adopt Johnny."

Her gaze was riveted to Mac's. The noise level in the cafeteria was high, but suddenly everything seemed to fade away—all sounds, all the people. She saw and heard only Mac. "Have you said anything about this to him?"

Mac shook his head. "And I won't until Mrs. Hocks has exhausted all her leads and Johnny feels at home with us. I'm hoping that won't be too much longer. You should have seen Amy and him today. They found some baby rabbits and decided to take in strays like Colt."

"What did you do?"

"On the way over here Colt returned my call. We discussed what we should do. The kids are sure the mother rabbit was killed. Colt told me they might survive if I can get them to eat. Before I left, Johnny fed them some milk with an eyedropper. The rabbits were sleeping when I left."

"How small are they?"

"They can't be more than a week or two old. One of them has his eyes open. The other doesn't. I could hold one in my palm."

For a few seconds Tess stared at his hand and remembered his gentle touch. Her stomach flip-flopped. "Then you're going to keep the rabbits?"

"I have a hard time resisting those two kids. Besides, I'm a sucker for strays, too."

"For animals in trouble?"

"People, too."

The intensity of his regard robbed her of her next breath. She swallowed several times, the tightness in her throat threatening to snatch her voice. She knew in that moment she didn't want to be one of his charity cases. She wanted more, and that frightened her. She looked away and concentrated on cutting her roast beef into bite size pieces, aware of his gaze on her. Her hands quivered.

"When I took my first psychology class in college, I became hooked on trying to figure out what makes people do the things they do." Mac sipped his coffee, peering at her over the rim of his cup.

"Some people don't like to be analyzed."

"Some people need someone to help them through their problems. They're too close to them. They can't get a good perspective of them."

"Is that what you do at the halfway house?" Tess asked, hoping to steer the conversation away from her.

"I told you I'm a good listener. That's what I mostly do. That and get people to understand why they're doing what they do."

"Stray people aren't like stray animals."

"But both need understanding and love."

When he said the word *love,* for a moment she allowed herself to wonder what it would be like loved by a man like Mac. Then she remembered the pain such intense emotions caused and pushed the dream away. "How are the puppies? Is Johnny taking care of his?"

Mac didn't answer her right away. He chewed his food slowly, his eyes narrowed on her face as though he were contemplating not letting her get away with changing the subject of their conversation. Finally he said, "Yes. I've been impressed with how well. Frisky sleeps in his room in a box. Sometimes I've found the puppy sleeping with Johnny when I check on him before going to bed. They're usually inseparable. That's why I should have known something was up when both Amy and Johnny put their puppies in the utility room this morning."

"It looks like your trip to Colt's farm may have triggered something."

"Yeah, I'm gonna have a house full of stray animals if I don't put my foot down." Mac cut into his pecan pie.

Tess watched him bring the bite to his mouth. Hers watered. "Wait till Casey hears about the rabbits. Your sister will encourage them."

"Yeah, that's what I'm afraid of. Amy's gonna be staying with Mom and Casey this weekend while I'm camping with Johnny and some of the kids from church."

"Chaperoning? You are a brave man."

"And I need a chaperone for the girls. Justin and his wife are coming, but Mary could use another woman to help her. Care to come along?"

"Me?"

"Yes. You could spend time with Johnny. He talks about you all the time."

"He does?"

"Come on. What do you say? I know you aren't working."

"How? Oh, never mind. Casey." The idea he was asking his sister about her made her blush. "Let me think about it."

"There'll be twelve children, seven boys and five girls, going, ranging in ages from ten to fourteen. Johnny doesn't say anything, but I think he's excited. I talked with his doctor, and he gave me the okay. Johnny's recovering quite well."

"Yeah, I know."

"Now all we have to do is work on his spirit. He's really taken to going to church with us, and this youth group has been wonderful for him."

Was that why she felt such a kinship with Johnny? They were both wounded in spirit. Tess knew she didn't want to pass up an opportunity to spend some time with the boy. She'd missed him these past few weeks. Talking to him on the phone wasn't the same thing as seeing him, making sure with her own two eyes that he was doing all right. Maybe it was time for her to stop trying to avoid Mac and let things happen naturally. Maybe it was time to face her fear of getting close to another man. Her life right now was certainly less than fulfilling.

"How did you convince Johnny to leave Frisky behind?"

"It wasn't easy, but Casey promised to take special care of her, and of course, Amy did, too."

"Will I have to hike much?"

"You probably do more walking on the pediatric floor than you'll do this weekend. Does this mean you'll go?"

Tess inhaled a deep breath and nodded. The smile that touched Mac's mouth sent her heart slamming against her chest.

"I just knew you wouldn't let—Johnny down."

A finely honed tension held Tess immobile. She felt as though she had plunged over a cliff without a lifeline. She was doing this for Johnny, she told herself and knew that was a lie. She was doing it for herself. She wanted to get to know Peter MacPherson, and it was time she did.

# Chapter Nine

Tess really wished she had asked where they were going to camp. In the middle of a mountain range wasn't her idea of a most ideal place to spend her weekend. But then she should have realized they would probably camp in the Rockies, since Denver sat at the foot of them. When she was around Mac, she sometimes forgot to think straight.

Adjusting her backpack, she followed Mac along the trail that would take them to their campsite. The excited voices of the children penetrated the morning silence. The scent of pine and earth saturated the air with a soothing aroma that seeped into Tess and eased her distress. The crystal-blue sky with not a cloud in sight promised the day would be a beautiful one. She listened to the snap of twigs and leaves beneath her boots and to the laughter of one of the girls ahead of her and felt content for the moment. She had always loved the mountains. Maybe she could put her memories behind her and enjoy the weekend for what it was—a time to get to know Mac and Johnny better.

Johnny's warm greeting when she'd climbed into Mac's car had given her hope. Mac was doing something right because she had never seen the child so happy, relaxed. His skin looked healthy, and his eyes were bright. Mac was a good father and deserved a household full of children. If Mac adopted Johnny, how would that affect her?

"Look, a hummingbird," one of the girls said, pointing toward a tree.

Tess paused to watch the tiny bird move its wings so fast it was hard to see them. It hovered for a few seconds then darted off. As she turned her gaze toward the trail, out of the trees came a deer, soaring across the path and bounding into the thick brush on the other side.

Not a word was spoken for a full minute as though everyone was waiting for another deer to cross, then all of a sudden every child began to talk and gesture toward where the deer had disappeared into the forest. A cool breeze stirred Tess's hair as she marveled at the grace of the animal and the beauty about her. She loved the outdoors and used to call it God's playground.

"I hope we see a bear," one of the older children said at the front of the line.

"I want to see a wolf."

"How about a mountain lion," Johnny added to the list.

Tess thought of those animals, and her eyes grew round. "Mac, are you prepared if we do?"

"Chances are we won't. Don't worry. Probably the biggest animal we'll see is that deer."

"I hope you're right. While all three of those animals are beautiful to look at, I prefer steel bars or glass between me and them. I know my limitations and how fast I can run."

"Running away from your problems isn't the best solution. They'll only follow you and take you over," he whispered to her. Then in a louder voice he said, "Let's keep moving. We have a ways to go to the campsite."

Mac's advice stayed with Tess the rest of the trip to the campsite. For the past two years she had been running away from what had happened in South America. She had tried to deal with it, but each time had felt overwhelmed with guilt and emotion until she had shoved it back in the dark recesses of her mind to examine later. Was later finally here? She asked herself that as she flung her backpack to the ground and scanned their home for the weekend, nestled under a canopy of pines and aspens.

Johnny came up next to her and shrugged off his backpack, too. "I've never been camping. Are there really bears and mountain lions around?"

"Nothing for you to worry about."

He puffed out his chest. "I ain't worried for myself. I don't want anything to happen to the—girls. All that screaming wouldn't be pleasant to the ears."

"I suppose you're right. Mac tells me I shouldn't worry."

"If one comes around, I'll protect ya."

She smiled at the boy. "Thanks." She noticed the pale cast to his cheeks and added, "I need to rest. Will you keep me company?"

He looked at the others sitting and said, "Sure. Then I'll need to help with my tent. Mac said something about finding firewood, too."

"If you help me put up my tent, I'll help you, then we both can look for wood."

"A deal." Johnny grinned, easing onto the ground with his legs crossed Indian-style. "Have you put up a tent before?"

"Yes," she answered, recalling other times she'd camped in the mountains a continent away.

"Is it hard?"

"A piece of cake."

An hour later Tess wished she had looked at the directions before declaring to Johnny how easy it was to assemble a tent. His was one of the big ones that would hold four boys. Finally Mac came to their rescue, taking the center pole that held the tent up and driving it into the ground.

"Okay, so I had the wrong pole. Anyone could make that mistake," Tess said while Mac continued to issue directions to Johnny, who scrambled to obey them.

The tent was erected in less than five minutes. Tess stood by and watched the whole process. Johnny gave

Mac a high five before making his way to her, pride in his step.

"The one I used in the past was entirely different," Tess said in her defense, pleased at how well Johnny was bonding with Mac. The boy needed a man in his life, and Mac was perfect for the job.

"Mac told me your tent is simpler, and I should be able to do it by myself."

In other words, stand back while I show you what I've learned. Tess was only too happy to let Johnny put the tent up by himself. She had learned quickly that the child had had few positive strokes in his life and responded to them when given appropriately.

While Johnny proceeded to work on her tent, Tess spied Mac talking to a child who had scraped his knee. Seeing him soothe the child, who was crying, she began to envision him with a horde of his own children surrounding him, her next to him. The picture nearly knocked the breath from her as she quickly looked away. Okay, he would make a good father—was in fact already a good father—but that didn't mean she had to be the mother. She needed to rid her mind of those thoughts, and quickly, before she did something risky— like fall in love with Mac.

Tess stared at the tent she was to share with Mary and couldn't bring herself to walk to it. A cool breeze blew down from the mountaintop, ruffling her hair and reminding her of other times. She shivered and pulled her light jacket close, folding her arms across her chest to ward off the chill burrowing deep into her bones that had nothing to do with the temperature.

All day she had kept herself busy with the children and hadn't had time to reflect. Now she couldn't ignore the thin mountain air, the feeling she was on top of the world looking down on life. She couldn't ignore the memories.

Tess looked around the campsite at the five tents set up in a circle with a large fire in the center. Not long before, the children had roasted marshmallows over that fire and Mac had told them Bible stories of Christ's journey to save humankind. There had been times Kevin and Tess had sat outside at night, listening to nature, breathing the fresh, clean air and discussing the Lord and their mission in South America.

What had gone wrong? What had she done wrong? Those questions taunted her, nibbling at her fragile composure. She shuddered, trying desperately to stop the flood of memories. This wasn't the time to remember.

"Cold?" Mac asked, sitting next to her on a log in front of the fire.

"A little."

"Here, let's move the log closer to the fire."

He stood and repositioned the piece of wood. Now if Tess wanted to, she could reach out and warm her hands over the flames. After zipping her jacket, she did just that and noticed their slight tremor.

"Better?"

"Yes. I forgot how cold it can get once the sun goes down even though it's the middle of May."

"Up on the top of this mountain there's still snow. You go high enough, you can leave summer behind in July."

Yes, it had been that way in the Andes, too, Tess remembered, and wished again she could forget that part of her life.

"But your sleeping bag will be warm," Mac added, poking the fire with a stick.

A few sparks spewed into the air, caught on the breeze and swirled. Tess watched them disappear in the darkness, wishing her problems could disappear, as well. "Thanks for loaning me one. I'm not equipped for camping."

"We do this several times a year with different groups of children. It's good for them to get away from the city and commune with nature, not to sit in front of the TV or play video games for hours. When I'm up here, I feel closer to God. He's always around us, but here His presence seems sharper and clearer to me."

Once she'd thought that very thing. Was that why she'd been sure the Lord would answer her prayer that day in the Andes? Tess looked again at the tent she was to sleep in. "I guess we should turn in. It's quieted down."

"Finally. I think the kids completely wore Mary and Justin out."

"Mary's pregnant. She tires easily."

"What's Justin's excuse for turning in early?"

"Sympathy exhaustion?"

Mac laughed. "Yeah, I could see my little brother doing that."

"You have a wonderful family. You're very close."

"There isn't anything I wouldn't do for them. My parents instilled in us how important a sense of family is."

"You're lucky to have such a large, warm family. I was an only child and always wanted brothers and sisters. I swore when I got married I wouldn't have just one child."

Mac tossed the stick into the fire and watched the flames lick at the wood for a few seconds before dying back. "There's nothing wrong with having just one child. There are advantages to being an only child."

"What?" Tess asked, remembering the times she'd played by herself because there was no one else around.

"You don't have to share as much."

"Peter MacPherson, I doubt very seriously you want Amy to grow up not knowing how to share. I've seen you with her."

He threw her a sheepish look. "Okay, you're right. But I'm happy with having just Amy—and Johnny, if it's the Lord's plan for me to adopt him."

"You're a young man. You could have more children." The second she'd spoken, she wanted to bite her tongue. "I mean you don't know what the future will hold for you."

"Some things I do have control over." A hard edge entered his voice.

"No one has control totally over their future. I've

seen you with the children today. You're a wonderful father. You have a lot to teach them."

"I can be around children as I am now and have an influence over them without being their father."

"Amy should have brothers and sisters. Take it from an only child."

Mac didn't say anything, the tight set of his jaw attesting to some inner struggle.

"Look how Amy has taken to Johnny. He tells me she follows him around."

"Does that bother him?"

"Are you kidding? He's never had a sibling and he's eating it up. She hangs on his every word."

"I know living with us has been an adjustment for him, but it's been good to have him at the house." Mac rose, extending his hand to help Tess up. "We have a full day tomorrow."

When his fingers closed around hers and he pulled her up, she came within inches of him. His scent drove all others away, centering her thoughts and senses on the man before her. In the golden glow of the firelight she saw his gaze soften as it took in her features, finally coming to rest on her mouth. Her lips tingled under the intensity of his regard.

He grazed his fingertips across her lower lip. "I'm glad you decided to come this weekend."

She couldn't say the words, *I'm glad, too.* They were stuck in her tight throat. She couldn't take her gaze from his. His eyes in the firelight appeared as two pieces of molten silver, mesmerizing her.

He cupped her face and leaned down, his lips brushing hers like a warm gentle breeze. The muscles in her legs liquefied. She grasped his shoulders to keep from collapsing against him while he slanted his mouth against hers and claimed her in a deep, heart-wrenching kiss. She felt it from the top of her head to the tip of her toes, like an electrical current that zipped through her body.

Nearby she heard an owl hoot, startling her. Gasping, she jumped back, her hand coming up to cover her mouth.

"I'm not sorry I kissed you. I've wanted to do that for a long time, Tess."

And she wasn't sorry he had kissed her. She wasn't even surprised by her intense reaction to his kiss. She'd anticipated it from the first time she'd laid eyes on him in the waiting room.

When she didn't say anything, he covered the distance that separated them and caressed a wayward strand of hair from her cheek. "Are you all right?"

The tenderness in his expression dissolved all rational thought. All she could do was stare into his eyes and want to become lost in them.

"Tess?"

One corner of her mouth quirked. "Sorry. I'm fine. Really. I was so wrapped up in you—your kiss—that the owl just surprised me. That's all."

"If you're sure?"

"Very. Now, I'd better get to bed or I'll be worthless tomorrow. I can bet the children will be up at the crack of dawn."

Tess took a shaky step back from Mac.

"I can guarantee it." He walked with her to the small tent she was sharing with Mary. "Good night."

Tess crawled inside, peering across the dying fire at Mac who stood in front of the tent he shared with his brother. She ran her fingertips across her lips and imagined the feel of his mouth on hers. Just thinking about it sent her pulse racing.

When she snuggled between the covers of her sleeping bag, she couldn't get the picture of Mac out of her mind. She closed her eyes but still saw him. She was afraid the man was going to haunt her dreams. Burrowing into the warmth surrounding her, she forced her thoughts away from Peter MacPherson for all of ten seconds. As exhaustion unfolded and spread through her, she felt herself sink into a world full of hopes....

*The harsh glare of lights and the heat radiating from them made rivulets of perspiration roll down Tess's face. She wiped her hand across her forehead and tried to smile at the audience. The corners of her mouth quivered from the strain.*

*"Now, Miss Morgan, the million-dollar question is—" the emcee paused for a few seconds, shuffling the index cards in his hands before selecting one and reading "— why were you allowed to live while everyone else was killed? You have one minute to come up with an answer."*

*The loud ticking of the clock started counting down her seconds.*

*Frantically Tess searched her thoughts for a reason, but all she could focus on was the ticktock of the clock reverberating through her mind. Why? Why me?*

*The buzzer blared. The audience quieted, waiting to hear her reply. She scanned their faces, desperately wishing the answer was written on them. Their features dissolved into blank masks.*

*"I don't know," she finally said to the emcee.*

*He thrust his face into hers and shouted, "Why don't you know? Why were you saved and not the others?"*

*The audience took up the chant. Why? Why?*

*"I don't know. I don't know."*

Tess bolted up in her sleeping bag, breathing shallow gasps of air, sweat pouring off her as though she had been standing under the glare of harsh lights. Her heartbeat thundered in her ears. Distraught, she looked around, trying to figure out where she was. Reality crept in. Tess stared at Mary sleeping next to her, the soft sound of her breathing suddenly reminding her of the ticktock of the clock in her dream.

Tess dropped her head, burying her face in her shaking hands while drawing in deep breaths to calm herself. She felt as if the tent walls enclosed her in a trap. Shoving back the sleeping bag, she grabbed a blanket and scrambled outside, not wanting to awaken Mary.

She inhaled deep, cleansing breaths, saturated with the scent of the mountain. Her heartbeat slowed to a decent pace as she walked to the log and sat. She wrapped the blanket around her, then rested her elbows on her knees, her chin cupped in her hands. In the moonlight that filtered through the trees she stared at the black pit where the fire had been and tried to find some kind of peace. It eluded her as though she tried to hold a snowflake in her palm.

"Can't sleep, either?"

She had been so deep in thought she hadn't heard Mac approach until he sat down beside her on the log, clicking off the flashlight he carried. Blackness surrounded them, giving the fantasy that they were alone in the middle of nowhere.

"Bad dream," she answered before she realized what she'd said.

"Want to tell me about it?" He lit a lantern, throwing a circle of light about them and shattering the illusion of isolation.

No—yes. She slanted a look at his profile, his gaze trained straight ahead. The glow from the lantern softened his features, coaxing her to tell him about the nightmare—about South America and Kevin. "For the past two years I've been running away and I've just come to the conclusion you can't, not from yourself. You're right. There's a time when everything catches up with you."

"Tell me about the dream."

"I'm a game show contestant and the emcee asks me the final question and I can't answer it."

"What's the question?"

The gentleness in his voice soothed her. She could do this. She looked sideways at him. "Why were you allowed to live while everyone else was killed?"

The question hung in the air between them for a few seconds. Then she heard Mac suck in a sharp breath, his gaze zeroing in on hers. "What happened, Tess?"

"I was a nurse at a mission in the Andes. My fiancé and I had decided to serve two years overseas before we married and started a family. Kevin had just finished his residency in family practice. We had been there for a year when a band of guerrillas came into the village. They killed everyone but me. They left me for dead, but I survived the gunshot wound." Her voice caught. She swallowed hard and continued in a tone that mirrored the trembling in her body. "I watched Kevin die, and there was nothing I could do to help him or anyone else in the village. The only way I made it was by pretending I was dead, too. Thankfully they didn't check."

Mac grasped her hand in his, the warmth of his touch a balm to her tattered nerves. "I'm so sorry, Tess. No one should have to go through something like that."

His comforting words reached out and caressed the pain in her heart. "When they left, I tried to help Kevin. I was too late. He died in my arms. After that, I passed out. The next thing I remember is waking up in a hospital bed in the capital."

His grip tightened. "Is that why you've turned away from God?"

She twisted, staring at him through glistening eyes.

"Don't you understand? Kevin was a good man. A good Christian who only wanted to serve the Lord and help people through his medicine. He had so much to give in the name of the Lord. More than me. Why did he die and I live?" One tear slipped down her cheek and fell onto their clasped hands.

"Sometimes God has plans for people that aren't what we think they should be. We have to have faith He knows what is best in the long run. Kevin is with God now. The Lord has something else in mind for you."

Tess squeezed her eyes closed for a long moment, wanting to shut the world out. "When I went to his funeral, his mother couldn't understand why I was alive and her son was dead. She fell apart in church. I barely managed to get through the service." Recalling that awful scene, she shuddered.

"You have much to give to others."

"But I don't save lives like Kevin did."

"There are ways to save a person that have nothing to do with medicine. Look how you took Johnny under your wing. If it hadn't been for you, Johnny wouldn't be living with Amy and me right now. The Lord hasn't given up on you. Don't give up on Him."

Still Tess could remember begging God to save Kevin or to take her instead. The memory haunted her. "I wish it were that simple."

"But it is."

The one thing that had nagged at her came to the foreground. "Kevin was a better Christian than me. He was much more devoted than me. So why did God take him and not me?"

"It's okay that you survived. You don't need to feel guilty."

"I wish I could believe that."

"You need to take a good hard look at the people you influence. Besides Johnny, Amy adores you, and I care about you very much. Then how about all the children you entertain with your clown therapy or help while they're in the hospital."

She pulled her hands from his grasp and rose, restless, as though her nerves were stretched beyond their limit and would break any second. "I might as well tell you everything." She let out a long breath. "Kevin was in the village that day because I talked him out of going to the capital until the following day. I thought it was going to rain and I didn't want us to get stuck traveling on the trail in a downpour." She whirled to face Mac. "He would be alive today if it wasn't for me."

Mac flinched as though she had hit him. In the dim light she could see his features pale. Now he knew the full extent of her responsibility in Kevin's death.

"So you see, Mac, there isn't much you can say to make me feel any less guilty. A good man died because of me."

Mac shot to his feet and gripped her upper arms. "Don't say that. *You* had nothing to do with it. You didn't pull the trigger. You can't foresee the future. You made a judgment call on the facts as you knew them. You are not to blame for his death."

She wrenched herself free, stepping away from him. "I saw how you looked at me when I told you."

"You saw my anguish over my wife's death in my face. Your words were so similar to what I felt right after Sheila died."

"What do you mean? Your wife died in childbirth."

"She didn't want to have a family. I'm the one who wanted to start having children and talked her into it. She would be alive today if I hadn't. So you see, you aren't the only one with guilt over another's death."

"Is that why you don't want any more children?"

"Isn't that enough?"

"Dying in childbirth isn't common."

"I won't be responsible for putting another woman in danger if I have anything to do with it. I can't risk that kind of loss ever again."

His confession stunned her. Words failed her. She clenched then flexed her hands. Slowly she curled her fingers into fists, her nails digging into her palms. So much pain. So much guilt—on both their parts. How would they begin to heal? To forgive themselves? Tess wondered.

"When Sheila died, I don't know what I would have done if it weren't for my faith in the Lord. The first time I held Amy I felt so lost. God gave me the strength to live each day. He can do the same for you, Tess."

She wanted to believe Mac, but she could remember her pleas that went unanswered in that mountain village. "What happened to me isn't the same as what happened to you."

"You're right. I had the support and love of my family to help me. I had a little baby girl to take care of. I imagine you were all alone to deal with your grief. What I'm trying to tell you now is that you aren't really alone. God is with us always. Let go of your guilt and embrace our Father."

She spun away, turning her back to him, hunching her shoulders as she drew in on herself. "I wish I could."

He laid his hand on her. "Let me help you. Come with my family to church again. Open your heart to the possibilities of the Lord."

Placing her palm over her heart, she felt its steady beat, evidence she'd survived that day in the mountains. She knew she had to do something to change the direction of her life. She loved nursing and dressing up as a clown to entertain sick children, but she was discovering that she needed something more. It was as though she had put her life back together after South America, but there were missing pieces to the jigsaw puzzle that left gaping holes in the overall picture.

"Both Amy and Johnny would love to have you accompany us."

Just Amy and Johnny? She wanted to ask, but bit her bottom lip to keep from saying what she really wanted to.

"Amy's still talking about our trip out to Colt's. And she wanted me to tell you again she was sorry about what Buttons did."

"Next time I know not to ask to hold the puppy."

His chuckles, close to her ear, whispered against her neck. "I never saw someone move so fast in the front seat of my car."

Tess faced Mac. "It's not every day I have the privilege of an animal using me like a piece of newspaper."

"She was just overexcited to see you."

"That kind of excitement I can do without. But tell Amy again for me that it wasn't her fault."

"Come to dinner next week and tell her yourself. I know they would love to show you the rabbits and how much the puppies have grown."

"Okay," she said, aware she was committing herself to more than dinner. She was risking her heart again. She knew she couldn't resist the lure of Mac and his family.

# Chapter Ten

Tess checked the address again, making sure she was on the right street. The houses needed fresh paint. One had a broken window patched with boards. Another had foot-tall weeds growing in its small front yard, which was littered with rusted car parts.

Tess spied Mac standing on the porch of a large two-story house on the corner. Painted recently, the halfway house had a new roof. The lawn was mowed, and the hedge in front was trimmed neatly. She slowed to a stop at the curb, craning her neck to stare at the shingled roof from which Mac had fallen and broken his leg. She shuddered at the long fall and thought how lucky he was that his leg was the only thing he'd broken that day. She climbed from her car, locked it then headed up the sidewalk. Mac descended the steps and met her at the bottom.

"I wish you'd let me pick you up. This neighborhood

isn't the best." Mac casually placed his hand at the small of her back.

"After what I've seen and lived through, this place is a piece of cake."

He grimaced. "That still doesn't mean I can't be concerned for your safety."

"I could say the same thing to you."

"Ah, a feminist."

She stopped at the front door and looked deep into his eyes. "No, a bullet will tear through your flesh as easily as mine. It doesn't know if you're male or female."

"Then I guess we will worry about each other."

"That's what friends do."

"Yes, friends," he murmured and pulled the door open to allow her to enter.

"I'm not surprised at the location of the halfway house. Have any of your neighbors complained?"

"A few. But there have been no problems in the two years we have been here, and the complaints have died down."

Some of the tension siphoned from Tess at that news. Part of the reason she'd decided to volunteer at the halfway house was that she wanted to see for herself what Mac did that was so important to him. The other reason was to check out the place. She could no longer deny that Mac was special to her. She needed to assess how safe he was. He came here almost every day. She cared about him and didn't want to lose him—as a friend, she added quickly, the hollowness of the declaration ringing through her mind.

"I think our good neighbors have learned to ignore us, and that makes it easier. One less problem to deal with." Mac motioned toward the living area. "Let me give you a quick tour."

Tess scanned the room. There were two comfortable, worn-looking couches and three overstuffed easy chairs, all surrounding a television set. Several end tables held lamps and coasters, and one had a stack of magazines. In the center of the coffee table, in front of one of the navy blue sofas, was a large Bible. Near the picture window that faced the street was a schefflera, a good six feet tall. One man sat in a chair watching CNN and chewing gum while another had propped his feet on the scarred coffee table with his head resting on the cushion, his eyes closed.

"Fred, anything happening in the world?" Mac asked the man in the chair.

"Nope. Not a thing," Fred answered between smacks of his gum.

"Well, I guess that's a good thing."

"No news is good news." The man cracked a smile, revealing one of his front teeth was missing.

"Is Harry asleep?"

"Guess so. He hasn't stirred since I've been here."

Mac frowned but didn't say anything. He signaled for Tess to follow him into the dining room, then the kitchen.

Once the door shut behind her, Tess asked, "Is everything all right with Harry?"

"He's new to the house. Came at the end of last week. I haven't been able to reach him like the others, but with the Lord's help I will." Mac passed through the kitchen, saying hello to Tom, the cook this week, and headed for the office in the back. "I counsel in here if the group is a small one or there's only one person. Sometimes we have large groups and we meet in the game room, through there." He pointed to a door leading from the office. "That's where you'll see anyone who has a medical problem. If you think they need to see a doctor, let me know. I can arrange that."

"How many men are living here?"

"Fifteen. We're almost to capacity."

"Do they stay long?"

"Not too long. This is a transition place for them. With luck by the time they leave here they have a job and have been off drugs or alcohol for a while."

Tess inspected the large office with a desk in one corner and a grouping of chairs in front of book-filled shelves at the other end. This was where Mac spent a lot of his time. The room reflected his character, from a Bible on the desk to a casual lived-in look that gave off no pretensions. "Are you the only counselor?"

"No, there are three of us who work here part-time."

"Do they all volunteer their time like you do?"

He looked uncomfortable. "Yes. The network of volunteers has grown since I've gotten to know some people at your hospital."

She noticed over the weeks she'd become better acquainted with Mac that he rarely wanted to talk about the good things he did for others. That was another part of his character she liked. He quietly went through life trying to right wrongs in the name of the Lord.

"Ready to get started?"

With a nod she walked toward the door Mac had indicated. "After I see everyone, what else would you like me to do?"

Mac smiled. "I imagine that will take most of the afternoon."

Tess had her doubts, since there weren't that many people in the house at the moment. Except for the television the place was quiet. She didn't hear any footsteps from the floor above. But according to Mac, they had a nurse conduct a clinic once a week, so he must know what he was talking about.

Several hours later Tess realized it wasn't just the men in the house who came to the clinic, but people who lived in the neighborhood. She saw several women and children with symptoms ranging from a cough to what she suspected was a broken arm. She set up that woman with an appointment to get her arm x-rayed immediately.

Mac stuck his head in the doorway and asked, "How's it going?"

"So this place serves as a free clinic to the area?"

"That's one of the reasons the neighbors don't complain much any more. Some of these people never get any medical attention except what we have here. Once a month a doctor comes to the clinic. Otherwise it's a nurse. They don't much care. It's more than they had before we set up shop."

"Your foundation funds all this?"

"This is one of my projects."

Tess saw Tom standing in the entrance with his head bowed. "Can I help you?"

The man looked up hesitantly. "I burned my hand a few days ago. I just wanted you to check it."

"Sure." Tess sent Tom a reassuring smile, hoping to ease some of his shyness.

Slowly he shuffled across the game room and sat in the chair in front of Tess. She waited for him to show her his hand. Hesitantly Tom raised his arm, his eyes downcast. She unwrapped the food-stained bandage, revealing a red and ugly-looking second-degree burn.

"This must have hurt bad."

"Still does, ma'am."

"Well, let me see what I can do to help you."

"I sure would appreciate anything you can do. I can't hold no knife in this hand, and I ain't too good with my left hand."

"Knife?"

"To cut up the vegetables for dinner, ma'am."

"Of course." Tess felt Mac's gaze on her as she worked to clean the burn and wrap it in a fresh bandage. She tingled from the touch of his eyes.

When she was through with Tom and he had left, she rose and stretched her cramped muscles, aware that Mac was still in the doorway to his office watching her. "I've enjoyed this. I don't know if I can volunteer every week because of my schedule at the hospital, but I would like to help out more."

Mac crossed the room. "That would be great. This place depends on its volunteers. I hope one day to expand services to the neighborhood. I'd like to have a doctor here more often and nurses here more than once a week." He stopped next to her. "You're very good with the patients, young and old. I like watching you work."

His praise wiped all thoughts from her mind. She felt the color in her cheeks flare at the same time a pleased feeling encased her in warmth. He reached toward her.

Shouts erupted from the living room. Without a second's hesitation, Mac spun and raced toward the yelling. Tess hastened after him, the loud voices suddenly too quiet. When she entered, she stopped inside the doorway, her gaze riveted to Harry, who stood over Fred in the chair. Anger marred the lines of Harry's face. His hands were fisted at his sides, his body conveying such rage that he appeared brittle, ready to break in two.

Mac moved close to the pair. "Harry, can I help you? Is something wrong?" His voice was soft, even.

His jaw clamped shut, Harry swung his gaze to Mac, a few feet from him. "He turned the station."

Fred, whose features were pale, spoke. "I thought he was asleep. I was tired of the news."

Harry glared at Fred. "Well, I wasn't asleep and I was listening to the news. Turn it back."

"I don't want to." The stubborn set of his mouth

attested to Fred's mounting bravery now that others were in the room.

Harry leaned down, placing both hands on the arms of the chair and caging the other man against the back. "Turn back to CNN."

He spat out each word slowly and with such fury that Tess stepped back. Her heart pounded against her chest. Her palms were sweaty. The air in the room churned with intense emotions as though someone had switched a blender on high.

Mac shifted forward. "Harry, I'm glad you're up. It's time for our counseling session. You can watch the news afterward." Mac pitched his voice low, a calming sound, meant to subdue.

"I don't wanna talk to you now. I want to watch the news." Harry bent closer to Fred, their faces only inches apart.

Tess held her breath when Mac laid his hand on Harry's shoulder. The man tried to shrug it off. When that didn't work, he spun and faced Mac, forgetting about Fred. Fred quickly squeezed out of his seat and scrambled out of the room while Harry glared at Mac for daring to interrupt him. The sound of Fred's fleeing footsteps on the stairs echoed in Tess's mind, competing with the thundering of her heartbeat in her ears.

"You'll be able to when we're through, Harry. You accepted counseling as a condition for living here."

Some the tension dissolved in Tess at the continual calming sound of Mac's voice, as though this type of incident happened every day and wasn't any big deal. She hoped Harry responded in a similar fashion. She gauged the man's reaction to Mac's words and saw a slight relaxing of the firm line of his jaw. Harry's sharp gaze mellowed as he instinctively followed Mac's example of taking deep breaths. Tess found herself doing it, too, and more of her tension eased.

Mac patiently waited for Harry to bring himself under control. Sweat beaded the man's forehead and rolled down his face. He clenched and unclenched his hands, but finally, after a few minutes of silence, his shoulders sagged and he dropped his head.

"Come on, Harry, let's talk about this in my office," Mac said, moving toward the doorway. "I know things haven't been easy for you since you came."

Tess stepped to the side and allowed both men to leave. When the room was empty, she collapsed onto the couch, all the energy draining from her body. When she'd looked into Harry's eyes, she'd seen hate and such anger she'd been frightened he would do something harmful to Fred—or Mac.

Thankfully Mac had deflated the man's rage, but what would happen next time if he couldn't? That question scared her more than the encounter she had just witnessed.

She headed to the game room, determined to stay until Mac emerged from his office safely. She glanced out the window and noticed it was getting late. She had a million things she needed to do at home, as well as errands to run, but she couldn't leave. The sound of

Harry's raised voice sent her across the room to hover near the door in case Mac needed her. She wasn't sure what she could do. Harry was almost as large as Mac, and she was sure Mac could take care of himself in a physical fight, but if anything happened to Mac— She wouldn't allow herself to finish that thought.

Thirty minutes later, Mac and Harry came out of the office. Harry hurried up the stairs while Mac watched him. Then Mac turned toward her, and she saw the weariness in his features. The dullness in his eyes and the tired lines on his face underscored how emotionally drained he was after the tension-charged encounter.

Tess went to him, only wanting to comfort and offer words of encouragement. "You did a great job of defusing the situation."

"Just part of the job." He shrugged off the compliment.

"How often do you have to do that?"

She hoped the panic didn't sound in her voice, but Mac looked at her sharply for a long moment before answering, "Not often, thankfully, but some of these men have a lot of emotional baggage to deal with. Until they do they often won't succeed in overcoming their addiction." He peered at his watch. "Why are you still here? Didn't you tell me you had to leave by four-thirty?"

She blushed. "Would you believe I wanted to make sure nothing happened with Harry?"

"And what would you have done?"

"I'm not sure. I didn't think that far. Call 911? Rush in and stop him?"

Mac grinned. "Let's see, you're five feet four inches and he's over six-two. How were you going to stop him? Jump on his back?"

"Okay. You can quit laughing. That man was very angry when you two disappeared into your office an hour ago. I wasn't about to leave you here alone."

"There are at least five other men here, Tess." The corners of his eyes crinkled. "But I like the idea you were going to save me. Not many women have said that to me."

"And I'm not going to make that mistake again."

He reached up and cupped his hand along her jawline. "You can protect me anytime you want." He stared long and hard into her eyes. "I need to leave soon. I'll walk you to your car."

"Are you trying to protect me now?"

"This isn't the safest neighborhood, especially as it gets darker."

Tess gathered her purse and the sweater she had brought. "As you know, I parked right out front."

"Are you still coming to the church festival on Saturday with us?"

"I'm looking forward to it. I miss seeing Amy and Johnny."

"They miss you."

"How are the rabbits doing?"

"Good. The kids agreed to take the rabbits to Colt's on Sunday."

"They're giving up on the idea of a shelter for stray animals?"

"Not exactly. They think the country is a better place for their rabbits than the city." He leaned around her to open her car door. "I won't be surprised if they find another stray animal soon."

The scent of sandalwood drifted to her, making her acutely aware of the man near her. "I think you're right."

"I just hope it's nothing too outlandish. I remember Casey finding a skunk once."

"Oh, that could be a problem." Tess slid behind the driver's seat.

"A smelly problem."

"Maybe you'd better stock tomato juice in the pantry just in case."

His laughter blended with the sounds of the neighborhood, a car starting down the street, someone mowing a small patch of grass. "Not a bad idea. We'll pick you up at three on Saturday. Be ready for some fun and relaxation."

With a nod, she turned her key in the ignition.

Mac stepped back and watched her drive away. Every time he was with her he felt another brick around his heart crumble. He'd started out with friendship in mind. He'd sensed her need for spiritual help. Now he knew he had been fooling himself. He was falling for her and he wasn't sure that was wise for either of them. She was afraid to risk her heart, and he realized after his marriage to Sheila that he could never settle for anything but total commitment from a woman. Tess wanted a large family, and he knew he wasn't prepared to give her that. Nope, it wasn't a good idea to get too emotionally involved with Tess. But was it too late? Mac wondered as he headed inside the halfway house.

"How many cups of coffee does that make for the day?" Delise said as she plopped down beside Tess at the kitchen table.

"Five, and before you say anything I know that isn't good. But it's that or I'm gonna fall asleep at the church festival. Better yet on the ride to the place."

"Yeah, what's been going on? For the past few nights I've heard you up and about at all hours."

"Bad dream." A chill shimmered down Tess's length when she thought about the nightmare she'd had after the incident at the halfway house. She shook her head as though that would rid her mind of the image of Mac dying in his office with Harry standing over him. She could still hear her screams.

"Well, it must be a humdinger to keep you up like that."

"I've had bouts of insomnia before. I'm sure that's all this is."

"Try a warm glass of milk."

"Yeah, I will." Tess couldn't tell her roommate she didn't want to go to sleep. She wasn't prepared to explain her nightmare to Delise. But worse, she was afraid Mac would see the dark circles under her eyes and probe for answers. He was much too astute for her peace of mind at times.

When the doorbell rang, Delise hopped to her feet. "I'll get it. Finish your coffee. I wouldn't want you falling asleep on your date."

"It isn't a date. Amy and Johnny are going to be with us."

Delise paused at the doorway. "Sure it isn't. He asked you to go with him. He's picking you up at your apartment. That sounds like a date to me even if the children are chaperoning."

Tess opened her mouth to reply, but Delise fled into the living room. Tess gulped the last few swallows of the lukewarm coffee, rose and put the mug in the sink. When she turned toward the door, Mac stood framed in it, looking incredibly handsome in a pair of blue jeans, faded and worn looking, and a striped red and blue polo shirt. His smile brightened his eyes and sent warmth coursing through her.

"Ready?"

She nodded, not trusting herself to speak. After snatching her purse and a floppy hat to wear in case the sun decided to peek out from behind the clouds, she walked with him to the front door. When she noticed his car was empty, she asked, "Where are Johnny and Amy?"

"Casey picked them up for lunch and a treat. She's bringing them."

"Oh," Tess said, sliding into the passenger side of the car, realizing this felt very much like a date, as Delise had so kindly pointed out.

After he started the car, he threw a quick look at her. "Having trouble sleeping?"

She knew he would say something. Why hadn't she prepared a response? She searched her mind for a reply that wouldn't lead to a lot of questions. None came to mind. "Yes," she finally answered, knowing what his next question would be.

"Why?"

Because I've been dreaming about you getting killed, she thought and gritted her teeth, her gaze trained on the road.

"Another nightmare about Kevin?"

"Yes, I've been having nightmares," she answered, deliberately not elaborating on the subject matter of her dreams.

"Tess, maybe if you talk with Pastor Winthrop, he might be able to help you put the past in perspective."

"Have you completely?"

Mac didn't answer for a moment. "Yes, I think I have. But—" he slid a glance toward her "—I had help. You're trying to do everything by yourself."

"You mean the Lord's help?"

"Yes."

But He's the one who took Kevin away, she wanted to proclaim as she had in the past. Instead she dug her teeth into her lower lip, knowing the truth wasn't that simple. "I'll think about it." That was all she could say.

"That's all I ask." He pulled the car into the church parking lot.

Tess noticed a crowd had formed on the lawn. A large tent offered shelter from the sun, or in this case the rain if the clouds blanketing the sky opened up. People manned the booths under the canvas with various products for sale from food to crafts. Several groups of children were playing games from catch to tag while others romped on the equipment in the playground. Some men milled around the barbecues, talking and peering at the dark sky. To the side of the grills a group of women arranged bowls of food on card tables.

Mac took Tess's hand and led her to the cashier to pay for the evening dinner of hamburgers and hot dogs with an assortment of salads and desserts. She saw several people she knew and waved to Mac's mother behind the table displaying jars of preserved fruit.

"What's the idea of the festival?" Tess asked Mac after he had gotten their meal tickets.

"It's a celebration of people's talents." He gestured to an older lady at the nearest booth. "Ruth loves to knit and makes beautiful sweaters. She sells them every year to help the church raise money. And Candace over there—" he pointed to a young woman who sat in front of an easel "—will draw your portrait for a fee. She's quite good. I'm going to have her do Johnny and Amy."

"Together?"

"Yes. Amy follows Johnny around everywhere. I keep thinking he's gonna get tired of it one day."

"He's never had much of a family. I think Amy's

hero-worshiping is a novelty to him." Tess caught Alice motioning for Tess to come over. "Your mother has a booth. Where's yours?"

"Doing what?"

"Well, let's see. You could teach children how to tackle."

"I think that comes naturally."

"You're a good listener. How about a booth where you listen to people?"

"Everyone can listen. That's not a talent."

Tess stopped, standing in Mac's path with one hand on her waist. "Peter MacPherson, being a good listener is very important and something a lot of people don't know how to do. It's a gift that's certainly appreciated by me."

He beamed with a wide grin, his eyes almost silver. "Next year you need to have a clown booth."

Next year. She liked the sound of those words. She returned his smile, feeling her whole face light up. "Yeah, children could threw pies at me."

"Just children?"

The gleam in his eyes made her laugh. "Maybe little old ladies, too." She started for his mother's booth.

"Can I persuade you to buy some of my preserves? It's like tasting a little bit of heaven with each bite. Want to try a sample?" Alice lavished some blackberry jam onto a piece of toast, then held the plate up.

Tess took a bite of the toast. "Mmm. This is delicious. Do you pick your own fruit?"

"Whenever I can."

"Hey, that's not fair. I want a taste," Mac said, his regard on the toast in Tess's hand.

Without thinking she lifted it to his mouth, and he ate the rest of the sample, his lips grazing her fingertips. Her gaze connected with his as though she were bound to him. The shared moment reinforced the attraction she felt toward Mac.

After a few seconds of silence, Alice coughed, and Tess glanced away from Mac, her face flaming, her legs weak. She gripped the edge of the table to steady herself.

His attention on Tess, Mac said, "Mom, I'll take two of every kind you have."

"At this rate I'll be sold out before the hour's up." Alice began boxing up the jars.

"I'll find the rest of the family and send them over." Mac finally looked at his mother. "Then you can join us at the picnic tables. I'm gonna stake one out for us."

Alice's brow arched. "Just one?"

"You're right, two. Any more and no one else will have one."

Relieved that Mac was no longer staring at her, Tess watched the exchange between mother and son and realized again how much she missed having a family to call her own. "Before you sell out, I'd like to purchase some."

"That's okay, Tess, I bought one for you and one for me." Mac lifted the box from the table.

"But I—"

"Just consider it a thank-you for sending us Johnny. I'm taking this to the car. Be back in a sec."

Mac disappeared through the crowd in the tent before Tess could open her mouth to refuse his gift.

"Hon, one thing I've learned over the years as his mother is to accept the gifts. He loves giving people presents for no reason at all. You're just going to have to get used to it. Besides, this is a donation to the church."

Alice's statement implied Tess would be the recipient of many presents in the future. That thought alarmed her. "He's really become attached to Johnny," Tess said, wanting to steer the conversation away from gifts and anything personal concerning her and Mac. She had always been uncomfortable with people giving her unexpected presents, or even on her birthday and at Christmas.

"He's crazy about the boy."

"What happens if Mrs. Hocks finds a relative?"

Alice shook her head. "It'll break his heart. When I talk with him now, he's always telling me something about Johnny as though the child was his own."

Again Tess thought back to the first day she'd met Mac. She'd been reminded of a gentle bear, and that impression was confirmed the more she was around him.

"He's had several losses in his life. I hope Johnny isn't one of them."

"So do I," Tess murmured, aware that Mac was heading toward them.

Tess followed his progress and noticed several members of the congregation stopping Mac to say something. He drew people to him with his easy ways and warm smile. There was nothing frightening about him even though he was very large and muscularly built. Her gentle bear.

Oh, my! Where had that come from? she wondered and turned her flushed face away before the man read what was in her mind. She wasn't ready. Was she?

"Let's go find Casey and the kids. See you, Mom, when you're through selling your wares."

When Tess emerged from the tent, she noticed darker clouds rolling in and the smell of rain in the air. A cool breeze picked up, whipping strands of hair about her face. "I think it might rain on this parade."

A drop splattered on top of Mac's head. "Yeah, I think you're right. We'd better get everyone moving indoors to the reception hall."

"But what about all this?" Tess swept her arm toward the tent and the grills set up for preparing dinner.

"I can't complain. We need the rain even if the timing isn't great. The festival will go on, just indoors. We're celebrating our good fortune and the talents God gave us. It doesn't make any difference where that happens."

Thirty minutes later Tess stood in the middle of the large reception hall surrounded by a mass of people crammed inside while thundered sounded and lightning flashed outside. The smiles and laughter attested to the festive atmosphere. Instead of being upset, everyone was glad of the rain, declaring its appropriateness because the children's play was about Noah's ark.

Mac and his brothers helped bring in chairs while Alice and Mary organized some of the churchwomen to prepare the food in the kitchen. Tess suddenly felt the need to escape the press of people. She wasn't sure where she belonged, where her place in this world was. Right now she felt as though she were on the ark in the middle of a sea with no sight of land. Noah found land. Would she?

Tess sought refuge in the sanctuary where the loud sounds of the festival were muffled by the thick, heavy double doors and walls of stone. Several soft lights illuminated the church in a warm glow of welcome. She walked toward the front and sat in a pew. The simple cross on the altar drew her attention. Staring at it, she thought of what Christ had done for mankind the day He had died on the cross. Slowly as her mind replayed Jesus's message, peace washed through her, cleansing her soul, erasing the guilt she'd carried around for so long.

She closed her eyes and listened to the sounds of the rain battering the roof of the sanctuary and sensed a feeling of safety, as if nothing could touch her inside these four walls. She hadn't experienced that in years, especially since the day in the Andes when her life had changed, when men had come down from the mountains and taken something precious from her. Now she realized she had allowed those men to rob her of not just Kevin, but her faith, as well. She had turned her back on the Lord when she should have been embracing Him, letting Him fully into her life to heal the gaping wound.

"Our Father, please give me the strength to see Your

plan for me. Help me to open my heart to You again and to forgive myself for living when so many died. I can't do it alone anymore. I need You."

After setting up the chairs for the play, Mac searched the reception hall for Tess. When he didn't find her, he checked the kitchen, then went back into the hall.

"I saw her go into the sanctuary." Casey came up to Mac.

"Her?"

"Don't try to pretend you don't know who I'm talking about. I saw you looking for Tess. When she isn't with you, you're always searching for her in the crowd."

"And what's that supposed to mean?"

"You're falling hard for her." Casey lifted her chin a notch as though to challenge her brother to deny what she said.

"Tess and I are friends. We—"

His sister placed her hands on her hips and shot him a disgruntled look. "Mac, quit fooling yourself. You've never done that before, so why start now."

"I'm trying to help her."

"Oh, good grief, Mac, get real. You are interested in Tess Morgan, and it goes way beyond friendship."

"You said she went into the sanctuary?" Mac asked, deciding to ignore his little sister's observation. She was only nineteen and had a lot to learn about the world.

"Yes."

Mac headed for the church but paused at the double

doors. Why had Tess gone inside? To speak with God? Should he disturb her? He looked around the quiet foyer, trying to decide what he should do. One of the doors opened. He stepped back.

Tess emerged from the sanctuary, a calm serenity touching her beautiful features as though the Lord had touched her. Her eyes glowed with an inner light when she peered at him. The smile that graced her lips melted his irritation at his sister.

"The most wonderful thing happened to me." Tess grasped his hands. "I talked with the Lord and He heard me." Tears welled up in her eyes and flowed down her cheeks. "Oh, Mac, you were so right. I should never have turned away from God when Kevin died. I should have turned to Him."

Mac took her into his arms and held her close to his heart. The pressure in his chest constricted his breathing. A lump lodged in his throat, and he had to swallow several times before he could speak. "I'm so glad you realize the Lord hasn't abandoned you."

She leaned back, her arms loosely about him. "But I abandoned the Lord."

"Remember the story of the shepherd leaving his flock to look for the lost sheep? He has found you and taken you back into the flock."

Through the shimmer of tears Tess regarded Mac, the tenderness she saw deep in his eyes. Emotions bombarded her from all sides, leaving her feeling drained but content. If it hadn't been for this man, she might never have found her way back to the Lord. She owed Mac a lot. Certainly her loyalty and friendship, but could she give him her love?

He held her face in his large hands. "You're special to the Lord and you're special to—"

"Mac, Tess, the play is about to start."

Tess shifted quickly away from Mac and turned toward Johnny, who rushed toward them. "Are you ready?"

"Yep, I've got my lines memorized. I've been helping Amy with hers."

"Do you need any help getting your costume on?"

"No, Casey's helping Amy then she's gonna help me." Johnny grabbed Tess's hand. "Come on. I want you two sitting in the front row. I had Mrs. MacPherson save you places."

"Okay, we're coming, buddy."

After Tess sat between Alice and Mac, she glanced down the row of chairs and saw all the MacPhersons. Tess felt honored to be included in the family event. All the children were in the play, with Johnny portraying Noah and Amy the white dove that found land.

"I wish we could open up the skylight and let the rain in. Then we would really have an authentic backdrop for the play," Alice whispered as the youth director came on stage to quiet the audience.

Mac leaned around Tess and replied, "I think we should just have it out in the parking lot."

A streak of lightning crackled the air followed by a loud boom that rocked the room. "I think I prefer staying indoors," Tess said, staring at the storm raging outside the window.

Amy shot out from behind the curtain on the stage and rushed to Mac, throwing herself into his lap and burying her face against his shirt. "Daddy, I don't like this," the little girl mumbled against him.

Another flash of light lit the darkened room, immediately accompanied by the sound of thunder. "Sweetheart, that's just the Lord shouting His joy to the world. If it didn't rain, life on Earth would cease to be."

"But, Daddy, it's so loud." She clapped her hands over her ears as thunder reverberated through the hall again.

"That's so everyone will be able to hear even from far away," Mac said when Amy cautiously uncovered her ears, her eyes round as saucers.

"It's just the Lord?"

"Yes, pumpkin. The sound won't hurt you."

She sat for a moment longer, her head cocked as she listened to the thunder rumble again. "You're right, Daddy. It doesn't hurt."

Mac hugged Amy. "You'd better get back behind stage. You're the most important part of this play."

Amy puffed out her chest. "I'm the one who finds land." She hopped from his lap and raced for the stage.

Tess touched Mac's hand. "I've always hated storms, too. Now I'll never think of them any other way than God's celebration of life."

"He does in many ways, small and large. It's all around us, Tess. The birth of a child. A new day."

"The miracle of love. A parent and child's love is a wonderful testament to the Lord."

The rest of the world faded from Mac's view. All his senses centered on the feel of her hand over his, of her scent of lilacs, of her beautiful features radiating with her renewed faith in the Lord. "Not just a love between a parent and child. There are all kinds of love. Each important in God's plan. Jesus's message to us was based on God's love for us."

Tears made her eyes glisten. "I'm just now rediscovering that."

So am I, Mac thought, sandwiching her hand between his. Was he brave enough to pursue this to the end? To discover what God had in mind for him and Tess?

## Chapter Eleven

"Don't be ridiculous. I don't mind taking you home." Tess braked at a stoplight and sent Casey a reassuring look.

"My car didn't start this morning."

"Cars, like computers, are wonderful until they don't work." Tess came to a stop at another light, scanning the intersection, the billboard—

In big, red letters, a message was written for all the world, or at least the people of Denver, to see. Tess, Will You Go With Me To The Circus Tonight? Yours, Mac. Her cheeks flamed the color of the letters.

"Your car isn't broken, is it?" Tess asked, aware the driver behind her was honking at her because the light was green and she hadn't moved. She pressed her foot on the accelerator, gunning through the intersection.

"I never said it was broken. I said it didn't start this morning. That's because I didn't try to start it. Mac brought me to work so I could get a ride home with you."

Tess's face still felt hot. "Why didn't he just call me up and ask me himself?"

Casey shrugged. "Not sure. You can ask him yourself. He's right there."

Tess pulled into Alice's driveway and saw the man in question leaning against his car with his arms folded over his chest and a pleased grin on his face. "I think I'll do just that."

When she approached him, the twinkle in his eyes erased any embarrassment she might have felt. After all, she wasn't the only one in Denver who went by the name of Tess, and surely there were lots of Macs who lived in the city. "I could be busy."

"Are you?" He lifted one brow.

"I should be, since you waited until the last minute to ask."

"I checked with Casey, and she said you weren't."

Tess frowned, remembering Casey drilling her yesterday about her plans for the week, including this evening.

"I wanted to surprise you. Do something different that you wouldn't expect."

"You got me there. I didn't expect the billboard or the circus."

"Amy and Johnny are coming, too. How about it?"

"You know I won't say no when you mention them," she said in an accusing voice that didn't sound very strong.

"A guy will use any means to get a gal to go out with him."

"You're that desperate?"

"You bet, where you're concerned. You've turned me down in the past."

"Not for a long time."

"In football I learned to anticipate every move of my opponent."

"Now I'm an opponent. That doesn't bode well for the date."

He chuckled. "I think this date will go just fine. You can call it research."

"Research? For what?"

"For your clown therapy, what else? There are gonna be a lot of clowns at the circus."

"Oh, so this was purely for my benefit?"

His easy laughter filled the air. "Hardly. Definitely it's for my benefit—and the children's, of course."

"You certainly know how to hit below the belt. You know how much I love being with Amy and Johnny."

"I hope not just them." His gray eyes glittered with that twinkle.

"No, not just them."

The air between them crackled with a finely honed tension. Their gazes remained bound while the world continued around them. One minute slid into two, yet Tess couldn't find the strength to walk to her car.

Finally Mac straightened as though suddenly remembering they were standing on a public street with only a few hours until their date. "I'll pick you up at six. Be ready to eat a lot of junk food and to have some fun."

Tess saluted. "Aye, aye, sir."

His chuckles drifted to her as she strolled to her car and climbed in. Something was in the air. She felt the charged atmosphere as though it were a palpable force. As she neared her apartment, her excitement grew. Their relationship was evolving to another level. She was no longer denying her attraction, and neither was he.

Tess stuffed the last of the chili dog into her mouth, chewed the gooey mess, then licked her lips. "My arteries won't thank you, but I do."

"Here, you missed some chili." Mac dabbed a paper napkin on her chin.

His gaze captured hers. Again, her surroundings faded and all her senses were centered on Mac—so close that he threatened her equilibrium. Because of him, she looked forward to each new day. She had re-discovered the Lord and her faith. Mac had become very important in her life.

She blinked, shattering the moment of connection. "I love these things, but they aren't easy to eat," she said to cover her disconcerting revelation.

Amy peered at her father. "When are the clowns coming out?"

Tess took one look at the little girl with chili smeared all over her face and grinned. "It's contagious."

She took a napkin and cleaned Amy. As she wiped

the child's chin, Tess couldn't shake the feeling she wanted to do this more often, on a regular basis. The knowledge left her shaken.

A man mounted the steps into the stands, selling cotton candy. Pulling on Mac's arm, Johnny asked, "Can I have some?"

"That's pure sugar."

"I know. That's why I love it."

"Why did I bother saying that?" Mac muttered to Tess and raised his hand to ask the man to pass down two cotton candies.

"A parent's duty is to be a voice of reason." Tess shoved the newfound emotions concerning Mac and Amy away to be examined in the privacy of her apartment. When Mac pulled out some money and paid for the cotton candies, Tess asked, "What about me?"

"You, too?" Mac signaled for another one.

"Afraid so. I have a big sweet tooth I try to keep under control."

"You're not succeeding."

"Nope." Tess took the cotton candy Mac handed her.

"Your dentist must love you."

"I don't have one cavity in my mouth."

He shot her a surprised glance right before the music swelled and the ringmaster announced the clowns.

"Daddy, look!" Amy pointed at a clown who had curly red hair and a big frown painted on his face.

He came running out and tripped over his large shoes, falling facedown in the arena. Two more bounded out, stumbled over the same imaginary spot, landing in a heap on top of the first one. Everyone in the audience laughed as the clowns tried to stand and ended up in a jumbled mess.

Halfway through their routine, Mac leaned across Amy and whispered to Tess, "Getting any ideas?"

"These skits require at least two people. Are you volunteering to get drenched with a bottle of water?"

"Since you're helping me at the halfway house, I guess I could help you if it doesn't involve putting on makeup. I have an image to uphold."

"I'll have to remember that the next time I'm entertaining the children on the floor."

His eyes sparkled with humor. "I'm gonna be up there day after tomorrow. I think I could manage being a straight man."

"Shh, Daddy, I can't hear."

"Sorry, pumpkin."

Tess tried to contain her smile, but every time she peered at Mac she pictured him with water dripping off his face. The wonderful part of that picture would be Mac's laughter. He enjoyed life.

"Somehow I get the feeling you aren't grinning about the performance," Mac whispered.

Pressing her lips in a straight line, Tess focused her attention on the center ring, but she felt Mac's gaze on her. She resisted the strong urge to look at him again. When the clown routine was over, she realized she couldn't remember a single thing any clown had done.

All her thoughts were fixed on the mischievous gleam in Mac's eyes.

When a couple of performers traversed the high wire on a bicycle, Johnny exclaimed with wide eyes, "I'd like to try that."

"Not without years of experience behind you," Mac immediately said. "Promise?"

Johnny nodded. "I didn't mean I would."

"How about me, Daddy?"

"Same goes for you. It isn't something to try at home. Understand, Amy?"

"I wouldn't. I don't like high places."

Mac sighed heavily. "I think that's one fear I'm glad she has."

At the end of the performance Johnny jumped to his feet and clapped. Amy quickly followed suit, pumping her arm in the air like Johnny. Tess realized in a short time Mac had made Johnny feel like a part of the family. For a few seconds she thought about him as a father—of her children. Quickly she pushed that from her mind but not before she acknowledged he would be an excellent one.

As they climbed down the stands, Amy took Tess and Johnny's hands. Mac linked his fingers through Tess's. Together—like a real family—they made their way through the crowd to the car.

When everyone was settled inside, Mac pulled out of the parking space. "Come back to the house with us. It's still early. I thought we could play a game, then put the children to bed. After that I'll take you home."

The scene he described fueled the image of being a family in Tess's mind. Its temptation enticed her to accept. "I can't stay up too late. I work tomorrow."

"One game."

"I want to play Twister," Amy said.

"Yeah," Johnny added.

"Then Twister it is."

"I'm gonna spin for everyone," Amy said with a shout of joy. "I do that real good."

Thirty minutes later Tess contorted her body to reach a yellow circle with her right hand.

Amy spun the wheel for her father. "Red, Daddy."

Mac twisted to look at the spinner, then plopped his left foot in the circle next to Tess. His face was inches from hers. Chuckling, he tickled Tess in the side, causing her to fall forward into Johnny, who managed to plow into Amy on the sideline. Mac jumped back, avoiding the pile of arms and legs, laughing at the sight of the entwined body parts before him.

"This reminds me of the clowns at the circus," he said, trying to bring his laughter under control.

Tess looked up. "I think it's payback time, kids." Pulling her arm free from the bottom of the heap, she rose, her gaze fixed on Mac with mischief in mind.

He began to back up, his hands out to ward off the advancing trio. "I'm sure in the rules somewhere it states no ganging up."

"I can't read, Daddy."

"Mac, it says nothing of the sort." Tess proceeded toward him with Johnny on one side and Amy on the other.

"Well, it should. It's highly unfair."

"And tickling an opponent is fair?"

Mac feinted a move to the right, then circled the group. Tess lunged toward his upper body at the same time the two children went for his legs. Mac went down with a thump. Sitting on her haunches, Tess let Amy and Johnny tickle Mac in the ribs. His laughter warmed her insides, confirming the feeling of closeness she'd had all evening.

"Uncle. Uncle," Mac called.

Reluctantly the children stopped, but Amy flung herself at her father, wrapping her arms around his neck.

"This has been the bestest day." The little girl kissed Mac's cheek.

"Yeah. I've never been to the circus," Johnny added.

"I'm glad you two enjoyed it. Now it's time for bed."

"Can't we stay up a little later?"

"No." Mac sat up, bringing Amy with him. "You two get ready and I'll be in to say good-night."

"Tess, too?" Amy asked.

"I wouldn't miss it for the world."

With slumped shoulders and bent heads, the two children left the room. Tess sat on the floor near Mac with her legs tucked against her chest and her arms wrapped around them.

"They're quite good at trying to make me feel bad that they have to go to bed," Mac said with a chuckle.

"Apparently Johnny didn't have a bedtime before coming here. You should have heard him the first night I told him it was time to go to sleep. Amy has since learned to do the same thing. The other day she told me she would be four soon and perfectly capable of staying up all night. That was said with her arms folded and her chin tilted as though daring me to deny the fact."

"Has she picked up any other habits from Johnny that you've had to contend with?"

"A few, but Johnny has been so good for Amy. She's quick to share her things with him. She doesn't even mind when I pay Johnny some extra attention. That worried me at first. She's thrilled to have him here."

"Have you heard from Mrs. Hocks about her search?"

The lines in his forehead deepened. He rose and began to pace as though nervous and not sure what to do with the extra energy. "Not in a few days. I have to confess I've started praying that she isn't successful. I don't want Johnny to leave here."

"Hopefully things will work out."

Mac stopped in the middle of the den and faced her, his arms straight at his sides. "What if they don't and Johnny has to leave?"

"Then you will deal with it. You're one of the strongest men I know. Your faith will sustain you."

Mac knelt in front of Tess and took her hands. "But when I think about the possibility—"

Tess pressed her fingers over his mouth to stop his flow of words. "Shh. Don't borrow trouble."

Mac's gaze snared hers and held it for a long moment. He started to lean forward when Amy called that she was ready for bed. "I guess that's our cue." Rising, he towered over Tess and offered his hand to help her to her feet.

"And I need to get home after I say good-night to Amy and Johnny." Tess tamped her disappointment. She'd wanted Mac to kiss her.

"That long day tomorrow?" Mac asked while they walked down the hallway.

Tess nodded and entered Amy's room. She sat in her white canopy bed with scores of books scattered over her pink bedspread.

"Daddy, I want you to read this one and this one and—"

"One, Amy, at bedtime. You know the rule."

She screwed her features into a thoughtful look and flipped through the books until she found the one she wanted. "Can Tess read it to me tonight?"

"Sure." Mac slid a glance toward Tess. "If she wants to."

"Are you kidding? I would be honored to read you a story."

Amy scooted over and made room for Tess. "Great."

"What about your prayers?"

Amy folded her hands and bowed her head. "Our Father, please watched over Daddy, Johnny, Grandma, Tess, Nina and all my uncles, aunts and cousins. Thank you for a great time at the circus. Amen."

When Tess heard her name included in the list of

people Amy wanted God to protect, her throat closed. It took a moment after the child finished her prayer to feel her voice was strong enough to read to Amy. Finally Tess began the story about a princess who was lost and trying to find her way home. By the time she came to the end and looked at Amy, the little girl was asleep, her head resting against Tess's arm. She closed the book and carefully slid off the bed while Mac shifted Amy to a more comfortable position then covered her with a blanket.

At the door Tess glanced at the child, the soft glow of the night-light illuminating her angelic face. She wanted children. Seeing Amy sleeping so peacefully underscored her desire for a family. For the first time in a long while she began to wonder if it might be possible for her dream to come true. Walking with Mac toward Johnny's room heightened the possibility in her mind. Mac is a wonderful father, she thought. She knew he had expressed reservations about having any more children, but surely if the right woman came along he would change his mind. Just because his wife had died giving birth didn't mean it would happen again. She hoped she could get him to see that.

When Tess entered Johnny's bedroom, she saw he was already asleep. Disappointment washed over her.

Mac switched off the lamp beside the boy's bed. "He still hasn't been able to manage staying up much later than Amy."

"It'll take a while for his strength to return completely. I'm pleased to see him doing so much," Tess whispered, making her way to the bedroom door.

"He's been pretty good about not overextending himself. I haven't had to say much at all to him about slowing down."

"He has a lot to offer."

"I'm hoping he's beginning to realize that."

"How could he not with you as the teacher, Mac? He's lucky you came into his life."

"I was thinking the same thing about myself. I needed Johnny. It was my lucky day when I discovered you crying in the waiting room."

The sincerity in his voice nearly undid her composure. "I think it's worked out for everyone." She started for the den, tired from the long day at work and content from the evening spent with Mac and the children.

He took her hand, and Tess found herself leaning into his strength, desperately trying not to yawn. His arm came up to cradle her close to him as she continued making her way toward the den.

"I'll drive you home before you fall asleep on me."

She did yawn then. "It isn't your company, I assure you." She laid her head on his shoulder.

"I know, Tess Morgan. I've seen you working. If I ever got sick, I'd like you to be my nurse."

"When was the last time you were sick?" She bent and snatched her purse from the floor by the couch.

"Not counting my broken leg—" he scratched his head "—you know, I can't remember. I've never had to stay in the hospital except that time I had my appendix out, and besides a few football injuries, I haven't been sick."

"Then it looks like my services won't be needed," she said with a laugh. "Thankfully, since men are lousy patients."

"Oh, I'm wounded." Mac clasped a hand over his heart. "Is that the female or the nurse in you saying that?"

She winked at him as she walked from the room. "I'm not telling."

"Colt, what brings you to the hospital?" Tess asked as she saw the big man approach the nurses' station.

"Me." Casey came up behind Tess and put a folder on the counter. "I found a collie mix the other day. I thought Colt's farm would be the perfect place for him to stay while I find him a home. Mom told me only one pet allowed at our place."

"I was coming to town so I offered to pick the dog up," Colt added quickly.

Tess looked from Casey to Colt and noticed a flush in her cheeks. Colt was shifting from one foot to the other. Tess realized Casey had taken the children to the farm a few weekends before. She had said because Johnny and Amy had begged her. Now Tess wondered if the kids had begged very much.

"I see," Tess said, taking the folder from the counter and preparing to leave them alone.

"We thought we would stop by Mac's and say hi, maybe go out for some pizza, all of us. Want to come along?" Casey asked, keeping her gaze averted from Colt's.

"I wouldn't want to intrude on—"

Colt dismissed her concerns with a wave of his hand. "You wouldn't be. Johnny and Amy love pizza, and I thought it would be fun for all of us to go to dinner, including you. Besides, what would Mac do if you didn't come along?"

It was Tess's turn to blush. She started to say something and realized she had no reply. The implication of what Colt had said thrilled her and scared her. Did the world think of them as a couple? Did Mac think of them as a couple? She and Mac had spent a lot of time together in the past few months. She had always told herself that they spent time together because of the children. She'd been lying to herself. She wanted them to be a couple.

"I guess I could. I need to go by my apartment first and change. After being in these all day, I'm ready to change." She gestured to her pastel green pants and shirt with small rainbows splashed all over them.

"Then we'll meet you over at his house." Casey retrieved her sweater from the back of her chair.

"Does Mac know you're coming?"

"No, but then that's part of the fun, surprising him. He expects it from me. Don't worry. By the time you get there, he'll know about the plans we have for him." Casey sauntered toward the elevator with Colt next to her.

Tess pulled up behind the row of cars in Mac's circular driveway, the sun heading down toward the mountains. Casey opened the front door.

"Sorry, it took me longer than I expected. Rush hour traffic is a bear today."

"Yeah, I know. We only arrived a few minutes ago ourselves."

"Where are the children?" Tess stepped into the large foyer.

"In the backyard showing off their puppies to Colt. Mac's out there, too." Casey added the last sentence with a gleam sparkling in her eyes as though to say she knew that Tess really wanted to know where Mac was. "And he's thrilled about this impromptu dinner, especially when he heard you were coming along."

"You know I noticed how close you were to Colt when you left work," Tess said as she walked next to Casey toward the back of the house.

"Just friends."

Tess glanced at Casey, realizing that was exactly what she had been telling everyone about her and Mac. "Sure. Keep telling yourself that. There are plenty of good shelters for animals in a city this size, I'm sure. Why did you call Colt about the dog?"

"A collie needs lots of room to run around." Casey fired the words back.

"And Colt dropped everything to come into Denver, an hour's drive, to pick up the dog from you." Tess reached for the handle of the back door.

"Okay. I won't say another word about you and Mac. But Tess, before I clam up, I just have to say I haven't seen my big brother this happy in a long time. You make him laugh."

"Must be the clown in me."

Casey stopped her from going out. "Does he make you laugh?"

Tess grew serious. "Yes."

Nodding in satisfaction, Casey smiled. "Good. Then I leave the rest in the Lord's hands."

In the backyard Johnny threw a ball to Frisky. The puppy chased it, stumbling over her own big feet. Buttons pounced on the ball, which set the two puppies fighting over it.

Amy put her hand on her waist. "I've been trying to teach them to share."

Mac laughed. "Honey, that'll take time. They are only a few months old."

The puppies tumbled until Frisky managed to take the ball and dart off with it. Buttons bounded to her feet and went after her sister.

Amy huffed, starting for the two puppies who were again vying for the ball. "They're family. They shouldn't fight so much. Johnny and me don't."

Mac saw Tess and strolled over to her with a smile in his eyes. "I'm glad you could come. The children are so excited about going out for pizza. You would think I don't feed them."

Tess leaned close to Mac to whisper, "Don't tell them, but so am I. I know pizza is mega calories a slice but I love it, too."

"Your secret is safe with me—for a price."

Tess arched a brow. "What?"

"That you come back with us and help me get the kids to bed. They don't put up a big argument when you're here. The other night was a breeze compared to most."

The idea of helping him put the children to bed pleased her. She felt a fluttering in her stomach, as though butterflies were beating their wings against her. "Sure. I can't pass up a chance to read another story to Amy."

"I doubt it'll be another story. She's been stuck on that one for the past two weeks. She could probably recite it to you."

Nina opened the back door and called to Mac. He jogged over to her and listened, his face tensing into a frown, the taut set of his shoulders indicating displeasure.

When he came back he said, "Mrs. Hocks is here to see me about Johnny. Will you come with me?"

"Have you said anything to her about wanting to adopt Johnny?"

"I called her this morning, but she was out of the office. Maybe this is her way of returning my call." He kneaded the back of his neck, his forehead creased in a frown. "Still, I've got this feeling—" He let the rest of his sentence fade into silence.

"Do you think something is wrong?" Tension vibrated from him, making Tess tighten her muscles until they ached.

"She's dropped by before unexpectedly, but— Oh, it's nothing. I'll feel better when I can get the proceedings started on the adoption." Mac called over his shoulder to the group in the yard, "Be back in a minute."

Casey and Colt were deep in conversation and barely acknowledged their departure. Johnny and Amy were busy chasing after their puppies and rolling around in the grass with them. Tess glimpsed the beautiful family scene and shuddered, Mac's worries becoming her worries.

Mrs. Hocks stood in the middle of the living room, staring out the picture window. She clasped her purse in one hand and a notebook in the other. When she heard them enter, she pivoted toward them with a smile on her face.

"I've got good news."

Tess felt Mac relax next to her, his features easing into his own smile of greeting.

"And I have good news, too," he said, beckoning for Mrs. Hocks to have a seat on the couch while he and Tess sat across from her on the other one. "What's yours?"

"I found a relative of Johnny's this afternoon who lives in California."

Without taking his gaze from the child welfare worker, Mac fumbled for Tess's hand and grasped it.

"Dottie Brown is his father's sister. She's coming to pick Johnny up. She didn't know about Johnny's mother's death. She lost touch with them a few years back. So isn't it great that Johnny will finally be with his family?" Mrs. Hocks beamed, delighted with her accomplishment.

The silence following her announcement pulsated with tension. Mac's grip tightened on Tess's fingers. The sides of the lady's mouth fell as she looked from Mac to Tess then back to Mac.

"I thought you would be happy."

Mac swallowed hard, a muscle in his jaw twitching. "And she wants to adopt him?"

"She's coming to Denver. She hasn't said yes yet, but I think she will. She hasn't seen Johnny in six years." Mrs. Hocks peered toward the entrance. "I wanted to tell Johnny about his aunt. Where is he?"

"He's out back playing with his puppy."

Mrs. Hocks started to stand.

"Wait," Mac said, halting the woman, who immediately eased down on the couch. "I'd prefer telling him, if that's all right with you."

"Well, I guess so."

Mac rose. "When should he be ready to meet his aunt?"

"Day after tomorrow. I'll bring her to the house in the afternoon. Have Johnny's things packed." Mrs. Hocks came to her feet, her brow wrinkled. "What good news did you have?"

Mac shrugged. "Nothing really. The doctor said he's still in remission and everything looks good."

"Great! That will certainly ease his aunt's mind."

Mac escorted Mrs. Hocks to the front door, then returned to the living room where Tess remained, stunned by the news. The anguish on his face when he entered said it all. She could feel his devastation even before he drew her to him and held her tight. It mirrored what she was experiencing.

"I know I shouldn't have, but I was beginning to think of Johnny as my son. What am I going to do?" He trembled with the force of his pain.

Mac's question tore her heart into pieces. There were no words to comfort him, to take his anguish away. Then she remembered the words of the twenty-third Psalm and began reciting them. She emphasized the words, "Yea, though I walk through the valley of the shadow of death, I will fear no evil: for Thou art with me; Thy rod and Thy staff they comfort me."

Listening to her softly spoken words, Mac drew in a deep, calming breath, then another. He pulled back and stared at her, his hands framing her face. "You're right. The Lord will guide me."

"Tell Mrs. Hocks your desire to adopt Johnny. Maybe it will make a difference. Maybe his aunt doesn't want to adopt him."

Resting his forehead against hers, Mac tunneled his fingers through her hair. "I love Johnny, but I can't deny him his true family for my selfish needs."

Tess gripped his forearms. "Don't say that. You're not selfish. You took him into your home and gave him a family when he needed it the most, when no one else wanted him. There was nothing selfish about that."

He gathered her again to him, so close she could feel his heart pounding. Its slow, tormented beat passed into her body, matching the rhythm of hers.

"Johnny may not want to go with his aunt. Have you thought about that?"

"Yes, but I can't influence him unduly. I have to give it a chance to work for Johnny. Family is important."

"Family is more than a mere blood relationship."

Mac sighed. "It would have been so much easier if Mrs. Hocks hadn't found any relatives."

"Life doesn't always follow the easy path."

"I know, but that doesn't stop me from wishing it would." He straightened away from Tess, shadows in his eyes. "God only puts what we can handle before us. We'd better return to our guests before they begin to wonder."

"Are you kidding! Johnny and Amy are too busy playing with their puppies, and in case you haven't noticed, Colt and Casey are too busy having eyes only for each other."

Tess walked beside Mac, his hand in hers. His earlier words about God only giving them what they could deal with made her take another look at what had happened to her in South America. She was a stronger person because of the tragedy, and with her recent return to the Lord, each day her faith grew. She realized that He had spared her because He had plans for her.

"Tess, don't say anything. I want to tell Johnny about his aunt after dinner. I don't want to spoil this evening."

"I'm not very good at acting."

"Neither am I, but we have to. It's important."

She squeezed his hand. "I know."

The minute Mac stepped outside, Amy ran up to him. "Daddy, I'm hungry. Can we go eat now?"

He scooped her into his arms and hugged her tightly

to him. "Of course, pumpkin. Where do you want to go for pizza?"

"Bear Country."

"I don't know why I bother asking." Shaking his head, he rolled his eyes. "That's the only place she wants to go out to eat. She loves the dancing bears, but her favorite part of the show is the singing chipmunk that pops up from the log. She laughs every time he performs."

"'Cause he's funny, Daddy."

"We can all pile into my car if you all don't mind close quarters," Mac said to the group.

Tess noticed his big grin, but she hoped she was the only one who saw the dull flatness to his eyes. This would be a difficult evening, but she was determined to stay as long as he needed her.

After the children put their puppies in the utility room, everyone crammed into Mac's vehicle. Colt and Casey didn't seem to mind being crunched together in the back with Amy in her car seat. The close quarters in front allowed Tess to place her arm around Johnny.

Fifteen minutes later they arrived at Bear Country Pizza House where loud noises during the shows made it almost impossible for any conversation to take place. Thankfully the next show wasn't starting for another twenty minutes.

After everyone gave their order to the waitress, Amy hopped down from her booster chair. "I want to ride the helicopter. Can Johnny take me?"

"Sure, if he doesn't mind." While Johnny stood, Mac

dug into his pocket for some quarters and came up with a fist full. "You two split this. The pizzas should be here in fifteen minutes."

Johnny took the money, then Amy's hand and they headed for the arcade area of the restaurant. Mac kept an eye on the pair as they went from ride to ride, his smile no longer on his face, the feelings he was holding at bay clearly visible in his eyes.

"Okay, I can tell something's wrong, big brother. 'Fess up."

"Mrs. Hocks found Johnny's aunt."

"That's gre—" Casey narrowed her gaze on Mac. "That isn't great. I thought that was what everyone was waiting for."

Mac peered at his sister for a few seconds before swinging his attention to the children. "I've come to think of Johnny as part of our family."

"Oh, Mac." Casey reached out and patted her brother's hand. "I'm sorry."

"Here they come. Not a word. Johnny doesn't know, and I don't want anything to ruin this dinner."

While the children settled into their seats, the waitress brought their pizzas. Mac said a quick blessing just as the show started. Loud music sounded from the speakers not too far from their table, drowning out all conversation.

Taking a slice with Canadian bacon and extra cheese, Tess watched the show while forcing herself to eat at least some pizza. But her food settled in her stomach like a rock and her heart wasn't in the fun songs and silly jokes. She tried to laugh at all the appropriate places, but she was sure anyone paying close attention could see the strain about her mouth and hear the brittleness in her laugh.

By the time they left the pizza parlor, Tess felt her nerves stretched to their limit and her stomach muscles constricted into a tight ball. A glance at Mac confirmed he was experiencing the same thing. Even Casey didn't chatter on the ride to Mac's house.

Tess knew Johnny suspected something when Mac said goodbye to his sister and friend, then asked Johnny and Amy to come into the den. The boy dragged his feet down the hall, and worry nibbled at his expression as he plopped down on the couch across from Mac.

"Did the doctor call or something? I feel fine. Honest." Johnny folded his arms across his stomach and got that defiant look on his face that had all but disappeared in the past weeks at Mac's.

"No, Johnny. You're still in remission. You're doing everything you're supposed to."

"Then what's wrong?"

"Mrs. Hocks came this afternoon to see me about you." Mac paused, cleared his throat, then continued, "She found your aunt, Dottie Brown."

"I don't remember her."

"She remembers you and is coming to see you the day after tomorrow."

Mac forced a light tone, but Tess could see the anguish each word caused. A nerve in his jaw jerked, and his hands were clasped together so tightly Tess could see his white knuckles.

"Why?" Johnny's defiant look wavered.

"She wants you to come live with her."

Johnny shot off the couch, his hands clenched at his sides. "I don't want to live with no stranger. I don't remember her."

"Perhaps when you see her—"

"No!" Johnny shouted and raced from the room.

"Daddy? Daddy, don't send Johnny away." Tears rolled down Amy's cheeks. "I don't want him to go. Please."

Mac held his arms out for Amy. "Honey, Dottie Brown is Johnny's family."

Amy ignored her father's outstretched arms. "No, we are." She ran from the room, her sobs echoing in the silence.

Mac dropped his arms to his lap. "I don't want him to go, either," he whispered, all the pain he felt lacing each word.

## *Chapter Twelve*

The doorbell sounded in the stillness like a death toll. Mac stiffened. On the couch, Amy grabbed Johnny's hand and held tight. Tess felt the beat of her heart pick up and thunder in her ears.

Mac signaled Nina to remain seated, then surged to his feet on the second chime, his features set in a neutral expression that Tess knew cost him dearly to maintain. The rigid set to his stance attested to the real emotions underlying his facade.

"She's here," Amy whispered so loudly she might as well have shouted the news.

Tess wanted to go to Johnny and scoop him into her arms. She wanted to declare to Mrs. Hocks and Dottie Brown that Johnny was perfectly happy where he was. Instead, Tess remained seated in the wing chair across from the boy, there for support for Johnny, Mac and Amy. This whole day, members of Mac's family had stopped by to see Johnny and say their goodbyes. Several times Tess had seen the boy nearly break down in tears, but somehow he pulled himself together with that stalwart expression that was on his face now as though nothing could touch him. Tess knew otherwise. She had been there herself and felt his pain as if it were her own.

Johnny watched as Mrs. Hocks and his aunt entered the den. Amy's gaze widened, and she leaned closer to him.

Tess forced a smile of greeting that quivered at the corners of her mouth and disappeared almost as quickly as it appeared. "Good day, Mrs. Hocks."

"Tess, it's good to see you," the older woman said.

Mac came in behind the two ladies, his eyes dark gray. "Johnny, do you have everything?"

The boy nodded but didn't move.

"Johnny, this is your aunt Dottie." Mrs. Hocks gestured to the woman next to her.

Dottie moved to the end of the couch, her expression restrained as she took in her nephew. "It's been a while since we last saw each other. Are you ready to go?"

Johnny looked toward Mac, and for a fleeting moment desperation edged its way into the boy's eyes before he masked his feelings behind his world-weary expression.

"Where's your suitcase?" his aunt asked.

Johnny pointed to several black pieces sitting near the doorway.

"Then we'd better get going. I'm sure these good people have things they need to do."

"Oh, no. We don't want Johnny to leave," Amy exclaimed, her body pressed against his side, her hand on his arm as though that would keep him there.

"Amy, we've talked about this."

"But, Daddy, we don't."

Mac positioned himself behind the couch and clamped his hands on Amy's shoulders while she released her grip on the boy. "Johnny, do you want me to help you with your stuff?"

"Yes, please." The boy jumped to his feet and raced from the room.

"Where's he going?" Dottie asked, alarmed at her nephew's sudden move.

"He probably forgot something," Mac said, taking Amy's hand and walking to the luggage.

Johnny reappeared a minute later with Frisky in his arms. "I'm ready to leave."

"A puppy?" Alarmed, Dottie looked at Mrs. Hocks. "You didn't say anything about a puppy. I—"

"I'll take real good care of Frisky." Johnny held the animal cradled against his chest, his face buried in her fur. "Won't I, Nina? She never has to clean up after Frisky."

Nina cleared her throat, started to say something, then instead, nodded, a sheen to her eyes. She spun away, pretending an interest in something on the coffee table.

Doubt clouded his aunt's expression. "We'll try her tonight and see."

Relieved, Johnny kissed his puppy's head, fighting the tears threatening him. For a long moment everyone just stared at the boy, the silence in the room deafening.

"Let's go," Mrs. Hocks said, the sound unusually loud.

Johnny took a step back and came up against Mac.

He laid a reassuring hand on the boy's shoulder, leaned down and said, "Don't forget to write. When you get settled, we'll call you."

Johnny nodded, his lower lip trembling.

"May I have a word with you, Mr. MacPherson, in private?" Dottie asked.

"You all go ahead." Mac motioned toward the children, Nina and Mrs. Hocks. "Tess, stay please."

Both Amy and Johnny hesitated.

"I'll just be a minute."

The children followed Mrs. Hocks and Nina from the room, leaving the three adults to face each other. Tess felt the tension emanating from Mac in waves and wished she could take his pain away.

"I want to thank you for taking care of my nephew. I also want to ask you not to call him. Let him settle in and get used to me first. I'll call you when I think he's ready."

Anger flared in his eyes. Mac opened his mouth to say something, clamped it shut and nodded curtly instead.

"Good. I'm glad we understand each other. From what I remember he can be quite a handful. I'm sure it hasn't been easy for you these past few months."

"Actually Johnny has been great. We've enjoyed his company," Mac said, his voice strained as though it would crack any moment. He snatched up the two pieces of luggage while he gathered his composure.

In the foyer Johnny had his face pressed up against

Frisky's wiggling body. He didn't look at Mac or Tess when they came out of the den. He didn't look at anyone. Tess's heart broke, anguish compressing her chest.

*Dear Heavenly Father, please give us the strength to get through this. Be with Johnny in his new home and help him to adjust to his new situation. He cannot do this alone. He needs You.* Saying the silent prayer gave Tess comfort in the midst of the turmoil that swirled about her. She did draw strength from the words and the knowledge that God was with them, especially Johnny in his time of need.

"Well, we must be going," Mrs. Hocks announced, withdrawing her keys from her purse.

Tears crowded Johnny's eyes. When he blinked several times, one lone tear fell. He sniffed and turned away from the group, his shoulders hunched, his head bowed as he clutched his puppy.

The constriction in Tess's chest expanded. She sucked in a deep breath to ease the tightness. Making her way to the small boy huddled in front of the door, so lost and alone-looking, she took him and Frisky into her embrace and kissed his cheek. She half expected him to say yuck and pull away. He didn't. He drew closer to her as though her nearness could give him the strength he needed to walk out the door.

"Remember, the Lord is with you. You aren't alone," Tess whispered.

He nodded once and finally pulled back, still clasping Frisky as though the puppy were his lifeline.

Tess moved to the side and allowed Amy, Nina and Mac to say their goodbyes. Amy cried, throwing her arms around Johnny and refusing to let go. Mac gently pried her loose and gestured for Nina to hold her while Mac turned to Johnny.

"It has been such a pleasure to have you in my house." Mac glanced at Johnny's aunt and added, "You're always welcome here." He hugged the boy, then backed away, his eyes glistening with unshed tears.

Tess took Mac's hand while Mrs. Hocks opened the door and Johnny and his aunt left. The click of the lock sounded in the deadly quiet and seemed to echo through the spacious foyer, announcing Johnny's departure as final. Amy's sobs cut into the silence and propelled Mac into action. He took his daughter into his arms and held her tightly against him, her cheek pressed against his chest, his chin resting on top of her head.

"Baby, we will see Johnny again. I know that in here." Mac touched the place over his heart. "God didn't bring him into our lives only to take him away."

"I don't know about you, Amy, but I could use a large glass of milk and some of the chocolate chip cookies I baked this afternoon." Nina stroked the child's back.

Lifting her head, Amy sniffled. "Cookies? Chocolate chip?"

"Your favorite. Ready to help me devour a whole plate of them?"

"I won't ruin my dinner?"

"Since when has that concerned you, young lady? Come on."

When Mac set Amy on the floor, she took Nina's hand and headed with the housekeeper toward the kitchen. Mac stared at the departing pair, his gaze clouded, a frown on his face.

"I'm calling Johnny. I don't care what his aunt said. I can't let that child think I've abandoned him. He's had enough of that in his short life." Mac flexed his hands, then curled them slowly.

Tess wrapped her fingers around one fist and brought it up between them. "Let Mrs. Hocks know you would like to adopt Johnny."

"Oh, I intend to first thing tomorrow morning. Dottie Brown may be Johnny's aunt, but we are more his family than she." He relaxed his grip, brushing one finger across her cheek. "Pray with me, Tess. I need all the help I can get."

"Of course."

Mac bowed his head. "Heavenly Father, I need Your guidance and help. I want Johnny to be a part of my family. Show me the way. In Christ's name, amen."

The simple prayer washed over Tess, renewing her faith in the Lord and easing any tension she felt with Johnny's departure. The Lord had brought Johnny and Mac together. Everything would work out for the best.

The insistent ringing pulled Tess toward wakefulness. She fumbled for the phone and brought the receiver to her ear. "Hello." She squinted at the digital clock and saw it was three o'clock in the morning. News in the middle of the night was never good.

"Tess, Mac here."

The haze clouding her mind evaporated, and she struggled to a sitting position. "What's wrong?" Her heart began to thump against her rib cage.

"Dottie Brown called and told me that Johnny is gone from the hotel room. She got up in the middle of the night and noticed his bed was empty. No one in the hotel saw him leave."

"Has she called the police?"

"Yes. She wanted to know if Johnny was at my house."

Tess heard the anger in Mac's voice and could imagine the grip he had on the phone. It would match hers. "What are you not telling me?"

"She all but accused me of kidnapping the boy. Nina and I looked, and he isn't here. Will you help me search for him?"

"I would have been upset if you hadn't asked me."

"I'll pick you up in twenty minutes. We'll check his usual haunts first. I have to do something. I can't sit and wait for the police to call."

"I understand. I seem to remember you keeping me company one night while I searched."

"I thought we'd gotten beyond this."

"A lot has happened to Johnny in the past few days. Running away is his usual way of coping. I should have figured something like this would happen."

"Be there in a while. Thanks."

Tess hung up, Mac's desperation and appreciation still sounding in her mind. She quickly switched on the lamp by her bed and got dressed in a pair of old jeans and a sweatshirt. It would be a long night, and comfort would be important.

So as not to awaken Delise, Tess waited outside her apartment for Mac to pick her up in his car. The second he turned into the parking lot, she hurried toward him, not wanting to waste a minute of their search time.

Inside she buckled up, saying, "Let's start in the warehouse district."

Before he backed out of the parking space, he gripped her hand, his gaze on her. "I should have said something tonight when Dottie Brown came. Johnny's run away because he thinks no one really wants him. After meeting the woman, I knew her heart wasn't in this. She told me tonight she was only taking Johnny in because of her duty to her brother. Johnny's a smart kid. He would have picked up on those vibes."

"Well, when we find him you'll have a chance to make it up to him and tell him you want to adopt him."

"If we find him."

Her grasp tightened on his hand. "We will. God brought you two together because He wanted you to be a family. Believe that." She heard him release a rush of air. "Johnny's in good hands."

The tension in his body relaxed. "You're right. The

Lord is watching out for him. He'll be all right until we find him."

Tess eased back in the seat, calmness descending. Her faith would sustain her through the search and help her be there for Mac.

"I want to be here when Amy wakes up, then we'll go back out looking for Johnny," Mac said as he let himself into his house, the bright light of dawn slanting across the front lawn.

Tess followed him to the kitchen. "I know he's okay."

"How?" Mac asked wearily, tossing his keys onto the counter by the coffeemaker.

"I just do. I can't explain it."

"I'm so tired, I could drink a whole pot of coffee and still fall asleep." Mac measured out several scoops and dumped them into the top of the small appliance. "These past few nights I haven't slept very well."

"Why don't you go lay down for a while? I'll let you know when Amy gets up." Tess took over the job of making the coffee and waved him out of the kitchen.

A yelp from the utility room caught Mac's attention. "I'll let Buttons out. She's getting pretty good about going to the bathroom in the back yard. She and Frisky were quite a pair." Mac's voice tightened around the last few words.

"Don't worry about her. I'll let her in when she wants in."

Mac picked up Buttons and strolled to the door. He

placed the puppy on the deck, then watched as she bounded across the wooden planks, coming to a screeching halt at the chaise lounge. Mac started to close the door, then took a good look at the chair. Buttons's barking filled the air.

"Tess!" Mac called as he raced for the bundle curled in a ball on the chaise lounge. Frisky poked her head up through the middle of the pile and answered Buttons's greeting.

Tess rushed out the back door just as Johnny stretched and sat up, rubbing the sleep from his eyes. Frisky leaped down and began to play tag with Buttons.

Mac drew the boy into his arms. "How long have you been here?"

Johnny looked around him and smiled at Tess. "A while. I didn't want to wake you guys up."

"I've been up most of the night searching for you."

The gruff sound to Mac's voice made Johnny frown and pull back. "I didn't mean to cause no trouble." His lower lip quivered, and he bit it.

"Trouble? Your aunt thinks I kidnapped you."

"I can leave." With his eyes unusually bright, Johnny chewed on his lower lip, not making a move to leave.

"No way." Mac hugged the child to him. "You're part of my family, and I'm gonna fight to keep you this time."

"You mean that?" Johnny said through the tears streaming down his face.

The thickness in Tess's throat grew. Her tears fell.

She pressed her hand on Johnny's back and said, "He means it. I can't begin to tell you how frantic Mac and I were last night looking for you."

Leaning back, Johnny stared at Mac. "Then why did you let me go yesterday with that lady?"

"She's your aunt. I thought you would want to be with your own family."

"I don't know her. She didn't want to keep Frisky. She kept sneezing and looking strangely at Frisky. She had the hotel put her in a dog kennel out back. Frisky didn't like it. I had to rescue her."

"Then you wouldn't mind me adopting you?"

"Really? You want me?"

"Yes, very much." Mac grinned. "I'll even take Frisky."

Johnny threw his arms around Mac. "You won't be able to give me back?"

"No, this will be for keeps."

Tess's smile matched Mac's and Johnny's. Her heart swelled with emotions she had cautiously allowed back into her life. Family, children were so important. She wanted it all, a loving husband, a house full of children.

"I'll be the best son you ever had."

Mac grew serious. "I want you to come to me if you're upset. Running away won't solve your problems. I will love you no matter what, and we can work through anything. Just don't run away again."

Johnny's expression equaled Mac's in gravity. "I promise I won't."

"Thanks. I think I lost five years tonight searching for you. I'm not as young as I used to be." Mac tousled Johnny's hair.

The back door banged open, and Amy raced outside, launching herself at Johnny. Mac caught her before she managed to topple Johnny onto the decking.

"You're back. I just knew you would be. I prayed real hard last night, and God heard me."

Mac cradled both children. "How would you feel if Johnny was a member of our family? Would you like a big brother?"

Amy's eyes grew round. "You mean it, Daddy?"

"Yep."

Amy jumped up and down, clapping her hands. "We're gonna be a family. We're gonna be a family."

Sadness intertwined with Tess's happiness as she watched the three of them bond. She took a step away from them, feeling as though she was intruding on them.

Mac glanced up and caught her backing away. "Where do you think you're going?"

She shrugged, not wanting to explain the feelings bombarding her. "I was gonna check on the coffee. Didn't you say you wanted a whole pot of it?"

"I'm wide awake now. I couldn't sleep if I wanted to. Let's get Nina and all of us go out for a big breakfast."

"Yes," the two children yelled and raced for the door.

Mac hung back, grabbing Tess before she followed the children into the house. "After I give Mrs. Hocks and Dottie Brown a call to tell them about Johnny, we're all going to breakfast, including you, then you and I are gonna talk. It's long overdue."

Johnny and Amy hit the house and sprinted for the utility room to get their puppies and go out back to play. Nina shook her head and trailed the children into the kitchen.

"I'm exhausted just looking at those two," Mac said, starting to toss his keys on the table in the foyer.

Tess stifled a yawn, feeling the exhaustion of a long night searching for Johnny and a morning spent celebrating his safe return to the MacPhersons.

Mac peered at her and closed his hand around his keys. "Come on. I'll take you home."

"What about our talk?" Tess wasn't sure she would be able to put two coherent sentences together.

"We'll talk on the way."

On the ride to her apartment Tess rested her head on the seat and listened to the classical music Mac popped into his CD player. Her eyelids began to droop as the sounds of Bach filled the car with soothing tones. The next thing she realized Mac was gently shaking her awake. Her eyes opened and her gaze connected with his. The tenderness in his expression quickened her heartbeat.

She sat up, smoothing her hair. "I'm sorry. I know you wanted to talk, but I couldn't keep my eyes open."

"I hated to wake you up. You looked so serene. Like an angel."

The huskiness in his voice prodded her heart to beat

even faster. "That's exactly what I thought Amy looked like the other night when I put her to bed."

"Yeah, she has her moments."

"She's wonderful. You're lucky."

"Yes, I am. It's been a while since I've thought that. You've made me realize that."

"How?" The question came out in a breathless rush.

"After Sheila died, I thought that part of my life was over. With you, Tess, I see it doesn't have to be." He raked his fingers through his hair and massaged the back of his neck. "I'm not doing a very good job of saying what I mean. I hadn't meant to say anything, since you were so tired. I was gonna wait till later." He clasped her hands, bringing her around to face him. "But here goes. Tess Morgan, I love you and want to marry you."

Her world exploded into bright lights and beautiful music. She felt like dancing and singing, all weariness slipping away. "Marry you?"

"Yes. Will you?"

Emotions she'd thought denied to her since Kevin's death tugged at her heart. She had to swallow several times before she could answer, "Yes. Yes, I would love to marry you."

Mac dragged her to him and settled his mouth over hers. Her heart soared, her pulse racing with elation. When he leaned back, the smile that graced his lips sent a warm tingling to the tips of her toes.

"This isn't how I had planned to propose to you,

Tess. You deserve flowers, a candlelight dinner and soft music. After all that's happened I couldn't wait for the perfect moment."

She framed his face with her hands. "This was perfect. You've made me the happiest woman alive. For years I've dreamed of marrying the man I love and having a family, the bigger the better."

His jaw tensed beneath her fingertips. A rush of air was expelled from his lips. "Amy and Johnny need a mother."

"Not just Amy and Johnny." Tess saw a frown carve deep lines into his face. "I know you have reservations about having more children, but—"

He jerked away, his body flattened against the driver's door. "I don't want any more children. I told you about my wife when we went camping in the mountains. Amy and Johnny are enough for me. My family is complete."

The steel thread in his voice underscored his words with a clarity that alarmed Tess. Because he was such a good father, she had never believed he wouldn't want to be a father again and again. The dream that had materialized in her mind vanished like a mirage in a desert. "Yes, you told me about Sheila dying during childbirth, but—"

"I will never be responsible for another death. I couldn't take that. It nearly killed me when Sheila died. I won't risk that kind of loss again."

"But you weren't responsible." She frowned, her exhaustion returning tenfold.

"She wouldn't have been pregnant if I hadn't talked her into it. She wouldn't have died giving birth if I hadn't persuaded her that we were ready for a family. You see, I wanted a large one. She wasn't sure she wanted any children. It was probably the one bone of contention in our marriage."

Dread wove its way through her body, making her limbs leaden. "But I want children. We agree on that."

"No, we don't. I've changed my mind."

The air in the car was stifling as though the last breath was being squeezed from it. Tess yanked on the handle and pushed the door open. She quickly stood and wished she hadn't. The world tilted and spun with her sudden movement. She gripped the car and closed her eyes, willing the spinning to stop.

She heard Mac slam his door. When she opened her eyes, he blocked her path, anguish in his features.

"I don't think I can do it, Tess."

"It isn't common for a woman to die in childbirth. I'm willing to take the risk."

"I'm not."

"Weren't you the one who once told me that life is a risk?"

"I've changed my mind where you're concerned."

Again that steel thread ran through his voice, and Tess was reminded of an immovable force. "I don't know what to say. I need to think."

"Do that. I want us to agree if we do get married. I won't go into a marriage again without that settled up front."

This should be the happiest day of her life, but instead she felt deflated, unsure what to do. She loved

Mac. But she wanted children badly. Yes, Amy and Johnny would be a part of her family if she married Mac, but she wanted to experience having children, holding and nursing a baby. She was afraid she would always feel incomplete if she gave in on this.

"But you need to think, too, Mac. Life *is* a risk, and you changing your mind won't alter that fact. Some things are important enough that you should take a risk. This is one of them."

"What if I don't feel that way?"

"Then we have a lot of thinking and talking to do before anything can be decided." She stepped around him, needing to escape to do that thinking. When she was with Mac, she wanted to give in to him, and yet she was afraid that would be the worst mistake of her life. One day she would resent giving up her dream of having children. "I'd better go inside. It's been a long night, and I'm very tired."

As she passed him, he grabbed her arm and held her still. He leaned into her, his face buried in her hair. He kissed the top of her head, then lifted her chin to caress her lips with his.

"I can't change how I feel, Tess."

"Yes, you can."

"But so can you."

"I see we're at opposite ends on this issue. Good day, Mac. I'll talk to you tomorrow."

"Promise?" He released her, a troubled look in his eyes.

"Of course. I agree we have to talk this out before we

decide on getting married. I'm working tomorrow, but we can see each other in the evening."

The long walk to her apartment felt as though it took an eternity. She sensed Mac watching her until she disappeared inside and collapsed against the door. Sliding to the floor, she curled her legs up and rested her forehead on her knees. She should be dancing and singing. Instead, she wanted to crawl into bed and bury herself under tons of blankets.

*Please, God, help me decide what is best for me, for Mac. I can't do this without You.*

# Chapter Thirteen

Exhaustion clung to Tess like cobwebs to a deserted house. She stared at the computer monitor at the nurses' station, the words about a new admission blurring. She rubbed her hands down her face to clear her thoughts. All night she'd tossed and turned, trying to come to a decision concerning Mac. Still the answer evaded her. Could she make a commitment to Mac knowing she would give up a lifelong dream?

"Tess, there's a call for you," the unit secretary said.

Tess glanced up from the computer, her brow furrowed.

"Line two."

Tess picked up the phone. "Tess Morgan."

"This is Joan in emergency. I think you should get down here. Peter MacPherson was just brought in. He's been in some kind of accident or something. I don't know the details."

For a few seconds Tess's mind went blank. Her

nerveless fingers dropped the receiver, and the sound of it hitting the counter resonated through the nurses' station, jerking her out of her trance.

She quickly snatched up the phone and said, "Is he—"

"He's lost a lot of blood. I don't know much beyond that."

"I'll be there."

Tess placed the phone in its cradle and leaped to her feet. She frantically scanned the area for the head nurse. When she saw Kathleen, she hurried to her and explained about the emergency, a sense of urgency taking hold.

She hadn't been able to say goodbye to Kevin. What if Mac— *Oh, Lord, please watch over Mac. Please don't take him from me.*

Two minutes later she was on the elevator, counting the floors as it descended. Her heartbeat picked up speed as she came nearer. By the time the doors swished open and she rushed out, maneuvering her way among people waiting to get on, her pulse hammered against her temples as though a kettledrum was inside her head.

Joan was waiting for her and pointed to Room Three. Tess shoved through the door and came to a halt just inside. Mac lay on a gurney with two nurses and a doctor hovering over him. Never before had the sight of blood made her light-headed. But seeing Mac helpless with his eyes closed and his face pale while the emergency room team worked on him caused her head to spin. Smells she should be used to assailed her, prompting her stomach to roil. She gripped the edge of the counter to keep from collapsing while trying not to hyperventilate.

"Tess, what are you doing here?" the doctor asked.

"He's a friend. What happened?"

"A gunshot wound to the left shoulder."

"Gunshot?" She didn't understand how something like this could happen to her Mac. He hated guns. He didn't have any in his house.

The doctor returned his attention to his patient. "You don't look too good. Why don't you sit in the waiting area? As soon as I have some information, I'll let you know. You might want to contact his family."

Part of her wanted to stay, try to help, but another part needed to leave the room before she fainted, something she had never done in her whole life. In the corridor she drew in deep breaths of the antiseptic-scented air. Normally the smell didn't bother her. Right now it made her stomach churn, and she fought the urge to throw up.

Visions of Kevin lying in his own blood, his life forces draining away while she held him cradled to her, hounded her all the way down the hall to the waiting area. People milled about, waiting on friends and loved ones. She joined them, crumpling into a chair where she could keep an eye on the door to Room Three.

She knew she needed to tell Mac's family, but she couldn't bring herself to get up and make that call. She didn't know what to say to them. She was afraid she would break down and cry, scaring them more than was necessary. As she twisted her hands together, she prayed as she had never prayed before.

*Dear Lord, please don't take Mac away. He's a good man with two children who depend on him. Please be with him and watch over him.* Two years before, she had whispered similar words concerning Kevin, and he had died. *Please, it can't happen a second time.*

Unable to sit still, Tess bolted to her feet, her breathing so rapid that the room tilted. She paused, willing herself to take calming breaths before she headed toward the nurses' station. She needed answers. She needed to do something before she went crazy, worrying and wondering if her past would repeat itself.

As Tess grabbed the phone to call Mac's mother, Justin arrived with Alice next to him. Justin headed for the nurse at the counter while Mac's mother strode to Tess. Alice gripped Tess's hands, her lips compressed in a worried expression.

"Are you all right, my dear?" Alice asked.

Her concern touched Tess. "Are you?"

"My son is in God's hands now."

Tess wished she had the self-assurance Alice did, but all she could think about was how Kevin had died and that history could repeat itself. "I was just about to call you. How did you find out so quickly?"

"Someone at the halfway house called me. Then I talked with a policeman. All I know about what happened is what he told me."

"Who did this to Mac?"

"Some man named Harry got upset and began waving a gun around. Mac tried to talk him into giving it to him."

All color drained from Tess's face. She thought of the scene a few weeks before at the halfway house when Harry had gotten upset. She could easily imagine what had happened an hour ago. The man was like a powder keg, only needing a spark to explode.

"Do Amy and Johnny know?" Tess asked, needing to focus on something other than her imagination.

"Not yet. I wanted to see Mac first. I only called Justin to bring me to the hospital. I was afraid to drive."

"I'd like to go with you when you tell the children."

"Sure." Alice sandwiched Tess's hand between hers. "He will be all right. I know it."

"Do you know he asked me to marry him yesterday?"

"That's great. I was praying he would."

"I haven't told him my answer yet." Tess cast a glance at the door down the hall, wondering what was going on in the room and yet not daring to find out. What if— She didn't want to think about what if. It only sent alarm streaking through her, making her realize how little control she had.

"I know it's a big step."

"Mac doesn't want any more children. I want children," Tess blurted, surprised she was telling Mac's mother the reason they weren't engaged.

Alice shook her head. "He still feels guilty about Sheila." She patted Tess's hand. "Give him time. He'll come around. He adores children and is a wonderful father. It would be a shame if he didn't have any more."

Tess didn't have a chance to reply to Alice. The doctor emerged from Room Three and headed toward them. His expression was neutral, giving nothing away.

"Tess." The doctor nodded toward her. "Is this the man's family?"

"Yes. This is Alice MacPherson, Mac's mother, and this is his brother Justin." Tess shifted to allow Justin to stand next to his mother.

"The bullet went through the upper left shoulder, nicking an artery but just missing the lung. He's weak, but barring any complications he should be fine. We gave him a transfusion and we want to watch him a few days. Rest and time should take care of him."

"When can we see him?"

"They're wheeling him up to surgery now to repair his artery. Once he's settled in his room you can see him." The doctor looked at Mac's mother. "I need some information, Mrs. MacPherson, and to go over a few things with you."

Tess sank back against the counter, feeling as if she had lost a pint of blood, not Mac. He should be okay, but what if an infection took hold and— Hadn't she promised herself not to think about what if? She had to have faith in the Lord to watch out and care for Mac.

Tess stood at the window, watching the sun disappear behind the mountains and the shadows of dusk descend.

Like the end of day and the start of night, she felt as though she'd come to a crossroads in her life. She leaned against the wall, her arms over her chest as though to protect her heart. Seeing Mac in a hospital bed churned up all the emotions she'd been desperate to suppress. Dread. Fear. Anger.

Yes, the doctor said he would be fine. But what if this happened again? Mac worked in a halfway house, counseling people who were often distraught, living on the edge. What was to stop some other person from getting upset and taking his frustration out on Mac? All the emotions she'd experienced when Kevin had died flooded her, crushing the breath from her. She sank onto the love seat and doubled over, hugging her arms tightly to her. She couldn't go through that a second time. She didn't have the emotional strength to fight those demons again.

The walls of the room seemed to press closer. She needed to get out before she suffocated from the stale, sterile-smelling air that so reminded her of how close Mac had come to dying. A few inches, and the bullet would have pierced his heart. She surged to her feet and headed for the door.

"Tess."

She froze. She heard Mac try to shift. The sound of his groan forced her to his side. "Don't try to move." She slipped into the chair by his bed, her hand on his arm to still him.

His eyelids fluttered. He licked his lips and swallowed several times. "I'm so thirsty."

Tess, glad to have some mundane task to do, quickly filled a plastic cup with water. Carefully she lifted his head and placed the plastic straw to his mouth, fighting the temptation to hug him to her, to check to make sure nothing else was wrong.

He took a few sips, then smiled, the gesture fading almost instantly. "Thanks. I'm lucky to have my very own private nurse."

The hoarseness in his voice magnified his situation in Tess's mind. Again the need to escape bombarded her. She fought the strong urge, knowing she couldn't leave.

"How do you feel?" she asked, putting the cup on the bedside table.

"Like a herd of wild elephants stomped all over me. Otherwise great."

She stiffened. "Don't!"

"Don't what?"

"Make light of what happened to you. You could have died. An inch or so to the right, and you wouldn't be here. You'd be in the morgue."

"But I'm not. I'm alive, Tess."

She clamped her mouth closed, refusing to say anything, afraid of what she would say if she allowed her emotions free reign.

Mac fumbled for her hand. "Tess?"

Tears stung her eyes. She blinked, and a few coursed down her cheeks. "What happened?"

"Harry didn't like how things were progressing at the halfway house. He wanted me to make some changes.

To be honest I don't think he intended to hurt me. I think things just got out of hand for him."

"Are you going back?"

Mac's forehead creased. "Yes, why wouldn't I?" He tried to shift again and winced.

"That's why. Look at what Harry did to you." She tried to keep the worry from her voice, but she knew Mac heard it.

"That was a freak accident."

"You breaking your leg was a freak accident. What Harry did wasn't." The force behind her words surprised her.

Mac sighed, his eyes drifting closed for a moment. "I'm gonna be fine, Tess."

This time, Tess thought, but kept her opinion to herself. "You need to rest."

"Will you stay until I fall asleep?"

He looked so vulnerable lying in a hospital bed with tubes attached to him. It took a great deal of effort to sit next to him and not fall apart at the sight of him. "I won't go anywhere."

His eyes slid closed. "Good. When I wake up, I want to talk about us getting married."

Tess watched his face relax in sleep. Pain contracted her chest as though she had been the one shot. Married. How could they? She wanted children. He didn't. He wanted to continue his work at the halfway house. She didn't want him to. She felt the gulf between them widen. One of the hardest things she would have to do was tell Mac she couldn't marry him. She knew her limits, and today she had hit a wall.

Tess ushered Amy and Johnny into the hospital room. Bright light poured through the window, accentuating the dozen arrangements of flowers Mac had received over the past forty-eight hours.

Propped up in bed, Mac grinned at the children. "It's about time you came to visit. I've missed you two."

Amy hopped up next to her father and hugged him. "Tess said you'll be coming home tomorrow." Her face screwed into a frown. "Why did that bad man hurt you, Daddy? I don't like him."

"He didn't mean to. He has problems I was trying to help him with. He isn't bad, just hurting and confused."

"I was scared." Amy snuggled close to Mac, sticking her thumb into her mouth.

"Me, too," Johnny mumbled.

"As you two can see, I am fine. There's nothing to be afraid of. I'll always be there for you." Mac looked over his daughter's head and straight into Tess's gaze. "Always."

The door clicked open, and Alice came into the room.

"Mom, I'm glad you're here. I bet these two would love to sample the ice cream sundaes they have downstairs in the cafeteria. I hear they are the best."

"Ice cream!" Amy's eyes widened. "Yes!" She pumped her arm in the air as she had seen Johnny do so many times.

"I can take—" Tess started to say.

"I want to talk with Tess for a moment. You two go with Grandma. I'll see you when you get back."

Amy planted a big kiss on Mac's cheek. Johnny gave him a quick hug, looking somewhat embarrassed by all the emotions being expressed. When the children followed Alice from the room, the silence that descended was thick and heavy. Tess could hear the hammering of her heart in her ears. She avoided looking at Mac for a long moment—just as she'd avoided being alone with him the past two days—but she knew the time for reckoning was at hand.

"Okay, Tess, what gives? You've gone to a great deal of trouble to make sure you're not alone with me these past few days. What are you not telling me?"

"This isn't going to work."

"What?"

The question hung in the air between them for a moment. "I'd rather talk later when you're feeling better."

"So you want me to be in good condition before you dump me."

The accusation cut through the tension that captured Tess and tore at her defenses. "I want children. You don't. I don't see a future for us." She looked away from the anger that sparked in his eyes, wishing their situation were that simple.

"Is that all?"

"Isn't that enough?"

"I think there's more to it than just not agreeing on the number of children we would have."

She bit the inside of her cheek. How could she tell him she would be afraid every day he walked out of the house that something would take him away? "You said yourself you wanted to settle the issue before getting married. Have you changed your mind? Do you want more children?"

His forehead wrinkled in a deep, thoughtful frown. "I don't know. I've been pretty out of it for the past few days."

"You wanted this discussion. I was willing to wait."

"To tell me it was over?"

"I don't see there's anything to discuss. We want two different things in life." She swallowed the lump in her throat, determined now that he had started the conversation to end their relationship so she could start healing. The road to recovery would be long, one she wasn't sure she would ever finish. Her heart ached with wants and needs only Mac could fulfill.

"I want to talk about it some more. I love you, Tess."

Emotions, all wrapped up in her love for this man, swamped her. But she remembered the terror that gripped her when she saw him in the emergency room, his blood everywhere as the nurse tore his shirt away to reveal his wound. "I just can't."

"Can't what?"

Johnny, Amy and Alice entered the room, saving Tess from having to answer. She fled before she broke down in front of the children. She felt the tears flowing down her cheeks. She saw people staring at her as she rushed toward the elevator. Sounds and smells faded from her consciousness. She focused her attention on one thing—finding a sanctuary.

Without realizing it, she ended up in front of the double doors that led into the hospital chapel. She pushed through them and sank onto a pew. Lacing her fingers together, she bowed her head. Her mind went blank for a few seconds, then the words poured into her.

*Dear Heavenly Father, I'm lost and don't know what to do. I love Mac so much. What if he had died the other day?*

The silence in the chapel amplified the loneliness she felt. What would she have if she walked away from Mac?

*Please, God, I need You. I need Your help. What do I do? What do You want from me?*

"Tess."

She pivoted in the pew and saw Mac standing in the doorway. He moved into the chapel, his gaze trained on hers, such tenderness and love in his eyes that her heart screamed out the injustice. The pallor of his features and the slowness of his gait attested to the ordeal he had been through, reminding her why she was afraid to commit.

He sat next to her, one corner of his mouth lifting in a smile. "I knew you would be here."

"How?"

"Because this is where I would have come."

"Oh," she murmured, the single word enhancing their bond more than anything.

"Tell me what is really bothering you. Let me help you."

"What if you had died?"

"But I didn't."

"You're going back to the halfway house when you're better. It could happen again."

"Yes, it could."

Pain stabbed her heart as though a bullet had ripped through her.

"But I could be sitting in my easy chair at home and die. When it's my time to go to the Lord, I will go, not one minute before. In the meanwhile, I can't stop living because I'm afraid of what might be."

"I don't want you to go back to the halfway house."

"Is that what you really want? Do you want me to turn my back on my ministry?"

"No—yes. I don't know."

Mac cupped his hand over hers. "I will if that's what you want."

Confusion reigned in Tess. She wanted to shout no, but the word wouldn't come out. How could she ask him to give up something that was so important to him? His strong faith and ministry were an intricate part of him and one of the reasons she loved him so much.

"Now, about having children?"

Tess twisted and pressed her fingers over his mouth. "I love Amy and Johnny as though they were mine." She paused, her throat clogged with emotions. "A family of four is plenty."

"So, we each give up what we want? You think that's fair? You think that's what God wants?"

"I love you, Mac. I'm not sure how this can work. You're right. I can't ask you to give up the halfway house."

"And I can't ask you to give up your dream of having children."

"It looks like we're at a standstill."

"Then we've come to the right place. Our Father will show us the way. We just have to open our hearts and listen to Him."

She wanted it to be that simple. Could it?

With her hand still linked to Mac's, Tess bowed her head. She wanted the fear gone. How could that happen when she had lived with it so long? She wanted a family. Could she make the emotional commitment without fear of being hurt?

"Our Father, guide us through this challenge You've laid at our feet. Help us to see Your path and to surrender our fear to You. Help us to put our lives in Your hands."

Mac's prayer held the key. The words weaved their way into her heart, and she felt the tension slip away. If she turned her life totally over to the Lord and trusted in Him completely, then she would no longer experience the terror she'd had on that mountaintop two years before. Wasn't that what true faith was all about?

*God is with me every step of the way. I will be all right.*

Tess angled her head to peer at Mac. Their gazes touched and she realized he felt the same way. A bond, forged through pain, solidified between them as she rested her cheek against his good shoulder and relished the moment of total peace and surrender.

In order to love God, to love Mac, she had to open herself up and let them in with no reservations, no conditions attached. Mac should continue his work because that was part of the Lord's plan. That was a part of Mac, the man she had fallen in love with.

Mac slipped his arm around her shoulder and she nestled into the curve of his body. "I love you, Tess Morgan. I want you to be the mother of my children. Together we both can let go of our fears. We can put our pasts behind us. You were right about life's risks. I can't stop living my life to the fullest because I'm afraid of what could happen."

"Because we will go to the Lord when our time is here, not one minute sooner."

"Yes, we both have to learn to risk in order to love. Grieving is an important process in life, but it should never take over as we both were letting it do. It should never control us to the point we turn away from what is truly important."

"The essence of our faith."

Mac placed a kiss on the top of Tess's head and cradled her closer. "That, and our ability to love another totally and unconditionally as we love our Father in Heaven."

"I do have one condition to place on you continuing your work at the halfway house."

She looked into his face in time to see him arch a brow. "Oh?"

The smile that graced her lips filled her with such love for the man next to her. "I want to volunteer alongside you. What is important to you is important to me."

"And I suppose you'll want me in the delivery room when our first child is born."

"Of course, holding my hand."

He bent forward and touched his lips to hers. "I'll be there every time."

# *Epilogue*

Johnny raced ahead of the large group emerging from the courthouse. "It's done. It's done. I am official."

Tess paused at the top of the stairs and watched the boy dance. Amy joined him, shouting her joy.

Mac came up behind her and wrapped his arms around her, resting his chin on her shoulder. "Do you think our son is excited?"

"No. What makes you think that?"

"Oh, the silly grin on his face, the fact he's waving the adoption papers around for everyone to see."

Tess turned her head slightly to glance at her husband. "Johnny's now legally a member of the family. He's still in remission with high odds in his favor that it will stay that way. You know this year can't get any better."

"I don't know about that." Mac laid his hand over her rounded stomach. "I'd say in about three months it will."

Amy ran up the stairs and tugged on her father's pant

leg. "Come on. Aunt Casey said we need to hurry. Remember the party? Everyone is waiting."

"What party?" Mac asked, his eyes bright with humor.

Amy twisted her mouth in a frown, her brow wrinkled. "The party to celebrate. I want some ice cream and cake before it's all gone."

Casey stopped next to Tess and Mac. "You know, the cake that says Welcome To The Family, Johnny and Colt."

"The MacPhersons are growing by leaps and bounds," Mac said, noticing Colt take his sister's hand.

Tess smiled at the thought of her family. "And I'm gonna be a beached whale walking down that aisle next month as your matron of honor, Casey."

Mac planted a soft kiss on Tess's cheek. "But a beautiful beached whale."

\* \* \* \* \*

Dear Reader,

My mother, who passed away recently, was a nurse all her life. I can remember her talking about her work and how much joy she got from being a nurse and helping others during difficult times in their lives. The story of Tess and Mac is a story about giving oneself to others and to God. Faith is what can sustain a person through those difficult times and even strengthen him.

I love hearing from readers. You may write me at P.O. Box 2074, Tulsa, OK, 74101.

May God bless you,

Margaret Daley

# SADIE'S HERO

Though he fall, he shall not be utterly cast down:
for the Lord upholdeth him with his hand.
—*Psalms* 37:24

I want to dedicate this book
to the people who work with Special Olympics
in Oklahoma and to a special coach, Laurie.

# Chapter One

Bachelor number forty-six: Andrew Knight, 37,
is a senior vice president of International Foods.
When not working, he likes to play golf and
read. With black hair and gray eyes he is any
woman's idea of a dream date, especially the
one he plans, dinner at Maison Blanche followed
by a concert on the lawn of Philbrook Museum
of Art in Tulsa.

Sadie Spencer read the description in the catalog, then
looked at the man who was number forty-six. He stood
on the platform in a black tuxedo that fit him perfectly.
Made for him, she decided as her gaze traveled up his
tall length to rest on his face, sculpted in clean, strong
lines. She had to agree with the catalog's description.
He did inspire dreams.

"The opening bid for our next bachelor offered on the

auction block tonight is two hundred dollars. Do I hear two twenty-five?"

"Two hundred twenty-five," a distinguished-looking woman in the front row shouted.

"I thought you wanted to bid on him," Carol West whispered to Sadie.

Her friend's urgent words focused Sadie on her mission. "Four hundred dollars."

Everyone turned toward Sadie, and for a few seconds silence reigned in the hotel banquet room. Leaning against the back wall, she shifted from one foot to the other, her throat suddenly very dry. The room seemed unusually hot.

"Sadie, are you crazy? I don't know why I even bother asking. Of course, you are." Carol's astonishment, mixed with her exasperation, was evident in her round eyes and furrowed brow.

"It's for a good cause—fifteen good causes, in fact," Sadie whispered, never taking her gaze off number forty-six. "I've got to have him."

"Four hundred fifty," the distinguished-looking woman countered, shooting Sadie a look of determination.

"Five hundred," she returned, mentally calculating how much she could bid and still have enough for the next month's rent. She really hadn't thought the bid would go so high, but she wasn't going to give in when she was so close to her goal.

"Five twenty-five."

Sadie turned to Carol. "Will you loan me fifty? I've

been trying for two months to get past his secretary. I'm a desperate woman. This plan has divine inspiration—well, not exactly divine, but when I saw his name on the list of bachelors for this auction, I knew my prayers had been answered. I know this will work. Please, Carol."

With a deep sigh her friend nodded.

"Five hundred fifty," Sadie said, aware all eyes were on her, including Andrew Knight's. His cool regard trapped her, momentarily wiping all reason from her mind. She tried to ignore the tingling sensation that streaked up her spine but she couldn't. Sweat broke out on her upper lip. She resisted the urge to wipe away the sign of her nervousness while *he* watched.

Determinedly she pulled her gaze from him. With a willpower she was beginning to think she'd lost, Sadie fixed her attention on the woman in the front row and silently pleaded for her to give up. She held her breath while waiting for the woman to bid again. If she did, Sadie would be forced to come up with another way to meet Andrew Knight. When the woman shook her head, Sadie relaxed her tensed shoulders.

"Five fifty once." The auctioneer's visual sweep of the room seemed minutes long rather than seconds. "Twice." Another pause, Sadie was sure for dramatic effect. "Sold to the lady in red for five hundred fifty dollars."

"I realize the man is gorgeous, but it isn't too late to back out." Carol's frown was deeply in place.

"His looks are beside the point. You know why I need to meet with him. His company is perfect for what

I have in mind." Sadie still felt his intense, piercing gray gaze on her and found herself drawn to the platform.

"There are less expensive ways to see Andrew Knight. I'm sure with your vivid imagination you'd have come up with a way to get past his barracuda secretary. You always do think of something in time."

Carol's words barely registered in Sadie's mind. Instead, she felt ensnared by assessing eyes and couldn't look away from the man her friend was discussing. Much to Sadie's dismay, she had the impression of being probed, cataloged and filed away in a matter of a few seconds by Mr. Andrew Knight. With a blush flaming her face, she averted her gaze, resolved not to look again. Apparently her vivid imagination was working overtime this evening.

"Carol, school will be over before I get in to see him if I don't do something fast. I've tried to get past that woman who guards his door as if her life depends on it. And perhaps it does."

"You're much too melodramatic for your own good. Life indeed!"

"I don't mean her life literally, but I do mean her job. It's his eyes and the way he carries himself." Sadie gestured toward the stage but didn't dare look at the man. "There's something about him that's so intense—almost brooding." *Or perhaps it's ruthless determination,* she concluded silently, not sure from where that impression came.

"You need an outlet for that imagination of yours. Have you ever thought about writing?"

"No," Sadie answered immediately, her smile vanishing.

"It's got to be in your genes," her friend continued as if Sadie hadn't said anything. "Your father's historical characterizations are great. He makes those people seem so alive and real. That last book he wrote about Napoleon was fascinating."

The air became stuffy, Sadie's chest tight with each breath. Standing in the back of the room with the other organizers of the annual fund-raiser, she took the opportunity to slip out the door into the hallway. As she inhaled deeply, Carol joined her.

"Are you all right, Sadie? You're so pale."

She waved her hand in the air, dismissing her friend's concern. "Too many people in there. Our turnout was much larger this year."

"Since you're on the board of Children Charities, you're in the position to get a larger room for the auction next year. Have you decided what you're going to say to Mr. Knight?"

"Me? Plan ahead? Only when absolutely necessary."

"In other words, you haven't the slightest idea how you're going to sell him on the work project."

"Of course, I know. I'm going to appeal to his soft vulnerable side, to his love of children. If I can convince IFI to go along with my project, then the other companies in the area will follow like cattle to the slaughter."

"From what I've heard there may not be a soft, vulnerable side to appeal to. I suppose he might love children, but he has been a confirmed bachelor for thirty-seven years."

"The first twenty don't count. Too young to marry. Something will come to me when I'm having dinner with him. If not, by the time he takes me to the concert, I should have come up with the right approach."

Carol's laughter rang in the silent hallway. "If anyone can come up with the perfect approach, it'll be you. Come on. We'd better get back inside. It sounds like the auction is over."

*Perfect.* The word stuck in Sadie's mind as she walked back into the room. All her life she had striven to be perfect because that was what her father had demanded. When she had brought home an A minus on her report card, her father had wanted an A. When she had brought home an A, he had wanted an A plus. She had always come up short in his eyes, never quite the daughter he wanted. Thankfully she had found salvation in the Lord. As a teenager, lost, hurting, she had turned to her church's youth group for solace when her father had been particularly tough on her self-esteem. Now she couldn't imagine her life without the Lord's guidance.

"I'd better pay for this date or I won't be going anywhere." Sadie made her way to the table at the side set up for that purpose.

"I see you won our number forty-six." Jollie Randall took Sadie's check. "You know, I was the one to recruit him for this auction. Most reluctant, though. Wanted to donate money instead. Don't scare him off, Sadie. We could use him next year."

"He could get married."

"Not likely. I work at IFI, and there have been many women who have tried to snare him, but he doesn't have the time for a serious relationship."

*Good,* Sadie thought. She didn't want a commitment, just his okay on her work project. "Then he's safe for next year.

"I'll send Mr. Andrew Knight back in one piece and you can save your money for next year's auction."

Jollie's eyes widened, and her mouth fell open.

Sadie felt pinpricks go up her spine. She slowly turned. Her whole face reddened as she stared into the subject of their conversation's unreadable gray eyes.

"As soon as you two ladies finish planning my future, I'd like a word with you." Andrew directed his comment to Sadie.

Intense might be too mild a word to describe Andrew Knight, Sadie thought as she continued to stare at him, her mind blank of any response to give him. She was sure her face rivaled her red dress.

His eyes warmed to a dove gray. "About the arrangements, Miss—"

"Sadie Spencer."

"Miss Spencer." He extended his hand.

When his fingers closed around hers, she wasn't surprised at the firm handshake that transmitted confidence and determination nor the warmth that spread up her arm at the tactile contact. For a few seconds she felt surrounded by him, a taut pressure building in her chest. Then he released her hand, and the tension eased, allowing her to breathe again.

"About the arrangements, Mr. Knight. May I have a word with you in private?" There was nothing she could do about the quaver in her voice, which signified the disruption this man caused to her equilibrium. She glanced about the room full of people, all talking at once. "I think there's a small room off this one we can use."

"Lead the way, Miss Spencer."

"Please call me Sadie. Only my students call me Miss Spencer."

He started walking beside her toward the room she had indicated. "You're a teacher?"

"At Cimarron High School. I teach students with special needs."

"That must be very demanding work that requires a lot of patience." Andrew opened the door for Sadie.

"My job is demanding, like a lot of people's, but I love working with my students. They're what make my job rewarding," Sadie said as she entered the room.

"I'm afraid I haven't been around any children with special needs. In fact, I haven't been around many children." Andrew shut the door, enclosing them in the suddenly small space.

Even though a few feet separated them, Sadie felt overwhelmed by his presence. He filled the room with his intensity. He leaned against a table and crossed his arms. An amused look softened his stern features as several minutes passed and Sadie remained silent, trying to figure out the best way to approach him about her work project. Nothing came to mind except the fact that he'd said he hadn't been around people with special needs. She needed to change that before approaching him about working with them, or his answer would probably be no even before she had presented the whole work project to him.

"Sadie." He finally broke into the quiet. "You said you wanted to speak with me in private. Since the hour is growing late and tomorrow is a workday—"

"But it's Sunday." *The Lord's day.*

He arched his brow and quirked his mouth. "Some people do work on Sunday. I get more work done on Sunday when everyone else is gone than I do two days during the week."

"Well, then." Sadie began to pace, nervous energy compelling her to move. "I have to confess I had a reason for bidding on you tonight." She stopped and faced him, deciding only to tell him about part of her plan. "I want IFI to help support Cimarron High School's Special Olympics program. Since you're the vice president of special projects and human resources, I thought you would be the person to see at IFI. For example, at the school we're in desperate need of uniforms."

"Why didn't you take the five hundred fifty dollars you spent on this date and buy uniforms with it?"

"Because we need continual support, not a one-time

shot in the arm. New uniforms will have to be purchased every year as our program grows. Fees to the
state games in May paid every year. Some equipment
purchased."

"I see. Wouldn't it have been easier to contact me at
my office?" His facade of cool businessman descended
over his features.

"I tried, but your secretary said you've been too busy
to see anyone right now. Something about being out of
town a lot lately on business. So when this opportunity
came up, I decided to bypass normal channels."

He raised one eyebrow. "Have you always been unorthodox?"

Sadie laughed. "I have been accused of that a few
times. Since I give to Children Charities every year, I
thought it was a brilliant plan."

"IFI is constantly being approached about donating
to good causes. Sometimes Mrs. Fox screens the
requests and the people seeking appointments not connected directly with IFI, especially when I'm particularly busy at work."

"Then you weren't out of town?"

"No, I was. Since you went to so much trouble, I'll
take a look at your proposal. Write up what you need in
the way of support and get it to me as soon as possible.
I'll have an answer for you by the time we go on our
date. I assume you still want to go?"

Sadie nodded, aware of the polite distance he was
putting between them.

Glancing at his watch, he straightened away from the table. "Would next Saturday night be okay? I have tickets for the concert for that night."

"Yes, that would be fine."

"I'll call you about the time closer to the day."

His tone of voice conveyed their conversation was over. As Sadie walked toward the door, she wasn't sure just how she was going to get him involved when he was so busy. Between now and their date she would have to come up with an offer the man couldn't refuse.

Andrew sat behind his massive desk in his office, staring out the window. The morning so far had been unproductive. He usually enjoyed these quiet times the most, but today he was restless, reflective. He rarely thought about his past because he felt it was a waste of time, something he didn't allow himself to do. But this morning he had to fight the memories he worked so hard to suppress.

No! He wouldn't permit his past to intrude now. He needed to turn around and concentrate on the Madison project. But he had one of those dreams last night, and afterward he always had a difficult time not giving in to his emotions.

At thirty-seven he was one of the four senior vice presidents of a large international food corporation. Most of his special projects he'd worked on involved enhancing IFI's reputation in the community and marketplace. His hard work the past fifteen years had paid off.

He should be elated, on top of the world. He wasn't. Lately he had felt more and more a vague restlessness, as though something was missing from his life, and when he did, he didn't feel in control. He wouldn't tolerate that.

A knock startled him from his reflection. He swiveled his chair to face the door. "Come in."

Bill, one of the guards on duty downstairs, came into the office, followed by Sadie Spencer. "Mr. Knight, she says she has an appointment with you. I told her you don't meet with people on Sundays. I started to send her away, but she persuaded me to check with you first. She said you're expecting some kind of proposal from her." Bill lowered his gaze to the carpet. "I didn't want to turn her away if that was true."

Andrew contained his smile at the sheepish look on the guard's face. After his brief encounter with Sadie Spencer the night before, Andrew could just imagine her unusual kind of persuasion. "Thanks, Bill. I'll take care of Miss Spencer."

"I hope you and Frank enjoy my chocolate doughnuts," Sadie said as the guard left.

Andrew chuckled. "So that's how you got the man to bring you up here. Bill and Frank usually guard my privacy like a mother hen guarding the chicken coop. I'm going to have to speak with them about women bearing gifts of food."

Sadie crossed the room, sat in front of his desk and placed several pieces of paper, a box and a thermos with two mugs before him. "I hope you aren't too angry with them. After all, you told me to get my proposal about Special Olympics to you as soon as possible. I stayed up last night so you could have it first thing this morning before I go to church."

"I'm impressed." He glanced at his watch. "It's only nine, less than twelve hours since I saw you last. I wish I could get my employees to work that fast." He picked up the papers and flipped through them. "You did all this last night after the banquet?"

"Yes. It's important."

He lifted his gaze from the proposal, locking with hers across his desktop. Her brown hair was pulled back in a French braid. Her face, with her pleasing features, held only a touch of makeup. She looked refreshed, ready to take on the world. But it was her eyes that drew him. They were dark, almost black. For a fleeting moment while they stared at each other, he sensed a haunting vulnerability she tried to conceal from the world. But he knew it was there beneath the surface and wondered what or who was responsible for putting it there. He felt a connection to her that momentarily stunned him.

He cleared his throat and looked away, dismissing the common bond. "I'll get back with you concerning your proposal as soon as I've studied it." His gaze fell to the box. "You said chocolate doughnuts? I must confess I have a weakness for chocolate."

"Chocolate has that effect on people. I, too, love it,

but I also have oat bran muffins with me. I don't want to be accused of feeding you only unhealthy food. I baked these this morning." She opened the box and began to withdraw all the goodies she brought.

Andrew watched, fascinated. Not only were there doughnuts and oat bran muffins, but also a coffee cake and cinnamon rolls. "You baked all these this morning!"

"Well—" she paused and peered at him "—after finishing the proposal at three, I couldn't go to sleep, so I baked. I like to cook. I find it soothing."

He watched her as she walked across his office and wondered where in the world she put all the food she cooked. There wasn't an ounce of fat on her. She had all the right curves for her small frame. "What do you do with the food you cook?"

"I eat it. That or I invite some friends over to help me." She closed the box and put it on the floor next to her chair. "Or I freeze it. Of course, I have to have a party periodically to clean out my freezer."

Her voice was tinged with laughter, and he felt himself responding to that. It was a rich sound that was comforting. It touched his restlessness and soothed him.

"Would you like some coffee?" Sadie asked, holding up the thermos. "I'd better warn you there's something a little extra in my coffee."

Before he could answer, she started pouring two mugs full. He eyed the coffee as she handed it to him. "Something extra?"

"I have several secret blends. This is what I call my morning pick-me-upper."

Andrew cautiously brought the mug to his lips, taking a deep breath of the wonderful aroma, and sipped. The coffee slid down his throat, warming him all the way. It was strong but smooth with no bitter aftertaste. "This is delicious. What's in it?"

She smiled, a smile that made her dark eyes sparkle like polished jet that caught in the sunshine. "A woman has to have some secrets. I'm usually an open book except for some of my special recipes." The smile deepened, bringing a playfully wicked gleam to her eyes. "I figured you would be ready for breakfast about now."

"How did you know I didn't have breakfast this morning?"

"Just a guess, but I bet food is unimportant to you."

"Why do you say that? We have to have food to exist." Andrew bit into a rich doughnut with melted chocolate dripping off it.

"I saw you eating last night at the banquet, and you hardly noticed the food you were putting into your mouth. You think of food as a way to keep yourself alive. I think of food as a delicious experience to be relished."

He began to chew the doughnut more slowly, taking notice of its sweet taste for the first time. He had never thought about his eating habits, but he supposed he did rush through his meals, rarely taking notice of what he ate, as Sadie Spencer pointed out after only one observation. Suddenly he was disconcerted that someone was able to read him so well in such a short time. He had worked hard not to reveal himself to others.

"I bet you usually skip breakfast, too." Sadie interrupted his thoughts. "If you have anything it's probably a cup of coffee when you get to work."

"Have you been following me?" He picked up an oat bran muffin and began eating it while she refilled his mug.

"No, but I've known many people just like you. Most have their biggest meal at night, when for weight purposes it should be either at breakfast or lunch. Breakfast is when I eat the most. That way I have all day to work off the calories." She stopped talking abruptly. "Excuse me. I have a habit of going on and on at times. It's the teacher in me. I teach nutrition and cooking to my students and can't resist talking about the subject. Just hold up a hand when you want me to stop. Breakfast is a great way—"

With his hand raised, he chuckled. Sadie Spencer was just what he needed to forget his melancholy mood. She swept into his office with mouthwatering temptations and a bright smile that dazzled a person. He was glad she had come, and he couldn't believe he wasn't upset that someone had interrupted him on a Sunday, which just wasn't done.

"You've sold me on the fact that breakfast is important." Andrew held up the cinnamon roll he was going to sample. "You're certainly more than a teacher."

"Why, of course. Everyone is more than what they do for a living. I'm sure in your spare time you do a lot of things. It just so happens that I love to cook in my spare time." Tilting her head to the side, she smiled again. "Well, one of the things I like to do."

"What are some of the other things you like to do?"

"Besides teaching, which I love, I'm involved in Special Olympics and Children Charities, but you already know that. I am also a Sunday school teacher—six- and seven-year-olds. I like to read anything having to do with history, and I do the usual sporting things, tennis, golf, swimming, skiing—"

"Whoa." Andrew raised his hand again. "When do you rest? I thought I was busy, but you're wearing me out listening to all your activities."

"Oh, what kind of hobbies do you have?" She snapped her fingers. "No, wait. The catalog said you like to play golf and read. So we do have something in common. What do you like to read?"

He frowned, trying to remember the last book he had read for pleasure. "Tons of stuff, all related to work. And before you ask about golf, when I do play it is for business purposes."

"Those aren't hobbies."

"I don't have much spare time."

"You work all the time?"

He straightened in his chair, his frown growing more pronounced. "I enjoy working."

She started to pour some more coffee, but he shook his head. "So do I, but I also enjoy my free time, too. All work makes—"

"Don't say it." Her teasing censure made him feel uncomfortable, as though he had wasted half his life climbing the corporate ladder. Andrew shifted the papers on his desk, then continued in a businesslike voice. "And speaking of work, I have a lot still to do today, and didn't you say something about going to church?" He didn't usually have to defend his work habits with the people he knew, and he didn't want to start now. His job had served him well over the years.

"Yes, but…" For a second, surprise flickered in her dark eyes. Quickly she lowered her lashes and busied herself cleaning up.

Andrew watched as she put everything into the box and closed the lid. He would consider her proposal, take her out on the date she'd paid for, and that would be all. It would end as quickly as it had begun. Relationships were always so much easier when they were kept on a friendly but impersonal basis. He had learned that painfully when he had been shuffled from one foster family to the next.

Sadie scooted the box toward him, then rose. "I've left you some food for later." She extended her hand across the desk, no expression in her expressive eyes now. "Thank you for taking the time to look at my proposal."

Her tone equaled his in stiff politeness. Rising, he accepted her hand, needing this meeting to come to an end as soon as possible. "I'll call you about the date later in the week."

After picking up her thermos and mugs, she started

to say something, but instead just stared at him. The darkness of her eyes intensified as a small frown knitted her brows. Andrew knew she was debating whether to speak her mind. He was surprised when she decided not to and turned to leave. His curiosity was aroused as he watched her walk toward the door. What had she wanted to say to him, and why hadn't she? He was sure she usually spoke her mind. She was probably not afraid of many people.

The sound of the door clicking shut reverberated through the office, and for a few seconds he felt totally alone, as though no one else existed in the world. A tight band about his chest tautened, constricting his breathing. Why did he feel as though he'd let Sadie Spencer down? And why did he care?

## Chapter Two

Sadie couldn't quite believe she was traveling to the Crescent City to have her date with Andrew Knight. That morning he'd called her from New Orleans, where a business negotiation had lasted longer than he'd thought it would. He would have to stay the whole day. He'd left it up to her—to come in IFI's jet, which was bringing a sales team to a conference or to wait until some indefinite time in the future for their date. She'd told him immediately that she would come to New Orleans, because she didn't know when the man would ever have the time to fit her into his work-consuming schedule. She wanted to get him involved with her students, but how was she going to accomplish that between all his business meetings?

Sadie was jolted from her musings when the stewardess announced the jet was preparing to land at New Orleans International Airport. She checked to make sure her seat belt was fastened, then tried to ready herself mentally for the landing, her hands gripping the arms of the chair so tightly her knuckles were white. She certainly wasn't destined to be a world traveler. She was fine in the air, but the takeoffs and landings always reminded her of how fragile life was and that at this moment she wasn't at all in control of it.

"Dear Lord, please give me the strength to persuade this man to give my students a chance at working in the community. Guide me and help me see Your path. In Jesus's name, amen," she murmured, the prayer taking her mind off the plane's descent.

When the jet touched ground, Sadie inhaled, then exhaled a deep breath. She tried not to think that she still had the return flight to get through. At least she wouldn't be alone and would be able to talk to Andrew to take her mind off flying.

As she descended the steps from the jet, she was accosted by the stifling heat of an October afternoon in New Orleans. The humidity blanketed her in a fine sheen, and she remembered all the time that morning she had taken to apply her makeup and to select the right sundress to wear. Ruined after one minute, she thought with a silent laugh.

At the bottom of the steps she scanned the area. No Andrew Knight. As she was trying to decide what to do, a white limousine approached the jet, and a chauffeur climbed out of the car.

"Miss Spencer?"

"Yes?"

"Mr. Knight sent me to pick you up. He regretted yet another delay, but by the time you arrive at the house, he will be through with his business."

"Where's Mr. Knight?" Sadie asked, puzzled about where his meeting was taking place.

"At Oakcrest Plantation. My employer owns the plantation. It's outside New Orleans. About a thirty-minute drive, Miss Spencer."

"Is your employer Mr. Madison?" Andrew had mentioned the man on the phone that morning. The negotiations must be taking place at his house.

"Yes, ma'am."

The chauffeur opened the back door for her, and she slid into the luxurious car, the soft feel of leather beneath her fingertips. On the ride out of New Orleans, she savored the distinctive sights of the river city. She particularly loved its history with its French and Spanish heritage. She should return one day and really see the city and its Southern culture. The romantic, as well as the historian, in her demanded it.

The gray shadows of dusk spread across the landscape as the limousine pulled into a long driveway lined with huge oaks that formed a canopy over the lane. Spanish moss dripped from their branches as though the trees were weeping. She felt like she was suddenly back in the time right before the Civil War and was going to a weekend ball at a neighboring plantation.

She was beginning to visualize herself dressed in a

hoop skirt made of yards and yards of silk material when the car stopped in front of the massive front veranda. Sadie looked out the window at the eight tall columns and white facade and fell in love with the place. She wished she had a home like this. Such a romantic, she chided herself and climbed out of the car when the chauffeur opened the back door.

Andrew came onto the veranda. The beautiful house behind him was eclipsed by his presence. Pausing on the steps, Sadie allowed her gaze to trek up his length, her earlier impression of his single-minded ruthlessness reconfirmed. What arrested her about Andrew Knight was the sense this man before her was tough, aggressive, individualistic, a man who controlled his own destiny. He would stand out in a room crowded with successful men. His regard held an intensity of purpose she seldom encountered.

"I'm sorry I couldn't make it to the airport, Sadie. I trust your flight was okay?"

"Yes," she murmured, suddenly not sure how to act. She was inundated with the feeling she shouldn't be here, that she was starting something that could hurt her in the end.

"Darrell and I just finished twenty minutes ago."

Sadie was surprised to find Andrew dressed casually in black slacks and a white polo shirt. She had expected no less than a three-piece business suit, since he had been working. In her brief encounters with him he'd seemed like a man who followed business protocol down to the last stitch of clothing. But then, if she thought about her presence in New Orleans, she would have to admit that her being here was a bit unusual in itself. She couldn't see him mixing business with pleasure. He was definitely a complex man, full of contradictions, she decided.

"Let's go inside, and I'll introduce you to Darrell and his wife."

Andrew motioned for her to go first, resting his hand at the small of her back. It wasn't an intimate gesture but a casual one. Even knowing that, Sadie couldn't help the quickening of her heartbeat as she entered the antebellum home.

Inside the foyer he dropped his hand. "They're in the den at the back of the house. Ruth and Darrell Madison, besides being good friends, don't stand on ceremony. They insisted I ask you to join us and were glad you decided to."

"Are we dining here tonight?"

"Yes. Mabel, their cook, is one of the best. I think you'll enjoy her creations."

"Only if we have a truly Cajun meal," she said with a laugh. "Otherwise—" She turned at the den door to stare at Andrew and forgot what she was going to say.

His clean scent, spicing the air, made her aware of his presence only inches from her. His handsome features erased everything from her mind but him and her together in a dim hallway.

"Otherwise what?" Amusement laced his voice while his gray eyes shimmered with laughter.

"Otherwise I might just have to insist on you taking me to Antoine's tonight."

"Without reservations on a Saturday night?"

"Don't you know somebody with pull?"

"Afraid not."

Sadie exaggerated a pout. "And all the way down here I couldn't get Cajun food out of my mind. I swear the minute I landed I thought I smelled seafood gumbo."

His chuckle slid over her as though they had been friends for years. "You're in luck. Mabel loves to impress guests with her Cajun cooking."

"I knew this would be my lucky day. One of my wishes has come true."

"One of them?" A thick brow rose as his smile crinkled the corners of his eyes. "That implies there's more than one. What is your other wish?"

Sadie had to step back. He overpowered her. "Now, if I told you, none of the others would come true," she replied, a breathless quality entering her voice, the distance between them still too close.

"Others! My, you're ambitious."

"I prefer the word hopeful."

He leaned nearer, reaching around her to grasp the doorknob. "When I return you to Cimarron City, I'd be interested in how I did with the others."

"Are you sure you want to know?" She was struggling to think straight with him so close. Her mind kept dwelling on his arm, which was brushing hers, his eyes, which were like molten silver as they looked at her, his mouth, which formed a half smile that was melting her insides.

"That sounds ominous. Exactly how many wishes are we talking about?"

"Only two others."

He turned the knob and pushed the door open. "That doesn't sound too overwhelming. I think I can handle that. I've got big shoulders."

Sadie entered the den first, followed by Andrew, who quickly made the introductions. Sadie shook Ruth's and Darrell's hands, immediately liking them. Their den reflected the couple, cozy, friendly, warm, the fragrance of fresh flowers filling the air from several arrangements on tables about the room.

"Andrew told us a little about this bachelor auction but not nearly enough to satisfy my curiosity," Ruth said as they all sat. "What a neat idea for raising money. How long has your organization been doing it?"

"Four years."

"It sounds like a dating game," Darrell said, scooting closer to his wife on the couch.

"It's all done in fun and for charity, but there have been several marriages that have come from the couples meeting at the auction. That might be why our turnout every year grows. We started with twenty bachelors, and this year we auctioned off fifty. The number of women attending has doubled just in the last year."

"I must confess when he told me I couldn't picture him

agreeing. How in the world did you ever talk Andrew into being one?" Ruth slipped her hand into her husband's.

"I didn't. Someone at IFI did, and from what I heard it wasn't easy. You might compare it to moving Mount Rushmore."

Andrew held up his hand. "Hold it. I have to say in my defense that I know how hectic my schedule can be. I didn't want there to be any problems."

Darrell's laugh was deep and hearty. "Like today. He drives a hard bargain, especially when he's under pressure to get the negotiations over with."

"I should also add in his defense he tried to buy off the woman who asked him by donating some money to the charity in his place. He just doesn't know how valuable a real live bachelor is."

"Now that sounds like the Andrew I know," Ruth said. "The true businessman to the letter. His time is much too valuable for something as trivial as a date."

Andrew bent close to Sadie and whispered loud enough for the couple across from them to hear, "Forget that I said Darrell and Ruth were friends."

Sadie hoped for once her face wouldn't flame. Andrew's nearness sent a shiver coursing through her. Her heartbeat and breathing were quickly becoming erratic. She added a fourth wish to her list; she wanted to know what one of his kisses felt like.

"Don't let Andrew fool you, Sadie. Darrell and he have been friends since high school. In fact, I guess we all three have been." Ruth rose, squeezed her husband's hand, released it, then said to Sadie, "Let's leave the men alone for a while. I want to show you the house. You should have seen it when Darrell and I bought it eight years ago. What a mess! I'm proud of what we've done to preserve a little history. I'll let Andrew show you the gardens and gazebo later."

Andrew watched Sadie leave the room, surprised at how glad he was she'd taken him up on his invitation to dine in New Orleans. Silence, thick and heavy like the humidity outside, fell between Darrell and him as the door clicked shut.

Andrew stood and walked to the mantel. "You can quit staring at me like that now."

"Like what?" Darrell exaggerated an innocent look.

"Like you're waiting for a confession. There's nothing to tell. I hardly know Sadie. She bid on me at the auction last weekend, and that was the first time I met her." Andrew recalled how she'd breezed into his office the following day and had nearly taken over in a short space of time.

"And you brought her here to New Orleans?"

"Is that supposed to mean something?"

"No." Darrell answered slowly, paused for a long moment, then asked, "Does she know you grew up not far from this house?"

Andrew stared at the empty grate in the fireplace. "That's not important. Irrelevant to the moment at hand."

"Is it?"

Andrew's head shot up and his gaze clashed with his friend's. "I'll have the contracts to you by the end of the week."

"Okay. As usual the past is off-limits. I just find it interesting that you brought a woman here. That's a first."

"When I make an appointment, I like to keep it."

"Business ones, yes, but ones for pleasure I doubt have that kind of devotion."

"In a way this is business between Sadie and me." Andrew kneaded the cords of his neck, feeling the tension beneath his hand. That was the only way he would consider the unorthodox invitation.

"Business? Is this how you're justifying this unusual move to yourself?"

Seated again on the couch, Andrew leaned forward, his elbows on his knees, his hands clasped loosely together. "Why do you want to read more into this than there is?"

Darrell shrugged. "Chalk it up to a friend who cares what happens to you. I've followed you through the years. I've watched you try to shake your past. I've seen you work incessantly up the corporate ladder. But I've witnessed the longing on your face when you visit here. There's a void in your life, and you don't quite know how to fix it."

"I'm fulfilling an obligation to take Sadie Spencer out. She paid for the date. That sounds like a business arrangement to me." When Andrew looked into his friend's face and saw the skepticism in his expression, he added, "Yes, I think she's an interesting woman."

"Just interesting? Have you gone blind since we last met?"

Andrew visualized Sadie. Her shoulder-length brown hair framed an oval face that was striking, with its satin-like skin, high cheekbones, full lips and dark intense eyes that could put a man in a trance. "Okay. She's beautiful, too. But that is all, Darrell. This date is as far as my relationship with her will go. I have too much still to do to complicate my life right now."

"The presidency of IFI?"

"Yes. Lawrence Wilson will retire in a year. I want the job."

"Along with several other vice presidents. It won't be an easy fight. The prize is a big one, if that's what you want."

"Yes, it's what I want," Andrew said, aware his voice held a defensive tone in it, which he knew Darrell heard, too. "Have I ever turned my back on a hard fight? The tougher the better."

"So you'll put your personal life on hold. You've been doing that for fifteen years. When will you take time for yourself?"

"Next year."

"You remember Gregory Hansom?"

"A year ahead of us in school?"

"Yes. He had a heart attack last week. Nearly died. The doctor told him if he didn't change his lifestyle and reduce his stress the next one would finish him for good. Is that what you want?"

"It's not going to happen to me. I exercise when I can and eat right." Andrew winced inwardly when he remembered how often he skipped breakfast and the fact that Sadie had called him on that.

"How often do you exercise?"

"Have we gone back in time to the Spanish Inquisition?"

"How often?"

"I try to get to the health club once a week."

"And do you make it?"

"Sometimes." Andrew rose, restless energy demanding a release. "I wonder what's keeping the women." He started for the door.

"You don't have to escape. I'll drop the questions. You're a big boy now and have to live your own life."

Andrew turned at the door, a forced smile on his face. "Thanks. Now I'll sleep better at night."

"Come on back over here and tell me what's going on at IFI. Let the women have some time to get to know each other."

The darkness caressed Sadie with its cool fingers. As she leaned into the lacework railing of the gazebo, she inhaled the jasmine-laden air with hints of honeysuckle woven in it. Listening to the night sounds, she cleared her mind of all her troubles and relished the moment for what it was—a small, peaceful heartbeat in time when everything was right with the world. A gift from God.

Andrew came to stand next to her. "I like to come out

here when I'm visiting. Ruth loves her gardens. She spends a lot of time working in them."

"I love a beautiful garden, too, but I'm afraid I don't have what it takes to be a gardener."

"Oh, what?"

"A green thumb." She held out her fist with her thumb sticking up. "Definitely black. I even killed a cactus once by under-watering it. But that character flaw doesn't stop me from appreciating a heavenly place, and this garden and gazebo are."

"Darrell built this for Ruth as a surprise when she was in the hospital having their daughter."

"How romantic," Sadie said, closing her eyes to hold the image of herself next to an attractive, intelligent man who captured more than she dared to allow.

"I suppose it was. Darrell and Ruth often do little and big things like that for each other. Even when they were dating in high school."

Sadie heard the envious tone in Andrew's voice and felt a kinship with him. All through dinner with the couple and their seven-year-old daughter, Sadie had sensed a deep caring and love expressed in their respect for each other. They had taken time for each other, never demanding, never criticizing. Carrie, their daughter, was lucky she didn't have to live up to her parents' expectations of her. As Sadie knew from experience, that was difficult on a child. It left emotional wounds that were hard to heal.

"How long have they been married?" Sadie finally

asked, realizing Andrew was staring at her, producing a tightening in her chest.

"Nineteen years."

"Nineteen!" Sadie pushed away from the railing, stepping back to face Andrew as he turned toward her. "They act like newlyweds."

His low, warm chuckle erased all other sounds and made everything so much more intimate. "Sadie, some people do stay married, even though I must admit it's not as common as it once was."

She tried to read his expression, but the dark shadows hid it. "You sound like a cynic. Have you ever been married?"

"Do you always speak your mind?"

"Yes. Have you?"

"No. How about yourself?"

She shook her head.

"I thought a die-hard romantic like you, Sadie, would have been by now."

"It's because I am that I've never married."

"Now who sounds like the cynic?"

She shrugged. "Darrell and Ruth are lucky. I've seen so many couples who aren't. Marriage is for a lifetime. I've just found that the dreams are usually better than the real thing."

"Then there are no disappointments?"

"Right."

"But you can't hold dreams."

Sadie shifted away from Andrew. She didn't like the

way the conversation was developing. Carol had told her that very same thing several times in the past year. She knew she had many friends but no one she wanted to get close to for the kind of relationship necessary for a marriage to work. "A relationship has its ups and downs, but that's what makes it exciting." Carol's words came back to Sadie. *But when you open yourself up to another, they see all your flaws.*

"I thought you were a die-hard workaholic," she said, trailing her hand along the wooden railing as she distanced herself some more. "When do you have time to squeeze in a relationship?"

His laughter blanketed the night like the cloak of darkness. "I deserved that. I don't, any more than you do. For different reasons we have something in common." Lounging against the railing, he folded his arms across his chest. "Actually, those were Darrell's words. He keeps hounding me to slow down and smell the roses."

"I think Darrell's right. Take a deep breath."

"What?"

"Really. Smell Ruth's roses. They smell wonderful." As she listened to Andrew inhale, she was drawn toward him until mere inches separated them. "When you came out here before, did you ever just enjoy the atmosphere, the flowers, the quiet?"

"Well, no. I like to come out here to think. It's a good place to work through a problem I might be having at IFI. Darrell has accused me of only visiting them to do just that."

"Sometimes it's nice to stop and savor a place for what it is. To wipe your mind clean of all thoughts and relish the moment of peace. I find that helps relieve my stress more than anything else."

"Attacking problems head-on works best for me."

"But I bet you're always at war, fighting something. Don't you ever get tired of it all?"

Andrew didn't answer for a long moment. When he did, his voice was stiff. "If you want something, you have to fight for it. The world isn't going to give you a thing."

His cold words reminded Sadie of why she was here in the first place. She knew the value of fighting for what she wanted. "Have you made a decision about my proposal concerning Special Olympics?" she asked in a no-nonsense voice.

"Yes, we'll be able to do what you requested."

"Oh, fantastic!" Sadie paused, took a deep breath, then said, "I have another favor to ask. Will you come Thursday night to the high school for a meeting and reception with the parents and students involved in Special Olympics? As IFI's representative you could formally give us the money at the meeting."

"I don't—"

"It would be good PR for IFI," she interjected, her stomach twisted with tension.

"What time?"

"Seven, in the high school auditorium."

"I'll be there."

"Thanks," she whispered, sensing his sharp gaze on

her as though he were trying to discern what was beneath her request.

She could come to care a great deal for this man beside her. He possessed a certain vulnerability that matched hers and pulled her to him, body and soul. Their outlooks on life were light-years apart. She doubted he went to church, if last Sunday at the office was any indication. Her faith was what sustained her. His work was what sustained him, she suspected, and yet she felt a common bond she couldn't deny.

# Chapter Three

"What are you not telling me, Sadie?"

Andrew's question cut into Sadie's thoughts and set alarm bells ringing in her mind. It was too soon to approach him about her work project. He was sharp, intuitive, no doubt two qualities that served him well in the business world. She couldn't let down her guard for a second around him. He endangered her peace of mind more than anyone had in a long time. This had to be kept purely professional—a working relationship, she vowed, as she placed some distance between them and faced him.

"Andrew Knight, it's just a simple request to meet my students. That's all." She pressed her lips together to emphasize her point and hoped he didn't pursue his question. She wasn't ready to tell him the main reason she had bid on him. She wanted him to see how capable her students were.

He started to say something when he heard his name being called from the house. "We'd better head back."

At the French doors that led into the living room, Ruth intercepted them. "Andrew, there's a call for you. You can take it in the den."

While he went to answer the phone, Sadie remained with Ruth, thankful for the timely interruption. "Your gardens are beautiful. I wish I could have seen more, but we need to leave soon."

"You're welcome at my home any time. Maybe you can persuade Andrew to bring you down again. Maybe even get him to take some time off. He works way too much."

Sadie knew the instant he reappeared even though she didn't see him come into the living room. Her body tightened with awareness as if every part of her were attuned to him. She glanced toward him and saw the frown that knitted his brow. "What's wrong?"

"That was the IFI pilot. He has to leave immediately for New York. He won't be able to take us back to Cimarron City tonight, like I had planned. We can either take a commercial flight or wait until he can pick us up tomorrow evening."

"Well, then it's settled," Ruth said. "Now y'all will be able to see more of Oakcrest. Y'all can stay here tonight."

Indecision clouded Andrew's eyes. He started to speak.

"Andrew, I won't take no for an answer. Sadie can use some of my clothes. What do you think?" Ruth turned to Sadie.

She looked from the woman to Andrew. "It'll be

okay with me. I don't have anything planned special for tomorrow. I can call a friend to teach my Sunday school class."

"Great. You can go with us to church tomorrow. I've been wanting to get Andrew to our little church, and this will be a perfect time to visit. I'll go get your bedrooms ready." Ruth hurried into the foyer as though afraid if she didn't rush Andrew would decline to stay the night.

The living room suddenly seemed small as Sadie faced him, not sure what he was thinking. His features had flattened into a neutral expression while his body was still tense. The silence between them stretched, marred only by the ticking of the grandfather clock. The rhythmic sound echoed in her mind, grating against her taut nerves.

"I'd forgotten how important Sundays at the office are to you. If you want to get a commercial flight, that's fine by me." Sadie welcomed the sound of her voice. It cut through the tension.

Andrew glanced at the grandfather clock in the corner. "It's too late. I've already tried."

Disappointment speared through her chest, leaving a dull ache in her heart. "Did you get reservations for tomorrow morning?"

"No. I had some things I needed to do, but by the time we got home the day would be half over."

"So you decided to take a day off?"

He nodded. "I haven't had one in several months."

"You have been busy. No wonder Mrs. Fox is so protective of you."

"We work well together. She's as ambitious as I am. I think she already sees herself as the executive secretary to the president."

"President?"

"Lawrence Wilson is retiring next year. I'm one of several being considered for the job."

"Oh." Her disappointment sharpened, and she knew she shouldn't feel that way. She should be happy for him. She had the impression being considered for the presidency was something he had worked years to achieve. But she also realized his time would become even more precious. She didn't want to become involved, but she did want some of his time to convince him of the merits of her work project. "No wonder you're so busy."

"Well, thankfully I brought some papers to work on down here. It won't be a total loss."

"Obviously you don't leave home without your briefcase."

A smile crinkled the corners of his eyes as he indicated she leave the living room ahead of him. "I suppose you're right. I don't. Never know when you can snatch a few minutes to work."

In the foyer, she faced him. "You really do have it bad." His attitude confirmed her need to keep her distance emotionally. Her father was a workaholic, and she knew how hard that was on a relationship.

"How so?"

"Here you've been given a golden opportunity to

kick back and relax in a gorgeous setting, and all you can think about is work." The second she saw his smile vanish, his body stiffen, she knew she had overstepped her bounds, but she had always spoken her mind and she wasn't going to stop now even if it meant angering him.

"I grew up here. I've seen it all."

"But I haven't. I've never been to New Orleans. I realize this wasn't part of the date, but can you forget IFI for one day and show me some of the sights after church?" Her heartbeat thundered in her ears; her hands were clammy. She was amazed at her boldness.

"First you talk me into going to a meeting Thursday night and now you want me to show you New Orleans?"

Her gaze coupled with his. "Yes, brazen of me, isn't it?"

"You know, I'm beginning to think your talents are wasted as a teacher. You should have been a negotiator."

"Then you will?"

"Yes."

"In that case, I'll say good-night. It's been a long day." She placed her foot on the first step, intending to escape as quickly as Ruth in case he decided to change his mind.

"Sadie, by the way, did all your wishes come true?"

He was directly behind her, his words a caress. Splinters of awareness shot through her as she slowly turned toward him. They were only inches apart. The silver fire in his eyes unraveled her, sending her heart clamoring. Her teeth sank into her lower lip while she clasped together her damp palms as though they would be an adequate shield between them.

"Did they, Sadie?"

She swallowed several times, afraid her voice wouldn't work when she spoke. "Almost."

"What hasn't come true yet?"

Her throat closed. Her fourth wish swirled in her mind like a kaleidoscope. "Bad luck to say."

"How can I help you if you don't tell me what it is?"

Her gaze slid away from the bright look in his eyes. She focused on a point beyond his shoulder and frantically searched for a way not to tell him what her fourth wish had been.

His finger whispered across her cheek, startling her. Her gaze flew to his face. "I know I shouldn't pry, but you have my curiosity aroused, Sadie. And since I got the impression I was involved in the wishes—"

"I wanted to eat a Cajun meal. I wanted you to support our Special Olympics program and come to the high school on Thursday night."

Sparks of amusement lit his eyes as he looked at her face. "That's not all, Sadie."

She could feel the heat of her blush. Why did her face have to be read like an open book? "You know, you must be a tough negotiator yourself."

"I wouldn't be where I am today if I wasn't." He cut the space between them even more.

Sadie swallowed hard and backed up the stairs. "Well, tomorrow is going to be a busy day so I'd better get to bed." She whirled and fled upstairs, aware of Andrew's gaze on her the whole way.

* * *

Swirls of fog obscured Sadie's view from the balcony. Wispy gray fingers slithered among the plants in the garden below, giving the landscape a ghostly appearance. She shivered and hugged herself even though the air was warm and peppered with the scent of flowers. She imagined the history this place could tell if it could speak.

The moment she thought about history her mind turned to her father. She didn't want him to intrude on her time in New Orleans, but for some reason she felt vulnerable, fragile, like a magnolia blossom. It had taken years to toughen herself to her father's expectations of her.

A memory, clear as if it had happened yesterday, imposed itself on her and whisked away what composure she had left. She'd been ten and learning to dive off a springboard. Over and over her father had worked with her to accomplish that feat one afternoon. After one particular attempt when she'd hit the water at an awkward angle and hurt her arm, she'd sat on the side of the pool with tears streaming down her cheeks. She'd rubbed her arm and looked at her father for some support and love. All she could remember was the anger on his face, his feet braced apart, his hands on his hips. He'd ordered her onto the diving board again. He refused to let her quit until she'd attained her goal. No child of his would ever quit, he'd declared, and they had stayed until the sun had gone down and she'd finally dived into the water with perfect form.

A sound penetrated Sadie's mind, whisking her away from her memories. She blinked, focusing on her surroundings, trying to slow the rapid beating of her heart.

"Sadie?"

She turned from the railing and saw Andrew walking toward her. Bold, tall, an imposing figure. She squeezed her eyes shut and wished he would go away—at least until she had control of her emotions. He was invading her life, making it impossible to keep her distance.

"I thought you were in bed." Sadie automatically fell back a few steps when she discovered Andrew dangerously close. Her heartbeat hadn't slowed its frantic pace, and she had to force herself to take deep, calming breaths of the moisture-laden air that smelled of night and flowers.

"And I thought you were asleep."

"I guess neither of us could sleep. Strange beds do that to me." And the fact she couldn't get him out of her mind, she thought, glad her face was in the shadows. "I was working and came out here to take a break."

"You allow yourself breaks?"

His chuckle was as warm and caressing as the night with its scents of roses and jasmine. "From time to time, especially when I was finding all I was doing was staring at the computer." He leaned close and whispered, "You want to know something? I was even wishing I had put some video games on my laptop."

"No? Really! Your secret is safe with me. I won't tell a soul that *the* Andrew Knight thought about playing a video game, especially when he should have been working."

His laughter filled the air. "You have corrupted me!"

"It must be the late hour. In the clear light of day I'm sure the old Andrew will be back."

"He better be. I have an important report due in two days."

Suddenly the lightheartedness evaporated between them replaced by a subtle tension that tautened Andrew's body. Sadie felt it move up him, and she didn't want the businessman to return just yet. "You said you were from this area?"

"Yes. I grew up near here and went to Tulane for college."

"May I see where tomorrow?"

"It's not on any tour of New Orleans I know of," he said, a strange huskiness in his voice.

Even though she couldn't see his expression clearly in the dim light from her bedroom, she instantly felt the subject of his childhood home was taboo. "What is on the tour?"

He shrugged. "What do you want to see?"

"I don't know. I've never been here. You're the tour guide."

"In that case I'll take you to the usual haunts. The French Quarter. The river."

"What did you do for fun when you lived here?"

The tension was no longer subtle. Sadie didn't need to see his face to feel tension seeping from every pore. The night sounds magnified the silence between them.

"I would escape to the bayou."

Escape? Sadie frowned. Visions of all the movies she'd seen located in the bayous flashed across her mind, and she shivered. "That's one place we can skip. Snakes are my least favorite animal. I know they are important in nature's scheme, but I prefer them behind two-inch-thick glass at a zoo." She forced a lightness into her tone, determined to ease the strain that had sprung up between them.

"How do you feel about alligators?"

"I have a healthy respect for their sharp teeth, their slashing tails. You used to see alligators?"

"Yep. We'd go looking for them."

"Why?" Her voice squeaked.

"For the thrill of it."

"When in the world did you pick up the hobbies of golf and reading?"

"When I grew up and became wiser," he said with a laugh.

"I'm not sure if I have."

"I think you've grown up. So it must be the wiser part," he murmured in the dark night.

She tried to think of something to say. But for once she was speechless. Definitely the wise part. If she were wise, she would have never come to New Orleans. If she were wise, she wouldn't be out here on the balcony with a man who had stolen into her life in a few short days. If she were wise, she would be on the next flight out of here regardless of its destination.

The blackness seemed to close around Andrew and

her, heightening her perception of him. She tried to inhale deep breaths, but each one was infused with his scent of sandalwood. The intensity of the moment was almost tangible, as if Sadie could grab it and hold it in her palm.

He moved toward her, his arm brushing hers. "Do you ever do things just for the thrill of it?" he asked, his question loaded with a hazardous potency she knew she should avoid.

She stepped back, coming up against a column. "Yes."

"Do you like to take risks?"

"Yes—within reason."

"Within reason? What limits do you set for yourself?"

He was a breath away, and she couldn't think with any kind of reason at all. She frantically searched her mind for an answer, but all she could think about was his nearness. Somehow she knew he was in a dangerous mood, as if he were challenging her to try to invade his privacy.

"When I take a risk, there has to be a reasonable chance it's worth it." She licked her lips nervously.

"And if you find out it's not after plunging in, what do you do?" He bent closer, one arm braced on the column near her head.

"I cut my losses. I'm a risk taker, not a fool." She hoped, she added silently, wondering if being here was a step in that direction.

"Interesting. I don't take risks in my life except in business."

"Why not? I don't see you afraid of much." Again she wet her lips, her teeth nibbling on the lower one.

"We all have our fears, Sadie. But to answer your question, I take so many in my professional life that there's nothing left for my personal one."

"Show me where you grew up." She threw the challenge out to defuse the charged moment, to force him to back off.

"You do like to take risks, don't you?"

Sadie gulped, sparks of danger charging the air. "Risks are what make me feel alive. Living would be boring if I never did anything a little daring. Once when I was careening down a mountain slope I wasn't ready to handle, my life flashed before my eyes. It didn't take long. I made it to the bottom and vowed there would be more than school in my life. I became active in my church. Took up several sports other than skiing. I decided to go to college and do what *I* wanted, not what my father wished for me."

"I had expected a yes or no answer." He chuckled, smoothing a strand of her hair behind her ear. "You're a woman of many words."

"Especially when I'm nervous." The high pitch of her voice conveyed her nervousness while she felt paralyzed against the column.

"I make you nervous?"

"Don't sound so surprised. I think you're aware of your effect on me."

His chuckle danced on the warm air again. "I do like your honesty, Sadie Spencer."

A blush tinted her cheeks. She hadn't lied to him, but

she hadn't told him the whole truth concerning why she had sought him out for a date. She would have to find the right moment and tell him soon before she lost her heart to him.

Andrew pulled away completely and grabbed her hand. "Let's go for a ride."

"Where?"

"You wanted to see where I grew up. I'll show you."

She stood her ground, forcing him to turn toward her. "Are you sure you want to?"

He shook his head. "You just asked me twice to show you and now you don't want to go. Make up your mind."

She straightened. "I sensed it wasn't something you wanted to do. I was just trying to be sensitive to you."

"I didn't want to at first. Now I do. A guy can change his mind."

"Why?"

"I'm not sure why, Sadie. I don't usually look backward. Maybe being here is the reason. Maybe it's you. I haven't shared my childhood with many."

"Then I'd be honored to see the house you grew up in."

"Actually we have two places to visit." His hold tightened around her hand.

"Just two. You were lucky. My father taught at several colleges before coming to Cimarron City University. We moved around a lot while I was growing up."

"Then we have something else in common. I did, too," he said, a strain in his voice that transmitted pain. "But these two places are the only ones that count."

* * *

Sadie stood staring at the vacant lot, overgrown, with the remains of a chimney poking through the lush undergrowth, and her heart throbbed with a slow beat. A lump was wedged in her throat, making any comment difficult.

"I haven't been able to sell this place. I should," Andrew said in a monotone as if he were reliving every horrendous moment. "I was ten when it happened. We were all asleep when the fire broke out. I got out. My parents and younger sister didn't. I watched as the flames destroyed my life."

Knowing words couldn't comfort, Sadie took his hand in hers and squeezed gently, letting the silence lengthen between them, the sound of crickets chirping filling the void.

"After that I was shuffled among half a dozen foster families over the next several years. I wasn't an easy boy to deal with. I had a lot of anger inside of me."

"You had no family?"

"No one who would take in a rebellious ten-year-old." He stared at the chimney, deep in thought. "Actually when I reached high school, I was put with Tom Dawson, and my whole life was changed." A smile graced his mouth for a few seconds before vanishing. "It wasn't easy at first. But Tom wouldn't give up on me. He made me understand that God had his reasons for sparing my life in the fire and that it was useless to fight His plan. I started going to the church where he was a pastor. For two years I had a relatively normal life, until..." His voice trailed off into nothingness.

"What happened?"

"For the second time in my life God took my family away. After that I gave up on having a family."

"And God?"

"I found it was better to rely only on myself. It's worked for the past twenty years just fine."

"Has it?" While she had been struggling to make her father accept her, failures and all, Andrew had had a far different childhood. Anguish twisted in her chest.

He turned toward her, grasping her other hand in his. "I didn't tell you this for your pity. My childhood toughened me. I don't let my emotions govern me and I'm much better off."

"Are you?"

"Yes."

"Why are you telling me this then? Are you warning me?"

"Yes." He inched closer. "I'm thirty-seven years old and have never been seriously involved with anyone. My work is my life and that is the way I've wanted it."

She didn't back away even though with each sentence he came a little nearer. She had spent a good part of her life trying to please her father and always failing. She had watched her mother doing the same thing. She had vowed years ago never to go through that again. Coming in second in a relationship was unacceptable to her. "Then you have nothing to worry about. My emotions are all tied up with my class. I have fifteen students who need me. I have no need for any other kind of relationship in my life except friendship."

"You know why I'm running away. Why are you, Sadie?"

## Chapter Four

How could she tell Andrew she was afraid to commit because of her parents, especially her father? Sadie wondered, remembering Andrew's story about his parents and the anguish he experienced losing them. With her fingers linked through his, she stared at the crumbling chimney and tried to form the words to explain her fear.

He released her hands and shifted away from her. "I'm sorry. I shouldn't have asked. I just warned you about me and then I turn around and ask such a personal question. Our—acquaintance doesn't warrant that."

Acquaintance, not relationship or even friendship. Closing her eyes for a few seconds, she could almost imagine the smell of the fire that had torn his life in two. He deserved an answer. She sucked in a deep breath of moisture-laden air and said, "I grew up in a home with both parents, but it was difficult being raised by a father who demanded perfection from me and my mother. I could never do anything to please him. I tried. I really did." Tears stung her eyes. She choked back the lump of emotions rising in her throat. She'd never told anyone else that, and surprisingly it felt right.

The stillness magnified the importance of what had happened. His expression showed disquieting astonishment, as if he couldn't quite believe they both had ignored years of holding secrets to reveal something of themselves.

Andrew drew her against him. "I propose no more journeys into the past. I know you didn't come on this date to relive bad memories. I certainly didn't. We look forward from here on out."

Listening to the steady beat of his heart soothed her tattered nerves. "Sounds like a deal to me. Where do we go from here?"

"I was going to show you Tom's house, but that's the past. Are you sleepy?"

She shook her head, leaning to look into his face. The gray light of dawn fingered across the eastern sky, declaring a new day.

"Neither am I." A smile graced his mouth. "I know a café not far from here that serves wonderful beignets and coffee New Orleans style. They used to make the best beignets in these parts. Do you think you're up for that?"

"Are you kidding? You can't come to New Orleans and not sample one, and some chicory coffee, too."

It was a fifteen-minute drive to the small café. Its

gray exterior with broken pieces of wood in the railing of the porch proclaimed it had seen better days. But inside, the place was spotless, the chrome shined and the wood polished. Sadie noticed the café was already crowded, and the sun had just risen. Sliding into a booth across from Andrew, she looked out the picture window at the golden light spreading rapidly across the land-scape. Through the branches of the large live oak tree with Spanish moss draped on its limbs, the sun illumi-nated the sky in streaks of orange, rose and yellow.

She stifled a yawn. "I know I'm going to regret this. I haven't stayed up all night like this in years—since college when I had to study for my finals."

"A cup of chicory coffee ought to keep you up." Andrew gave their order to the waitress who stopped by the table on the way to the booth next to them. "I think I can remember pulling a few all-nighters back in my college days, even though that seems a lifetime ago."

"You're not *that* old." Sadie smiled at the harried waitress as she poured their cups full of the steaming coffee, then rushed away.

"I sometimes feel older than my thirty-seven years."

"Then you should teach high schoolers. They keep me young."

"Now *I* have to say *you* aren't that old."

"I figure I'll be saying that when I grow old and gray-headed." Taking a sip of her brew, Sadie relished the strong flavor that indeed would help keep her awake.

The waitress slapped the plates of beignets on the

table and hurried to another booth. The bell over the door chimed as more customers came into the café. The smell of coffee and fried food infused the air while the sounds of different conversations floated to Sadie.

She allowed her beignet to cool for a minute, then gingerly picked it up between her thumb and forefinger. She took a breath, and white confectioners' sugar flew everywhere.

"Oh, my, you should have warned me," she said with a laugh, noticing the powder adorning the black shirt she'd borrowed from Ruth.

"And miss the initiation?" Andrew raised a brow as he carefully took a bite of his beignet.

After tucking a napkin into her shirt like a bib, Sadie savored the sweet taste of her food between sips of coffee. The tastes complemented each other, making this New Orleans breakfast an experience she would remember. But she knew the main reason she would remember and relish this trip was the man sitting across from her.

When she'd finished three beignets, he asked, "Want any more?"

She shook her head.

He reached across the table and brushed the side of her cheek with his napkin. "You still had some sugar there. I think in the short time I've known you I've had more breakfasts than in all of last year."

Sadie glanced at her empty plate with a dusting of white all over it. "I don't think we should classify this as a true breakfast, or the one I fixed you last weekend.

One day I'll prepare you what I consider a true breakfast." The second she extended the invitation she wished she could retract it. She bit the inside of her cheek to keep from making the situation any worse.

His gaze captured hers. "I just might have to take you up on that when my life settles down."

"After the fight for the presidency?"

"Yes."

"You think your life will be simpler then?"

"I hope so."

"That doesn't sound like a man eager to take on more."

"I'm a man eager to move on to the next challenge."

"And work is the only challenge you see?"

His jaw clenched, a nerve in his cheek twitching. "Yes—and that's the way I like it."

He might as well be wearing an off-limits sign around his neck. Sadie finished the last sip of coffee. "I find my work a challenge, but I like to balance it with other things. I enjoy my church and coaching Special Olympics." She lifted her arm to glance at her watch. "Speaking of church, when does it start? I don't want to hold up Ruth and Darrell."

Andrew tossed some money on the table. "I'm not sure, so we'd better go. I don't want to hold them up, either. I've faced Ruth's wrath before, and it's an experience I would like to forgo."

The quaint small church, freshly painted white with forest green trim, sat nestled among live oaks, tall pines and magnolia trees. As soon as Darrell pulled into the parking lot at the side of the building, Sadie felt waves of tension emanating from Andrew, who was next to her in the back seat.

Carrie leaped from the car while Darrell and Ruth gathered up their belongings and followed their daughter. Andrew remained in the back seat, the taut set of his shoulders and his fisted hands indicating something was terribly wrong.

Sadie slipped her hand over his clenched one. "Want to tell me about it?"

"Tom was the pastor of this church. I attended it when I was young."

"And you haven't been back?"

"Could never bring myself to. I don't think I can go inside."

"Do you want me to sit with you?"

"No." His answer was clipped, said through clamped teeth. He sucked in a deep breath, held it for a moment then released it slowly. "No, it's about time I put the past behind me."

Sadie laced her fingers through his and walked beside him up the stairs and into the church. Everyone was standing and singing the opening hymn, the rafters of the sanctuary vibrating with the sweet tones of "Amazing Grace." Immediately Sadie felt at ease, as though she'd come home.

The inside was simply decorated. The most ornate aspect was the eight stained-glass windows depicting scenes from the Old Testament. Light poured in through the floor-to-ceiling windows and danced on the polished wooden floor. Lemon wax and various perfumes scented the air. Sadie scanned the church for the Madisons.

Andrew's grip on her hand tightened as the organ swelled for the final notes of the song. Sadie slanted a look toward him and noticed the tense set to his expression, the taut line of his body and wondered if he would stay. Indecision played across his features.

The hymn ended, and the congregation began to sit. Sadie spied Darrell and motioned to Andrew. He again fortified himself with a bracing breath and moved down the center aisle toward the middle. Her heart ached with what Andrew must be going through. Wrestling with memories was hard, and she suspected he didn't often do it. To him the past wasn't something to relive.

The service flew by. Sadie enjoyed the sermon about overcoming fear. The pastor quoted Isaiah 41:13. "For I the Lord thy God will hold thy right hand, saying unto thee, Fear not; I will help thee." She felt Andrew's fingers close about hers. The gentle pressure of his touch through the rest of the sermon brought tears to her eyes. By the time she sang the final hymn, she had herself under control.

At the end Andrew hung back and let everyone else file out, even Darrell and his family. He told them he would be along in a moment. His friend took one look at Andrew's expression and nodded.

Sadie stood beside Andrew, searching for the right words to say. *Lord, how do I help him through this?*

When the church was empty, Andrew sank down onto the pew, his shoulders hunched, his head drooping. Sadie reached out to lay her hand on him, but didn't. She didn't have the right to intrude, and yet she realized she wished she did. Instead, she dropped her arm to her side and bowed her head. *Heavenly Father, give me the insight I need. He is hurting, and I want to be there for him.*

The silence of the church echoed through Sadie's mind. In the distance she heard the murmurs of the congregation just outside the open double doors. The cool autumn breeze blew in, carrying with it the hint of moisture and honeysuckle. She waited, still not sure what she could do to ease Andrew's burden.

He lifted his head and stared at the altar. "I should have come back before this."

"Why didn't you?"

"I didn't know if I could handle it. Now I know I can." His gaze swung to hers. "I can put my past behind me, where it belongs, once and for all. I've let it control me more than I thought. Now it won't."

The tone and finality of his words took her by surprise.

"I should be angry at Darrell and Ruth. They didn't tell me they went to this church."

"Perhaps they didn't realize how much it affected you."

"We went to high school together. They knew."

"Then they thought it was time you dealt with what happened to Tom."

"Death is what happened to Tom. It's that simple."

"Is it?"

"I learned early not to care too much." Anger, suppressed but under the surface, sounded in his voice as he fought to erase any emotion in his expression.

"Then why did it bother you to come back here?" she asked, realizing she was intruding on his private life.

"Memories." His grin was lopsided, self-mocking. "I guess I'm mortal, like everyone else. Until Darrell pulled up to this church, I didn't realize just how much it would affect me. Now that I think about it, I probably wouldn't have said anything to him at the house. I would have shrugged and thought it wasn't a big deal."

"But it was?"

His look was sharp. It pierced her. "Yes, it was, but not now. Tom is gone. My family is gone. There's nothing I can do about those facts. But I can't let them govern my life."

"So they won't? I wish I could get a handle on my life that easily."

"Life moves forward, not backward."

The determination in his voice underscored his feelings more than the words he'd spoken. Sadie wished she could separate her past from the present, from the future. But who she was was wrapped up in that past. And the same was true for Andrew. What was going to happen when his past finally caught up with him and he was forced to deal with it?

"I have goals, plans."

"What about God in all those plans? Have you made peace with Him today?"

"I'm not at war with Him." Andrew surged to his feet.

"Then you don't blame Him for your family and Tom's deaths?" She rose, standing only a foot from him.

"I don't blame Him. I don't depend on Him, either. God exists. That's all."

"It's that simple," Sadie countered, wanting to shake some sense into the man.

"Simple? Life isn't simple. Death is, but not life." Andrew signaled with a wave of his hand for Sadie to step to the center aisle. "Darrell and Ruth will wonder what's happened to us. We'd better leave."

Sadie saw his closed expression and knew he'd shut down his emotions. He was very good at doing that. Coming to New Orleans opened a door on his past that he usually was very successful at keeping locked.

The breeze from the river ruffled the stray strands of Sadie's hair, making them dance, enticing her to let down her guard and relish the beautiful day. She loved being on the water. The sounds of a steamboat cutting a path toward a far-off pier and a gull overhead insinuated their way into her mind. She relaxed against the railing…

*"It's not that difficult, Sadie, to learn to ski. I don't have all day."* Her father's words rang above the roar of the motorboat. *"This is the last time. If you can't get up, that's it."*

Her limbs ached with fatigue. She squinted and tried to make out the figure of her father, leaning over the side of the boat as he shoved the loose ski toward her. The *glare of the sun caused her eyes to burn. She saw the ski slide past her and grabbed for it. She missed, her hand grabbing a fist full of water.*

*"Sadie, hurry up. It's getting late."*

*She swam toward the ski and struggled into it. Her arms shook. Her legs felt as though they were made of rubber. But she would stand up on the skis this time or— She wouldn't complete the thought. She would just do it. Her father didn't allow for any option but success. And he didn't like to waste time obtaining that success.*

*The boat darted forward. Her arms jerked straight. She locked her elbows and prayed.*

*When she rose out of the water, she wanted to shout her joy. She wobbled. Tensing, she focused all her attention on staying up for longer than a second.*

*Minutes later she crashed into the water. Elated that she'd finally gotten up on her skis after only four tries, she was ready to go again. She wanted to fly over the wake like her friend Sally did.*

*"We need to head back, Sadie. Come on in." Her father reached out to help her into the boat.*

*She whipped the wet hair out of her eyes and grasped her father's hand. "I did it!"*

*Her father didn't say a word. All Sadie could remember was the frown carved deep into his tanned features as he hoisted her out of the water....*

The sound of the steamboat's horn jolted Sadie from her memories. Leaning on the white railing, she watched the people on the pier and tried to compose herself before having to face Andrew.

He shifted next to her. "You were a million miles away," he murmured close to her ear.

"No, just a journey into the past." She glanced at him and saw the puzzled expression in his eyes. "I guess this is a day for that."

"I thought this was your first trip to New Orleans?"

"It is. But it's not my first time being on a river." She hoped her crisp tone conveyed her reluctance to discuss her past. They each had memories they didn't want to delve too far into.

"What did you think of this ride?"

"I could get used to this mode of transportation. It's slow, relaxing. I like listening to the paddle wheel. Sorta like a waterfall. I could fall asleep listening to it." She twisted to face him squarely. "I doubt I'll be very good tomorrow at school. Think we can bottle this sound and play it later on our way home?"

He smiled. "I'll check the musical repertoire on the plane. Maybe there's something that'll help. But to tell you the truth I don't even know if it has a sound system."

"You don't?"

"I'm always working."

"The story of your life?"

Momentarily a dark storm edged into his expression. "There's nothing wrong with that."

"I think we've had this discussion about all work and no play. I have no intentions of trying to change you."

"You don't?" Skepticism was evident in his question and the lift of his brow.

"Nope. You're a big boy now. If you want to work your life away, that's your business. Of course, at the end of a day you might ask yourself what you'll have for it in, say, twenty years."

Andrew didn't reply but turned away as if he were interested in watching the docking process. Sadie thought he was going to ignore what she'd said until he looked at her and declared, "After I get the presidency, I'll have that time to play."

She arched a brow, much as he had a moment before. "You will? You keep saying that. Are you sure you won't just substitute another goal that will drive you to work even harder?"

His frown furrowed his brow, his lips compressed into a slash. "I think it's time for us to leave the boat."

He started to walk toward the gangplank. Sadie placed a hand on his arm to halt him. "Forget what I've said, Andrew. I don't want those careless remarks to dampen the rest of the afternoon. I've had such a good time so far. The French Quarter was wonderful. Everything I thought it would be. Is it a deal? Next time you can just put your hand over my mouth to stop me from putting my foot in it."

The tension eased from his shoulders. He stuck his hand out for her to shake. "That's a deal I'll accept. Now let me understand. I can put my hand over your mouth anytime I think you're going to stick your foot into it?"

She narrowed her eyes in mock anger. "No. Only when referring to your diligent work habits and nonexistent play—"

He pressed his hand over her mouth, the rough texture of his palm warm against the softness of her lips. "You were saying?"

She glared at him and mumbled, "Funny."

"I try to be, in rare moments of playfulness." He hooked his arm through hers and began to lead her toward the gangplank.

"Then you think I should savor this rare moment?"

"Funny," he said, mimicking her tone and look. "We need to hurry if we're going to make this next stop before it's too late."

She glanced at her watch. "It's a little early for dinner. Where are we going?"

"Why do you think I'm going to tell you when I haven't all afternoon? I like to surprise you."

"Did I tell you I hated surprises? I actually open all my Christmas presents ahead of time then rewrap them so no one knows."

His laughter filled the air with a richness she could get used to. "I think my family figured it out, though. They don't bother to wrap them anymore. They just give me mine in a bag with a token amount of tissue to cover the gift."

"I can just picture you getting up when everyone else in the family is asleep and sneaking into the living room to open your gifts."

"That's why my parents could never get me to sleep on Christmas Eve. I couldn't wait for Santa Claus and those presents I didn't know about. It used to kill me. My curiosity is a horrible burden I must bear."

"Somehow that doesn't surprise me."

"Do I note a touch of sarcasm?"

"Never from my lips."

Darrell and Ruth's driver was waiting for them by the curb. Sadie had a strong suspicion the man knew Andrew's plans. The driver went about his duties in silence as though Andrew had mapped out everything before they had started. Of course, he had. Andrew wouldn't know any other way to do it. Spontaneity wasn't in his vocabulary. She would have to see if she could change that—at least for this one day.

When they pulled up to a tall building by the Mississippi, Sadie wasn't sure what to expect. When they arrived at the Top of the Mart, Sadie was charmed by the spectacular view it offered of New Orleans. She saw the wide river winding through the Crescent City, the haze that clung to the horizon. The late afternoon sun was sinking in the west as they were shown to a table. The day's shadows lengthened over the city as though they were fingers reaching out to all its parts.

"This is beautiful. What a way to see a place." Sadie craned to look as far as she could.

"This is definitely a different perspective of New Orleans than the one a person gets from the French Quarter or the river."

"It's romantic. I didn't know you had it in you," she said without thinking, regretting the words the second they were out of her mouth.

"Ouch, I think."

"What I mean is that you are so practical and…" Her voice faded into silence as her gaze found his.

She looked away, forcing herself to concentrate on the sights of New Orleans at dusk. The yellow-orange western horizon set the sky on fire. Streaks of various shades of red ribboned across the heavens like streamers on a colorful package, enticing her to open it.

The silence between them lasted until after the waitress took their orders. When Andrew leaned forward, his words returned her attention to his face. "I have to admit that I don't usually have time to be, as you say, romantic. But in New Orleans I find it easier. This city lends itself to romance."

"Yes, it does have a certain flair."

"But you are right about me being practical. I'm a businessman first and foremost."

She heard the warning in his voice. "Are you saying a businessman can't be romantic? Is there something you take in college that wipes that from your system?"

"No, I believe it's in my genes. You're right, I can't speak for other businessmen."

His chuckle flowed over her, and she wished again that he would laugh more. Sadie liked the way he relaxed when he smiled. His whole face lit, warming every inch of her. "Being practical doesn't mean you can't be romantic. I would say being romantic was very practical. A few romantic gestures can go a long way in a relationship. That can make life much easier, don't you think?"

"I'll keep that in mind when I have time for a relationship."

"Ah, yes. Your fight for the presidency. Why do you want to be the president of the company?"

His eyes widened. He waited until after the waitress had placed their coffee in front of them before answering. "Why not? I've done just about everything else I wanted to at IFI. It's the next logical step."

"You sound like a restless man. Never satisfied with what you have."

"You make ambition sound like a dirty word."

"Are you satisfied?"

"Yes," he answered without a thought. "If I weren't, I wouldn't be doing what I'm doing. There's one thing I don't do. I don't waste my time."

"Has today been a waste?" Sadie couldn't believe she was asking the question, but often, to her regret, she spoke her mind.

His probing look snared hers. He brought his cup to his mouth and took a sip, never breaking eye contact with her. "No. Contrary to what you believe, I sometimes do recognize the need to get away from the office."

Sadie was the one to look away first. She studied the darkening landscape of New Orleans, which glittered with lights. It reminded her of Christmas, her favorite holiday.

"In fact, Sadie, I'm grateful that you stayed. I'd forgotten what New Orleans could be like. I've enjoyed seeing my birthplace through your eyes."

The warmth in his regard robbed her of coherent thought. From across a crowded room, his gaze had a way of drawing her toward him, and suddenly she was frightened by the power this man was beginning to have over her. She had never given another human being that kind of power since she had given up trying to prove herself to her father. She prided herself on being her own person, never depending on anyone for emotional support. But the newfound feelings swirling inside of her were making a mockery of that declaration. Were she and Andrew more alike than she cared to acknowledge? Neither wanted to admit depending on another. But whereas he prided himself on standing totally alone, she sought the Lord's guidance.

When they left the restaurant in the French Quarter, Sadie took a deep breath of the cool night air, enhanced with Cajun spices and the scent of the river nearby. "I'm stuffed. That was delicious."

Andrew started to guide her toward the limousine waiting by the curb, but she hung back. "I need to walk this dinner off, Andrew. We're not far from the river. When do we have to be at the airport?"

"The plane doesn't have to be back until tomorrow morning."

"You mean we could stay out all night," she whispered as though she were a teenager plotting to foil her parents.

"I thought you had school tomorrow."

"I do, and I suppose after not sleeping much last night I would regret it. But it's fun to defy the laws of nature every once in a while."

Andrew walked to the driver, said a few words to the man, then came back to Sadie. "I told him to take my luggage to the plane and to tell the pilot we'll be a while longer. We'll take a cab when the mood strikes us to leave. What do you want to do? It's your turn to show me what you want."

It took a supreme effort for Sadie to keep her mouth from dropping open. "What about your plans?"

He snapped his fingers. "Erased."

"At the stroke of midnight you aren't going to turn into a pumpkin?"

"No. And I suspect I require less sleep than you do."

She tucked her arm through his, liking the feel of him at her side. "Then let's walk. I believe I remember that Jackson Square isn't too far from here."

When they arrived at Jackson Square, Sadie surveyed the crowd of people milling about, the artists displaying their work, some musicians entertaining the tourists with the blues. The aroma of various foods vying for dominance saturated the air. The sounds of laughter and conversations wafted to her. "I want something to take back to Cimarron City. Let's get our portrait drawn."

"Together?"

"Yes, cheaper that way." Sadie tugged on his arm.

After negotiating a price for their portrait, Andrew sat

slightly behind her and to the right. "I hope this doesn't take too long. I'm not very good at just sitting," he whispered into her ear, sending tingles down her neck.

"Why doesn't that surprise me? Now be good. This isn't a painful process."

Ten minutes later Sadie had her doubts about that. It was pure torture to be sitting so close to Andrew, breathing in his clean scent, which mingled with the aromas of the river, Cajun spices and flowers in the park. Feeling him along her back and side, she decided this was definitely not a good idea and scooted away from him. His hand clamped on her shoulder and stopped her movement.

"Sit still. I thought I was the one with the problem," he whispered. "I don't want to have to sit here any longer than necessary."

Andrew started to remove his hand from her when the young man drawing the portrait said, "No. I like that better. Drape your arm like this." He came up to them and positioned Andrew's arm along hers so he cradled her to him, as though they had been friends a long time.

Okay, so she had made it worse rather than better by trying to put some space between them. She could do this. Surely it wouldn't last much longer—she hoped. But ten minutes later her nerves were as taut as a stretched rubber band about to snap. She was tired. That had to be the reason for this unusual reaction to Andrew, that and the spell New Orleans had cast on her.

"There. Done," the man said, a smile of satisfaction on his young face.

Sadie was almost afraid to look at the portrait. She knew what she would see, and she was disconcerted when she finally stood and peered at the drawing. The dreamy expression on her face spoke volumes that she wished she could have masked, but she had always been easy to read. A burden she had to bear, she decided as she slanted a glance at Andrew to gauge his reaction.

He studied the portrait, his brow knitted with a thoughtful expression as if he had just discovered something he wasn't sure about. She knew that feeling. The portrait before them showed a couple who looked perfect together, a couple who belonged together, two halves of a whole. What had been captured on the canvas in such a short time exposed her to the world, and that bothered her more than she cared to acknowledge. This definitely hadn't been one of her better ideas. All she wanted Andrew to do was pay the young man, wrap the portrait up and never peer at it again.

"Do we have time for one more thing?" Sadie asked when they were walking away from the man who had drawn their picture.

"I'm afraid to say yes for fear of what you'll come up with. After all, you were the one who bid on me at the auction just so you could see me about Special Olympics. That should have given me a hint when you told me that. And to think I turned the rest of the evening over to you."

She waited until it was clear to cross the street before answering him. "I just want to see the river at night. There's nothing wrong with that."

Again she was proven wrong when, a few minutes later, she was standing on the Moonwalk by the edge of the river enfolded in a velvety night, the cool breeze stirring the strands of her hair, the scents of beignets and coffee drifting to her from a café not far away. She shivered.

"Cold?"

She didn't reply. Andrew drew her against his length and enveloped her in his arms. She felt as though she had come home in his embrace. Oh, no, she was in trouble again.

"We probably better leave," she murmured, the statement not coming out with any force while her gaze was transfixed by the romantic spill of moonlight on the river.

"Yeah, probably." His whispered words were close to her ear, tickling its shell.

Neither made a move to leave.

She snuggled against him, seeking his warmth. He hugged her closer. The stars, the river, the night cast their magic over her, making her believe anything was possible. And maybe for this one day, it was. Tomorrow they would be in Cimarron City, and life would proceed.

When he turned her to face him, she didn't say a word. Instead, she tilted her head to look into his eyes, hidden in the shadows of night that had woven a spell around them. This was not reality, Sadie repeated silently. They wanted different things from life. They led different lives. And yet, she was drawn to him. She wanted to heal his broken heart, help him see that God hadn't abandoned him all those years ago.

Andrew cupped her face, his fingers combing through her hair. "I enjoyed myself, Sadie."

"But?"

"But we need to leave for the airport. Tomorrow we'll regret staying so long in New Orleans."

Regret? No, she doubted she ever would. "When we're at work trying to stay awake?"

"Yes, exactly." He stepped away, his arms falling to his sides.

Somehow she didn't think that was what he'd really meant. He was already reining in his emotions, closing totally down. She didn't have to see his expression to know how he looked. She could tell by his distancing, his stance that held him apart.

# Chapter Five

The second the seat belt snapped closed, the strap secure about Sadie's hips, she felt trapped, perspiration beading on her upper lip. She gripped the arms of her chair and stared straight ahead. The plane began to taxi to the end of the runway. Her fingernails dug into the cushioned padding.

*Breathe,* she told herself, but the tightness in her chest attested to the fact she couldn't. *Remember the pastor's sermon today about fear.*

"Sadie, are you okay?"

Andrew's question seemed to come from afar, as though he spoke to her from the other end of a long tunnel. Her mind was blank. She was unable to form a coherent sentence. *The fear of man bringeth a snare: but whoso putteth his trust in the Lord shall be safe.* The words from Proverbs 29:25 gave her the strength to turn toward Andrew and offer him a ghost of a smile.

He covered her hand with his, rubbing his warm palm across the backs of her fingers. "Are you afraid of flying?"

"I'm trying not to be."

"I thought you were a risk taker."

"Only when I am in control. I thought about learning to fly—but only for a millisecond."

"That long?"

"Okay, we've established I'm afraid of flying. Please let's not talk about it anymore." Again she recited silently the words from the Bible and again she felt more capable of dealing with this fear.

"Whatever you say." Andrew continued to massage her hand as though he could impart his courage into her. "What would you like to talk about? The weather?"

"Not at the moment, since it directly affects flying," she quipped, glad she could joke about her fear.

"Then tell me about Thursday night. What do you expect me to do?"

She focused her thoughts on her plan to get Andrew involved with her students. For a moment it took her mind away from the fact that the plane was barreling down the runway. "This is an organizational meeting. I want you—" The jet lifted off the ground, and Sadie choked back her next words.

"Don't leave me hanging in suspense, Sadie. You can't say that to a man and not complete the sentence." He pried her hand loose from the padded arm and held it cradled between his palms.

The plane's ascent left her breathless, her heart

speeding as fast as the jet through the air. Sweat popped out on her forehead and rolled down her face. *I am not alone. God is with me.*

"Take a deep breath, Sadie. You look like you're going to faint. How in the world did you make it to New Orleans?"

Sadie followed his advice, and slowly her lungs filled with stale air and her heart eased its frantic beating. "I prayed a lot. I hate to fall apart around others."

"But with me it's okay?"

"Something like that. You should be flattered. I feel comfortable enough around you to fall apart."

"Thanks, I think."

She felt his gaze on her and turned to meet his look. "You're welcome."

The jet leveled off, and her body's reaction to the fact they were thousands of feet in the air settled into a slight case of the nerves. She wiped her free hand across her forehead and upper lip.

She attempted a smile that quivered about the corners of her mouth for a few seconds before disappearing. "I'm not afraid of many things, but flying is one of them. I'm okay, usually, between takeoffs and landings."

"So we have a few hours."

"If the weather holds."

"So what do you expect of me on Thursday?"

"I want you to present the check from IFI and say a few words. That's all. You don't have to stay, but I would love for you to have pizza with us afterward. That is, if you have the time."

"Pizza? Isn't that fattening? I'm surprised a teacher who teaches nutrition would encourage such a dish."

Sadie responded to the teasing tone in his voice with a laugh. "Pizza covers four of the five food groups. If you happen to like pineapple on your pizza, it can cover all five. I think that's pretty nutritious. Besides, you work with what you've got. Teenagers have distinct appetites and are particularly attracted to sugar and fats."

"Then I'll be at the high school at seven with a check, a few words and an appetite for pizza." He unlatched his seat belt and shifted in the chair to a more comfortable position. "Now that the date is almost over, what was your fourth wish?"

The question caught her by surprise. Her eyes widened, and her throat went dry. She remembered her foolish fourth wish, to be kissed by him, and blushed. "Nothing to concern you." She squeaked the words out.

"I don't believe you, Sadie. You're ten shades of red."

"Okay. It does concern you. But that's all you're going to find out." She pressed her lips closed to emphasize her point.

"Oh, now you have my curiosity aroused. You know I'm not going to let this drop."

She narrowed her eyes and folded her arms across her chest.

He laughed. "I think I get the hint. Okay, if you won't tell me what it is, then at least tell me when it is fulfilled."

She nodded, feeling the heat in her cheeks spreading. She needed to get their conversation away from wishes and onto a safer topic. "I had two reasons for bidding on you at the auction. One was IFI supporting our Special Olympics team, and the other—" she heaved a sigh and plunged ahead "—the other involved a vocational training program I'm developing at the high school."

Andrew stiffened, his expression neutral.

"I have a student who will be graduating this year." She hurried ahead with her explanation before she lost her nerve. "I would like to place him in a job in the community before he leaves high school. He's a wonderful, hard worker who would be an asset to any company that hired him."

"And you want IFI to hire him?"

"If I can get the biggest employer in Cimarron City to participate in the program, others will follow. I want to try him out on a trial basis for a few hours each afternoon. There's a funding source that will pay his salary while he's training."

"What if it doesn't work out?"

"Then you don't hire him after graduation. But if you agreed to this program, it would be with the serious intention of hiring him when he's out of high school."

"Is this why you couldn't get by Mrs. Fox?"

"Yes."

He frowned, rubbing the back of his neck. "I don't know about this, Sadie."

"Please meet Chris first before you decide."

"Will he be there Thursday night?"

She nodded.

"Now I know why you didn't take your donation and just buy uniforms."

"What I said was true. We need a sponsor, but I won't kid you. My main reason for betting on you was for Chris. If I didn't think this would benefit everyone, especially IFI, I wouldn't have pursued it so vigorously. I just need a chance to prove this job program can work and my students can be a valuable asset to a company."

"This means a lot to you."

It wasn't a question, but she said yes anyway.

"So this whole date was really work to you?"

"It started out that way, but quickly changed last night."

"When?"

"When you took me to see your home."

Silence descended between them, the hum of the engines the only sound.

"You know, I should be angry with you. But how can I be when you've just proven you're more like me than you think?"

"How so?"

"Your work—your students—they're very important to you. Your life revolves around them, I suspect."

"I do have a balance."

"And I don't?"

"What do you think?"

"I don't." He lifted his briefcase onto his lap and opened it. "Which reminds me, I have work to do."

Sadie watched him shuffle through some papers before he pulled out a stack of them. He had effectively shut a door in her face, and she couldn't blame him. She was afraid her plan had backfired.

"That concludes our business. Now I would like to introduce Mr. Andrew Knight from IFI, who has an announcement for us." Smiling at Andrew, Sadie stepped to the side.

He walked to the podium in the high school auditorium and waited for the applause to die down before saying, "Miss Spencer, I appreciate the opportunity to come here tonight and present Cimarron High School Special Olympics team with a check from IFI for two thousand dollars. We are proud to be a sponsor of such a fine endeavor."

Surprised at the generous amount, Sadie took the check from Andrew while her students and their parents cheered and clapped. "On behalf of the team, I want to thank IFI for their support and you for coming tonight." After shaking his hand, she continued, "I hope to see everyone at Mitchell's for pizza."

Several of her students swarmed her and Andrew, wanting to see the check. Sadie held it up for them to look at it, then said, "I don't know about you all, but I'm starved."

"Me, too," a small girl who didn't weigh more than eighty pounds said.

"Does this mean we get new shirts?"

"Chris, this means we get new uniforms." Sadie folded the check and put it into her pocket.

"New ones?" A tall, thin boy with freckles and a ready smile asked.

"Yes, Kevin."

"In time for soccer?" Chris asked, his optimistic gaze fixed on Andrew.

"Not for soccer, but hopefully in time for basketball. Our soccer tournament is next week." Sadie began walking toward the back of the auditorium, where some of the parents were waiting for their children.

Andrew slowed his pace, allowing the students to go ahead of them. "Is that the Chris you want to work at IFI?"

"Yes. He's twenty." Sadie stopped halfway up the center aisle, realizing Chris's small stature might make him appear younger to some people. Only five feet tall, Chris Carter had dark brown eyes, slightly slanted at the corners, and a broad, flat nose. The most appealing part of his appearance was his wide smile, which came readily to his face.

"You comin', Miss Spencer?" Chris called as he started for the back door with his mother.

"Yes, we'll be along." She waved the group on, then turned to Andrew. "Have you made your decision yet?"

"I thought you wanted me to get to know Chris first."

"Yes, of course. Then we'd better hurry." She started forward.

"Why?" Andrew hung back.

"So we can sit at the same table as Chris. He's very popular."

"Does he know about this job you want to get him?"

A few feet away, Sadie pivoted toward Andrew. "He knows I'm looking for a job for him."

"But not at IFI?"

"I didn't want to get his hopes up."

"His hopes up?"

"His father worked at IFI until he died."

"Who was his father?"

"Harold Carter."

"Harold Carter?" Andrew creased his brow. "Didn't he die a few years back from a heart attack?"

"Yes. He was only forty. Chris took it very hard."

The auditorium door slammed shut, and Sadie realized they were the only ones left. She stared at Andrew, drinking in the sight of him in a three-piece gray pinstripe suit with a dark red tie, a bold statement in his otherwise conservative attire. She'd missed him these past few days and often had found herself daydreaming about their thirty-hour date in New Orleans.

"Then we'd better get to Mitchell's. I want to meet this young man. I won't agree to the pilot program unless I think he has a good chance of employment after graduation. That's only fair to everyone."

"What kind of pizza do you like? I'm buying," Sadie said as they left the auditorium.

"Nonsense. I can—"

"You are my guest, Andrew Knight. It's the least I

can do for you, for coming here to present the check in person."

"Canadian bacon. How about you?" Andrew held her car door open for her.

"A supreme with everything on it except anchovies. I'm not big into fish, especially on my pizza."

"Then we agree on something. I'm not either."

"If you don't watch out, before you know it we'll be in complete agreement."

"I doubt that will ever be the case. We look at life entirely differently."

"Ah, but that adds spice to the mix."

"Sometimes too much spice can lead to heartburn."

"At least you know you're alive." Sadie started her engine. "I'll meet you at Mitchell's."

On the short drive, Sadie reflected on what Andrew had said. She'd grown up in a household where her mother had agreed with everything her father said. She often wondered if her mother had an original thought since she'd married. There were times she found herself wanting to stick up for her mother and having to bite her tongue to keep from saying anything. Perhaps her mother and father were very well matched. Or perhaps her mother had discovered it was easier not to disagree. Sadie knew one thing from watching her parents' marriage— she could never be involved with a man who didn't accept her differences. Was there even a man like that?

Sadie pulled into a parking space near the front of the restaurant. Inside Mitchell's, she scanned the tables and saw that Chris and his mother were still alone. While heading toward them, she noticed Andrew enter.

"Mind if we join you?" Sadie asked, aware of Andrew weaving his way through the crowded restaurant toward them.

"Oh, no. It gives me a chance to personally thank Mr. Knight for the generous donation." Amanda Carter removed her purse from a chair so Sadie could sit down.

"Me, too." Chris chimed in as Andrew pulled out the chair next to Sadie and eased into it. "We needed uniforms for ages. Thank you, Mr. Knight." A grin split his face almost ear to ear.

"You're welcome."

"You know what we want, Chris. Do you want to order for us?" Amanda asked, opening her purse for some money.

Chris leaped to his feet. "Sure. Can I have a large soda?"

"No, not so close to your bedtime."

Sadie started to rise. Andrew placed his hand on her arm to still her movements. "I'll order for us. It gives me a chance to talk to Chris."

"Well, then here's—"

"I'm paying."

"But—" Sadie was protesting to a retreating back. She snapped her mouth closed and thought of how heavy-handed her father could be at times, never considering her wishes. Was Andrew like that? Then she realized she was overreacting. Most gentlemen would do exactly what Andrew had done.

"I remember Mr. Knight from when Harold worked at IFI. He'd just been promoted to his new job in human resources, and everyone was glad. They thought he would be fair and willing to try new things. I also heard he works twenty-four seven. How were you able to persuade him to come to the high school tonight?"

Sadie glanced at the man in question and noticed he was talking with Chris. Her student, who had a big grin on his face, laughed and gave Andrew a high five. "It wasn't that difficult. I asked. He accepted," she answered, her gaze still fixed upon Andrew and Chris, deep in conversation.

"Then maybe he isn't immune to a pretty face. At work it was always strictly business with that man, if the rumors are to be believed."

Sadie felt the heat of a blush slowly rise on her face. She remembered Jollie's comments at the bachelor auction and wondered if everyone—at least the women—sat around discussing Andrew Knight. There was an air of vulnerability about him, but he guarded that secret. To the world he presented a confident, controlled facade, which she had glimpsed cracks in.

"I wouldn't know anything about those rumors." Sadie waved to one of her students sitting with her whole family.

"They're coming back to the table. I see Chris has made a new friend. He doesn't know what the word stranger means."

That was one of the things Sadie was counting on.

Chris probably knew all fifteen hundred students at the high school, if all the greetings he received in the hallways were any indication.

"Miss Spencer, Mr. Knight is gonna come see us." Chris slipped into his chair.

"When?"

"I told Chris I would try to come see his soccer match next Friday," Andrew said, setting the drink on the table.

Her eyes widened. "You did?"

"He's never been to a soccer game." Chris stopped one of his friends, who was going back to his table. "This is James. He's one of the goalies."

James mumbled something, his eyes downcast.

"Mr. Knight's coming to see us," Chris announced to James and another student going by.

"Only if I can get away," Andrew tried to explain, but Chris had already jumped up from the table and left to spread the word.

Sadie sank her teeth into her lower lip to keep from smiling. Andrew didn't know what to do to stop the rumor of his visit from flying around the restaurant. He started to rise, then shrugged and relaxed in his chair.

"I guess I'd better try to make it."

She decided to give him an out. "If you can't make it, they'll understand. They love playing in front of people, and you're their newest hero."

"Hero?"

Sadie nearly laughed out loud at the stunned expression on Andrew's face. "They've been wanting new uniforms for quite some time. Wait till you see their old ones on Friday. That is, if you can come." She quickly went on to cover the uncomfortable silence. "They've been practicing for the past month with their special partners."

"Special partners?"

"Students in regular education classes. We play unified soccer. Half the team are students who are Special Olympians and the other half are special partners. Everyone has a lot of fun even if we don't always win."

Five minutes later, Chris came to the table. "They just called our numbers. I'll bring our pizzas."

While standing at the counter waiting for his order, Chris saw a group of high school boys come into Mitchell's. He greeted each one with a high five. Chris dragged one of the students to the table.

"Mr. Knight, this is Cal. He's on the team, too. He practices with us."

"Did you forget our pizzas?" his mother asked, shaking her head as though she were used to this from her son.

Chris smiled sheepishly. "Sorry."

Before Cal returned to his friends, he said, "Nice meeting you. Chris is excited about the new uniforms. He said you're buying them for the team."

"Well, not exactly. IFI is," Andrew said, taking a large sip of his iced tea.

"That's great! My dad works for IFI." Cal joined his friends while Chris carried the first pizza to the table, then retrieved the second one.

The aroma of baking bread and sizzling meats that permeated the restaurant made Sadie's mouth water. Her stomach rumbled. The minute Chris placed her pizza between her and Andrew, she scooped up a large piece and took a bite.

"I know pizza is mega calories, but nothing beats it," she said after washing down her food with a sip of her soda.

For the next ten minutes silence prevailed at the table while they all satisfied their hunger. Halfway through her third piece, one of Sadie's students stopped by the table.

"Miss Spencer, I'll see ya tomorrow." The girl threw her arms about Sadie and hugged her. "You're beautiful."

"Thank you, Melissa. You've made my day."

Chris leaned over the table as though imparting a secret. "Melissa always thinks everyone is beautiful. But she's right about you, Miss Spencer."

"If I wasn't blushing before, I'm sure I am now."

"Yep, you're a nice shade of red," Andrew said with a wink. He lifted his glass and downed the rest of his iced tea, his gaze linked to hers the whole time.

She grinned. "Which clashes with my maroon shirt."

"Oh, no, Miss Spencer, you look great. I like what you're wearing." Chris waved to another student across the room. He rose and tossed down his paper napkin. "Mom, I'll be over there."

Chris left, threading his way through the crowded dining room. Sadie chuckled. "And people ask me why I teach students with special needs. They're absolutely great for the ego."

"I'm beginning to get the picture." Andrew watched Chris for a moment before continuing. "Is there anyone he doesn't know?"

"Not at Cimarron High."

"I can attest to that. Our phone is constantly ringing. Thank goodness I don't have a life outside the home or I would never hear from them." Amanda gathered her purse and stood. "I'd better pull Chris away. Tomorrow is a school day, and it will take him at least an hour to calm down after your news, Mr. Knight. Thank you for the donation." Amanda held out her hand, and Andrew shook it.

"I'm glad IFI could help."

While Chris's mother made her way across the restaurant to get her son, Sadie finished her pizza, suddenly not sure what to say to Andrew. She surveyed her few students who were still eating with their families and friends. Their open, guileless faces confirmed her reason for teaching in the first place.

"Because I want this pilot program to work, I want to run this by Mr. Wilson. If we're going to do this project with your school, I want to do it right."

What would her students say if she followed Melissa's lead and threw her arms around Andrew? She refrained from doing that, but she could feel her whole face beaming with a smile.

"Don't say anything. It's not official, Sadie."

"Not a word from this mouth until you tell me I can."

"Now that's an intriguing idea."

"Let me rephrase that. Not a word from this mouth about the project until you tell me I can. Is that better?"

"No, I like it the other way." His eyes danced with a twinkle.

"If I didn't know better, I would think *the* Andrew Knight is teasing me. I didn't think you had a playful bone in your body."

"I have my moments. And speaking of time—"

"We were?" Sadie couldn't help asking, knowing where the conversation was leading.

"I need to leave. I still have some work to do tonight. I'll walk you to your car."

"You don't have to. This isn't a date."

"Still, I'll walk you to your car."

The firmness underlying his words reminded her again of the control the man exhibited. He wasn't used to people denying him anything. He definitely needed his cage rattled.

"Okay," she said slowly, trying to decide what to do. "I need to say good-night to my students who are still here."

"Fine." A wariness crept into his voice as he watched her push back her chair.

Sadie made the rounds of her five students and their families left at Mitchell's, refusing to look toward the table where she'd had dinner with Andrew. If she caught his hard gaze, she'd probably lose her nerve to teach him a point.

She held Melissa's baby sister for a few minutes, contorting her face into silly expressions to get the child to laugh. She took an extra moment to go over the plans for the soccer tournament the following week with Kevin's mother. By the time she returned to the table twenty minutes had passed. She expected to see Andrew fuming or gone, but he sat calmly, bent over his paper napkin, writing some notes on it.

"I didn't think you had it in you," Sadie said, standing over him.

He peered up, surprised to see her. "What?"

"The patience to wait."

"I have a lot of talents you probably aren't aware of. When you travel as much as I do, you learn real quickly, if you want to keep your sanity intact, ways to occupy your time when you're unexpectedly delayed."

She laughed. "Touché."

He arched one of his dark eyebrows. "Were we having a contest?"

"I think you know very well we were."

In one fluid movement he rose. "Who won?"

"I think we both made our point."

"You don't like someone telling you what to do, and I am capable of going with the flow when I need to. Not such a hopeless case, am I?"

"I never said that." She winked and turned to leave.

Before she had a chance to thrust the restaurant door open, Andrew stepped around her and held it for her. She hurried into the cool night air, glad for its refreshing crispness.

At her car he lounged against the front fender and crossed his arms over his chest. Sadie paused, her hand on the handle, aware she couldn't very well drive away with him leaning against her Honda.

"I thought you had to get back to work."

"I do. I wanted to stop for a moment and—what was it you said? Smell the roses."

"I think you enjoy teasing me."

"It's hard to resist when you make it so much fun."

"I didn't know that word was in your vocabulary."

"You know, if I wasn't such a laid-back kind of guy I would take offense at your constant insistence I don't know how to have a good time."

She almost said, "Prove it," but suppressed the words.

His chuckle floated on the light breeze. "You're too easy to read. I'm just going to have to show you I can have a fun time, like the next guy."

"Oh?" Her doubt drenched that one word.

He shoved away from the fender and straightened, his large presence looming before her and exuding power. "Let's make a deal. If I come to the soccer match, you have to go out with me that evening. I'll show you what I like to do the rare times I do kick back and relax."

"Will you have an answer about the work project by then?"

His chuckles evolved into laughter. "Persistent, aren't you? Yes, I should. What do you say, Sadie? Do you dare find out what I think is fun?"

"I thought the date I bid on was your idea of a fun date."

"Oh, no, far from it. Now, the change in plans to New Orleans was closer to the truth."

Fascinated, against her better judgment, she nodded. "But I have to warn you that I'm usually pretty exhausted after one of these tournaments."

"I'll keep that in mind while planning our date." Andrew gripped the handle and opened her car door. "Till Friday, Sadie."

She slid behind the steering wheel and clasped the cold plastic so tightly her hands ached. What was he up to?

If he hadn't tied it to him coming to the tournament, she could have said no. Who was she kidding? She couldn't say no to his invitation no matter how it was issued. This man intrigued her more than she cared to acknowledge. She was sure if she was around him that could change. After all, he was much too domineering and commanding for her. She'd lived with her father's demands. There was no way she would ever become involved with a man who wouldn't allow her to be herself.

# Chapter Six

Sadie didn't have to turn around to know that Andrew had finally arrived at the beginning of the last game of the tournament. She seemed to have a sixth sense when it came to him. She felt his gaze upon her even before she glanced to see him strolling across the field toward her.

In a three-piece navy blue suit, Andrew looked out of place, and yet he didn't. She suspected it wouldn't make any difference what clothes he wore. He had an air of confidence about him that announced to the world he set his own rules, and that wearing business attire to a soccer match was perfectly acceptable.

A roar from the stands pulled Sadie's attention to the game unfolding without her coaching. Kevin dribbled toward the opposing team's goal, came to a halt and swung his foot toward the ball. He missed. An opponent stole the ball and headed toward Chris, Cimarron High's goalie.

"Chris, you can stop it," Sadie shouted, moving down the line toward him. "Cal, set the defense up."

When the Tulsa team made a shot at their goal, Sadie held her breath while Chris dove toward the ball and landed on top of it. The parents and benched teammates stood, yelling their excitement.

Sadie clapped and cheered, pumping her arm into the air. "I knew you could do it."

"If you don't watch out you won't have a voice left." Andrew positioned himself next to her with his hands in his pants' pockets.

"I usually don't. It's a good thing these games are on Friday. It gives me two days to get my voice back. I'm an interactive coach."

"I can see that."

"What I see is that you made it—barely."

"Would you believe that a meeting at work held me up?"

"Yes. Thirty more minutes, and all bets would have been off." Sadie noticed her team had lined up on the field for the kickoff, and she hadn't even realized it. "Go sit down and let me concentrate on the game."

"Do I fluster you, Sadie?"

She rolled her eyes skyward. "You're a distraction— an unwanted distraction."

"I think you wounded my male ego."

"Go." She waved him toward the stands and then focused her attention on the game proceeding without her.

Distraction was an understatement, Sadie decided at

the half as her team was running off the field. Thank goodness they were playing well without the benefit of her coaching, because she couldn't seem to concentrate.

"Get water, everyone," Sadie called to her players. Out of the corner of her eye she saw Andrew strolling toward her. "You all are doing a great job. We're ahead by two goals." *No thanks to me,* she added silently, beads of perspiration popping out on her upper lip.

She removed her white hat and fanned her face. This was worse than the time her parents came to see her coach a game. She felt the pressure weighing her down and wished she had discouraged Andrew from coming. He stopped next to her.

With his usual big grin, Chris approached Andrew. "I'm glad you came. We're winning! Did you see me stop that goal?"

"That was perfect," Andrew said.

At hearing the word perfect, Sadie cringed. "You need to get some water. The game will be starting soon."

"Can I play forward? I want to score."

"Change places with James."

Chris ran off to get some water and sit between two high school girls who had accompanied the team as cheerleaders. Sadie shook her head, amazed at the ease Chris had conversing with anyone. If he got the job at IFI, he would do fine.

"Any word about the work project?" she asked, needing to put business between her and Andrew.

"It's a go. When do you want to start the program?"

"As soon as possible."

"That's what I thought you would say. I need you to meet with the person in charge of the mail room. I cleared a time Monday afternoon. We'll meet with Mrs. Lawson in my office at four o'clock, if that's okay with you."

*Thank you, Lord. With Your help this will work.* "I'll be there. When can I tell Chris and his mother?"

"When we've worked out the details with Mrs. Lawson."

"But—" She clamped her mouth shut on the protest. She wanted to shout her good news to the whole world, but she would wait.

"For this to work you'll need to sell Mrs. Lawson on the idea."

"Yes, of course. May I ask one more favor?"

"You do know how to push a guy."

"Will you or Mrs. Lawson interview Chris for the job? I want him to experience the whole process, starting with filling out an application."

"I will, but he'll also talk with Mrs. Lawson."

Andrew's gaze strayed to the young man in question, who was smiling at the pretty girl next to him as though he were the cat who had swallowed the canary. "I have to warn you, Mrs. Lawson is rather stern. She runs a tight department and doesn't tolerate any playing around."

"Chris will adjust," Sadie said with more conviction than she felt. Chris always did best with a person who was nurturing and easygoing. She had a lot riding on how well Chris did, but she would never let him know that.

The referee blew his whistle, signaling the start of the second half. Her team lined up, positioned to accept the kickoff.

"Do I have to sit in the stands? I promise I won't say anything to distract you."

She didn't think that was possible, but that wasn't his problem. He couldn't help it if she was attracted to him. "Fine," she answered, and glanced toward him. A mistake, she discovered when her gaze was trapped by the warmth in his eyes and the humor in his expression.

She missed the first few plays of the second half. Forcing herself to look away from Andrew and toward the field, she determinedly ignored the man next to her—for all of ten minutes. When Chris broke loose from the pack with the ball, Andrew's cheers sounded above everyone else's. He headed down the line as Chris headed for the opponent's goal.

"Shoot," Andrew called when Chris had a clear shot on the goal.

The twenty-year-old brought his foot back and sailed the ball through the air. It whizzed by the goalie's head and into the net. Sadie jumped up and down, and before she knew it, she was being crushed against Andrew, whose enthusiasm matched hers.

Then suddenly he realized he held her and she realized she held him. They broke apart. A flush crept up her face. "I—I—" She stammered and couldn't form a coherent sentence. She turned away, shaken and flustered.

"I think I'll sit in the stands," Andrew said, as stunned as she was.

With a quick glance, she saw him settle next to one of her students, Melissa, who proceeded to chatter. It took a few seconds for him to wipe the amazement from his expression and fix on what Melissa was saying to him. Then the team manager, Tina, joined in the conversation. Sadie knew he would be occupied with those two. He would have to focus hard to understand Tina and even then would probably only understand a word or two. His brow was furrowed in concentration.

She relaxed and riveted her full attention on the last few minutes of the game. A member of the Tulsa team dribbled toward James, who crouched low, his arms out to the sides as though he were going to bearhug his opponent. The girl punched the ball past James, who watched it bounce into the net, still perfectly poised. He fell to his knees and bent over. He remained like that even as the teams lined up to kick off. The referee blew his whistle, announcing the game was over.

While everyone formed a line to shake the Tulsa team's hands, Sadie heaved a sigh and walked onto the field to retrieve James. She knelt next to him, placing her hand on his hunched back.

"We won. You need to congratulate the other team on a good game."

"I miss. I miss." James mumbled and pounded the dirt, tears streaming down his face.

Sadie captured his hands and held them, forcing him

to look at her. "It's okay. Remember it's not if you win or lose but how you play the game. You played a good game, James." Sadie stood and extended her hand. "Come on. I need to say a few words to the other coach. Will you come with me?"

James sniffed and clasped her hand. "No like goalie."

After talking to the Tulsa coach, Sadie walked with James to the sidelines where the rest of the team was drinking water and high-fiving each other. She searched the crowd for Andrew and found him still sandwiched between Melissa and Tina, both talking to him at the same time, Tina waving her hands as she tried to pantomime what she was trying to tell him. He whipped his attention between the two girls, but Sadie saw the dazed look in his eyes. Taking pity on him, she headed toward them.

"Tina, as our team manager you need to get our practice balls. Melissa, please help her so we can leave right after the awards presentation."

The pair hopped up and hurried to do their jobs. Sadie sat next to Andrew, suddenly tired, her throat parched.

"I think Tina was trying to tell me about going to the ballet in Tulsa."

"She did, last weekend. She tells anyone who will listen. It left quite an impression on her."

"Well, Melissa wasn't going to let her hog the conversation so she started in on telling me about her camping trip last summer."

"Melissa and Tina are best friends, but they're competitive when it comes to getting someone's full attention.

When Tina first came to my class, she didn't speak a word. Now I have a hard time keeping her quiet. I love it, even if I can only understand every third or fourth word."

"You don't understand her? I was worried maybe it was just me. Melissa didn't seem to have much trouble understanding Tina."

Sadie laughed. "Yeah, they sometimes complete each other's sentences."

Andrew rose. "I'll pick you up tonight at six. Wear something casual."

"Where are we going?"

"It's a secret."

Sadie pushed to her feet. "You know I don't like surprises or secrets. I thought I made that clear in New Orleans."

"Yep, crystal clear. But you aren't gonna find out from me. You're just gonna have to wait. I know you have lots of patience. I've seen you with your students." His pressed lips and smug expression underscored his intention to keep their destination a secret.

"You're enjoying this way too much," Sadie said, starting for the shelter at the park where the awards ceremony would be held.

"Yes, actually I am having fun." He fell into step next to her.

"I have to warn you I'm pretty tired." When he didn't say anything, she added, "Your plans don't involve a lot of exertion, do they?"

"Well, that depends on what you call exertion. You'll

just have to wait and see." With a cocky smile and a salute, Andrew headed for his car.

Sadie peered at Andrew as he negotiated the streets of Tulsa, amazed that he even owned a pair of jeans, let alone a faded, worn pair that obviously meant he hadn't gone out and bought the jeans that day.

At a stoplight he turned his attention—and charm—on her. His face lit with a smile, and he looked every inch a relaxed man. The classical music playing and the comfortable temperature of the warm autumn night lent further soothing strokes to the evening. Then why was she wound as tight as—

Her eyes grew round as Andrew pulled into the parking lot of an amusement park. The large roller coaster loomed before them, and lots of lights sparkled in the darkening night.

She riveted her gaze to his face. "This is your idea of fun?"

"In some people's books fun and amusement are synonyms."

"But not yours!" Her voice rose, and later—when she was thinking and acting rationally—she would attribute it to exhaustion. She loved amusement parks. He couldn't. It was necessary they didn't have anything else in common. Otherwise, it would be very difficult to fight her attraction to this man. "When was the last time you went to an amusement park?"

He smiled a bit too smugly. "Last summer."

"Last summer! How long did you stay?"

"Several days."

"Really?" She knew Andrew Knight was a complex man, but his answer emphasized it even more.

His eyes gleamed. "Really."

She searched her mind frantically for an explanation that would fit with her image of Andrew. "Why did you go? I thought you never took a vacation."

He pinned her with his penetrating gaze. "It was a business trip."

"I knew it!" Sadie said, relieved that her image was still intact. "That's an unusual place for a business trip."

"Theme parks serve food. It's perfectly logical when you work for a food company."

"Yes, logical," she murmured, the world righting itself. "Back to my original question. When was the last time you were at an amusement park for fun?"

"When I was nine. I used to love to go. I haven't been to one since my family died."

Her heart expanded, and any triumph she felt that she'd figured him out vanished. She shifted so she could face him. "I'm sorry. I didn't mean—"

He pressed his fingers to her lips. "Shh. This is a night of fun. I thought it was about time that I recaptured some of my youth and I couldn't think of anyone I would like better to share it with."

She beamed, her exhaustion completely gone. "Then by all means let's head for the midway. I haven't had cotton candy in ages."

Hand in hand they walked to the ticket booth, and Andrew paid for them to get in. Inside, the scents of popcorn and hot dogs drifted to Sadie as the sounds of bells, clangs and laughter punctuated the air.

"What do you want to ride first?" Andrew asked, looking up and down the long midway.

"You pick. I come to the amusement park at least once a year."

"By yourself?"

"No. Usually with my students. That way I have an excuse for acting like a kid and going on every ride there is."

"Nothing makes you sick?"

She patted her stomach. "Tough as nails. Coated in iron."

"Well, in that case let's do the Ferris wheel first."

From the gleam in his eyes she had expected him to ride the most challenging one first. "Ferris wheel?"

He chuckled. "Don't worry. We'll work our way up. Before the evening is over you'll be thoroughly spun, twisted and twirled until you won't know which way is up or down."

"Promise?"

His chuckle evolved into full laughter. "Yes." He grabbed her hand and tugged her toward the Ferris wheel.

Two hours later, full from eating two hot dogs and one cotton candy washed down with a large soda, Sadie stood next to Andrew staring at the huge roller coaster, known for its thrilling ride.

"This is the last ride. Ready?" Andrew asked, tossing the last of his drink into the trash.

Sadie positioned herself at the end of the line waiting to get on the ride, with Andrew right behind her. "I'm glad we saved the best one for last."

"What I can't figure out is how a woman who loves to go on any ride—some that look as though they defy the laws of nature—can't stand to fly."

"When you figure it out, please let me know. Fears are often irrational. I used to say it was because I have no control when I'm flying, but then I really don't have any control on one of these rides, either."

"Not an ounce."

"So I guess that's not the reason. What are you afraid of?" She shuffled forward when the teenage boy running the ride allowed the people in front of her to sit in the cars.

"Let's go to the back." Andrew steered her through the small crowd and claimed the last car.

After they were secured, the metal bar across their laps, Sadie said, "You haven't answered my question."

"Fire, and there's nothing irrational about that fear."

For a moment Sadie was hurled back to New Orleans. She stood in front of the charred remains of his home, and her heart ached for a little boy who watched his family perish. Saying she was sorry wasn't adequate. She was glad when the roller coaster started, because there was nothing she could say to take away his pain, and she wished there was.

She covered his hand on the bar as the cars chugged

upward for the first drop. He linked his fingers through hers, his gaze bound to hers as they reached the top. For a few seconds high above Tulsa with the lights glittering below them, Sadie felt suspended, stopped in time. Andrew leaned toward her and brushed his lips across hers, soft as the warm breeze.

Then the car plunged downward at an alarming speed. But all Sadie could think of was the light feel of his lips against hers. For a few seconds they had been connected on many levels. She wondered in that moment if he had captured her heart.

Thankfully—because she didn't want her emotions to be tangled up with him—the wind rushing by her, the screams of excitement and fear and the sensation of leaving her stomach at the top of the roller coaster brought her back to reality. After that, she experienced the ride, relishing the breeze blowing through her hair, the sudden drops, the exhilarating speed. When the car came to a stop at the end, Sadie closed her eyes for a moment while her pulse quieted.

"I told you I'd tell you when my fourth wish came true. It did," she said, not really thinking clearly, or she wouldn't have admitted it.

"To ride a roller coaster?"

"No." His gaze touched hers, and the feel of his lips feathering across hers replayed in her mind. "I wanted you to kiss me."

For once it seemed Andrew was speechless, surprise dominating his expression.

Sadie quickly stood, her legs shaky. She grasped Andrew to steady herself. "I think my exhaustion is finally catching up with me. Friday night is usually my meltdown night."

"Meltdown night?"

"I go home after school, get takeout from a restaurant and collapse after a long week of teaching. I must confess it's the one night I vegetate in front of the TV. I'm not even sure what I watch half the time. I often wake up at two or three in the morning in my lounger in front of the TV with some awful show on that is only on in the middle of the night."

"Interesting."

"I guess you never do something like that." Sadie walked next to him toward his car, aware of his penetrating regard on her face.

"Can't say that I do. I don't think I've watched television in months."

"What do you usually do on Friday night? We've already established it isn't going to an amusement park."

"Work. I leave IFI about seven or eight, grab something at a fast food place and go home and work some more."

"No dates?"

He stopped at his car and faced her. "Occasionally. I'm here right now, aren't I? How about you? No dates on Friday night?"

"Occasionally. I'm here with you, aren't I?"

"Yes, delightfully so."

She inclined her head. "Thank you."

"About that kiss—"

She covered his lips with her fingertips. "If I hadn't agreed to tell you when my fourth wish happened, you'd never have known. But I'm a woman of my word. No more discussion." *Please,* she silently added.

He looked at her long and hard for a breath-held moment, then opened her door before going around to his side and climbing into the car. "I had a fun evening."

"So did I," she said with relief, glad he was dropping the subject of their brief kiss and her wish. "I didn't think about anything important."

"I have to admit until just a moment ago I didn't think of IFI once," he said with a touch of amazement.

"Now you know it can be done."

He slipped in another classical CD, this time the soothing sounds of Brahms. Sadie settled her head on the cushion. The motion of the car, the warm wrap of darkness, lured her to sleep.

An hour later Andrew shook her awake. "You're home and you have a visitor."

Sadie jerked up and saw her mother sitting on her porch swing and a suitcase next to the front door. "Oh, no. Something must be wrong."

Sadie scrambled from the car before Andrew had a chance to come around and open the door for her. She hurried to the porch, aware that Andrew was behind her, matching her quick steps.

Stunned, Sadie came to a stop in front of her mother on the swing. "Mom, what's wrong? Why are you here?"

"I've left your dad and I'm moving in with you."

"What happened?" Her stomach knotted.

"He didn't like the dinner I fixed him. He left to eat out and that's when I left him." Her mother fixed her gaze on Andrew. She rose and extended her hand. "I'm Abby Spencer."

"Nice to meet you, Mrs. Spencer. I'm Andrew Knight—a friend of Sadie's."

"Ah, you're the young man she bet on at the auction."

Sadie hadn't thought it possible Andrew could blush, but he did. "Come in, Mom. We need to talk."

"This is my cue to leave. Thanks for the fun evening, Sadie."

"Don't leave on my account. Come in, Mr. Knight, and I'll fix us some coffee. I have a feeling it will be a long night."

That was an understatement, Sadie thought, the knot in her stomach constricting even more.

"Some other time. I have work that I've neglected."

"Thanks for everything. I'll see you at four on Monday." Sadie watched Andrew leave before unlocking her door and waving her mother into her house.

"He seems like a nice young man. Are you two dating?"

"No, Mom."

"Then what were you doing?"

"We're friends. That is all. His company is going to be a work site for one of my students."

"Then it was business tonight?"

Sadie remembered the shared laughter, the brief kiss. "No, we went to the amusement park in Tulsa."

"In my day, that was called a date."

"Mom! Tell me what happened tonight."

"I already did. Your father threw my beef stew out and left. For over thirty years I have cooked and cleaned for that man, and that's how he treats me. He's never done that."

Sadie dug her teeth into her bottom lip to keep from saying what she wanted to. From where she'd stood as a daughter, her father had never treated her mother the way a husband who really loved his wife should. Granted, he might not have thrown her dinner out, but he'd done many things far worse—like ignore her mother, who worked hard to make his home comfortable.

Tears crowded her mother's eyes. She sank onto the couch in the living room. "I know it didn't taste great." She swiped at a lone tear coursing down her cheek. "But I deserve better than that. I—" She hiccupped. "Sadie, I think he's seeing another woman. I can put up with a lot of things, but not that."

Sadie gathered her mother into her arms and held her, stroking her back. "Why do you think he's seeing another woman?"

"Because he's never home anymore. He was supposed to be at the university the other night working late and when I called no one answered his phone in his office. Where was he?" Her mother leaned back, tears flowing freely down her face. "I know I've put on some weight and I might not be as interested in history as he is, but—" Her words faded into silence.

"I think you need to talk to Dad about this. There may be a logical explanation for the other night."

"It's not just that. I came in on him yesterday on the phone. He was very secretive and hung up quickly. And just last week I received several calls and no one was on the phone. I've read Ann Landers. I know the signs. What should I do?"

Her mother was asking a woman who was afraid to have a committed relationship with a man, who was afraid she could never fulfill a man's ideal, who would rather be alone than expose her flaws to another. "Why don't you talk with Reverend Littleton? I know he counsels married couples all the time. I also think you need to talk with Dad about your suspicions."

Her mother rubbed at the evidence of her tears. "I'm afraid, Sadie. I'm not brave like you."

"You think I'm brave. Mom, I don't know how to open myself up to a man."

"Maybe Reverend Littleton can help you, too." Her mother clasped her hand and patted it.

"Does Dad know where you are?" Sadie asked, instead of commenting on her mother's suggestion. The minister at her church was a kind older man who was renowned for his counseling, but she couldn't see herself opening up to anyone. It seemed so much safer to keep her face hidden.

"No. I didn't even leave him a note."

"Then at least call and leave a message on the answering machine. He'll worry about where you are."

Her mother harrumphed. "I doubt it."

"Then, Mom, do it for me. You can stay as long as you need."

"I'll leave a message. But if he answers, I'm hanging up."

When her mother rose to walk to the phone, Sadie noticed Abby's hands were shaking. Her heart went out to her mother. Sadie had issues with her father, but she didn't want to see her parents' marriage of thirty-two years break up. Marriage was for a lifetime, and that was why she could never see herself married. She was too scared to trust her heart to someone for the rest of her life.

## Chapter Seven

"It's so good to see you, Sadie. Come on in." Andrew held his office door open for her, a pleased look on his face.

As Sadie headed toward him, she wanted to do a victory dance in front of Mrs. Fox, who more than once had refused to let her talk to Andrew. Instead, and to her amazement, Sadie walked into the office at a dignified pace with a gracious expression upon her face.

"How's your mother doing?" Andrew asked while gesturing for Sadie to be seated in a comfortable-looking chair in front of his desk.

"She's staying with me for a while, but at least she and Dad are talking, not always in a calm voice, but talking." Sadie sat, relieved to be off her feet after spending all day standing. It was a rare moment she could sit at her desk as Andrew did and work, not when she had so many students all working on something different. "And they've both finally agreed to see Reverend

Littleton. I didn't think Dad would, but last night he told Mom he would go with her tomorrow. Of course, he's only committed to one session and he made sure she knew that." When she saw Andrew's grin, she added, "I'm doing it again, aren't I? Giving you more information than you care to know."

"Nervous?"

"Yes. I want this program to work."

His gaze connected with hers. "So do I. I think it would be good for everyone involved."

The warmth in his expression relaxed her. She leaned back in the chair and drew in a deep, fortifying breath.

"Mrs. Lawson is rarely late for anything. I'm sure she will be here any second."

"Can you tell me a little about her—"

A firm knock sounded on his office door, then it swung open and a tiny woman, no more than five feet tall, with black hair pulled back in a tight bun, entered the room. She covered the distance to the other chair next to Sadie in precise, long strides.

"I'm sorry I'm late. There was a mix-up in the mail room that I had to straighten out before I could leave." Mrs. Lawson sat with her back ramrod straight and her hands folded in her lap.

Sadie looked at the older woman and trembled. She half expected to see frost hanging off her eyelashes. *Lord, show me the way to make this work.*

"Mrs. Lawson, this is Sadie Spencer, the teacher at Cimarron High School I told you about."

Sadie started to offer her hand to the woman, but something in Mrs. Lawson's demeanor stopped her. "It's nice to meet you, Mrs. Lawson." Somehow she got the impression no one called the woman by her first name, not even Andrew.

"I understand that you have a student with mental disabilities you would like to place here in the mail room."

Sadie nodded, her throat dry.

"Can he read?"

"Yes, about third-grade level."

"Can he alphabetize?"

"Yes. I'm been working with him, and he's getting quite good."

"Quite good isn't good enough."

The woman's mouth was pinched into a frown, and Sadie felt all her time and energy had been wasted. How was Chris going to succeed with a boss like her? Again Sadie found herself turning to the Lord for guidance, silently sending a prayer for strength to deal with this new challenge.

She looked Mrs. Lawson directly in the eye and said, "Chris is very capable. He'll make any employer a valuable employee with some on-the-job training."

"When is Chris starting in the mail room?" Mrs. Lawson asked, turning her attention to Andrew as though what Sadie had said was unimportant.

"He'll start next Monday. I'll interview him, then send him to you by one o'clock."

"I understand he'll work half days from twelve to four."

"Yes," Andrew said to Mrs. Lawson.

The older woman glanced away for a few seconds, then returned her attention to Andrew. "And if I have a problem with him, what is the procedure I follow? Do I treat him like the other employees?"

"Yes, but inform me if there's a problem."

Sadie gripped the arms of her chair. Mrs. Lawson's tone underlined the wariness the woman felt toward this arrangement. Chris would be a great ambassador for the work program, but Sadie wasn't sure any student would please Mrs. Lawson.

The woman rose, her back stiff. "Then if that is all, I have a lot of work that needs to be done." As she turned, her gaze fell on Sadie. "It was nice meeting you."

Again her tone negated the meaning behind her words, and Sadie's doubts grew. "Thank you for taking Chris."

Mrs. Lawson nodded curtly and headed for the door. When it clicked shut, Sadie released her pent-up breath in a rush and relaxed her tight grip on the arms of the chair. She flexed her hand to ease her aching fingers.

"Andrew, I don't know if the mail room will work."

"It's a good place for Chris to start. Let's give it a chance."

"Will you let me know if there's a problem? I'll be checking periodically, but Mrs. Lawson might not say anything to me until the problem is unsolvable. I've found that happens sometimes."

"I'll call you if she says anything to me." He leaned

forward, resting his elbows on his desk, his gaze intent on her face. "I want this to work."

"Thank you for trying this program." Sadie stood, clutching her purse in front of her. "I'll have Chris here next Monday at twelve for the interview and to fill out the paperwork." She turned to leave.

Andrew pushed to his feet. "Sadie?"

She stopped, peering at him.

He walked from behind his desk. "Mr. Wilson, the president of IFI, is having an informal reception at our Grand Lake lodge for the candidates for the presidency this Saturday night. Will you go with me?"

"You're asking me out on a date?"

The corners of his mouth twitched up. "Yes, that's what it sounds like to me. As I told you, I do occasionally go on dates."

"How informal?"

"Casual attire. It's a barbecue."

"Yes, I'll go."

"I'll pick you up at five." He lounged against the desk, crossing his legs at the ankle. "I probably need to warn you that it will be a working evening. Mr. Wilson is hosting this reception for the board to meet the candidates."

"Am I supposed to be surprised?"

"No, just wanted you to know what you were getting yourself into for the evening."

"In other words, I might not see much of my date."

"I'm the only one not married. It would seem odd if

I was the only one who didn't show up with a date for the evening."

"This evening affair is sounding more appealing by the second."

He grinned. "I figure with you I don't have to pretend. You know exactly where my interests lie."

Through a valiant effort, Sadie kept her disappointment from showing on her face. She didn't want a relationship with Andrew, but for some reason being reminded he wasn't interested in a relationship hurt more than she wanted to acknowledge. "Yes, I know. You're after the presidency of IFI. Everything else in your life has been placed on hold."

"Exactly." Pushing himself away from the desk, he escorted her toward the door, his hand lightly touching the small of her back. "I'll see you Saturday."

He walked with her all the way to the elevator. Even through the sweater she wore, she felt the warmth of his fingers on her back. For a fleeting moment she wondered what it would be like to lean on this man for support. He was strong, independent, two qualities she admired in a person. And beneath his tough exterior there beat a soft heart, a quality that endeared him to her.

"Mom, he's gonna be here any minute. Help! What does casual mean to you?" Sadie held up a pair of jeans and some black pants. "Do I wear this or this?" She thrust each selection out in front of Abby.

Her mother leaned against the doorjamb. "Honey, there are many degrees of casual. What did he say?"

"Informal. That's all. Why didn't I quiz him more about what he meant?" Sadie tossed the jeans onto the discarded clothes stacked haphazardly on her bed. "I probably should go with the black pants. You can dress black up or down. Now, what kind of top should I wear?" She turned to her closet and began rummaging through her clothes.

"I've never seen you this nervous. Is something going on with you and Andrew that I should know about?"

Sadie whirled. "No!"

Her mother quirked a brow.

"Honestly, Mom, we're just friends. That's all."

"And you obsess on what to wear with your friends?"

"This reception is important to Andrew. I wouldn't want to be the cause of any problems for him."

"I see." Her mother folded her arms across her chest, the smug expression on her face saying more than her words.

"What do you think?" Sadie held up a white silk blouse then a leopard print shirt. "Which one?"

"The white."

"Yeah, the other makes too bold a statement. I need to play it low-key. This is Andrew's show. I certainly don't want to draw attention to myself."

"You should never do that."

Sadie paused in tossing the leopard print blouse on the growing pile of clothes and eyed her mother. "You're enjoying this."

"Yep. I rarely get to see you falling apart over something as minor as two friends going to a reception. Now if this had been a date, I could understand."

Sadie put her hands on her hips, the leopard print blouse bunched up in her fist. "This is not a date."

Her mother straightened from the doorjamb. "No, dear."

Sadie started to protest some more when the doorbell sounded.

She gasped. "I'm gonna be late."

"I'll entertain Mr. Knight while you finish getting dressed."

"Mom, don't say—" Sadie didn't complete her sentence because her mother had disappeared down the hall.

Sadie listened while her mother let Andrew into the house with a cheerful greeting. Sadie leaned her head into the hallway, conscious of the fact she wasn't completely dressed, and tried to hear his reply. They had obviously walked into the living room, and the sound of their voices was too muffled for her to understand what was being said. That prompted Sadie to hurry and throw on her clothes.

No telling what her mother would say to Andrew. There were times she could have an impish streak. Sadie remembered once in high school her mother regaling her date about some of her antics while she was growing up. She had come into the room just in time to stop her mother from pulling out the albums and showing him pictures of her as a baby in less than appealing snapshots.

Ten minutes later Sadie appeared in the living room, ready to yank any albums out of her mother's grasp. She hoped her French braid didn't have too many hairs sticking out and that her lipstick was on straight. Glancing at her clothes, she was pleased to see that at least she looked all right even if inside she felt less than together.

Sadie rushed forward. "Sorry I'm late."

Andrew lifted his head and snared her gaze with his assessing one. "The wait was worth it."

She noted his tan slacks and black polo shirt and breathed a sigh of relief. His idea of casual was the same as hers. "Ready?"

Andrew rose, saying to her mother, "Thank you for the invitation to Thanksgiving dinner, but I'd hate to intrude on your family time."

"Nonsense. It will be a small gathering this year so you're more than welcome. I hate to hear of anyone spending Thanksgiving alone. It's meant to be spent with family—and friends." Her mother winked at Sadie.

She nearly choked.

"Don't you think so, Sadie?"

Her mother looked at her with such innocence in her eyes that Sadie could only nod her agreement.

"You see. Even Sadie feels you shouldn't spend Thanksgiving alone."

"Then it's a date. Thank you for inviting me."

Behind Andrew her mother smirked. "Yes, it's a date."

Sadie stifled her moan, but she knew she would have

to talk with her mother tomorrow about trying to match-make, because that was what she was doing. She was clearly going to have to define friendship for her mother.

"We'd better get going. I wouldn't want you to be late for the reception." Sadie grasped Andrew's hand and practically hauled him toward the front door.

When they stepped outside, the autumn air caressed her cheeks, cooling the heat that suffused her. She was thankful beads of sweat hadn't popped out on her forehead and run down her face to ruin what little makeup she had on.

"If you don't want to come to Thanksgiving dinner, Andrew, you don't have to."

At the car he opened her door, his gaze trapping her. "Do you want me to?"

The intensity in his regard wiped any rational thought from her mind.

"I meant it when I said I didn't want to intrude, Sadie."

The vulnerability she occasionally glimpsed in him surfaced for a brief second. She covered his hand on the door and said, "You could never intrude. I would love to have you spend Thanksgiving with my mother and me."

"Not your father?"

She tilted her head to the side and thought about that. "You know, Mom hasn't said anything about that. He might be there. Their counseling session with Reverend Littleton wasn't a rousing success, but at least they're talking."

"That's good."

Sadie climbed into his silver Lexus and watched as he rounded the front and slid into his seat. "My question to you is will you mind coming to dinner if my father is there? The atmosphere may not be very relaxed." Sadie refrained from telling Andrew it rarely was when she was with her father. She had told Andrew more about her life than she usually said to anyone, which was a surprise in itself.

"Do you know what I was going to do Thanksgiving?"

"Work?"

"You got it. I was going to go into IFI and work on some reports. There are always reports that need doing." He peered at her through a half shuttered gaze. "My dinner that evening would have consisted of a frozen TV dinner of turkey."

"Not very appetizing."

"No, but that's my idea of Thanksgiving if I don't go to Ruth and Darrell's."

"Why aren't you this year?"

One corner of his mouth lifted in a self-mocking grin. "Not enough time."

A dull ache pierced her heart. "Is it all worth it to you?"

"Sadie, I don't know anything else but work, so I have to say yes."

"You don't have to say or do anything if you don't want to."

"That's a pretty naive way to look at life." He started the car and pulled out of the driveway.

"I've never considered myself naive."

"Don't you do things that must be done?"

"Well, yes. Everyone does at some time in his life, but people do make their own choices, you included."

"Exactly. I choose to work. I find comfort in work."

"Because it doesn't require an emotional commitment?"

He sucked in a deep breath. "You do know how to hit below the belt. But then maybe that's because we are alike."

"I know how to commit emotionally. I do to my students."

"Not the same thing as a relationship with a man. You know why I won't commit. Why won't you?"

"Haven't found Mr. Right," she quipped.

"Are you looking?"

"Do you want to be a candidate?" she asked, hoping to shut this conversation down quickly.

"Touché. I'll be quiet. That's what you want."

For the next forty-five minutes silence reigned in the car while the landscape sped past. Sadie was glad for the reprieve. She felt emotionally overloaded from their brief conversation. He had a way of getting past her defenses. She was constantly finding herself having to shore them up when she was around him.

When Andrew pulled into a gated driveway that led to the lake, she noticed his demeanor change. A new tension hung in the air, as though he were preparing to do battle. She could almost see him running through a list of tasks in his head.

"Is there anything I should know, do?" she asked, wishing she could ease his burden.

"No, just be yourself."

"Are you sure about that?" Laughter tinged her words.

He quirked a brow at her. "Should I be worried?"

"No, I'll be on my best behavior. Promise. I would never do anything to ruin your chances of becoming president."

"Now I am worried."

But the expression on his face belied his statement. His features relaxed into an easy grin, and he took her hand as they approached the front door. Her impression of IFI's cabin on Grand Lake was one of a sprawling structure of glass and rustic wood that blended with the surrounding water and woods. The only things out of place were the expensive cars that lined the circular drive, underscoring the purpose of the evening's reception. Tension whipped down her as they waited for someone to open the front door.

When she stepped into the foyer, she felt drawn to the panoramic view from the floor-to-ceiling windows in the living room, which overlooked the lake. The setting sun tinted the water a rosy hue while the colorful fall leaves on the trees along the shoreline danced in the light breeze. The beautiful vista reminded Sadie of the power in God's creation, in His love. That thought brought peace to her, and she knew everything would be all right this evening. She discarded her tension like an unwanted cloak, determined to enjoy herself even if she felt out of her element.

Taking her elbow, Andrew directed her to a small group near the floor-to-ceiling windows. "I want you to meet Lawrence Wilson, the president of IFI. This is Sadie Spencer."

She shook Mr. Wilson's hand. "It's nice to meet you. This place is beautiful."

"I like to entertain here. A much more relaxing environment."

Andrew went around the group, introducing her to the other two candidates for the presidency and their wives. Charles Benson and his wife, Elizabeth, greeted her with smiles and a warmth Sadie found herself responding to. The Edgars, Stephen and Linda, were more formal but nice.

When another man and his wife entered, Lawrence Wilson said, "Now that everyone is here, I have an announcement to make."

The room quieted, and people turned toward him, waiting for him to continue. Andrew enclosed her hand within his, his arm touching hers.

"As you probably all know, since there seem to be no secrets at IFI, I'm retiring next year. What you don't know is that I'm retiring earlier than you think. I will be stepping down in six months instead of nine, and I've gathered here tonight the three men I think are capable of running IFI after I'm gone." Lawrence gestured to each man as he introduced them.

Andrew's hand tightened when his name was announced. She felt his tension as though it were a part of her.

"Over the next few months the board and myself will be taking a careful look at each man to determine who will be the best one to run IFI in the twenty-first century. Good luck."

Sadie felt as though she were at a horse race, watching the colts contend for the purse. After that announcement the room buzzed with noise as everyone began to talk at the same time—except Andrew, who remained unusually quiet next to her.

He scanned the people and leaned toward her to whisper, "Let the games begin."

She smiled. "I was thinking more along the lines of a horse race."

He tipped his head back and laughed. "I've been called many things but never a horse." His gaze was riveted to hers. "Thanks, Sadie, for making me laugh. I needed that." His stance relaxed, his grip on her hand a loose connection. "I guess I'd better start making my rounds."

"I think I'll escape outside to the deck."

"Already? The evening's only begun."

"But the sun is setting, and the sky is beautiful. Later I won't be able to see a thing from the deck."

"True. Want me to come with you?"

"That would amount to stumbling at the starting gate. No, you need to woo some board members."

Sadie watched Andrew weave his way through the small crowd, stopping to converse with several people.

Mostly she noticed he listened intently to what the others were saying, interjecting a comment when necessary. Any tension he felt wasn't evident, and Sadie thought he was in his element, much as she was teaching her students.

She slipped outside, smiling at several people who were also taking time to absorb the beauty of the sunset slanting across the waters below. The scent of meat roasting on a grill and the sound of water lapping against the shore drifted to Sadie. She wished she could bottle this moment. The breeze rustled the leaves of the maple and oak trees. She shivered in the darkening light, hugging herself.

"Cold?"

She whirled, surprised that Andrew was standing behind her holding a sweater for her.

"I borrowed Mrs. Wilson's sweater. I thought you might be getting cold."

"But you're supposed to be in there wooing the powers that be."

He moved close and draped the sweater over her shoulders. "I have plenty of time to woo. Besides, if my hard work and record don't get me the presidency, then I don't deserve it. I didn't want you to enjoy the sunset by yourself."

She laid her hand on his forehead. "What did you do with Andrew Knight?"

He chuckled. "Nothing. He's in here somewhere."

She turned and noticed that the sun had sunk below the trees. "Oh, it's gone. You missed it."

"That's okay." Andrew gripped the railing, leaning into it and slanting a look at her. "Tell me about it. I'd rather see it through your eyes, anyway."

"I—" She couldn't think of a thing to say to that statement.

"Sadie Spencer, don't tell me you're speechless. That's got to be a first."

"You're getting awfully good at teasing me."

The smile that touched his mouth went to her heart. "Yes, you have a gift of bringing that out in a person."

"I think that was a compliment. Thank you."

"It was. You were perfect to bring tonight."

Perfect. There was that word again. She hated it. What would happen when Andrew discovered all her flaws?

The urge to pace Andrew's outer office was strong, but Sadie remained seated next to Chris, her hands gripping her purse as though any second someone was going to dash into the room and snatch it away. Thankfully Chris was flipping through a magazine, oblivious to the turmoil churning in her stomach.

She heard footsteps approaching and glanced up to see Andrew hurrying into the office. He threw her a grin before turning to his secretary and giving her a stack of papers.

"I need these to go out immediately." He snagged Sadie's gaze and nodded toward his office. "Give me a few minutes. I have to make a quick phone call."

After Andrew disappeared into his office, Sadie took

the magazine from Chris and replaced it on the coffee table. "I want you to do this by yourself. I know you think Mr. Knight is a friend, but Chris, when you are at work, remember you greet him with a handshake, not a hug."

"I remember, Miss Spencer."

"Speak slowly and clearly. Don't mumble."

"Why aren't you coming?"

"Because this is something you need to do by yourself. I'll be right out here when you're through."

Andrew opened his door and motioned for them to come inside. Chris stood and walked toward him. "You aren't joining us?"

Sadie shook her head and watched her student enter Andrew's office. For a second her heart stopped beating. This was so important to Chris and to her. She closed her eyes and turned to the One who gave her strength. *Heavenly Father, watch over Chris and be with him. Help him through the interview and the first days on the job. Please help Mrs. Lawson to understand the worthiness of an employee like Chris.*

Fifteen minutes later Sadie had scanned the three magazines on the coffee table and was trying to decide how to occupy her time until Chris was finished. She pushed to her feet and started to walk down the hall to the water fountain when the door to Andrew's office opened and Chris came out with Andrew behind him. Chris grinned from ear to ear.

"You should see how high up we are," Chris exclaimed. "I can see the river from his window."

Sadie suppressed a moan, realizing Chris would never lose his enthusiasm for the small things. "How did everything go?" Her gaze skipped from Chris to Andrew.

"I'm taking him downstairs to meet Mrs. Lawson right now. Would you like to come along?"

Sadie agreed. She followed the pair to the elevator. She wanted to pull Andrew to the side and find out how well Chris did, but she didn't.

"This goes fast," Chris said as the elevator came to a halt on the ground floor.

When they entered the mail room, Sadie noticed everyone was at work. The only sounds were the shuffling of paper and the copy machine running. Chris paused for a moment to survey his new work area. A young man looked up, and Chris grinned and waved at him.

"Come on. Mrs. Lawson's office is this way." Andrew motioned to a closed door with a large window next to it that afforded Mrs. Lawson a view of the mail room.

Again Sadie's reservations surfaced. This would work if the environment was conducive to Chris. She worried about the extra-tight rein Mrs. Lawson seemed to have on the people who worked for her. How would Chris fare when he was so openly friendly and social? Sadie threw a glance over her shoulder at the workers in the room going about their jobs. Her doubts multiplied.

Inside Mrs. Lawson's office Chris sat between Sadie and Andrew while the older woman perused his application. A tiny frown knitted her brow.

Sadie's chest tightened with each breath she dragged

in. She flexed her hands, then gripped the arms of the chair and waited for the woman to say something.

Mrs. Lawson looked at Chris. "You will have to clock in and out every day. I will show you where when we leave here. You will have a fifteen minute break at two. If you don't understand something, ask for help. I will have you work with Bert until you learn the job. You'll be delivering and picking up mail as well as sorting it. Do you understand your duties?"

Chris nodded, a big grin on his face.

Andrew rose. "If you don't have any questions for Miss Spencer or me, we'll be leaving then."

"Who'll be picking him up?" Mrs. Lawson asked, standing, too.

"I will, this first day, with his mother. After that his mother will. Today we'll come up with a place for Chris to be when she comes."

"I suggest the lobby."

"Of course." Sadie got the distinct feeling the woman didn't want anyone disrupting her routine in the mail room.

When Mrs. Lawson didn't say anything else, Andrew opened the door and waited for Sadie to leave first. She hated walking away from Chris. Chewing on her bottom lip, she gave Chris one last glance before exiting.

In the lobby Andrew faced her. "It will work out. Mrs. Lawson comes across as being stern and inflexible, but she does a good job running her department."

"But how happy are her employees?"

"I don't receive any complaints. She'll make sure that

Chris is trained properly in his job. Will you trust me on this one?"

She nodded. "You know IFI better than I do. I guess I just feel like a mother hen."

"Chris did fine in the interview with me, and he'll do fine with Mrs. Lawson." He began walking her toward the doors that led outside. "What time do you want me to come on Thanksgiving?"

"My father will be there. Mom asked him, and he agreed."

Andrew halted a few feet from the door. "Does that make a difference in me coming or not?"

"No, I just wanted to warn you. My father can be difficult at times."

"And yet you're upset about your mother walking out on your father."

"It seems my feelings concerning my father are all tangled up."

"I don't have to come. I always have work to do here."

She grasped his arm. "I want you to come. I only wanted to warn you about what you might be getting yourself mixed up in. Come around twelve."

"You're going to have turkey and all the trimmings?"

"Yes."

"Then I'll be there. It's not that often I get a home-cooked meal."

Her mouth quirked up. "Then you'll have something to be thankful for."

As she left the building, she sensed Andrew watching

her, but she didn't glance back. For the first time in a long while, she was looking forward to Thanksgiving Day. She tucked that knowledge away to examine later when she was alone and had time to reflect.

# Chapter Eight

"How do I look?" Abby stood in the doorway of the kitchen and spun around. Her silk peach dress fell in soft waves about her knees.

Sadie noted she was wearing high heels and hose. Since Sadie could remember, her father had insisted they all dress up for Thanksgiving, giving the day a formal touch. "Mom, you look fine. You always do." She went back to sautéing the onions and celery for the dressing.

"Here, let me do that while you get dressed." Her mother took the wooden spoon from Sadie.

"You don't think I'm dressed?" she asked with a laugh, gesturing at the old pair of sweats she had on with evidence of the day's cooking spattered on it.

"While I think you're cute dusted with flour and who knows what, I think if you want to impress that young man you might want to change."

Sadie frowned. "I'm not trying to impress Andrew."

"Then what was that scene a few weeks ago when you were trying to decide what to wear on your date?"

"Mom," Sadie said with a deep sigh, "I was trying to impress the people he works for. IFI can become a valuable workplace for my students."

"Of course, dear." Abby focused her attention on the skillet.

Sadie stared at her for a moment, then sighed again and left the kitchen, realizing she would never convince her mother Andrew was just a friend. For years her mother had tried to get her married, even fixing her up with blind dates. After the third disastrous one Sadie had put a stop to the blind dates.

Nevertheless Sadie was determined to prove a point to her mother. She pulled out a pair of black jeans and a red turtleneck sweater. She wanted to set an informal and casual tone for the afternoon, and she would start with what she wore.

As she brushed her long hair, deciding to leave it loose, she heard the doorbell ring. "I'll get it." She hurried to answer the door. Since her father wasn't due for another hour, Andrew must be a few minutes early.

When she swung it open, her smile faltered. Her father stood on her porch, dressed in a suit. "You're early." It was all she could think to say.

"Yes, I am." He moved past her into the house. "I see you aren't ready yet."

Peering at her attire, she bit on the inside of her

cheek, a coldness embedded deep inside her. "I decided to go casual this Thanksgiving."

"Does your mother know?"

"Know what?" Abby came into the foyer, wiping her hands on her apron.

Her father waved his arm toward Sadie.

With a glance from Sadie to Robert, her mother straightened her shoulders and said, "Since this is her house, she sets the tone."

Shock flared in his eyes. "Very well." He continued into the living room.

The bell rang again. Sadie quickly answered the door, glad to have something to do. She forced herself to smile as she greeted Andrew. She was glad to see him, but she didn't know if his coming to dinner was a good idea.

His gaze skimmed the length of her. "You look beautiful."

She blushed under his intent look, any chill she felt gone. "Thank you. You don't look half bad yourself." She took in his attire, black pants and turtleneck with a tan and black sweater.

"Thank you, ma'am. Now that we have the pleasantries out of the way, what's for dinner?"

"I'll give you three guesses, and if you don't get it on the first try, I'll have to tell my mother to forget what I said about you."

Andrew stepped closer, the intensity in his gaze sharpening. "And what was that?"

He was so near that Sadie felt surrounded by him.

Tilting her chin up, she licked her lips and said, "That you were a very smart man."

His eyes glittered. "I'm curious."

"I thought I was the only one around here allowed to get curious."

"Nope." He shook his head slowly. "Why were you and your mother talking about me?"

"Now if I told you everything, that would be way too easy and dull." She spun to go into the living room.

Andrew captured her arm and halted her movement. He spoke into her ear, his breath feathering her neck. "There's nothing wrong with easy and dull."

"Oh, yes, there is, Mr. Knight. As you well know, there's nothing wrong with hard work if something is worth it."

"I'll have to remember that when I'm working late at night. But frankly, Miss Spencer, I can't believe I heard those words from your lips."

"My motto is to expect the unexpected."

She heard her father's raised voice coming from the living room and tensed, the imp inside her vanishing. Suddenly she was reminded of the day to come. There would be nothing easy or dull about this Thanksgiving.

"Let me introduce you to my father, then I need to finish putting the dinner together."

"Can I help?"

She flashed him a smile. "Chicken. Afraid to be alone with my parents?"

"I was hoping to sample some of the food before it

made it to the table." He glanced away then at her, a sheepish look on his face. "I forgot to eat breakfast."

She placed her hands on her hips. "Where were you before coming here? This is a holiday, Andrew Knight."

He hung his head. "Guilty. I was at work. I just had one report to get out."

"Tsk tsk. You are a hopeless case, but I'll take pity on you and let you help me in the kitchen. You're familiar with what you do in a kitchen, aren't you?"

"I can microwave a dinner and open a can and heat it on the stove."

"I'm impressed."

"Come on. Introduce me to your father before I have no ego left."

Sadie moved into the living room with Andrew at her side. Her parents were seated on the couch, arguing. Her mother saw Sadie and clamped her mouth shut. Her father twisted to stare at Sadie and Andrew, clearly not happy to be interrupted.

"Dad, I want you to meet Andrew Knight. Andrew, this is my father, Robert Spencer."

The two men shook hands and retreated to their respective corners, sizing each other up. Sadie wanted to squirm but held herself straight, waiting for something to happen.

"It's a pleasure to meet you finally, Mr. Spencer."

"I didn't realize we were having a guest for dinner."

Sadie shot her mother a glare. "You were supposed to tell Dad."

"I forgot." She shrugged. "Other things on my mind. Did I tell you all I have applied for a job at the university?"

"A job! Doing what?" Robert asked, surprise and anger lacing his words.

"I'm going to work in the library. I love books and I decided it was time for me to do something I love."

Sadie tugged on Andrew's arm and pulled him toward the kitchen. As the door closed behind them, she could hear her father demand her mother quit.

"I'm sorry. My mother doesn't always have the best timing."

"I think your mother has perfect timing."

Sadie stared at Andrew for a moment. "I suppose you're right. That's a piece of news she probably didn't want to tell him. At least with us here my father will temper his response." She went to the stove and removed the skillet. After pouring the onions and celery into a large mixing bowl, she added the other ingredients for the dressing.

"It does seem most unusual that Mom would get a job now after all these years of not working. I always thought she liked staying home and taking care of the family."

"Maybe she needed more." Andrew scanned the kitchen. "What can I do to help?"

"Sit over there."

"And?"

"And nothing. I don't have time to teach a novice."

"I'm a quick learner."

"Don't worry. I'll let you sample some of the food.

I'll even let you carve the turkey—that is, if you know how to."

Andrew puffed out his chest. "I know how to."

"Really?"

"Well, how hard can it be? You take a big knife and cut the meat off."

"Have you ever done it?"

"No, but I'm sure I can manage."

"On second thought, you sit there and keep me company. I'll carve the turkey."

He placed his hand over his heart. "Oh, you've wounded my ego again."

Sadie opened the oven and checked on the turkey, its aroma filling the kitchen. After placing the casserole dish with the dressing inside, she closed the door and started for the refrigerator.

"Will we get to sample any of that baking you like to do?"

"I made some rolls and a pecan pie. Is that enough for you?" She rummaged in the refrigerator, looking for the ingredients for a salad.

"It is for me. What about you and your parents?"

Sadie popped her head up and slanted a look toward Andrew, who sat comfortably at her kitchen table with a wide grin on his face.

He winked. "I do believe I'm getting the hang of this teasing."

"I'll just have to invite you to one of my parties when I clean out my freezer."

"Promise?"

Suddenly she realized what she had said, implying their personal relationship would go beyond today. She straightened, then dragged out spinach and lettuce. "Yes, the next one I have, which—" she swung the freezer door open to reveal a stuffed compartment "—won't be long. I don't know what I'm going to do about leftovers."

"I'll try to eat more than my share. That ought to help you out."

"Mr. Knight, you are so obliging. Whatever did I do before I knew you?"

"I don't know, but I'm glad I could be of help." He surged to his feet. "And speaking of help. I can wash lettuce and spinach. That doesn't require a culinary degree."

Sadie handed the items to him, then went to the refrigerator to retrieve the rest of the salad ingredients. Seeing Andrew standing at her sink rinsing the lettuce gave her a moment of pause. He looked so right in her kitchen, as though he belonged. For a few seconds she fantasized what it would be like if they had a relationship that was more than friendship. Then she remembered the struggles her parents were going through. She remembered where Andrew had been before he had come to her house for dinner—work, which was where he spent most of his waking time. She shook the fantasy from her mind and set the rest of the salad fixings on the counter.

\* \* \*

Seated at the dining room table, Sadie took her parents' hands and bowed her head. "Dear Heavenly Father, please bless this food and each person at this table. This is a time for thanksgiving, and we have much to be thankful for. Watch over the less fortunate and be with us in our time of need. In the name of Jesus Christ, amen."

Lifting her head, she caught Andrew staring at her from across the table. She realized in that moment she was very glad he was spending Thanksgiving with her. The dread she usually experienced mellowed as his gaze took her in.

"I would have carved the turkey, Sadie." Robert Spencer cut into the silence while forking several pieces of the meat onto his plate.

"That's okay, Dad. I wanted to give Andrew a lesson on how to, and besides, this is my first time to cook Thanksgiving dinner for you all." Sadie thought of the time she and Andrew had spent alone in the kitchen while she finished the meal preparation. His presence would make the next few hours bearable.

"Yes, well, we should have been eating at home. That's how we've always done it."

Her stomach constricted into a huge knot. Sadie gripped the serving spoon for the broccoli casserole, her chest expanding with a deep breath. "Maybe it's time to start a new tradition." After taking some of the vegetable, she passed it to her mother, not sure she would be able to eat it.

"Perhaps when you marry might be a better time to start a new tradition."

Sadie was so close to blurting, "If your marriage is any indication of what it's like, then I want nothing to do with marriage." But she kept her mouth shut, her teeth digging into her lower lip while she took the platter of turkey from her father.

"I understand from Sadie, sir, that you're a history professor at the college. What area is your specialty?"

"Nineteenth-century Europe."

"History was one of my favorite subjects in school," Andrew said, taking a sip of iced tea.

Surprised at that bit of information, Sadie said, "I would have thought something like math would have been."

A smile slowly curved Andrew's mouth. "No. To better understand today, you need to understand yesterday."

"My thoughts exactly." Her father tore off a piece of his roll and popped it into his mouth. "I wish more young people felt like you do."

Sadie refused to look at her father. She heard disappointment in his voice. He'd wanted her to go through the graduate program in history and follow in his footsteps, teaching at the college level. He never stopped letting her know she'd let him down.

"Of course, I feel people must do what's important for them," Andrew continued, his silent support conveyed by the expression in his eyes, directed solely at her. "There are many things important in this world. Thankfully there are people like Sadie who love to teach our children. I couldn't do it, but I know we need good teachers like her."

"Right you are, Andrew," her mother said, patting Sadie's hand. "Robert, did I tell you that Sadie was named teacher of the year at Cimarron High School? She'll be competing with others from the elementary and middle schools for teacher of the year for the whole district. She just found out yesterday."

"That's wonderful." Andrew lifted his glass. "Here's to the best."

"Yes, the best," her mother said, raising her iced tea and clicking Sadie's glass.

Sadie turned her attention to her father, almost afraid to see the expression on his face.

"When will you know?" he asked, cutting his turkey into bite size pieces.

"After the new year there'll be a dinner to introduce the individual schools' teachers of the year, and then they'll announce the district one at that time. That person will go on to the state competition."

"Let me know what happens." Her father forked a piece of meat into his mouth.

*Okay, Sadie. What did you expect? A twenty-one-gun salute?* "I will," she murmured, her stomach so tight she didn't think she could eat another bite. Even if she won the teacher of the year for the whole country, she doubted it would be enough for her father. That thought caused her spirits to plummet.

"Personally I don't know how you do it."

Andrew's voice pulled her gaze to him. The look of admiration on his face sent her heart beating rapidly. He smiled at her, a gesture that suddenly seemed to wipe everything from her mind but him.

"I've seen you with your students, and you're amazing. If their opinion counts for anything, you'll win hands down."

"I agree, Andrew," her mother said. "She devotes a lot of time to her students."

Sadie glowed under their praise, trying to dismiss the fact that her father said nothing. She knew he thought she wasted her time working with students with special needs. She didn't think she would ever be able to change his mind. Where she saw loving, giving students who had every right to a full, productive life, her father saw students who would never be complete, contributing members of society.

"I don't care who wins in January. It is an honor to have my daughter representing the high school. Andrew, would you like any more dressing?" Her mother held up the bowl.

He shook his head. "I'm stuffed. This was delicious, Mrs. Spencer."

"Oh, please call me Abby, and I didn't do much. Sadie was up at five this morning getting the turkey ready to go into the oven. I mostly watched this time. It was nice. I don't get to do that often. This was certainly a treat."

Suddenly silence blanketed the room, each person intent on moving food around on the plate. Sadie searched her mind for a safe topic that would put an end to the discomfort at the table. Her mind went blank.

"Dr. Spencer, I understand you write books. Are you working on one right now?" Andrew asked.

In that moment Sadie could have kissed him. Her father's favorite subject was the books he wrote. She forced herself to eat a bite of dressing, waiting to see what her father would reply.

"I'm nearly finished with a biography of Prince Albert. I've spent more time on him than I usually do. I wanted to do justice to the man behind the throne." Her father launched into a discussion about how much influence and power Prince Albert had as the husband of Queen Victoria.

Sadie breathed deeply the rich aromas of the foods about her and relaxed in her chair. With Andrew asking pertinent questions the conversation flowed between him and her father as though this were a normal dinner, not one rife with tension. She observed the ease with which Andrew conversed with her father, the great detail of knowledge he had in a field where her father was an expert.

When there was a lull in the conversation, Sadie rose. "Would anyone like a piece of pecan pie with vanilla ice cream?"

Andrew chuckled. "This from a woman who prides herself on eating well-balanced meals."

"I never said I didn't indulge in tempting desserts from time to time. Remember all those things I bake. Not all of them are oat bran muffins."

"Come to think of it, not many were."

"Have you been invited yet to one of her parties when she empties out her freezer?" Her mother stood, too, and started gathering dishes.

"Not yet, but she has promised to invite me to the next one."

The twinkle in Andrew's eyes melted Sadie's tension completely. "Okay, I don't normally plan one of these parties more than a day in advance, but how about this Saturday night? I need to clear the freezer out. Christmas is just around the corner."

"You're on."

"I've seen what's in her freezer. You're in for a treat."

"Mom. Dad. Do you want to join us?" Sadie stacked the plates to carry into the kitchen.

"Oh, no, dear. Your dad and I have the Henderson party to go to."

Her father's eyes widened. "I thought you said you couldn't make—"

"I've changed my mind. If we're going to work out our problems, we'll need to spend some time together." Her mother marched into the kitchen with her hands full of dirty dishes.

"Any pie?" Sadie asked, realizing her mother's real motive.

Andrew scooted back his chair. "I need to walk some of this delicious food off before I indulge."

Her mother entered the dining room. "Andrew, that's a good idea. Why don't you two go for a walk while your father and I clean up? That's the least we can do, since you prepared the dinner."

Her father's eyes grew rounder. He rarely stepped into the kitchen unless it was to eat, certainly never to clean up. Sadie decided to take her mother up on her offer.

"Yes, I think I will." Sadie hurried into the kitchen and put her stack of dishes on the counter.

When she came into the dining room, she noticed an uneasy silence had fallen again. She grabbed Andrew's hand and started for the front door, snatching a sweater as she left.

Outside she paused on her porch and drew in deep breaths of the cool fall air, perfumed with the scent of burning wood. The sky was cobalt blue with not a cloud anywhere. She tilted her face to the sun and relished its warm rays.

"I doubt you've ever had a Thanksgiving like this one," she said when she felt Andrew's probing gaze on her.

"No, but then I don't usually spend Thanksgiving with a family."

"Not Darrell and Ruth's?"

"When I can get away for a couple of days."

"Which isn't that often."

"Not in the past few years." Andrew began walking.

Sadie fell into step next to him, and his strides shortened to accommodate her. "I'm sorry. My father can be difficult at times."

Andrew slid a smile toward her. "Actually I enjoyed our conversation about Prince Albert. As I said, I like history."

"Then you and my dad have something in common."

"You don't like history?"

"Well, yes, I do."

"Then you and I have something in common."

The idea they had more things in common than she thought nonplussed her, causing her step to slow. Andrew went a few feet in front of her, stopped and turned toward her.

"Is that so hard to imagine, Sadie?"

"That we have things in common? No, I guess not. It's just that you and I live our lives so differently."

"Do we?" He held his hand out for her to take. "I think we live our lives very much the same—all or nothing. I've seen you with your students, and you throw yourself completely into it."

The warmth of his fingers on hers was like the rays of the sun on her face. She savored the feel, realizing somewhere that day she had given up the notion that they were just friends. It was more than that, at least on her part, and that thought scared her more than a confrontation with her father.

They continued their walk, their hands linked. Andrew steered them toward the park.

"If you're going to be a good teacher, you have to give a part of yourself to your students."

"And if I'm going to be a good executive, I have to give a part of myself to the job and the people who work for me."

"But I can draw the line between work and pleasure."

Andrew took a few more steps without saying a word, then he said, "Tell me about your relationship with your father."

She shrugged. "What's there to tell? You saw how we are close up and personal."

"Has it always been strained?"

Sadie thought over her childhood. There was a time when things had been different. She halted in the middle of the path. "No. Everything changed when Bobby died." Why hadn't she seen that before?

"Who's Bobby?"

"My baby brother. He was three and I was nine. He died of a massive infection that had started out as a spider bite."

He came to her, grasping both her hands. His scent chased away all others. "I'm sorry we have that in common. Losing a sibling is so hard."

"But until this moment I never thought about Dad changing. He was always demanding, but loving and caring, usually. After Bobby's death he got worse, never satisfied with anything I did. It was never good enough for him. I always felt I had let him down, that I wasn't the son he had wanted."

"Maybe he's scared."

"Dad?"

"Yes. When you lose someone close to you, sometimes you shut down, afraid to feel anything for anyone."

"Is that experience talking?"

He ignored her question and began walking again, his

pace faster. She started to pursue the question, but the firm set to his jaw proclaimed the subject was off-limits. She clamped her mouth shut. She didn't need him to say yes. She had seen the truth in his eyes before he masked his expression. His feelings shut down the day he lost his family, and Tom's death only cemented Andrew's determination not to care for another. When he was young, all the people he loved had died. How could she combat that?

## Chapter Nine

"Everyone, I want you to meet Andrew, my knight in shining armor," Sadie announced to the group of friends sitting in her living room.

"Okay, you have managed to embarrass me," Andrew whispered in her ear.

"But it is true," she said with a laugh, trying to ignore his breath tickling her neck. "You've saved my work program. I've already recruited another business because IFI is participating."

"I know it hasn't been quite two weeks, but Chris seems to be doing a good job. He's got his route down for the mail run. He always has a smile for everyone. When he comes into my office, he usually stops to say hello if I'm not busy with someone."

"Good. He does brighten a person's day." She swept her arm in a wide arc. "Mingle. I'll let everyone tell you their names. I still have a few more things to put on trays so I can bring them in."

"Need any help?"

"Oh, no. I'm not gonna let you hide out in the kitchen."

"Madam, I never hide out. I was trying to fulfill the role of knight in shining armor and help." The corners of his mouth twitched.

"Sure, Andrew. These are just a few of my friends from school." She gently shoved him toward the group of eight people who were seated in the living room.

"You are cruel, Sadie Spencer."

The laughter in his voice contradicted his words. She gave him a little wave, then headed for the kitchen. She quickly finished preparing the trays and took the first one into the living room, halfway expecting to see Andrew off to the side by himself. Instead, she found him in the middle of the group, laughing at something Sally said. Then Carol made a comment that set everyone off.

"I hope you all have worked up an appetite. I have lots of food to get rid of." Sadie placed the tray on the coffee table and started for the kitchen.

"I'm not sure it's a good thing when a cook announces she must get rid of food," Andrew said, relaxing in the easy chair.

At the door into the kitchen, Sadie said, "Dig in at your own peril. Be back in a sec with more goodies." She heard people moving, and someone sighing with pleasure as he tasted one of her chocolate chip cookies.

She picked up another tray and headed for the door. It swung open. Andrew entered, finishing a brownie.

"I thought the least I could do was help you carry the trays to the living room. This brownie is to die for."

Sadie beamed. "Thanks—I think."

With Andrew's assistance the food was set up on the coffee and end tables so everyone could munch while talking. When Andrew tried to have Sadie sit in the easy chair he'd occupied, she shook her head and sat cross-legged on the floor in front of it.

"Okay, what game do you have for us this time?" Carol asked, taking a sticky bun from a plate.

"Truth or dare?" Sadie waved away the platter of assorted cookies making its rounds.

Sally and Ted groaned.

"How about Trivial Pursuit?" Nathan suggested.

"I'm brain dead. Besides, I got creamed the last time we played." Carol tore off a piece of the sticky bun and popped it into her mouth.

Ted laughed. "You always say that."

"I refuse to remember trivial facts. They clutter up my mind." Carol pointed a finger at Ted. "And not a word from you about that last comment."

Sadie held up her hand. "I guess as usual I'll have to settle this lively debate. We're gonna play charades. We haven't played that in a long time. The guys against the gals."

"Yes! We're gonna cream you," Joyce said to Ted.

Andrew leaned down and whispered into Sadie's ear, "We could just talk."

She shook her head. "You saw the debate about what game to play. You ought to see some of our discussions. Not a pretty sight. This is much safer."

"Did I hear the word safe?" Sally's husband, Mason, reached for another piece of fudge. "Sadie, if you think playing charades will be safe, you've got another think coming. Remember the reason we haven't played it in a long time. The gals cheat."

"We do not!" All of them spoke at the same time.

"We haven't played because you guys are sore losers." Sadie rose and went to a cabinet to retrieve the bag of choices. "And since we won last time, we get to pick which category." She produced a red cloth bag. "Movies it is."

When she sat down next to Andrew, he moved forward on the edge of his chair. "What if we haven't seen a movie in years, have no idea what is current?"

"No problem. Most of these are oldies. Late night TV fare."

"Worse. I don't watch TV unless it has something to do with the food industry. I don't even own one."

Sadie's attention was riveted to him. "You're kidding. You don't watch any shows."

"Nope. Don't have the time to watch."

"You do work a lot." He really did have this work thing bad, Sadie realized. She patted his arm. "Well, do the best you can."

"I think you're gloating, Sadie Spencer. I have to tell you I am a fierce competitor. That should make up for my lack of knowledge."

The glitter in his eyes could only be described as predatory. She shivered. "So am I."

"Then may the best man win."

"You mean woman."

Andrew winked. "We'll see."

An hour later half the food was gone and the score for charades was tied. Sadie and Andrew were the last ones. They were seated across the room from each other. Sadie eyed Andrew in the middle of the group of men and decided she'd created a monster. He'd immersed himself in the game with relish, and even though he hadn't watched many movies, he had come up with a surprising number of right answers.

Sadie shoved her hand into the red bag and drew her selection. She read it and wanted to moan. *Zulu.* Mason flipped the egg timer over, giving her one minute to think of what she would do. What in the world was *Zulu?* A war movie? How was she going to act this one out?

"Time's up," Andrew announced with more glee than he should.

Since everyone knew it was a movie, she held up one finger to indicate one word, then she motioned how many syllables and that she was giving them the first one. Hunching over, she made her arms swing back and forth like a trunk on an elephant—at least that was what she hoped it looked like.

*"Hunchback of Notre Dame,"* Sally shouted.

"Yeah, that's one word with two syllables," Mason said.

"No comments from the peanut gallery." Carol moved closer to Sadie, as though that would enlighten her.

Sadie decided to portray another animal. She got down on all fours and acted like she was roaring—silently, of course, because the men would have declared foul for saying something. Surely she looked regal as she pranced as though she were the king of the jungle.

Joyce jumped up. "Cat."

Sadie lumbered to her feet to encourage Joyce to expand her answer.

"Tiger. Jaguar. Lion."

Sadie spread her arms wide as though to take in everything.

*"Lion King,"* Carol said.

Ted chuckled. "Two syllables, not two words."

Another animal. Sadie began leaping around the area, pounding on her chest and scratching her sides.

"Ape," Sally yelled.

Sadie nodded.

"Ape-man?"

"Is that supposed to be a movie?" Nathan asked, a smug expression on his face. "I thought you might say *Planet of the Apes.*"

Joyce flashed her husband a too sweet smile. "Can't. That's more than one word. Can't you count?"

Mason whistled. "I think she got you there, Nathan."

Before the whole thing fell apart, Sadie quickly went to the second syllable, noticing that over half her time was gone. She pantomimed washing her hands.

"Clean. Dirty."

"Eat."

Sadie continued with putting on makeup.

"Face."

"Beauty."

She tried brushing her hair.

"Bathroom."

Sadie waved her hand to get Sally to say more.

"Restroom? Women? Men?"

The timer went off. Sadie's shoulder slumped and she plopped down on the couch. *"Zulu."*

*"Zulu?"* Carol wrinkled her brow. "I guess the first was animals for zoo, but what was the last part?"

"Loo is the British word for restroom."

Sally rolled her eyes.

"I was desperate," Sadie said in her defense.

Andrew stood and dug into the bag for his selection. "If we win this, we win it all." He looked at his slip of paper and smiled, then handed it to Sadie.

*Battle of the Bulge.* Okay, the gals might still have a chance—if the sun rose in the west. She passed the paper down the row of women, hearing the groans as it made its way to the end.

After disclosing how many words in the title, Andrew launched in with the first one. He punched the air.

"Fight." Mason waved his hand. "I know. *Fight at Okay Corral.*"

"At least my husband can count."

"No, he can't. The title is *Gunfight at the O.K. Corral.* That certainly is more than four words." Joyce crossed her legs and brushed imaginary lint from her jeans.

Andrew began firing a pretend machine gun.

*"The Guns of Navaronne,"* Ted shouted.

Andrew held up one finger.

"Oh, sorry."

Next Andrew acted like he was fighting with a sword.

"Duel."

*"War and Peace. War of the Roses."*

Andrew shook his head.

"Battle."

Andrew nodded vigorously, pointing to Ted. Then Andrew indicated the fourth word. He puffed out his cheeks and held out his arms as though he weighed four hundred pounds.

Mason leaped up. "Fat. Obese. *Battle of the Bulge.*"

"Yes!" Andrew pumped his arm in the air.

She should have been upset that the women lost, but Sadie couldn't take her eyes off the huge grin on Andrew's face or forget the fact that he was high-fiving all the men as they congratulated themselves for their victory.

When the group settled down, Sadie found herself next to Andrew on the couch. Her side was pressed against his while four of them crammed themselves on the large sofa. Andrew shifted and placed his arm along the back cushion, which caused Sadie to be cradled in the crook of his arm. It felt right, she decided.

"I thought you said you didn't watch movies," Sadie said, content within the shelter of his arm.

Andrew smiled, a warm gleam in his eyes. "I don't, but I do love a good puzzle. In fact, I'm quite good at solving puzzles."

"Well, I dare say the guys will be wanting you to come back the next time."

"But not you?" Mischief brightened his eyes.

"I didn't say that."

"I could always restrain myself."

"You? Never. That's not in your nature."

His gaze pinned her. "What is in my nature?"

Suddenly Sadie felt as though they were the only two people in the room. Everything faded from her consciousness but Andrew and the intensity of his look. "You like to control the situation, be in charge. You thrive on challenges." She tilted her head to the side. "You're a loner, but I'm not sure that's what you truly want to be."

One brow arched. "And how did you come to that conclusion?"

She shrugged. "Woman's intuition?"

"When a woman doesn't want to answer a question, she falls back on that."

"What does a man fall back on?"

"Silence."

"You're quite good at that."

"It has come in handy from time to time."

Sadie chuckled. "I bet."

"Care to share what's so amusing?" Sally asked while sharing the easy chair with her husband.

Sadie slanted a glance toward Andrew. "We were discussing the differences between a man and a woman."

"Hold everything. I want this evening to end on a friendly note. I'm afraid if we go down that path my wife's radical views will start a war." Mason squeezed his wife to him, affection in his expression.

"We could always have Andrew act out the word *war.* He was getting quite good at the end." Sally leaned forward and grabbed another brownie.

For the next hour the discussion ranged from how different men and women were to the weather, which Sadie insisted was a safer topic of conversation. Slowly the evening wound down and her guests started to leave. When she closed her front door on Sally and Mason, she turned into the living room to find Andrew was the only one left. He transferred the few cookies on one tray to another, then stacked them to carry into the kitchen.

"You don't have to help clean up."

He glanced toward her. "I know. I want to."

Sadie tried to cover her surprised expression, but she realized she didn't.

"With both of us cleaning up, it won't take long." Andrew headed for the kitchen with the trays.

Sadie remained in the middle of the living room, still trying to shake off the shock. Her father never helped her mother clean up a thing. Even Thanksgiving Day she and Andrew had returned to the house to discover her mother doing all the work with her father watching.

When Sadie finally roused herself to follow Andrew into the kitchen, she found him searching under the sink for some dishwashing soap.

"What are you gonna do with the leftovers?"

"Give them to you?"

His laughter saturated the air like a warm coat in the dead of winter. "I think you spend half your time trying to fatten me up. I'll take a care package, but I'm only one man. There's no way I can finish all this off." He motioned toward the two trays still half filled with goodies.

"Thankfully I have a class who loves sweets. I'll take the rest to school and let them indulge on Monday."

"They must love you."

She blushed under his ardent perusal. "They do like it when I clean out my freezer."

"Come over here and dry." Andrew dunked the first tray into the soapy water.

"First, let me fix up your care package and put the rest into plastic bags."

They worked side by side in silence for a few minutes. Again the feeling of rightness descended over Sadie. When she picked up a towel to dry the large trays, she watched Andrew wipe down her counter and thought how much he looked at home in her kitchen. That realization brought her up short. She sucked in a deep breath and held it until her lungs burned.

While she put away the trays, Andrew prowled the room, coming to a stop at her desk. He stared at the pad, then lifted it and studied it.

"Is this scenery for a play?"

She nodded, bending to push the last tray to the back of the lower cabinet. "I'm in charge of the Christmas play at church this year. I'm trying to come up with the scenery needed. As you can see, I'm not a good artist."

For a few seconds a faraway look came into his eyes. "I used to be in stagecraft when I was in high school. I enjoy—" He bit off the rest of his sentence.

"You used to enjoy making scenery?" She straightened, facing Andrew.

"Yes. I used to like working with my hands. Something about it—" he paused, creasing his brow "—was comforting."

"Well, then, do I have a deal for you. I don't have anyone to build the scenery yet. I sure could use your help."

He shook his head. "I don't think—"

She walked to him and pressed her fingers across his mouth. "Please. Wouldn't it be nice to see if you still feel the same way?"

He sighed, his breath fanning her fingers.

She dropped her hand to her side and waited. Suddenly it was important that he became a part of the Christmas play.

"Okay, if I can find the time."

"Good. The first rehearsal is tomorrow afternoon.

You can come and get an idea of what we're gonna do. Some of the high school youth group will be there. A few have volunteered to help with the pounding of nails. I just need a leader to direct them. And you have such good leadership qualities."

He laid his arms on her shoulders, trapping her in front of him. "And you have such good persuasive qualities. I think I'm doomed."

"We could always have real animals. That should be entertaining." Andrew stretched his long legs out in front of him and relaxed in the chair in the recreational hall at the church.

"Not to mention messy," Sadie said with a glance at him. "No, I think your idea of making animals would be better. With a cast of thirty first, second and third graders, I think that's about all I can handle in any one day."

"Okay, I can get some plywood and make animal cutouts, then have the high schoolers paint them. Didn't you say Cal was a budding artist?"

She nodded.

"Think he could do a cow, sheep and donkey?" Andrew drew in his legs as a small child ran in front of him and leaped over them.

"Jared, no running," Sadie called to the first grader. "Yes, Cal can handle that."

"While he's doing that, Chris and I can build the manger."

"Then you'll make the scenery?" Sadie sat next to Andrew.

"Yes, and I'll definitely have the easier of the two jobs." Andrew surveyed the large room filled with the thirty children waiting for Sadie to direct them. "Where's your help?"

"Carol should be here soon."

"It will just be you and Carol?"

"And now you," she said with a grin as she pushed to her feet and started for the group of children.

"I didn't say anything about working with the kids," Andrew called.

Sadie kept walking as if she didn't hear him when Andrew knew she'd heard every word he had uttered. He watched her gather the older children to her and begin giving instructions, her voice firm but caring.

A natural teacher. She'd make a good mother to his— He put an immediate halt to that thought, shoving the longing to the back recesses of his mind. He had no business visualizing any kind of relationship with Sadie beyond friendship. When the New Year came, he would be drowning in work. Right now, before the holidays, he had a reprieve—a very brief one.

For the next hour Andrew worked with the four high school students, who included Cal and Chris, making plans for the scenery. When Sadie announced play practice was over, the room erupted with children talking and laughing. They had been relatively quiet during the practice, which still amazed Andrew.

"I'll get the wood, paint and supplies. We can start putting everything together next Saturday afternoon at two." Andrew closed his pad, where he had written down the materials he needed.

"Mr. Knight, I'll help you get them."

Andrew started to say he could take care of it himself, but one look at Chris's eager expression and he replied, "Sure. I'll pick you up at noon next Saturday."

"Great!" Chris leaped to his feet. "I'll be a big help."

As he hurried toward his mother, who stood in the doorway into the recreational hall, Sadie approached. "The least I can do is help, too."

"Now you offer to help with the scenery." Andrew looked skyward.

"I've been told I have great timing."

Andrew threw back his head and laughed while thirty young children ran, walked and skipped out of the hall.

"Besides, I have the money to purchase the materials."

"No, I'll take care of it. Consider it my donation." Andrew raked his hand through his hair and scanned the empty hall, silence prevailing for the moment.

He took a deep breath and caught a whiff of Sadie's perfume. He thought of Ruth's rose garden, and memories of the time they'd spent in New Orleans inundated him. The warning signs had been there. He'd never taken another person to his old homestead. Sadie had a way of working her way into his life without him even knowing it until it was too—

Whoa! He put a stop to that thought, too. He was in

control. His emotions concerning Sadie were nothing more than friendship.

"Up for a cup of coffee? I don't want to go home yet." Sadie threaded her arm through his.

"Why?"

"My dad is over at my house talking with Mom. I figure I'll give them some space."

He covered her hand on his arm. "Are you avoiding your father?"

Her fingers tightened. "Yes. I don't want to complicate the situation. They're working on their problems. My presence might make things more uncomfortable."

He would have given anything to have a family. He still missed his parents and sister after all these years. He usually didn't allow himself to think about the past, but Sadie and her situation with her parents had forced the memories to surface.

"Have you ever talked with your father about how you feel?"

She halted her progress toward the door. "No, I wouldn't know where to begin. And don't tell me at the beginning. You saw how Thanksgiving dinner was."

"I didn't say it would be easy, but ignoring your feelings or keeping them bottled up inside of you can't be good."

"This from the man who has such a firm control over his own emotions."

"But I don't have a father I need to come to terms with."

Her gaze locked with his for a few seconds before it slid away. "I'm afraid."

"What could be worse than what you are going through now?"

"An out and out rejection." She hung her head, her shoulders slumping.

He lifted her chin and peered into her eyes. "That's a risk I think you should take. You told me your relationship with him changed after your little brother died. I know losing a loved one can change a person inside. Perhaps your father is suffering more than anyone knows."

She heard the anguish in his words. She doubted he realized it. Through a blur of tears, she laid her hand over his heart, feeling the slow beat beneath her fingertips. "And you've got no one to talk to about what happened to you all those years ago."

"There's nothing for me to talk about."

His heartbeat increased, negating his words. "Are you sure about that, Andrew? Maybe you should have a conversation with God. I think He's the one you're angry at."

He stepped back, his expression closed. "I'm not angry at anyone."

"You aren't? Then why don't you attend church? You used to. What happened?"

"Life. Work."

"That's a cop-out. If it's important, you make room for it in your life."

"I'm here now." He gestured wildly at the foyer leading into the sanctuary.

"That's not the same thing. When was the last time you spoke with the Lord?"

He took a bracing breath, visibly fighting for the control that was so important to him. "It's not going to work, Sadie. You're good at changing the subject when you don't want to discuss something."

"And you aren't?"

One corner of his mouth lifted. "Yes, we both are."

She grasped his hands in hers and held them up. "I'll make a deal with you. I'll speak with my father if you'll come to church with me and speak with God."

He closed his eyes for a moment, his chest rising and falling rapidly. "I'll come to church with you, but I can't guarantee anything beyond that."

"It's a start."

"And how about your part of the bargain?"

"I'll talk to my father."

"When?"

"Soon. That's all I can promise."

"I can live with that."

"Now, how about that cup of coffee and maybe a slice of pie, too?"

"If I hang around you too much longer, I'll have to start watching my weight. I still have several goodies from last night."

"You'll just have to start exercising more." Sadie linked her arm through his and started for the door, a lightness to her step. She liked the idea of him hanging with her—probably too much, if she wanted to avoid heartache. The problem with that was her heart was already involved, and she didn't think that was going to change any time soon.

## Chapter Ten

"You can stop laughing now." In the church's recreational hall, Sadie took another step back from the cow she'd put the finishing touches on.

Andrew pressed his lips together, but his eyes held merriment deep within them.

"But, Miss Spencer, you got paint all over you," Chris exclaimed, not able to contain his laughter.

"Okay, so I got carried away. The cow is done. You and Cal are still painting the donkey." Sadie pointed her brush at the plywood animal in question.

"That's because this is gonna be a work of art. Right, Chris?" Cal dipped his brush into the bucket.

"Yeah, a work of art."

"And what is this?"

Andrew burst out laughing. "I think if we turn it around we can paint the other side and no one will be the wiser. When are the children going to be here?"

"In a few minutes. You aren't trying to get rid of me, are you?"

"Never." The gleam of merriment in Andrew's eyes brightened.

Sadie narrowed her gaze and directed its full force on the exasperating man. "My cow isn't that bad."

"I've never seen a brown and white one quite like that. The markings look like big polka dots."

"It's a Holstein."

"They're black and white, and their dots aren't that round. Besides, I doubt a Holstein was in the manger the evening Christ was born."

"Well, that will be the last time I offer you a little help while I'm waiting for the children to arrive."

"Promise? I think I hear the children in the foyer. You'd better check."

Glancing toward the door, Sadie cocked her head to the side. "I don't hear anyone."

When she looked at Andrew, he'd turned the plywood around to show the unfinished side, and all three of them had moved to stand in front as though that would block her view. She fisted her hands on her waist, screwed her mouth into a mock frown and tapped her foot against the tiled floor. "Do I have to remind you guys that I'm the director? Therefore I am in charge."

Andrew stalked toward her, his brush still in his hand. She eyed it, then looked into his face, set with determination. She took a big step backward and came up against a chair. When he stopped in front of her, she licked her dry lips and thought about making a mad dash for the door.

"If you stay, I can't be accountable for my actions. I have this overwhelming need to paint a polka dot—" with lightning speed he lifted his hand and brushed black paint on her cheek "—here, to match your cow, of course."

"Oh, you didn't!" She brought her hand up to her face and felt the wet paint.

"He did, Miss Spencer," Chris called, laughter in his voice. "Way to go, Mr. Knight."

"Chris, don't forget who your teacher is." Sadie started around Andrew, stumbled into him, grasping his hand with the brush before he realized it and snatching it away. As quickly as she secured the brush, she wiped it across his face from forehead to chin then scrambled away.

Andrew spun. Chris and Cal's laughter echoed through the recreational hall.

"You look like a zebra," Chris said.

"No, Chris. He doesn't have enough stripes—yet." Sadie went to the bucket and immersed the bristles in the black paint. "But I wouldn't want to be accused of not being authentic in my work." She held the brush up and strode toward him.

Andrew's eyes glittered. That should have been a warning to Sadie that she was in big trouble, but she was too elated at getting his brush that she ignored his stance, which spoke of a man ready to do battle.

Before she had a chance to raise her arm, he pinned

it flat against her side. She couldn't move. "I think I do hear the children."

"Too late. Where do you want it?"

"What?"

"The stripe."

"I—" She swallowed her words.

"Don't care, do you?"

"Andrew, the children!"

His gaze trekked downward. "Have you taken a good look at yourself? I don't think it will matter what I do."

Sadie glanced at her old, faded jeans and gray sweatshirt. For the first time she noticed how much brown paint she'd managed *not* to get on the piece of plywood.

"Oh!" Her gaze slipped to Andrew's face. "I was never a neat painter in school. My teachers were always complaining."

"I can see why."

The door to the hall burst open, and several children raced into the room. Sadie turned a pleading look on Andrew.

He leaned close until she felt surrounded by his scent. "This isn't over, Sadie. Just postponed."

"What are you going to do?" She moved an arm's length away.

"I have to think on that one. In the meanwhile, I need to scrub this stripe off." He casually walked past the people filing into the hall as though he wore a black line down his face every day.

But Sadie did see him tense when snickers erupted

from the children he passed. *Oh, my, I'm going to have to stay out of his way.* She wondered how long it would take for him to forget about the stripe.

Then she saw several little girls pointing to her face and giggling behind their hands. That was when Sadie remembered the big polka dot Andrew had painted on her cheek. She hurried after him, saying to the gathering group, "I'll be right back. Sit in the chairs and wait on me."

Ten minutes later, with her face scrubbed, she entered the recreational hall to find the children running around the room and Andrew trying to calm them down and get them into their chairs. The dismay reflected in his expression told her more than anything that this man wasn't used to being around six-, seven- and eight-year-olds. She stood by the door for a few minutes to give him a chance to subdue the masses.

After one seven-year-old boy knocked over a chair, Sadie took pity on Andrew and hurried forward, stopping next to him. Over the din he said, "Don't ever leave me alone with them again."

"I didn't leave you alone. Surely a few children aren't fright—"

"Don't say it. I will readily admit I'm scared of anyone under the age of fifteen and I'm definitely out of my element."

"With some practice you'd get the hang of it. You're a smart man."

"A smart man would have taken one look at the chaos and run the other way."

Sadie laughed, put her two fingers into her mouth and blew a loud whistle that immediately got the children's attention. They stopped where they were and faced her, the noise level down to a low murmur.

"That's much better. Now I would like the shepherds to sit over here, the wise men here." Sadie pointed where she wanted them. "Angels in this row and Mary, Joseph and the innkeeper in front."

All the children dutifully made their way to their designated area.

"I'm amazed. They listened. Where did you learn to whistle like that?"

"My first year coaching. It's a great way to get children's attention. It's one of many survival techniques that I learned early on."

"Since you have everybody under control, I'll just return to the scenery and correct a few things."

Andrew left Sadie standing in front of the children and hurried to the half assembled scenery. After fixing Sadie's cow, he peered up to see her working with the angels. With a smile on her face and a calm demeanor, she looked like an angel herself.

He watched her give them their instructions and marveled at how they listened to her when only fifteen minutes before they were wild. He had thought they had been incapable of settling down. Another thing he was wrong about. With Sadie he was discovering that a lot.

He started to return his attention to the crib he was

constructing when he saw a little boy with tears streaming down his face run to Sadie. She knelt so she was on the child's level and comforted him as he told her how he had bit his lip and it was bleeding. She withdrew a tissue from her pocket and dabbed at his mouth, her words low but soothing. The child calmed down and hastened back to his group.

Sadie Spencer would make a great mother and should have children of her own to love and care for. That thought popped into Andrew's mind, and he couldn't shake it, or the disconcerting feeling that washed through him. Picturing her with another man didn't sit well with him, either. That realization sent his mild discomfort into a full-fledged panic.

He had no claim on Sadie, and yet he couldn't shake the feeling he wanted to. There was no room in his life for a wife, and he couldn't see Sadie as anything but that. Yes, right now he had more time than he usually did, but that was only because it was the holidays, and work at IFI slowed down. Once the new year came he would be so busy he would lose track of whether it was night or day.

Nope, he had no business even thinking of Sadie in any terms except as a friend. She might be mother material, but he wasn't father material.

"Chris, I'll tell you when to pull the curtains open." Sadie paused by the young man and peeked into the audience to see if everyone was seated. Her parents and

Andrew were in the front row. Her mother slipped her arm through her father's and leaned over to whisper something into his ear. Her father smiled.

Her mother had returned to her own home a few days ago on the condition that they continue in therapy. Much to Sadie's surprise her father had agreed, even coming to her house to help her mother pack and move home. Sadie hoped everything worked out for her parents, but she didn't know if that was possible. Her father wasn't having an affair; he was just consumed with his work. He'd never seemed in the past to be willing to make any changes. It had always been her mother bending to his will.

"Miss Spencer?"

A shepherd tapped her on the arm to get her attention. Sadie blinked and looked down. "Yes, Joey."

He crossed his legs and screwed his face into a frown. "I've got to go to the bathroom *bad*."

Sadie glanced at her watch and noted it was time to begin. "Hurry. I'll wait for you to come back before we start."

"I'll be fast."

She surveyed the stage to make sure everything was in place, including the cast. One angel scratched her head, and her halo fell to the side. Joseph pulled on his fake beard, and it caught on his chin. Sadie quickly corrected the problems, then stepped to scan the area again.

She encountered a solid wall of flesh.

Andrew steadied her. "I was sent back here to check and make sure everything was okay."

"Who sent you?"

"Your mother. She remembers when she was the director of the pageant and figured you might need some help."

"I've got everything under control."

The second she said that, Joey raced back, yelling so loud everyone in the audience must have heard, "I'm done going to the bathroom, Miss Spencer."

Sadie winced.

Joey slid to a stop but not before colliding with a cow. It crashed to the floor, dust flying everywhere. One of the angels jumped back and fell against a donkey, which toppled, causing a chain reaction. Sadie squeezed her eyes closed and listened to the falling scenery, flinching every time she heard another piece hit the floor.

Then there was total silence, not even a sound from the audience on the other side of the curtain.

Afraid to look, Sadie pried one eye open.

All the children stood amidst the fallen scenery with their eyes round as saucers and their mouths agape.

"I'm sorry, Miss Spencer," Joey cried, tears coursing down his cheeks.

Practicing her deep breathing, she hurried to Joey and knelt in front of him. "That's okay. I know you didn't mean to do this." She tried not to look at the chaos around her, but her gaze—as though it had a will of its own—skimmed over the mess. "We'll put it right, and the play will go on."

"Okay, kids. Pick up any pieces near you and stand them up." Andrew strode among the children and helped where needed.

Sadie watched as the stage was once again transformed into a stable. She marveled at how efficient Andrew was in getting the cast to assist him. While Andrew was dealing with the cleanup, Sadie parted the curtains and quickly stepped out in front, raising her hands to signal for the audience to quiet down.

"There has been a slight delay. If everyone will remain in their seats, we should be starting very soon."

"That sounded more like an earthquake struck," a man in the back called.

"We had a minor mishap with no injuries."

"Do you need any help?" her mother asked, her brow creased in worry.

"No, I have everything under control." She crossed her fingers behind her back and hoped she was right.

When she looked backstage, the scenery and the children were standing in their proper place. "Okay, it's time to begin." She moved off the stage with Andrew and signaled to Chris to open the curtains.

As they parted, Sadie whispered to Andrew, "I thought you didn't know anything about children."

"I don't, but I do know how to deal with a crisis."

"You have the makings of a father," she said without thinking, and immediately regretted the statement.

Andrew tensed, his expression shuttered. "You have to be around to be a father."

\* \* \*

Reverend Littleton cut the birthday cake for Baby Jesus, then handed the plate to the first child in line. Sadie poured the little girl a cup of punch. When she gave her the drink, Sadie's gaze found Andrew in the crowd. The intensity in his eyes took her breath away. She nearly spilled the next cup. Determinedly she kept her attention on her task, but the hair on the nape of her neck tingled. If she glanced up, she would find Andrew looking at her. That thought disconcerted her but at the same time sent a thrill through her.

"The play was lovely, dear," an older lady said as she stood behind her grandson in line for refreshments. "Of course, when I did it, Joseph didn't forget his lines, and we used a live sheep."

"Yes, Henrietta, I remember that sheep well. Didn't it eat the hay in the manger, then baa the whole way through the play?" Robert Spencer asked, coming up behind Sadie.

The older woman turned beet red and hustled her grandson away with his drink and cake.

"You remember that?"

"Yes. That was the year you were Mary."

"I didn't know you came. I thought you couldn't make it."

"I was in the back and had to leave right after the performance, but I was there to see you woo the audience."

Sadie flushed, never expecting to hear those words from her father. She slanted a look at him and wondered what had happened to him. He didn't compliment. She continued to fill cups with punch, deciding she had better not say anything about this out-of-character action. Instead, she basked in the praise.

"Can I get two glasses for me and your mom?"

"Yes," she said, quickly pouring for her father.

"We're going to leave, but we'll see you tomorrow. Invite your young man if you want, Sadie. I like him."

Her father left her staring at his retreating figure, stunned at what had just transpired.

"Miss Spencer, I'm thirsty," Joey said, thrusting a cup toward her.

"Oh, sorry." She quickly refilled his glass, then finished serving the rest of the lineup.

When she was through, she poured herself and Andrew a cup and headed toward him. Reverend Littleton paused beside Andrew, said a few words, then moved on toward a group of men near Andrew. He watched the reverend progress through the crowd, a thoughtful expression on his face.

As Sadie neared Andrew, their gazes locked, and she felt as though the rest of the people vanished, leaving only her and Andrew in the hall. She remembered her father's words. *Your young man.* Suddenly she realized she wished that were true. She liked Andrew, too, much more than she should. She was afraid she was even falling in love with him.

"What did the reverend want?"

"That he hoped to see me at church."

"I hope you're thirsty." She handed Andrew his cup, not sure what to say. The fact she was falling in love wiped everything from her mind but the man before her.

"I saw your parents sneaking out of here."

Sadie glanced toward the double doors and visualized her and Andrew doing the same. She wanted to be alone with him to explore this new revelation. "Mom says Dad is trying to be more responsive to her needs. She thinks her leaving him really shook him up."

"I'm glad it's working out for them."

"So am I. I hated the idea of them divorcing."

"That seems to be the trend."

"Not in my book. My word means a lot to me. If I pledged myself to another, I would want it to be for life." She thought about her growing feelings for Andrew and panic took hold. If she fell totally and completely in love with him, she could never see herself in a relationship with another man—even if Andrew didn't return her love. She needed to back away from him before it was too late.

"Your pageant was a success."

"I couldn't have done it without your help."

"Yes, you could have. You're a very capable woman."

She warmed under his compliment. She was capable and independent, but she realized she'd enjoyed working on the pageant these past few weekends with Andrew, sharing duties, brainstorming the best way to do something. It was nice not being alone for once.

"I'm glad it's over with. I intend to relax for the rest

of my Christmas vacation. The end of the semester at school and all the holiday preparations have exhausted me. Ready to leave?"

"Yes. I like the idea of relaxing." Andrew tossed down the rest of the punch, then took her cup and threw both cups away.

As they made their way toward the door, Sadie asked, "Is my hearing correct? You said you like the idea of relaxing?"

He placed his hand at the small of her back and guided her from the recreational hall. "Yes, you heard me. You must be rubbing off on me."

"Don't say that too loud. Someone might think you went off the deep end."

"If I do, you're going with me." Clasping her hand, he stepped into the night.

Large snowflakes swirled on the light breeze, dancing in the lights in the parking lot. "We might have a white Christmas! It's been years since we have." She breathed in the crisp, cold air laced with the scent of burning wood.

"This might spoil some people's plans."

"I don't think it will snow much, and I doubt the children will much care. They'll be having too much fun, sledding and building snowmen."

"Is that what you did as a little girl?"

"Sure. Didn't—"

Andrew shook his head. "Remember, I grew up in New Orleans. I don't remember seeing snow until I moved here."

"I like snow as a change of pace in the winter, but I wouldn't want to live too much farther north. I want my snow to fall, then melt in a few days." Sadie emerged from the overhang and turned her face toward the heavens, relishing the feel of snowflakes melting on her cheeks.

Andrew came up behind her and grasped her shoulders. "I still haven't grown accustomed to the cold weather. Let's get in the car before I freeze."

"It would have helped if you had worn a coat." She peered at him, dressed in a nice pair of black slacks with a black turtleneck and a multicolored wool sweater.

"It wasn't snowing when I left my house."

"Don't you listen to the weather?"

"Nope. I usually don't have the time. Besides, I figure what's going to happen will happen. So many times the predictions weren't right that I gave up on believing them."

"True. But that's Oklahoma weather for you. It's hard to predict."

"Then why listen?"

She shrugged, starting toward his car. "Habit."

"Do you do a lot of things out of habit?"

"I wouldn't say a lot. I like to be spontaneous."

Andrew chuckled. "I can vouch for that."

"Since you don't have a spontaneous bone in your body—"

"Hey, I think I resent that. I can go with the flow with the best of them."

"Oh, please, Andrew. Only when it's going your way."

He opened the passenger door for Sadie. "I will admit I prefer being in control to going with the flow."

She waited until he rounded the front of the car and slid behind the wheel before speaking. "You probably have a five-year plan that you haven't wavered from since you came up with it."

"What's wrong with having goals?" He started the engine and slowly backed out of the parking space.

"Nothing. Goals are fine so long as you keep them in perspective. Life happens. Changes occur."

"I know that. I met you, and you were nowhere in my five-year plan."

A sudden silence fell between them, thick and heavy. Sadie didn't know what to say to that revelation, and from the frown on his face, she was sure Andrew hadn't meant to admit something like that to her.

"I'm not sure how to take that," she finally said.

"It's a compliment. I don't allow many things to affect my five-year plan."

"And I do?"

"You've made me question my path, my goals."

"What conclusions have you come to?"

"The jury is still out."

The temperature in the car soared, and it had nothing to do with the heater. Hope blossomed in Sadie's heart, and for a moment she allowed it to grow. But then her doubts began to surface. She didn't think she wanted to be responsible for anyone changing the direction of his life. That put too much of a burden on her.

"I enjoyed going with you to church tonight. Reverend Littleton has a gift for inspiring others." Andrew pulled into her driveway.

"I love the early Christmas Eve service. The children take such a big part in it."

"I like the idea of a birthday celebration afterward. Nice way of reminding the children and adults why we celebrate Christmas."

"It's still early. Do you want to come in for some coffee—the decaf kind?"

"Love to."

When Sadie entered her house, the scent of pine and cinnamon assailed her. Her live tree dominated the living room, and the aroma from baking cookies hung in the air. She plugged in the lights before heading for the kitchen to make the coffee. Andrew followed.

"Your home is so inviting."

"I love to decorate. I probably go overboard."

"You think?" Andrew scanned the kitchen, filled with Christmas items, from the towels hanging on the stove to the canisters on the counter to the Christmas cards on the refrigerator.

"Okay. I do go overboard. But in my defense, it's hard not to get wrapped up in the holidays with the students I teach. A lot of the ornaments on the tree are made by them. Every year when I put them up, I think about the students who made them. To me it's like a photo album of memories. Do you have a tree?"

"No. I'm not home much to enjoy it."

His words evoked a sadness in Sadie that she couldn't shake. She wanted to put her arms around him and tell him this Christmas he wasn't alone. Instead she prepared the coffee, her hands trembling, her throat tight. Andrew had lost his sense of family and home. The day of the fire, his house was not the only thing destroyed.

*Dear Lord, help me to guide him back to You. He needs You. He needs to believe in belonging again.*

The aroma of brewing coffee spiced the air, lending a homey warmth to the room. Sadie faced Andrew, leaning against the counter. Her smile quivered at the corners of her mouth. "If I had known that, Andrew Knight, I would have brought a tree to your house and helped you put it up."

"A pine without any decoration would have looked strange in the middle of my living room."

"You don't have any?"

He shook his head.

Sadie knew then what she would give him for Christmas, in addition to the mystery she had bought him. "Then you can enjoy my tree tonight and my parents' tomorrow. They wanted you to come to dinner. I think my father will behave this time."

"Are you gonna be there?" His eyes crinkled in a smile.

"Yes, and I would love for you to join us."

"Then in that case, I will."

"Good." Sadie twisted to pour two cups of coffee, then handed one to Andrew. "Let's sit in the living room."

She opened the blinds over the French doors that led

to the patio so they could watch the snow fall. With all the lights out except those on the Christmas tree, the room was dim and cozy, a magical feel to the atmosphere. Sadie sat next to Andrew on the sofa and let the silence between them lengthen.

"Do you have trouble driving in the snow?" she finally asked as the white on the ground deepened.

"No. I may be from New Orleans, but I manage to get around okay. In fact, I'll pick you up tomorrow morning to go over to your parents."

"I appreciate that. I may be from here, but I don't do well driving in the snow. I got stuck once on a hill. My car slid all the way down and into a ditch. I had to abandon it and walk to a store to call my father to come rescue me." The memory blazed across her mind, reminding her of yet another incident where she hadn't quite lived up to what her father had thought she should be able to do. He hadn't been pleased that she had interrupted his writing time.

"That can happen to anyone."

"Yes, I suppose it could," she murmured, pushing the memory into the background. "But still you'd better not stay too long. I don't think I could rescue you."

"I think you could do anything you set your heart to."

Sadie placed her half empty mug on a coaster on the coffee table. "I appreciate the compliment, but I'm still not gonna get out in this weather to tow you out of a ditch."

"Chicken."

She looked him directly in the eye. "Yes, and proud of it."

His laughter wove its magic about her. In that moment she knew the possibility she was in love with him was a reality. She also realized her heart would probably be broken by this man.

He put his cup down, too. "I think I'd better go. I wouldn't want to be tempted—to call you if I needed to be pulled out of a ditch."

She rose at the same time he did. They stood a foot apart between the sofa and the coffee table with little maneuvering room. "I—" She swallowed several times. "Will you go with me to the teacher banquet in a few weeks?"

"The one where they announce the teacher of the year for your school district?"

She nodded, acutely aware of the man so close she could reach out and touch the lines of his face.

"I'd love to. And when you win I intend to embarrass you with my applause."

A blush heated her cheeks. "I might not win. There are some good teachers up for the honor."

He moved closer and clasped her upper arms, his fingers rubbing circles. "If you don't win, that's their loss."

She thought for a moment he was going to kiss her, but instead he squeezed by her and walked toward the front door. On the porch he stopped and glanced at her.

"Drive safely, and call me when you get home."

His eyes widened for a few seconds. "I don't think anyone has ever said that to me."

"Then there's a first time for everything."

She watched him get into his car and pull out of the

driveway. She waved to him, then waited until he was at the end of her street before she went into her warm house. She leaned against the front door and closed her eyes, imagining him with the snow falling around him, his footprints to his car marring the pristine white landscape.

She wanted him in her life. Would he disappear like his footprints in the continuing snowfall? She felt her heart crack with the answer.

## Chapter Eleven

"I should have realized you had an ulterior motive when you insisted I bring my heavy coat." In Sadie's parents' foyer, Andrew zipped up his jacket and fitted his gloves on his hands.

"Trust me. You'll enjoy this. When I was growing up, I couldn't wait for a snowfall. I got out of school, but I also got to play in the snow. Everyone should at least once in his life build a snowman." Sadie tugged open her parents' front door and stepped into the crisp, cold air.

"I suppose if this was summer you'd have me running around catching fireflies and putting them in a jar."

"Oh, no. I don't believe in that. But I do like to watch them on a summer's night." She paused on the porch and scanned the blanket of white, the snow muffling any sounds.

"So where are you going to build this snowman?"

She quirked a brow at Andrew. "Me?"

"You don't seriously expect me to roll balls of snow around on the ground, do you?"

"Yes."

"Oh, all right." He exaggerated a sigh. "Let's get this over with."

"You don't have to act like this will be torture." Sadie marched down the steps and trudged into the yard. "We'll put it here." She bent over, packing some snow into a ball, then she began to roll it along the ground.

Andrew watched her for a good minute, then followed her lead. "I hope no one from the office drives by."

"This is a dead-end street. I think you're safe."

Fifteen minutes later Sadie had the bottom part done. Sweat beaded her forehead, and she swiped her gloved hand across her brow. "I forgot how much work this was."

"I thought we were playing." Andrew lifted his large snowball and placed it on top of hers.

"We are. Sometimes playing can be hard work."

"Are we through?"

"We are if you want a headless snowman. Tell you what, go inside and ask my mom for a carrot and a box of raisins. I'll finish the last part."

"And have your mother think I'm crazy? No, you go inside and get those things. I'll make the last ball."

"Mother's used to strange requests from me."

"Now that doesn't surprise me." Andrew started on the last snowball.

Sadie hurried inside and found the food she wanted to make the face. On her way out she noticed her father stacking logs in the fireplace. She loved sitting in front of a warm fire after being outside in the cold. She couldn't wait to share the cozy moment with Andrew and give him his presents.

When she emerged from the house, she found Andrew positioning the last snowball. He stepped back to examine his efforts. Sadie stuffed the carrot and box of raisins in her pocket, then leaned over, scooped up a handful of snow and packed it into a ball. Straightening, she threw it at Andrew. The snow sputtered against his overcoat. She quickly made another and aimed for his chest. The ball hit him in the side of the head because he moved at the last moment—toward her.

"I didn't mean to hit you in the face."

He kept coming, his intentions to get even clearly written in his expression. "That's okay. And I'm not gonna mean to do what I'm gonna do."

"What's that?" She squeaked the words and took a huge step back.

With lightning speed he closed the space between them, barreling into her and sending her into a snow pile. "This."

His massive body covered hers for a few seconds before he rose and offered her his hand. She gathered some snow and hurled it at his chest. His eyes widened, then narrowed on her.

"I was trying to be a nice guy, but this is war. I still remember the paint incident at play rehearsal."

Quickly he made several balls, then launched them

at her. One hit her in the back as she scrambled to her feet, the other on her leg as she ran toward the porch. He stalked her, bending down every few feet to form another snowball and toss it at her. She managed to dodge the third one, but the fourth ball got her in the chest.

"Uncle! Uncle!" She glanced over her shoulder to see if Andrew had stopped his pursuit.

He was still coming with a relentlessness that must pay off in the business world.

She almost made it to the front door when he halted her escape inside.

He leaned close and whispered, "Where are you going? We haven't finished what we started."

"That depends on what you're talking about."

"The snowman. What else is there?"

His breath tickled the skin below her earlobe. She trembled, even though sweat ran in rivulets down her face. "You're not going to throw any more snowballs?"

"I won't if you won't."

"A deal." She released her hold on the doorknob and turned toward him. He smashed a ball into her face.

"You lied."

"I didn't. I didn't throw a thing."

She wiped the cold snow from her while peering at his other hand to make sure he didn't have anything in it.

"We're even now." He backed away, holding his arms out. "I'll be good unless you decide to take me on again."

"I've learned my lesson. You fight dirty."

"I fight to win. I learned that long ago, Sadie."

His words, spoken with a hard edge, embedded coldness like a sweeping blizzard deep inside her. She needed to remember that. He was after the presidency of IFI, and nothing and no one would stand in his way. Heartache chipped at her composure.

Sadie quickly finished the snowman, arranging the carrot for the nose, two pieces of bark for the eyes and the raisins for the mouth. After sticking two broken limbs for arms into the middle snowball, she stood back and inspected their creation. He leaned to the left, and the balls weren't proportional, but she didn't care. Andrew and she had made it together, and even with his grumbling, she suspected he hadn't minded. He could play when forced to.

A cold breeze sliced through her, reminding her that her backside was wet from lying in the snow. She shuddered and hugged herself. "I think I need to get inside and warm up."

"I probably should be going soon. I certainly enjoyed the dinner. I appreciate your parents including me."

"And this time my father behaved himself." Sadie started for the house.

"Have you talked to him yet?"

She halted, as stiff as if a cold wind had ripped through her and frozen her. "I haven't found the right time."

"Don't wait too long, Sadie." Andrew came up beside her and took her hand. "I've never told anyone this, but my dad and I had a fight the evening of the fire. I ran up to my bedroom after shouting at him that I hated him.

I never got to tell him I loved him, that I didn't mean what I'd said that night. I would give anything to be able to take those words back. But I can't, and it's too late to ask him to forgive me."

She grasped his other hand. "He knew you loved him and he forgave you. Children say things they don't mean. Parents know that."

"It doesn't change the way I feel. There's an emptiness inside of me that I can't fill."

"Seek God's guidance. He'll help you fill that void."

"I don't know if that's possible. I've lived so long with this hollow feeling." He brought their clasped hands to his chest, covering his heart.

"You're always welcome to go with me to church. The children love you, and Reverend Littleton is a wonderful listener. Look what he was able to do with my parents."

"Maybe your dad was ready and just needed a push."

"And maybe you're ready. Faith is a great healer, Andrew."

He cupped her face. "I'll think about it if you'll think about talking with your father."

"That was our deal." Emotions swelled in her parched throat. "Now, I have something for you, and I can't wait another minute to give it to you."

"You got me a present?" Surprise laced his voice.

"Yes, I like to give presents to my friends."

He slid his hand into his pocket and withdrew a small wrapped box. "So do I."

"You got me a present?" The same surprise was in her voice as she took the gift from him.

"I started to give it to you ahead of time, but then I remembered you saying something about unwrapping presents before you should then rewrapping them so no one knew you peeked early."

"So you took the temptation away from me. Now that's what I call a friend."

Inside Sadie shed her overcoat, gloves and hat, then opened the closet door to retrieve his gifts. She handed them to him. "Let's open them in the living room."

When Andrew stepped into the room, he froze, every line of his body tensing. His gaze was riveted to the fire raging in the hearth. Emotions flooded his face, usually so controlled.

He swung around and left. "I can't."

Sadie hurried after him and caught him in the foyer as he was shrugging into his coat. "I'm sorry about the fire. I wasn't thinking. I should have said something to Dad about it. We always burn a yule log on Christmas Day."

"And you should. It's part of your tradition."

"Please don't leave just yet."

He inhaled a deep breath and held it. "I don't usually look back, and these past few days I've done more reflection than…" His voice faded into silence as he glanced away from her. "I can't stay, Sadie. I need to be alone."

He wrenched open the front door and walked away, leaving her staring at his retreating figure. She wanted to run after him; he had thrown up a barrier between them, erected over the years to protect his heart. Tears blurred her vision as she swung the door closed and felt the emptiness of the foyer.

Then she remembered the gift he had given her, still clasped in her hand. She carefully unwrapped it and lifted the lid. Beautiful gold earrings with hearts dangling from hoops lay nestled in red tissue. A small card was in the lid.

Sadie read the words, and her tears ran down her face. *To a lady with a heart of gold.*

Andrew sought refuge in his house with not one Christmas decoration to adorn its sterile decor. He slowly turned in his living room and scanned his possessions. The oak furniture was utilitarian and simple. The tables were devoid of knickknacks. The room reminded him of any number of suites he'd stayed in while traveling for business. Nothing personal. Nothing to tie him to the place. That was always how he'd wanted it—until now. Until Sadie. Now he dreamed of more.

But he wasn't good at relationships. For years he'd kept his emotions so tightly bottled up inside him that he'd lost the ability to express his true feelings. Because of that he certainly couldn't see himself getting married. With Sadie that would be the only way.

His gaze fell to the two wrapped presents she'd given him. He didn't make a move toward them, afraid to open the gifts because they would be personal—not like those he received from acquaintances and business associates. The presents on his coffee table mocked him, demanding to be opened.

He reached for them, a slight tremor in his grasp. He picked up the flatter of the two and quickly tore the paper away to reveal a mystery book by a popular writer. He flipped open the book to find that Sadie had inscribed a message to him. *For the day you decide to take a vacation and relax.*

His chest felt tight, each breath he inhaled searing his lungs. The tight lid on his emotions popped off, and a few leaked out.

When he unwrapped the second present, he took his time, wanting to prolong the discovery of what lay beneath the green foil for as long as he could. He opened the box and nearly dropped it. Inside was a hand-painted Christmas ornament with his name on it and a message that said, "The first of many."

Many what? Christmases together? Ornaments from her? He pushed the box away. What lay inside demanded too much of him. Didn't she know he wasn't capable of giving himself?

Andrew unlocked his front door and stepped to the side to allow Sadie past him. He wanted to give her something of himself—his time. It was a small gesture to arrange a special dinner for her, but he suspected she would appreciate it. "You really don't have to do this," Sadie said, entering Andrew's house for the first time, a delicious aroma of baking food drifting from the kitchen.

"Yes, I do. You've cooked for me on numerous occasions. Now it's my turn."

"But you can't cook."

"But I know how to order." Andrew held up his forefinger. "This is very good at dialing."

"I like a resourceful man."

"I aim to please." He showed her into the living room, taking her coat and laying it over the back of a chair.

Sadie stopped and stared at the Christmas ornament she had made for Andrew. It hung from a stand on an end table. Except for a beautiful hand-painted lamp, her gift to him was the only thing on the table. In fact, as she surveyed the room, the only other items that indicated this was a person's home were a photograph of Ruth, Darrell and their little girl and some magazines, all business related, scattered on the coffee table. This glimpse into Andrew's private life made her sad.

"Thank you for the gifts." Andrew sat on the black leather couch and motioned for her to sit also. "But I have to admit your ornament looks kind of lonely sitting over there by itself."

"I was hoping you'd feel that way and add to your collection of one."

"Stranger things have happened."

"With a few touches of color, a couple of pillows, this room—" she began with a wave of her hand.

"Don't, Sadie." Andrew pressed his finger against her mouth to still her words. "I'm rarely here. I spend more time in my office than here."

"What I saw of your office, you could use some color there, too, and a few knickknacks to personalize the place."

"Why? They only collect dust." He relaxed on the sofa.

"I guess that's one way of looking at it. I prefer to think of the various items I have around my house as mementos of my past."

"But you forget I don't dwell in my past."

"Don't you?"

"What do you mean by that?"

"I think your past very much dictates how you live now. You say you don't look back, but what happened to you in the past is what has made you the man you are today."

A frown creased his forehead, and he pinched his mouth into an unyielding line. "I suppose you have a point."

"I have my moments." Sadie sat up straighter, twisting so she faced Andrew on the couch. "Listen, about Christmas Day. I'm so sorry about the fire. I wasn't thinking."

He held up his hand to stop her flow of words. "I know you didn't mean anything by it. You would think a grown man could be in the same room as a fire, and usually I can. But for some reason I felt as though the walls were closing in on me."

"My parents missed saying goodbye to you."

"Please give them my apologies."

"I already have. They understand."

For a moment an uncomfortable silence pulsated between them. She felt as though she could hear his heart beating, and its fast tempo matched hers.

"How long did the snowman last?" Andrew shifted on the couch, sliding his arm along the back cushion behind Sadie.

"About twenty-four hours. It toppled over before it completely melted. I'm not sure naturally or from the two boys across the street. Either way, it bit the dust. All that was left was the carrot and two pieces of bark. I think the birds took the raisins." She realized she was chattering, but she was nervous, as though this evening something would change between them.

The sound of her stomach rumbling drew a raised brow from Andrew. "I suppose you're ready to eat."

She nodded, a sheepish smile on her face. "I forgot to eat lunch today."

"No! Not you? The woman who lectured me on what a proper breakfast was?"

"I spent all day taking down my Christmas decorations. It was a huge task."

"I can imagine, after seeing your house. Was there any room you didn't have something in?"

She thought for a moment, her head tilted to the side. "Nope, not that I can think of. As a teacher I collect a lot of things at this time of year. I have to find somewhere to display them."

Andrew pushed himself off the sofa and turned to help her up. "A few of the decorations did look homemade."

She placed her hand in his and rose. "Those are my favorites. Anyone can go out and buy something. It means a lot to me when one of my students makes me something for the classroom or my house."

"I noticed you collect angels."

"And snowmen. Those were in the back bedrooms. I'm thinking of doing one of those Christmas villages."

"I think you're a kid at heart."

"Teaching students keeps me young."

"That from an old lady of thirty."

"I'll say that when I'm fifty. It's hard to be around young people and not be caught up in their exhilaration, their youthfulness."

"That's your fountain of youth?"

"You know, I never thought of it that way, but you're right. But I also need food, so lead the way."


"I must say you do a good job of ordering a delicious dinner." Sadie folded her napkin and placed it beside her empty plate. "What's for dessert?"

"You ask that after eating a healthy portion of prime roast beef, potatoes au gratin, steamed carrots and a Caesar salad, not to mention two rolls?"

"Yep. I always save room for dessert."

"Where? Your big toe?"

"Didn't you notice I ate extra slow? That way I have more room for what I'm sure will be something chocolate."

"You're very sure of yourself."

"You've admitted a weakness for chocolate just like me."

He scraped his chair back and gathered their plates. "Coffee?"

"Yes, please. Can I help?"

"No, you're my guest. Sit back and relax. I'll be just a minute."

Sadie took in her surroundings. The mahogany dining room table shone with a high polish, reflecting the chandelier's many crystal pieces. There was no china cabinet, but there was a buffet table with a silk flower arrangement that matched the one in the center of the table. The room dripped elegance, but again she felt its impersonal touch.

Andrew shouldered the kitchen door open and entered with two plates of chocolate fudge cake. After putting them on the royal blue place mats, he went back for the coffee, poured them a cup and sat down.

"Now this is what I call a real dessert," Sadie exclaimed, leisurely sliding the first forkful into her mouth and savoring the luscious taste.

When she'd finished the last bite, Andrew smiled and asked, "Another piece?"

"I'll take a rain check on that. Better yet, you can send a slice home with me. One for the last day of the old year and the first day of the new year."

"You have everything figured out."

"Not by a long shot." She rose. "Let's get these dishes cleaned up so we can greet the new year in proper style."

"And what's that?"

"I brought hats and horns for both of us."

"I haven't worn a silly hat since a birthday party when I was eight."

"Oh, good. Then you know how much fun we'll have," Sadie said as she pushed her way through the swinging kitchen door. She took the plates to the sink, and when Andrew entered, added, "This is one of the cleanest kitchens I've ever seen."

"That's because it's rarely used. Even tonight all I had to do was heat up the dishes. Simplicity is my middle name."

"I'll rinse the dishes while you put them in the dishwasher. You do know how to do that, don't you?"

"I'm not that hopeless in the kitchen."

"No, the dinner was heated to perfection."

"See, there's hope for me." Andrew took the first plate she rinsed.

Twenty minutes later, the kitchen was spotless again. Sadie dried her hands on a paper towel and tossed it into the garbage can under the sink. "I didn't realize it was so late. We only have twenty minutes until midnight."

"We got a late start, and you ate slow."

"Hurry. I want to get our hats."

"I was hoping you forgot about them," Andrew grumbled as he followed her into the living room.

She produced a bright gold hat with a point and red glitter, she set it on her head, then gave him one that was silver with blue sparkles. Next she pulled out of her bag two horns and some confetti. "Now we're ready, with fifteen minutes to spare."

"Do we just stand here and wait or can we relax on the sofa?"

"When was the last New Year's Eve party you went to?"

"Last year. I'm not as hopeless as you think."

"Did it have something to do with IFI?"

He looked uncomfortable, a tiny frown furrowing his brow. "The president gave a party for all the executives."

"That doesn't count."

He stepped toward her. "Yes, it does. A party is a party."

"Okay, maybe half." She moved closer to him.

They stood in the middle of his living room, their gazes trained on the clock on the mantel. Silence ruled as the minutes ticked by.

"Five. Four. Three. Two. Happy New Year," Sadie said, blowing her horn and tossing confetti into the air.

As bits of paper drifted down, Andrew closed the space between them and drew her into his arms. He bent forward and kissed her, his embrace tightening.

Her emotions swirled as though they were confetti caught in a breeze. His arms around her felt so right. Andrew Knight in her life felt right.

When he touched his forehead to hers, she breathed in the scent of him and knew there would never be another man for her. She framed his face and compelled him to look her in the eye. "I love you, Andrew. I can't pretend otherwise any longer."

Everything came to a standstill for a long moment.

It seemed as though her heart stopped beating, her breath trapped in her lungs.

Then all of a sudden he moved away from her. He placed several feet between then, tearing the silver hat off his head. Something akin to fear shone in his eyes as he stared at her. Then he shuttered his look and turned away.

"I'd better drive you home now. I have work to do tomorrow. And yes, I know it's New Year's Day and a holiday, but the work still has to be done." Andrew took her hand and squeezed it, his expression softening for a few seconds. "Things will start to heat up now that the holidays are over. I've played long enough."

Sadie felt a door slam shut in her face. He was securing his emotions against her, and she wasn't sure there was anything she could do about it. The crack in her heart widened.

## Chapter Twelve

"I'm glad you could come so quickly, Miss Spencer." Mrs. Lawson motioned for Sadie to have a seat in front of her desk in her office at IFI.

"You said something about Chris having some problems at work that you wanted to discuss with me. What's wrong? Chris seems happy working here."

"Perhaps too much. That's the problem. When he delivers mail, I've seen him hugging some people in the offices or high-fiving others."

"I know he can be a bit enthusiastic when he sees someone he knows. Has anyone complained?"

"No, but that's not proper in a place of business."

"Have you talked with Chris about this?"

"No, I thought I would discuss it with you first. I've never dealt with someone—" the woman searched for her next words "—like Chris."

Sadie shifted, her hands clenching the arms of the chair. "Do you want me to talk to Chris?"

"That might be best," Mrs. Lawson said with relief in her voice.

Sadie rose, silently counting slowly to ten. She started for the door but stopped and pivoted. "Mrs. Lawson, Chris is just like anyone else working for you. If he's doing something wrong, I've often found him eager to change. He likes to please people."

Sadie left the woman's office before she said something that would ruin Chris's chances of working at IFI after graduation. She walked straight to Chris's station, touched his arm and indicated he follow her outside.

In the hallway Sadie pulled Chris over to the side for privacy. "How's it going?"

"Great. The people are nice."

"I'm glad you like it here. Chris, Mrs. Lawson feels you're too friendly with people when you greet them. Remember what I've always said about shaking people's hands."

"But I like them. I thought you hug people when you care."

"Not at a place of business. Can you remember that? It's important when you greet someone to say hi and shake his hand. No hugging or high-fiving. High-fiving is fine for school but not here."

"Yes, Miss Spencer. I'll remember."

The smile he gave her reassured her that he would

try his best. "Good. Now, you'd better get back to work. I'll talk with you tomorrow at school."

"See you." Chris waved before going back into the mail room.

Sadie glanced at the bank of elevators at the end of the hall and wondered if Andrew was in his office. She wanted to tell him what time the dinner on Saturday started. Being a spur-of-the-moment kind of person, she headed for the elevator and rode up to his floor.

When she saw Mrs. Fox manning her desk, Sadie inhaled a deep, fortifying breath and approached. "Is Andrew busy?"

"Yes." Mrs. Fox looked up, her mouth pinching into a thin line.

Sadie suspected the woman wasn't too happy about how she had circumvented her to get to Andrew. "May I see him?"

"Just a moment." Mrs. Fox buzzed Andrew and announced Sadie was in the reception area. "Go on in, Miss Spencer."

"Thank you." Sadie flashed the woman a huge smile and walked to Andrew's door.

When she entered, he was already halfway across his office. "I won't keep you. I just wanted to tell you when the teacher's dinner is."

"This Saturday, isn't it?"

"Yes. It's at seven at The Garden."

"Then I'll pick you up at six-thirty. I should be through with my meeting by then."

*Through with his meeting?* A rift of unease shivered through her.

His phone rang. Andrew held up his hand and said, "Just a moment."

Striding quickly to his desk, he snatched up the receiver and spoke low into it. Whatever the person on the other end said clearly upset Andrew. His mouth slashed into a frown, and his grip tightened. He turned his back to her and finished the conversation.

She had no right to feel shut out of his life but she did. The barrier she had experienced New Year's Eve seemed higher, and she was aware the man she had gotten to know over the holidays was retreating and the businessman was firmly back in place.

Andrew put the receiver in its cradle with such control that another tremor shuddered down her. She wanted to ask him what was wrong, but again the sense that she was intruding where she shouldn't was underscored by the tight expression on his face when he pivoted toward her.

"If you want, I can meet you at The Garden if you're gonna be pressed for time." She clutched the straps of her purse until her hands ached.

"No, I should be all right. I'll be there at six-thirty." He strode forward, taking her by the elbow, his features softening somewhat. "But I am pressed for time now. I need to be in the president's office in ten minutes and I still have some information I need to gather."

"I understand," she murmured, one part of her

mourning a loss as though Andrew had told her he never wanted to see her again. "I look forward to seeing you Saturday."

The sound of the door closing as she left his office reinforced the feeling of being shut out of his life.

Sadie paced from one end of her living room to the other, glancing at her watch for the tenth time in three minutes. Andrew was late. It was six forty-five and— The ringing phone startled her, and she jumped. Quickly she answered it, praying nothing had happened to him. "Hello."

"Sadie, I've been delayed," Andrew said in a whispered rush. "Hopefully I'll be able to make the dinner later. Please go to the restaurant without me."

Sadie heard some people talking in the background. "I'll save you a seat. Good—"

The phone line went dead. Sadie stood in the middle of her living room holding the receiver and listening to the dial tone. Then, as if she finally realized she was going to be late for a dinner in her honor, she hung up the phone, snatched her purse and hurried to her car, pushing her swirling emotions to the background. She didn't have time to feel—to fall apart.

Five minutes after seven, she entered The Garden and the hostess directed her to the back room where the dinner was being held. She found the table her parents were sitting at and slipped into the empty chair next to her father.

"Where's Andrew?" he asked, passing her the basket of rolls.

"He'll be late. He got tied up at work."

"At Christmas he was telling me about the demands of his job. He has a lot of responsibility at IFI."

"Yes, he does." She heard the tension in her voice and wasn't surprised at her father's probing look.

"Are you two serious?"

"We're just friends, Dad. As you said, Andrew is too busy for much of a life outside of his work."

"There's nothing wrong with a man working hard."

She was thankful the waitress started serving the main course of roasted chicken so she didn't have to reply to her father's statement. He would feel that way, since most of his life he'd buried himself in his work, often to the neglect of his family. She already felt wrung out and certainly didn't want to get into that with her father.

Every time the door opened to admit someone into the private dining room, Sadie looked, expecting to see Andrew. By the time the waitress removed the main course and brought out the dessert, Sadie gave up.

When the superintendent rose and went to the podium, her stomach twisted into a huge knot. This was a big moment, and she wanted Andrew sitting next to her. Her father reached over and took her hand, squeezing it as the man spoke about the honor of being selecting as a teacher of the year from a school. Then the superintendent described each candidate up for teacher of the year from the Cimarron City public schools.

"Our candidate representing the high school has many roles as a teacher of special needs students. Within her classroom she has faced many challenges that most would never dream of dealing with. She has gone beyond her role as a special education teacher to set up a peer tutoring program for regular education students at Cimarron High School. It is heartwarming to see these peer tutors forming friendships and helping with students who have special needs. Outside the classroom she is a coach for Special Olympics and enjoys taking her team to many sports activities throughout the year. She also is the vocational coordinator, visiting job sites where her students work as well as developing potential job sites for possible employment opportunities for her students. Please give a round of applause for Sadie Spencer."

Blushing, Sadie stood. She was never comfortable with compliments. After she resumed her seat, the superintendent went through the rest of the candidates.

"Each one of these teachers would be a great representative for our school district. Now I have the good fortune to announce…" He paused and tore open an envelope.

Sadie's mother leaned in front of her father and whispered, "I feel like I'm at the Academy Awards. Good luck, sweetheart."

"She's the best. She doesn't need luck," her father said. "If she doesn't win, it's their loss."

Sadie's gaze fastened onto her father.

"The winner is Sadie Spencer from Cimarron High School."

"I knew you would win." Her father winked at her.

She sat in her chair, speechless, not having prepared anything to say. She heard the applause, but the sound seemed far away.

Her father nudged her gently in the side. "You'd better go up to the podium."

"I didn't write a speech."

"You'll think of something. It's rare that you don't have something to say."

On the long walk to the front of the room the one thing that kept repeating itself in her mind was how much she wished Andrew was here to share her good news. She glanced at the door one last time before stepping up to the podium.

"I'm speechless," she said into the mike.

"We know better than that, Sadie. You're never speechless," a fellow high school teacher called.

Sadie smiled. "What I meant is that I didn't write a speech. The other candidates were so deserving that I didn't allow myself to think about winning this honor, and indeed it is an honor to represent this school district for Oklahoma Teacher of the Year. Cimarron public schools are simply the best in the state."

Applause erupted, and a few cheers.

Sadie waited until the noise died down to continue. "I have a lot of people to thank for me being here tonight, but without God's guidance and support I wouldn't be standing here receiving this honor. He is the first one I must thank. The next are the students I'm privileged to teach. I have learned so much from them and hopefully in the process have taught them some life lessons. Then, of course, I must include in this list my parents and the staff I work with at Cimarron High School. Thank you."

Amidst clapping and a standing ovation, Sadie took the plaque from the superintendent and shook his hand. She started to walk to her chair when he stopped her.

Leaning into the microphone, the superintendent said, "That speech is one of the many reasons we chose Sadie Spencer for this honor. She will represent our school district well at the state level. Thank you, Sadie, for teaching our children."

Sadie made her way toward her table, pausing to shake people's hands and to exchange a few words with some people she'd taught with for years. When she arrived at her chair, her father rose and hugged her, then her mother. Tears welled in Sadie's eyes. Her father rarely embraced her, and certainly not in front of so many people. This should be one of the happiest moments of her life, and yet there was a part of her that was sad, as though the evening wasn't totally complete without Andrew. When had she come to depend on him to define her happiness?

"Honey, you were wonderful up there," her mother said, kissing her on the cheek. "Don't you think so, Robert?"

"You couldn't have prepared a better speech, if you ask me." Pride oozed from his voice. "You really enjoy teaching your students, don't you?"

"Yes, Dad, very much." Peering into his eyes, she finally saw understanding about her choice to become a teacher for students with special needs.

"I guess I never stopped to really listen to you."

Tears cascaded down her cheeks. She wiped them away, only to have more replace them.

"After this is over, we need to celebrate. Where would you like to go, Sadie?" her father asked, his arm around her shoulders.

"Home." She needed to leave before she totally broke down in front of everyone.

"We can do that. I believe your mom baked a cake this afternoon for the occasion."

It took Sadie twenty minutes to make it to her car. She hoped she murmured the right words to everyone's congratulations, but she wasn't sure. She felt confused, at loose ends, when she should be flying high. The realization of how important Andrew was to her, someone who had prided herself on her independence, distressed her.

She followed her parents to their house and pulled in behind them in the driveway, upset that even as she'd weaved her way through the crowd at the restaurant, she had kept looking for Andrew to appear. By the time she entered her parents' home, anger at being stood up tangled with her worry that something had happened to Andrew.

"I need to make a phone call." Sadie sought the privacy of her father's office.

She dialed Andrew's office, but there was no answer. She called his house and got his answering machine.

Her worry mushroomed. She decided to check her messages to make sure he hadn't left one.

"Sadie, I'm sorry I can't make it to the dinner after all. There's a problem I need to see to personally in Seattle. I'm leaving tonight. I'll call you when I get back."

The aloofness in his voice chilled Sadie. She hung up but remained sitting at her father's desk, immersed in conflicting emotions. She knew he had warned her about what was happening. His work came first and always would. He hadn't promised her a thing, and yet she had secretly hoped for more. And now she would pay for it. Her heart broke, the deep ache making each breath difficult.

The tears flowed unchecked down her face as she leaned back in the overstuffed chair and closed her eyes.

"Sadie? What's wrong?"

Surprised to hear her father's voice, she bolted up, her eyes snapping open. "I—I—" She couldn't find the words to explain the anguish she felt.

"What happened? Something with Andrew?"

The concern in her father's voice unleashed more tears. His image shimmered as he strode to her and reclined against the desk, his hands gripping its edge.

She sucked in a gulp of air. "Andrew's okay."

Her father remained quiet, waiting for her to continue.

"Daddy, I'll always be alone." Fresh tears burned her eyes as she spoke for the first time her biggest fear. She had pushed people away because she was afraid they would do it first. Andrew and she were alike in that respect.

"No, you won't." He clasped her arms and drew her

to her feet. "You will always have me and your mother. I know that I haven't been the best dad in the world, but I do love you."

With her head against his shoulder, she remembered Andrew's encouragement to talk with her father about how she felt growing up. She swallowed hard, but her throat was still tight and dry.

"Dad, I'd like to talk to you about something." Her voice was raspy.

"What about?"

She pulled back. "Not being perfect," she blurted, her breath bottled in her lungs.

His brow wrinkled. "I know you aren't perfect. No one is."

"But you were never satisfied with my accomplishments. You always wanted me to do better."

"Of course, I wanted you to do better. I want the best for my daughter, but that didn't mean I wasn't proud of you."

"What if I don't get Oklahoma Teacher of the Year? How will you feel?"

He looked as though she'd punched him in the stomach. "You don't think I would be proud of you anymore if you don't win the next level?"

She nodded.

"You couldn't be more wrong, Sadie. I'll be disappointed that the committee couldn't see you're the best in the state, but I'll still be proud of you. I—" Her father's eyes grew round. He twisted away and began to pace, plowing his fingers through his hair. "I never said it, did I?"

"No."

He stopped and faced her. "I'm sorry."

Never once in his life had her father told her he was sorry. Her throat closed, emotions buried for years surfacing.

"Your mom says that's something I need to work on. I've made quite a few mistakes with this family. Reverend Littleton is helping me to see that I shut down after your little brother died. I turned away from your mother, from you. I never properly grieved his death."

"Oh, Daddy." Sadie rushed to her father and hugged him.

He held her tight. "I've caused you a lot of tears, haven't I? I hope you can forgive me."

"We're family." His comfort soothed her troubled soul. She knew they still had a long way to go in developing the kind of father-daughter relationship she dreamed about, but this evening was a start.

"Am I the reason you're crying right now?"

"No." She could hear his heart pounding and drew strength from him. "I wish Andrew could have come tonight."

"What happened to him?"

"Business called him away from Cimarron City."

"I'm sorry about that, Sadie, but with a man like Andrew, who is dedicated to his work, that kind of thing will happen. You have to learn to accept that."

It might have been possible for her to accept his work schedule, but Andrew wasn't giving her a chance. He was pulling away. She had heard it in his voice. She needed to protect herself before there was nothing left to protect.

A pile of papers sat on Andrew's lap, but all he could seem to do was stare out the airplane window at the dark night—and see Sadie's face when she heard her message from him. On the ride to the airport he could have gone by the restaurant and talked with her personally instead of taking the easy way out. But he'd been afraid if he had seen her disappointment he would have stayed, and he couldn't. He was the one at IFI who was supposed to get the negotiations with the union back on track.

He rubbed a hand down his face, wishing he could scrub away the disgust he felt toward himself. He hadn't wanted to hurt Sadie, but he knew he had. He had warned her he wasn't a settling-down kind of guy—but for a while there he had pictured himself with Sadie as his wife, living in a house with a white picket fence, a dog and children. These past few weeks, since the New Year, he was reminded of the type of work schedule he had. There was no room in it for a wife and family. The only decent thing left for him to do was end it with Sadie.

His chest hurt with the thought. But he was no good at relationships and long ago he had stopped dreaming about having a family. Work didn't demand an emotional commitment, people did.

* * *

This time last week Sadie had been summoned to Mrs. Lawson's office because there was a problem with Chris. Now she stood in the middle of IFI's large lobby, undecided whether to see Mrs. Lawson first, or Andrew. She peered at the doors that led into the mail room. Business first. While the reason she was here to see Andrew was certainly not pleasure, it was personal.

With determined steps she covered the distance to the mail room and thrust open the door. Sadie waved to Chris as she headed for Mrs. Lawson's office. After one sharp rap the woman admitted Sadie.

"I won't keep you long, but I was in the building and wanted to check on Chris and the problem we discussed last week. Are things better?" Sadie remained by the door.

"Chris seems to be conducting himself properly."

"Are there any other problems I should know about?"

Mrs. Lawson shook her head. "He's eager to learn and works hard while he is here."

Surprised at the softening in the older woman's features, Sadie relaxed her taut body and smiled. "I'm glad he's working out."

Mrs. Lawson returned her smile. "Yes, better than I thought when Mr. Knight approached me about this program."

Sadie turned toward the door, glanced back and said, "Thank you, Mrs. Lawson. If you have any other problems concerning Chris, please free feel to call me."

Sadie briefly spoke to Chris before leaving the mail

room. Her gaze slid from the glass doors that led outside to the bank of elevators. She knew that Andrew had returned home sometime yesterday because he had left her a message on her answering machine, congratulating her on becoming the teacher of the year. Nothing else was said, and the silence after his message had been deafening.

What to do? Andrew was a friend, and when she was in a building where a friend worked she always stopped by to say hello. Her rationalization worked for all of one minute, but she knew by the time she had punched the button for his floor that she really wanted to see him to put an end to this roller coaster ride she had felt herself on these past few months.

"Hold the elevator," a woman called.

Sadie pressed her finger on the open door button. Jollie stepped onto the elevator, surprise evident in her expression.

"So the rumors are true," the other woman said.

"What rumors?" Sadie asked, knowing what Jollie was going to say.

"That you and Andrew Knight are an item. Is he another bachelor we're gonna lose for next year?"

"We are friends. He's safe," Sadie said, realizing she would probably have to get used to that idea, except that she didn't think she could be Andrew's friend. Being around him and not showing her love would be too much for her to handle. She wore her emotions on her face, and she wasn't that good an actress.

"Then why are you here?"

"I have a student working here."

"Yes, I heard, in the mail room. In fact, Chris comes into my office every day. What a breath of sunshine. All the employees like him and look forward to his afternoon visit."

Sadie responded to the woman's words with a smile, glad that something was going right. "He likes working here."

"I'm going to have an opening in my department soon. Would Chris be interested in working in receiving?"

"I'll talk with him about it."

"He'll have to apply, but I hope he does. I know how difficult Mrs. Lawson can be to work for, and if Chris is doing okay for her, he'll be an asset for my department."

"I'll get with Andrew about it."

"Great. See you at our first organizational meeting for the auction." The elevator doors slid open, and Jollie left.

The next floor was Andrew's, and Sadie quickly exited the elevator. She couldn't believe her good fortune when she saw that Mrs. Fox was away from her desk. Without debating, she went to Andrew's door and knocked, entering his office when she heard him say, "Come in."

Andrew glanced up from a pile of papers he was reading. Surprise quickly followed by joy flitted across his features, only to have a neutral expression descend by the time she'd crossed the office.

"How did you get past Mrs. Fox?"

"Easy. She wasn't out there. How was your trip? Successful?"

"Yes, the negotiations are back on track and should be wrapped up in a few days."

"I'm glad."

Silence fell between them, thick and heavy like a sudden summer storm. Sadie sat before her legs gave out on her. The width of his desk separated them, but she felt as if they were worlds apart. She searched for the right words to say, but his unreadable look wiped all thoughts from her mind.

"Andrew, I find being direct the best way to go through life," she began, her mouth parched as though she had stuffed wads of cotton in it.

"I find that a good philosophy."

"Then I think we should talk about us."

"Us?"

Her gaze coupled with his. "You and I both know there is an us, or there was until just recently."

Andrew surged to his feet. "Yes. We do need to talk." He strode to the large picture window that afforded him a wonderful view of Cimarron City. "I told you from the beginning I had no time for a relationship, that my life would be tied up with my work. That hasn't changed, Sadie."

His back was to her, and she needed to see what was in his eyes. She walked to him and leaned against the windowsill, fingertips digging into the ledge. "So what was December all about?"

"It was a lull in my busy schedule because of the

holidays. Even IFI slows down at that time of year." He ran his hand through his hair, then rubbed the back of his neck. "I don't want to disappoint you again like I did Saturday night."

"I see."

"Do you? Do you really see?"

"Yes, I do. You're afraid to make a commitment. I believe you use your work as an excuse to justify to yourself that you have no time for anyone in your life. That's easier than risking getting hurt in a relationship."

"You have it all figured out."

"No, far from it, but I do know one thing. I'm not perfect. I have faults, and that's okay. I used to think it wasn't, that no one could see my flaws and still like me. These past few months I've come to realize differently. I have to be with a man who will commit to me one hundred percent. You can't do that, and I think you're right that we should end whatever we had between us."

Andrew straightened, quickly scrambling to conceal the anger that flashed in his eyes. "Good. Then we agree."

Sadie started for the door, determined to remain in control. "Oh, by the way, Jollie wants Chris to apply for a position in the receiving department when it opens up."

"I'll look into it." His reply was cold.

At the door she paused and said, "I'm gonna ask you again. Have you thought about what you'll have in, say, ten or twenty years? Will it be enough to satisfy you? What happens when you retire and there is no more work?"

With those questions spoken, Sadie slipped out of the office, feeling Andrew's penetrating stare shimmer down her back. She had to go back to school for a meeting. *Please, Lord, give me the strength to make it through the rest of the day without falling apart.* She uttered the prayer over and over as she felt her heart shatter into a thousand pieces.

## Chapter Thirteen

Andrew started to knock, hesitated and dropped his arm to his side. Turning away, he walked a few paces down the hall, then stopped and twisted, staring at the door. When Sadie had left his office the day before yesterday, he'd felt as though she had sucked the air from the room and taken it with her. Her questions still rang in his mind, demanding answers he didn't have. He needed help and had run out of places to go.

The door opened, and Reverend Littleton appeared in the hallway. "Andrew? What brings you to the church?"

Andrew stared at the man, two nights without sleep dulling his mind. He couldn't get Sadie out of his thoughts, especially the devastation he'd glimpsed in her eyes that last time he'd seen her in his office.

"What's wrong, my son?"

Andrew flinched. He could remember Tom saying those very words to him when he'd first lived with Tom.

Over the two years he'd lived with Tom, he'd learned to put his trust and faith in the man and the Lord. Then Tom had been taken away just as quickly and disastrously as his family, and he'd felt himself floundering for a safety net.

Tunneling his fingers through his tousled hair, Andrew approached the reverend. "I need your help."

Reverend Littleton stepped to the side. "Come into my office and let's talk."

Seated in a comfortable chair across from the older man, Andrew closed his eyes for a moment, gathering his scattered thoughts into a coherent pattern. Finally, at four in the morning, he had come to the conclusion he needed more in his life than what he had. Sadie was right. There was nothing there that would mean anything in the years to come.

Andrew took a deep, cleansing breath. "How do you find your way back to God?"

"Son, I think you've taken the first step today by coming here and asking that question."


"This is an unexpected visit, Andrew. Is something wrong with the union negotiations?"

Andrew remained standing in front of Mr. Wilson's desk. "No, I've come to withdraw my name from consideration for the presidency of IFI."

"May I ask why?"

"My goals and plans for the future have changed these past few months."

"They still involve IFI?"

"Yes, but not as its president. I want to start a family."

Surprise flitted across Mr. Wilson's features. "Are congratulations in order?"

"I haven't convinced the lady yet."

"If I know you, Andrew, that's only a technicality. Who do you like as the next president?"

Andrew pulled up a chair and sat, more relaxed now that he had told Mr. Wilson his wish. "Charles would be excellent."

"Would you be willing to take on a different role at IFI?"

"What?" Andrew asked, wary that he would be trading one all-consuming job for another.

"I want to divide your job and expand the special projects part. With you heading that section, someone else can oversee the human resource department. I like this project you're doing with Cimarron High School and their vocational program. Connected to this position, of course, would be community awareness of IFI here in Cimarron City as well as globally. Image in today's market is everything. What do you think?"

Andrew shifted, leaning forward, enthusiasm building inside him. "I like it. Tell me more."

The hairs on the nape of Sadie's neck tingled. She scanned the gym at the University of Oklahoma, her gaze skipping from Special Olympics participant to coach to spectator. She saw familiar people, but no one staring at her. Still, the sensation someone was looking at her plagued her as she walked with her team toward the court they would play on.

She placed her gym bag on the floor. "Let's stretch and warm up first."

The eight team members formed a circle. Chris went into the middle and demonstrated one stretch. Everyone followed his lead. Sadie bent over and touched the floor along with her players. As she straightened, again the feeling someone was staring at her inundated her. She looked from side to side. When she glanced behind her, she saw him.

Andrew smiled at her, nodding his head in greeting.

Shock swept through her. Andrew was dressed in gym shorts and a T-shirt with a whistle around his neck. He would be their referee. Her shock quickly turned to confusion. Why wasn't he working? Just because it was Saturday didn't mean it was a day off for him. He had no days off.

Ignoring his heartwarming smile, she focused her attention on the stretches her students were performing. But each time she lunged, reached or twisted, she couldn't shake the prickly sensation Andrew was following every move she made.

Halfway through the exercises, she slipped away from the circle to confront the man. She marched up to him, fisted her hands on her waist and demanded, "Why are you here?"

"I'm volunteering."

"Don't you have work to do or something?" She winced at the panic in her voice and wished he hadn't heard it. She knew he had. A gleam entered his eyes.

"No. I took the weekend off."

"Why?"

"To volunteer at the Winter Games for Special Olympics. I thought that was obvious."

"Nothing about you is obvious. Are you refereeing our game?"

He nodded.

"Then I'm gonna protest."

"Why?"

"I'm sure this is a conflict of interest."

"You don't think I can be fair-minded?"

"I—" She suppressed her retort. "Yes, I guess so."

"Besides, all the other referees are busy, and they're shorthanded as it is. I thought you would be happy to see me. You're the one who convinced me that Special Olympics is a good cause to donate my time to."

She narrowed her eyes, wishing they could pierce his thick skin. He was enjoying her discomfort at his presence. "You could have volunteered for one of the other sports being played at the winter games."

"But I know how to play basketball. I thought that was important if I was gonna referee." He peered over her shoulder at her team. "They have five more minutes before the game starts. I need the captain to call the coin toss."

"I'll send Chris over." Sadie marched to the circle of

players, aware of Andrew's gaze assessing her, and told Chris to meet with Andrew.

Chris's face lit with a bright smile. "Mr. Knight is our referee?"

"Yes."

"That's great. He'll get to see me play. I told him about this."

So that was how Andrew knew about the winter games. Sadie wanted to discover just how much Chris and Andrew had talked about this weekend. Did Andrew mention her? Why was he here? As her thoughts began to run rampant with all the possibilities, she put a halt to the questions. Showing up for one day didn't mean anything. Special Olympics was a great cause, and she was tickled pink Andrew was giving his time to something other than work. But that was all. One day isn't a lifetime commitment, she reminded herself as she prepared her team for the start.

The game was excruciatingly slow. The seconds dragged into minutes, and Sadie could hardly keep her mind on her team. Her gaze kept returning to Andrew in the middle of her students, looking as though he was enjoying himself. He appeared relaxed, the tense lines in his face gone.

"Spencer, in?" Donnie tapped her on the shoulder and pointed toward the court.

"Okay, but remember that goal is the Chargers'. Don't shoot at that basket," Sadie said, waving toward a hoop.

The score was tied eight to eight with their opponents

getting some help from Donnie, who had made a basket for the Chargers. When Donnie ran onto the court, Sadie shouted, "Remember this is our goal." She pointed to the north end again.

In Donnie's excitement at getting another chance to play, he rebounded the ball and immediately took a shot at the Chargers' goal. The ball circled the rim and dropped through the net. Moaning, Sadie buried her face in her hands while their opponents exploded with applause. She thought of taking Donnie out and decided not to. He loved to shoot baskets and was quite good. Maybe he could make a few for them, too.

Two minutes later, the score was eleven to ten in the Chargers' favor. Andrew blew the whistle, announcing the end of the game. Donnie went up for a shot and made yet another basket for the Chargers. Thankfully this one didn't count. The team shuffled off the court, their heads hanging. Donnie still stood at the basket, rebounding and shooting.

"Coach, we should have won," Chris said, throwing a narrow-eyed look toward Donnie.

"Everyone gets to play. You know that, even Donnie. He made five of our baskets."

"Yeah, and seven for them."

"Did you enjoy playing?"

"Yes."

"Then that's all that counts. We're here to have fun and make new friends. Now, we have some time before our next game. Why don't you get some water and rest?"

"Can I have my face painted?"

"We'll do that later."

"Good. I want Sooners here." Chris pointed to his left cheek. "And Cowboys here." He gestured to the other side of his face.

Sadie laughed, tousling his hair. "Covering all your bases," she said in reference to the two big universities in the state. Chris was a huge fan of both.

Sadie returned to the court to retrieve Donnie before the next teams played. He didn't want to leave. Andrew came up behind Sadie and caught the ball as it bounced off the rim. Donnie frowned at him.

"Sorry, buddy. The next game is gonna start soon. You can shoot some baskets later."

Donnie stared at the ball clutched in Andrew's grasp, then stomped off to sit on the sideline. Sadie started to follow her student.

"I'm not refereeing this next game. I have a break. Can we talk?"

His question halted her progress toward the sideline. She didn't turn and face him. She didn't want to look into his eyes and find her resolve to get on with her life melting. "I'd rather not. I have strategies to form. We have to win all the rest of our games to win the tournament."

"You should have no problem winning if you just leave Donnie under your goal, tell him not to move and get the ball to him. Problem solved."

She heard the snap of his fingers and whirled, her anger rising. "And your specialty is solving problems."

"Yes—except my own. I haven't done a very good job there."

She placed her fisted hands on her waist. "And what problems do you have? I thought you had your life all planned out five years in advance."

The sound of balls slapping against the floor and hitting the backboard, the cheers when a person made a basket, the murmurs of voices in the crowd filled the air. Scanning the area, Sadie saw the next teams coming onto the court her students had been playing on, but none of that mattered. Her whole being focused on Andrew several feet away.

"A big one." He shortened the distance between them. "I've made a mess of my life. I've discovered the plans I made don't fit the new me."

Her eyes widened. "The new you?"

He grasped her arm. "Can we go somewhere less public to talk?"

Again she took in her surroundings, her students sitting with their families drinking water and talking. "I can't go far. We have another game soon."

"How about outside in the corridor?"

"Andrew—"

"Please, Sadie, this is important."

The beat of her heart picked up speed. Hope began to blossom in her, and she had to stamp it down before she got hurt any more than she already was. "Fine. I can spare ten minutes."

She followed him from the gym and down the

corridor until he found a less crowded area. The sound of people cheering could still be heard, but Sadie felt as though the rest of the world had disappeared with only her and Andrew left. Her emotions lay bare and exposed. But as she recalled the life he'd chosen, she shored up her defenses and faced him in the alcove.

"What is it you need to tell me?" she asked, hearing the steel thread running through her words. *Dear Lord, I have to be strong. I can't deal with another rejection.*

He drew in a deep breath, glanced away for a few seconds, then directed his look at her, an intensity in his gaze. "I was wrong. I thought I could live without you. I can't."

Sadie raised her hand to stop him from saying another word. "Don't, Andrew. You were right from the beginning. It won't work for us. We want different things from life."

"No, we don't. I'd convinced myself I didn't need anyone to make me happy. That work was a good substitute. Then you came along and forced me to examine my life. I didn't like what I saw, what I'd become. I want what Tom had taught me was important—family, God."

Tears burned in her eyes. She'd longed to hear those words ever since she'd met him. Still, years of holding her emotions inside for fear of being rejected kept her quiet.

"When Tom died so unexpectedly, in my grief and anger, I turned away from the Lord, from all that Tom had shown me. Give me a chance to prove I can make a commitment, Sadie. I love you and want to spend the rest of my life proving to you what a good husband and father I can be."

Tears streamed down her face. Emotions clogged her throat, making it impossible to say anything.

Andrew caressed her cheek with his forefinger, brushing her tears away. "I met with Mr. Wilson and withdrew my name from consideration for the presidency. I made it clear to him that my priorities have changed." His touch lingered, one hand cupping her face while the other clasped her arm to bring her closer. "Say something."

Sadie swallowed hard. "I'm afraid, Andrew. Work has driven you for years."

He brought his other hand up to frame her face. "Have faith in me, Sadie. People can change if they want it bad enough, and I want this very bad."

She inhaled then exhaled slowly. "I don't think I can do anything else. I love you, Andrew Knight. God has taught me the importance of faith and giving people second chances. Yes, I'll marry you."

A smile transformed his serious expression. He feathered his lips across hers, then deepened the kiss while winding his arms around her. "You'll learn one thing about me hasn't changed. When I set my mind to do something, I do it. We will have a good life, Sadie Spencer."

# Epilogue

With her arms folded over her chest, Sadie leaned against the wall in the hotel ballroom and watched the next bachelor step onto the stage. The door opened near her. She turned to see who had entered.

"Where's that man of yours?" Jollie asked, slipping into the place next to Sadie along the back wall. "The least he could do is return to the scene of his downfall."

Sadie laughed. "I hope he doesn't see it that way." With a quick look at the door, she saw another person enter the ballroom, but that man wasn't Andrew, either. "He's late."

"He's probably at work." Jollie cocked her head to the side. "On second thought, he's usually left before me these past few months. You've definitely changed that man. I never thought I would see the day he didn't burn the midnight oil."

"How's Chris doing?"

"He's working out great. I'm glad he transferred to

my department. The people love seeing him come to work. He brightens the place."

Again someone pushed the door open, and Sadie glanced toward it. A smile lit her face when she spied Andrew in the entrance to the ballroom. She waved, and he headed toward her.

Jollie leaned toward her. "I should be angry you took the most eligible bachelor off the auction block. But after all the men he persuaded to donate their time to this charity auction, I can't complain."

"Neither can I." Sadie slipped her hand in Andrew's. "It's nice to see you, Jollie."

"I'd better get back to the table I'm manning. See you two later."

"Sorry I'm late. I got detained longer than I thought at the church with the appropriation committee meeting, then the contractor called and needed to see me about our house."

His whispered words fanned her neck in warm waves. She shivered, and he brought his hands up to pull her against him. "Is there a problem with the house?"

"Not anymore. Ready to leave?"

"Leave? I thought we were staying to eat dinner."

"Nope. I've made other plans for us. This is our first anniversary."

Sadie twisted, looking at Andrew. "We were married six months ago."

"But this is where we first met, this time last year." He took her hand and tugged her toward the door.

"Where are we going?"

"It's a surprise." He opened the car door for her. "Sit back and relax."

Sadie reflected on the past year. She hadn't thought her life could get any better. Today at the doctor's it had. Laying her hand on her stomach, she smiled. Remembering the money she'd spent at the auction the year before, she decided that was the best five hundred fifty dollars she'd ever spent.

Andrew parked his car in the driveway of a home under construction. "We're here."

"At our house?"

"Come on." Andrew unlocked the door and switched on the light.

Sadie entered the almost completed house, her heels clicking on the concrete slab. Soon the carpet and hardwood floors would be put in. Soon she and Andrew would move in.

In the middle of the living room a table set for two with a white tablecloth and candles beckoned. She crossed to the table and ran her hand over a china plate.

"You thought of everything."

"Surprised?" He came up behind her and drew her against him.

"No, not really. I'm discovering how romantic my husband can be." She turned in his loose embrace so she could face him. "It's been a wonderful year."

"It's been a life-altering year."

The warm look in his eyes, so filled with love,

melted her against him. "And the life-altering part isn't over with."

A silent question entered his expression. "You went to the doctor?"

"Yes, I couldn't wait until tomorrow. You know me and surprises. He confirmed we're going to have a baby."

Andrew's shout for joy echoed through the empty house as he whirled her around.

"I take it you're happy about the baby," she said when he settled her feet on the concrete floor.

\* \* \* \* \*

Dear Reader,

For many years I have worked with students with special needs. I wanted to write about the students I am fortunate to work with each day. I wanted to show what a wonderful gift these students are to society. They have hopes and dreams like everyone else. They enjoy working and they enjoy playing sports. I have coached Special Olympics for years and think this organization is a worthy one. I have gotten such joy from seeing one of my students participate in a sport, and whether he wins or not doesn't matter. You can volunteer with Special Olympics in your state. They can always use a person to congratulate an athlete when he has crossed the finish line whether he is first or last.

I hope you enjoy Sadie and Andrew's story and the blessings a student with special needs can bring to a person. Again I want to thank God for giving me the chance to teach students with such a zeal for life and an unconditional love for others. I love hearing from readers. You may write me at P.O. Box 2074, Tulsa, OK 74101.

May God bless you,

Margaret Daley

# *Love Inspired*
## SUSPENSE
### RIVETING INSPIRATIONAL ROMANCE

# SECRET AGENT MINISTER
## *Lenora Worth*

**Things were not as they seemed...**

The minister of Lydia Cantrell's dreams had another calling.
As his secretary, she knew the church members adored him,
but she was shocked to discover Pastor Dev Malone's past as
a Christian secret agent. Her shock turned to disbelief when
Pastor Dev revealed he'd made some enemies—
and that he and Lydia were in danger.

*Available September wherever you buy books.*